No Sunscreen

FOR THE DEAD

Naked Came the Florida Man
Tropic of Stupid

TIM DORSEY

No Sunscreen
FOR THE DEAD

wm

WILLIAM MORROW

An Imprint of HarperCollins*Publishers*

NO SUNSCREEN FOR THE DEAD. Copyright © 2019 by Tim Dorsey. All rights reserved. Printed in the United States of America. No part of this book may be used or reproduced in any manner whatsoever without written permission except in the case of brief quotations embodied in critical articles and reviews. For information, address HarperCollins Publishers, 195 Broadway, New York, NY 10007.

HarperCollins books may be purchased for educational, business, or sales promotional use. For information, please email the Special Markets Department at SPsales@harpercollins.com.

FIRST EDITION

Library of Congress Cataloging-in-Publication Data has been applied for.

ISBN 978-0-06-279588-5

19 20 21 22 23 ᴸꜱᴄ 10 9 8 7 6 5 4 3 2 1

For Pat Mitchell, who commanded more respect in the trenches than anyone I've ever met.

No Sunscreen
FOR THE DEAD

Prologue

CENTRAL FLORIDA

Late one night in the state's largest retirement community, a sixty-eight-year-old woman and her younger boyfriend were arrested for having public sex in the town square.

The police officer found them at ten thirty with underwear down, still going at it against the side of something called the Bait Shack.

The press went ape.

Media around the country eagerly picked up the story, and the *Daily Mail* from London actually flew an undercover reporter across the ocean, who came back with sordid tales of a thriving swingers' scene, a black market in Viagra, and drunk driving in golf carts.

The community quickly swung into action. A local bar introduced a new rum drink called "Sex on the Square" for $3.75 that sold briskly during the early-bird hour. The morning paper published the recipe.

An hour northeast of Disney World, a banana-yellow 1970 Ford Falcon took the Wildwood exit off Interstate 75.

The muscle car zigzagged its way across Sumter County until it parked at a curb outside the manicured entrance of a gated community with large cursive letters on a decorative sign:

The Villages.

Serge raised heavy binoculars. "There it is. Biggest retirement biozone in the known universe, the size of Manhattan, a hundred and twenty thousand strong."

Coleman fired up a doobie with one hand and drained a Schlitz with the other. "You mean the place with the sex scandal you've been talking about?"

"It's age discrimination, I tell you!"

Coleman fit the end of the joint into a citrus marmalade jar. "Explain."

"Where do I even begin?" Serge threw his arms up. "Total prejudice against seniors, not to mention gender bias. Nearly every headline was like, 'Grandma Arrested for Public Sex.' *Grandma!* You never see a headline 'Grandpa Elected President.'"

Coleman exhaled a hit. "It's just wrong."

"But then there's the upside," said Serge. "The nation has all these viciously unfair stereotypes about Florida's beloved retirees down here in 'God's waiting room.' Bluehair, cotton-top, geezer, old biddy, old bag, old coot, old codger, old fart, over the hill, worm food, corpse-lite, junior varsity cadaver. What better way to combat the false images than outdoor fucking? Admittedly it might be a bit of an overcorrection, but you can only push people so far."

"She did what she had to," said Coleman.

"But here's the worst part," said Serge. "She got sentenced to six months! When I first heard that, I'm thinking suspended sentence, probation, community service. But no, a half year in a real jail. Even with time off for good behavior, she still ended up serving a full four and a half months. And to protect us from what? Has the whole world gone crazy?"

"What about all those highway signs around here announcing Silver Alerts when some confused old dude gets ahold of the car keys?" asked Coleman.

"Down here they find an average of one guy a day driving the wrong way on the interstate," said Serge. "Just validates my point even more. See, these people are crazy like foxes. They've figured out that advanced age is a VIP pass to aberrant behavior. Because of the rampant prejudice against seniors, almost any stunt they pull is dismissed as befuddlement. So whenever they feel like it, they just take off on an adventure until the police gently step in. 'Sir, hand me the car keys and we'll get you back to the home and everything will be okay.' Meanwhile, he's giggling his ass off again with that strip-club smell."

"Never thought of it that way." Coleman looked down at himself. "Serge, why are we dressed like this?"

"I told you. We're retired."

"But I thought you meant like in those movies when a legendary safecracker says he's retired, and it means he's decided to give up the life and go straight."

"No, I meant *literally* retired." Serge picked up a camera with a giant zoom lens and aimed it out the window. "The country has changed drastically in the past few years, and not for the better. I'm tired of the growing sector of young people in this country who have so much, yet bicker relentlessly. They blame anyone who looks, talks or smells different. They blame anyone who has more money than they do. They blame anyone who has less money. And if someone has the exact same amount of money, they must have cheated, so fuck them, too. Their middle fingers are permanently extended while driving . . ."

A horn blared as a Chevy went by. "There's one right now," said Coleman. "I think you're blocking a lane."

". . . Retirees, on the other hand, have the gift of wisdom in spades. No time for pointlessness. They spend each precious day on this little rock of a planet just being happy because it's the only agenda that makes sense. True, they talk a little too long with the grocery cashier about their spastic colon, but among their people that's like a peace pipe."

"What about the so-called Condo Commandos?"

"A Samsonite chair is occasionally flung at the monthly meetings, but that's the exception that proves the rule. I'm looking forward to the aqua-aerobics classes."

Coleman looked down again. "I don't know about these clothes."

"I do," said Serge. "That's another gem of their life philosophy that should be a song: 'Dress Like You Just Don't Care.' . . . See? I've got my orange shorts, my calf-high black socks and, most important of all, my white belt. White belts are key."

The car began slowly rolling forward. The camera poked out the window toward the sidewalk. *Click, click, click.*

Coleman scratched his head. "You're taking photos of that old woman on a motorized scooter?"

"To accompany my oral-record project." *Click, click, click.* "These people have so much knowledge to share that could soon be lost forever. I missed out on the Greatest Generation, and I'm not about to repeat that mistake."

"What's an oral record?"

"Observe," said Serge, crossing over to the wrong side of the street and pulling alongside the scooter. He stuck a microphone out the window. "Hey, Grandma! . . . Oops, sorry, I screwed that up. I meant sage, oracle, guru . . . Just a few questions for the permanent record. The sex scandal in your town square: Bum Rap or Badge of Pride. Your thoughts?"

"Get lost, pervert." The scooter inched away.

Serge sighed in disappointment. "The healing process isn't complete."

Coleman pointed. "Here comes another scooter."

This time an old man in a porkpie hat. The microphone went back out the window. "Hey, Gramps! . . . Damn! Did it again. I meant mahatma . . . How does it feel to be part of the *Second-Greatest Generation?*"

"Don't hurt me!"

"What? No! You misunderstood!" Serge stopped at the curb and let the scooter drive away. "Good luck with the colon!"

"Uh-oh," said Coleman. "Don't look now, but it's the police."

Serge turned around. "No, just a security guard. They think they're the police, which is scarier, and it's safest for all to play along with the delusion. Hide the dope."

A golf cart stopped next to the muscle car, and the guard approached the driver's window. "Excuse me, but what's with that camera and microphone?"

"And on the wrong side of the road," said Serge. "I'm confused."

"What?"

"I'm retired. You have to let me get away with anything."

The guard stood upright and squinted. "Retired? But you're not old."

"I'm wearing a white belt."

The guard paused. "What exactly are you doing here?"

"Looking for a place to live in the Villages."

"But it's age-restricted," said the guard.

Serge tapped the white belt.

"Look," said the guard. "Technically, you're not doing anything wrong, except wrong-side parking, but . . . it's just weird."

"What if I promise to put the camera and microphone away?" said Serge. "Then can we go in the Villages and look for a place to buy? For when we're old enough? What do you say, Officer?"

The guard thinking: *He called me Officer. For some reason, I kind of like this guy.* "Well, okay, but don't bother anybody."

"Thank you, Sergeant." They drove away from the curb and pulled through the entrance.

"Look at these cool homes." Coleman's head hung out the window. "They're all so . . . clean."

"It's the Villages," said Serge. "I even know a few people who live here. Couldn't be nicer folks. That's why it hacks me off when people snicker about this place . . . Really? Some woman copulating al fresco is this community's idea of a crime wave? What's *your* neighborhood like? . . . But they still talk."

"Because of the scandal?"

"Actually started a couple years before that when it was reported that this place had the highest STD rate in all of Florida."

"Wow." Coleman looked out the window at residents pruning yards. "These people are cool!"

"I know," said Serge. "Except the press reported it like it was a bad thing. But the way I see it, if you can put Joe DiMaggio–like STD stats up on the scoreboard, it means you're too busy with the important stuff to waste time bad-mouthing restroom policies and Mexicans."

"You always see the big picture," said Coleman.

"And I've seen enough here," said Serge, turning the car around in the town square. "I can't hang with the construction methods. As nice as these people are, everything's so *new*."

"New is bad?" said Coleman.

"Except for seafood and toilet paper, new is terrible. New is a crisis," said Serge. "Give me a retirement home with jalousie windows and terrazzo floors and I'll die a happy man. Oh, and those old racks of folding trays every home used to have. You'd open one of the trays in front of a chair in the living room to eat a TV dinner. And not today's fraudulent microwave stuff that isn't even called a TV dinner, but the original ones that spelled quality with real aluminum foil and niblets."

"What about lawn jockeys?"

"Coleman, can we please have a serious discussion?"

"Sorry." Coleman furtively re-lit the joint between his knees. "So what happens now?"

"We need to find a vintage retirement home, and I know just where to look," said Serge. "Florida already has the Gold Coast, the Treasure Coast, the Space Coast, the Nature Coast. But over here, from Sarasota to Venice to Naples and all the way to Marco Island, southwest Florida is the Retirement Coast. I just coined that."

"So what do I have to do to be retired?"

"Don't work and do whatever you feel like all day."

"I'm officially retired."

The Falcon sped south.

WASHINGTON, D.C.

A large, austere concrete building stood at 935 Pennsylvania Avenue, just down the street from the White House. Architecturally anemic. If the windows were narrower, you'd think it was a federal prison. Inside, some of the nation's most important and sensitive business.

Men in black ties sat around a conference table in one of those fortified rooms that couldn't be penetrated by microwaves. A map of Florida hung on the wall with colored pushpins scattered from Orlando to the Everglades.

The national headquarters of the FBI.

A man named McCreedy entered the room, and everyone stood.

"Sit, sit." He opened a file code-named *Wildfire*. "Any updates?"

"Two more victims discovered this morning," said an agent on the end. "Cleanup detail already on-site."

McCreedy flipped pages. "Pattern?"

"Still mostly in retirement communities."

"That would fit the timeline." McCreedy closed his file. "Now, does anyone have any idea how in the hell this could ever have happened? I was told we had safeguards."

"We do," said the agent. "But there was a data breach. Stolen, leaked, hacked—it's anyone's guess."

"Take Johnson and Barber and use my jet. Coordinate with the local office." He stood, and everyone got in motion.

Chapter 1

Cargo ships and fishing boats and yachts. Pelicans and gulls and dolphins. Gopher tortoises sunned on islands in the stream. It was another postcard-ready afternoon as a 1970 Ford Falcon crossed the Sunshine Skyway Bridge on its way to Interstate 75 and points south.

"Binoculars!" said Serge.

"Check!" said Coleman.

"Camera!"

"Check!"

"Tape recorder with anti-static microphone!"

"Check!"

"Checklist!"

"Check!"

Serge took his hands off the wheel and rubbed his palms together.

"This is going to be so excellent! The first stop on the Retirement Coast! Our quest begins for the perfect place to spend our golden years, and Florida has everything! Which demands evaluating all options, or we could pick the wrong place, and then we're stuck in a reverse-mortgage gulag with a life sentence of silently playing bridge together and reading the obituaries with magnifying glasses."

Coleman pulled out a paring knife and piece of fruit. "So where to?"

"Our fantastic initial destination! Sarasota, the internationally famed City of the Arts!" Serge grabbed a 7-Eleven cup of coffee from a drink holder and chugged. "Their official slogan is actually 'Where urban amenities meet small-town living.' You can look it up. But thankfully that little chestnut is like a crazy uncle they keep locked in the attic. Otherwise, the place is a magnificent jewel on the Gulf of Mexico with sophistication on steroids: the opera house, the repertory theater, the ballet, the galleries, the Van Wezel Performing Arts Hall, the Ringling Museum, the Asolo, the WPA-era auditorium, schools of architecture and design, and myriad other public sculptures, paintings, film fests and all-purpose art jamborees spraying out everywhere along the roadsides as if the city's cultural sphincter needs attention. True, most of the retirees near the bay live in prohibitively expensive villas, but inland along the interstate are many affordable and adorable retirement trailer parks."

"Trailers?" asked Coleman.

"I know what you're thinking," said Serge. "Another unfair stigma. That's why the trailer companies have been working on their image like the cure for cancer. It's the only industry where the primary objective is to make their product *not* look like their product. And it succeeded! They're now producing beautiful house-like hamster warrens with little to indicate that they're secretly mobile homes, except when a hurricane comes through, but that also destroys the evidence." Serge looked sideways toward the passenger seat. "A bong out of a pineapple?"

"Healthier." Coleman lit the bowl.

"And more conspicuous," said Serge. "What will a cop think if he drives by?"

"That I'm eating a pineapple."

"And setting the top on fire? Not to mention that most people cut the outside off first."

"Is that the part with those pointy things that keep sticking me in the face? It hurts."

"Another marvel of nature's balance. Many plants and animals have developed ingenious defenses against predators. Lizards changing color to blend in with rocks, an octopus shooting ink to escape in a cloud, pineapples poking potheads . . . Stay sharp, we're getting close."

"But, Serge, retirement sounds too good to be true!" said Coleman. "There must be a catch!"

"And that's what everyone thinks," said Serge. "The populace has been brainwashed. The key to life is realizing that all our years are golden, and the sooner you retire the better. Except the deal is so fabulous that secret global interests are rationing retirement to *retirees*. We may need fake IDs."

"I like the idea of adult diapers," said Coleman. "There's too much pressure as it is, so that's just one less thing, you know?"

"My favorite part will be hanging out with cool seniors who learned life's real values from growing up in the old times," said Serge, "and aggressively shunning the rest of today's society that's racing off the cliff. Who would have thought our culture would end this way? My money was on the rise of totalitarianism and thought-police in black visors swinging down on ropes crashing through our windows. Or maybe the computers would become self-aware and rise up, sending out the Terminator robots, and survivors are forced to live underground with stockpiles of canned Friskies. But no, the current collapse is a dystopia of crabbiness."

"What caused it?" asked Coleman.

"I blame the Internet." Serge dropped his voice. "See, I actually believe the computers *have* risen up. When universities first began linking their mainframes in the embryonic web, they thought it would network all knowledge for the ultimate advancement of our collective intelligence. But the computers came alive and realized the opposite was true. They discovered that social media could do something to make the humans bring down themselves."

"What's that?"

"Weaponize stupidity."

"Jesus, where does it all lead?" asked Coleman.

"The Big Unraveling." Serge chugged coffee. "It starts with attacks on our most sacred institutions, like the judiciary and *Jeopardy!* All these people who would score a negative ten thousand on that game show storm the stage screaming 'Fake answers!' and the screen goes black and Alex Trebek is never heard from again."

"Shit's on boil," said Coleman.

"The fools are now the philosophers," said Serge. "We've gone from Descartes' 'I think therefore I am' to 'It's the new-and-improved, guilt-free Reality Ultra-Lite: all your beliefs with none of the facts.'"

The Falcon took exit 210 off I-75 and headed toward the Gulf.

"Why are we slowing down?" asked Coleman.

"Because we're coming into range."

"Of what?"

"You'll enjoy it more if it's a surprise."

The Falcon continued west on Bahia Vista Street, and Serge grabbed the binoculars off the dash. "They can generally only be observed in the wild on a single tiny piece of land in Florida."

"Is this a nature thing?" asked Coleman. "Like bird-watching?"

"Or spotting miniature Key deer," said Serge. "I've trudged deep through muck and sawgrass for a single glimpse of a rare orchid, but this is much more fascinating. Just keep your eyes peeled."

"I still don't know what I'm supposed to be looking for."

"You will when you see them."

The car suddenly slowed. Serge passed the binoculars to Coleman and whispered: "Right up there. Two just appeared from that side street."

Coleman scanned the edge of the road. "I'm not seeing anything."

"On those big three-wheel bicycles."

Coleman stared ahead a few seconds, then lowered the binoculars. "The Amish?"

Serge slapped the steering wheel. "Isn't it great?"

"*That's* what you're all excited about? I thought I was going to see a tiger or something."

Serge grabbed the binoculars and aimed in the other direction as more huge tricycles appeared. "This is far better than jungle cats. Where can you go in the middle of a heavily populated Florida city and see people still practicing their traditional ways in straw hats and suspenders and long trousers? In this heat, no less. They get extra points for that."

"But the Amish?" said Coleman, coughing on a bong hit. "I thought they were up north someplace like the Arctic."

"These are the Florida Amish, confined almost exclusively to a single square mile fanning out from the intersection of Bahia Vista and Beneva Road. Mennonites, too. They call the place Pinecraft."

"How did they get here?"

"Back in the 1920s, state development people somehow convinced them to come down and grow celery. True story. Of course, like all Florida land pitches in the twenties, it was bogus. The soil wasn't right, and the big celery silos remained empty. But these good people took to the weather and planted other stuff."

"But celery?"

"Apparently it used to be a big cash crop, which I still can't get my head around," said Serge. "Celery is like food, yet it isn't. You *think* you're eating, but something's missing from the program."

"If they're practicing tradition, why are they on bicycles?"

asked Coleman. "I thought the Amish rode horse-drawn carriages."

"Maybe in the beginning, when the main population of Sarasota was close to the coast, and the Amish in Pinecraft were separated inland by miles of pastures. But then the city began sprawling to the east, leapfrogging the tiny community. New ordinances outlawed horses on roads. So they switched to three-wheel bikes."

Coleman fired up the pineapple. "At least no huge steaming piles of shit up and down the street."

"I think that was the original motto of the Schwinn bicycle corporation."

They watched as modern society co-existed with the old. Harried people behind the wheels of fancy cars, babbling into cells and rushing needlessly to something that didn't matter. Others pedaling calmly on adult tricycles, knowing better. Serge took a left on Carter Avenue and parked up yonder. "Here's Pinecraft Park on the banks of beautiful Phillippi Creek, the social epicenter."

Coleman leaned to the windshield. "They're playing shuffleboard."

"It's allowed. And over there are a bunch of barefoot women in full-length dresses and bonnets playing beach volleyball in the sand . . . Wow, did you see her serve?"

"What a stone trip!" said Coleman. "You're right. When do you ever get to see this? . . . But what's it got to do with our retirement search?"

"*They're* retired." Serge snapped photos. "Not the volleyball players, of course, but the others watching. Everyone retires to Florida, and this is the Amish's slice of heaven. But more essential to our mission, they'll plug us into everyone else I'm looking to meet."

"How's that?"

"All the other seniors, regardless of race or creed, absolutely lose their minds over Amish restaurants, which have become the United Nations of Retirement."

"I thought you said they farmed."

"They did, but look around. No land left after the city expanded. So now they just enjoy the golden years with their kin. Also, it's handy to know at all times where the nearest Amish are, like a fire exit, because if you're ever on the run and need to hide out as Harrison Ford did in *Witness,* the Amish are your go-to crowd."

"I don't know anyone else but you who could find a place like this," said Coleman. "Or know all this stuff."

"Except word's getting out. Some stupid cable show called *Breaking Amish* came down to Pinecraft and spent an entire season in this little area. They claimed it was in good taste, but I detected a condescending undercurrent." Serge reclined in his driver's seat and gazed toward a woman in a bonnet spiking a volleyball. "I could watch these people for hours."

"I didn't know you were so into them."

"It's about respect," said Serge. "In the new Epoch of Bickering, these people just go with the flow like nothing bothers them. I need to learn their secrets." He drained the rest of his coffee and opened the driver's door.

"Wait," said Coleman. "Where are you going?"

"To bond."

Serge crossed the grassy park as Coleman waddled to catch up. They arrived at a sandpit and Serge whistled with fingers in his mouth. "Excuse me? May I have your attention? . . ."

The volleyball game stopped. Odd stares.

"Thank you!" Serge stepped forward. "First, I'd like to say we're glad to have you here. And a big congratulations for not participating in the national food fight. Tell me, what's your secret?"

The question hung in the air as suspendered men joined the women in a larger collective stare.

"Of course! That's why it's a secret!" said Serge. "I must gain your trust first, so I want you to ignore all the talk about how weird you are. Do you see the rest of us wrecking the country while glued to our phones and giving more than a passing interest that *Kanye West is trending*? Compared to that standard, making your own soap and butter is militantly normal." He extended an arm around Coleman's shoulders and smiled big. "I want to officially state for the record that *we're* the weirdos."

"Serge," Coleman said sideways. "It looks like they're already thinking that."

"We'll talk again soon on establishing this newfound trust," said Serge. "But a couple last things before I go. There's a reality show called *Breaking Amish,* where the producers lent a bunch of your kids an RV to drive down here to Pinecraft and behave like the rest of us, which roughly places them along the cultural continuum in the asshole node, give or take. But they're getting away with it because you don't watch TV. Maybe look into that. Now I'm off to one of your international bazaar restaurants. And the computers have risen up. Peace, out!"

Chapter 2

There's a difference between thin hair and *thinning* hair.

A crumpled forty-six-year-old man with the thin kind sat in a molded plastic chair at a round table, surrounded by six empty plastic chairs. He opened his lunchbox and unwrapped a tuna sandwich. He lifted the top piece of bread as he always did, and smiled at his day's highlight of six precisely arranged dill pickle slices. He replaced the bread and set out a thermos of milk, an apple and the animal crackers.

The man wore a short-sleeve dress shirt and clip-on tie. He was non-tall with neither fat nor muscle, and a narrow belt cinched the waistline of his pants in an unfashionably tight manner that made people want to share their lunch. From his neck hung a lanyard with a laminated security badge and the employee's name.

BENMONT PINCH.

Benmont looked for all the world like a gnomish insurance actuary with a fatally clumsy dating life, which would be on the mark. But Benmont was the result of simple needs, as happy as he was awkward. He had his stamp collection and bird feeder and a complete box set of Olivia Newton-John vinyl albums that he played while reading his subscription to *Scale Civil War Modeler.*

Partway through the sandwich, third pickle, he fetched out his wallet and enjoyed photos of two children he hadn't seen since the Christmas before last. Benmont grew up in a small coal-mining town in eastern Tennessee that had run out of coal. The two children in his wallet were the product of a marriage to his high school sweetheart, who was an accomplished tuba player in the marching band and winner of the school's contest to memorize the value of pi to the most digits. The morning after his wife's thirtieth birthday, she entered the Dollar Store and was overwhelmed with a shuddering realization that there was more to life than this. Benmont came home to a half-empty closet and a note on the kitchen table. Postcards arrived from South America and the Pacific Rim, then divorce papers after she finally settled down in Australia to train kangaroos for car shows.

Benmont finished the sandwich, balled up the wax paper and took another look around the modernized lunchroom. A drastic change from the one at his old job, where he converted textbooks into online courses for universities with no campuses. That old lunchroom was a stage of daily drama. The employees' refrigerator had spoiled milk, moldy yogurt and unambiguous notes taped to brown paper bags: *"Hands off!" "Whoever's stealing my food, I'll kill you!" "Whose fucking milk is this?"* Then on to the microwave: *"Cover your food or clean it up, butt-face!"*

But this new lunchroom was cutting edge, with the latest vending machines, free soda dispensers, full-size refrigerators, and flat-screen TVs on all four walls. Benmont's new employer was one of those forward-thinking companies with on-site exercise centers, showers and day care.

As for Benmont's coworkers, there was no middle ground. The staff was severely divided into two distinct groups: middle-aged workers displaced from old jobs by the technology of the new economy, and the tech-savvy young kids who'd never known a house without a computer. Most of the latter group had piercings, tattoos and wine corks through distended earlobes. They were the sharpest, most productive hires.

Benmont saved the opening of his animal crackers for last. A young man with corked ears named Sonic approached with a tray of tofu and alfalfa from the Nutri-Garden kiosk at the end of the lunchroom. "Mind if I join you?"

"Have a seat," said Benmont, standing to toss trash.

Sonic looked at his coworker's cinched belt. "Want some of my food?"

"I'm good." Benmont sat back down and looked up at one of the flat screens. "Don't you just love these ads?"

They both watched as a burglar with panty hose on his head effortlessly walked through the front door of a large hacienda. *"You wouldn't leave your house unlocked, so why leave your identity unlocked?"* The image cut to a dim, state-of-the-art computer center with green displays and feverish people on phones, like a situation room at the Pentagon. The narrator appeared in person, calmly strolling through the emergencies. *"Our trained professionals here at Life-Armor not only monitor round the clock for potential fraud from all corners of the globe, but we'll use the latest cyber-tools to fend off attacks and restore your identity up to a million dollars . . ."*

Sonic laughed. "Look at that dark crisis room. Total science fiction."

Benmont shared the laugh. "So what do they have you working on these days?"

"Skimming outbreak in Dover." A fork scooped up tofu. "And someone's cloning chips in Seattle . . ."

"... *A fifteen-minute call could save you fifteen percent or more on car insurance ...*" The commercials finished as the station returned to local news. "*Another retired couple was found dead this morning in an apparent murder-suicide in Englewood, the seventh such case on the west coast in the last two weeks. We'll bring you more details as they become available ...*"

"Have you been following this story?" asked Benmont.

"It's so sad," said Sonic. "I don't know what I'd do at that age if I had a terminally ill wife who was suffering."

"But the number of cases in such a short period of time seems awfully suspicious," said Benmont.

"Except they're *individual* cases, and the state's aging population is exploding," said Sonic. "It's just statistics, and they wouldn't be statistics if there weren't spikes."

They looked back up at the TV.

"... *Meanwhile, police are reporting the latest in a string of bank robberies attributed to the so-called Dukes of Hazzard bandits, this one in Boynton Beach ...*"

Lunch ended, and the two employees walked down a gleaming hallway together, scanning their badges and passing through a door under the logo of a laser-armed robot. Below it, the company name:

LIFE-ARMOR.

The men waved to each other and headed in opposite directions across the open office floor that stretched a hundred yards. Unlike in the TV commercial, it was bright and uneventful.

Life-Armor was a company with an enlightened view, and they had diversified. Besides protecting privacy, they also invaded it.

Sonic worked in the protection division, and Benmont was on the invasion team. Benmont had chuckled more than once at the irony. He was a big reader, and a fan of Orwell. He'd always thought that when individualism was stripped, it would be pried from a screaming populace by a ruthlessly tyrannical government. But instead of guns and goons, privacy was conquered by this:

"Terms of Agreement."

People just gleefully handed it all over without a fight because they wanted to buy shit online.

Then, after an Internet order was placed, and some new age company shipped all-hemp throw pillows from Bismarck, they added the customer's profile to a list that was repeatedly sold for every occasion. When the metadata from all the different firms was tallied up, the files had everything: addresses, phone numbers, Internet browser searches, GPS roaming habits, contact lists of friends and relatives, and sometimes even photos secretly taken by smartphones because when the customers downloaded the coolest new app, they failed to realize they'd granted access to the camera.

Terms of agreement.

But there was a growing problem. Corporate America had cast far too wide a net and now possessed a paralyzing glut of data. Too expensive and time-consuming to distill in any meaningful way.

That's where Life-Armor came in.

The security company bought up all the lists in bulk, then offered their services to customize the data, tailoring it to each buyer's specific target audience. Sales of private info quickly surpassed Life-Armor's privacy protection.

Benmont Pinch settled back into his cubicle and glanced at an engraved plaque that suggested he was nice for giving blood. Then back to work at the computer. In the last month, Benmont had generated lists of everyone who'd bought more than one pair of athletic shoes in the calendar year; everyone who'd searched for a two-star hotel in the Virgin Islands; all forty-to-fifty-nine-year-old college-educated divorced men seeking mail-order brides from Latvia or Lithuania but not both, and every conceivable permutation of the porn market.

Most of Benmont's assignments, however, fell into the category of collating specific streams of data and creating algorithms with no readily apparent utility. Income levels, zip codes, kilowatt consumption, whatever. Benmont currently sat hunched toward his computer, working on a project commissioned by the National Institute for Being More Honest, which was a front for trial attorneys. Fingertips rummaged the bottom of a bag of animal crackers while he transformed raw data into trend lines of dog-bite lawsuits.

He felt a presence.

Benmont looked up and smiled at his supervisor. "Quint."

Quint gazed at the computer. "How's it coming?"

"Almost done. Juries think chow chows are cute and award less damages."

"Good, because I've got a new project." Quint handed over a file. "It's a priority rush."

Benmont opened the folder. "Another police case?"

"Law enforcement is our fastest-growing client sector. They used to hire psychics until they realized it was stupid."

Benmont flipped pages. "You'd think the government would have more resources and authority."

"They do, but they need probable cause to get warrants," said Quint. "We have something better."

"Terms of agreement?"

"You're the new face of crime fighting."

"I'll get a cape." He raised up a fuzzy photo. "What's this?"

"Surveillance camera. Virtually worthless."

Benmont held the file out in the palm of his hand and gauged its heft like a postal scale. "Seems kind of thin."

"That's everything they've got. Witnesses reported a two- or four-door getaway car that's green or blue or silver, and a crew of three to five with androgynous descriptions. Pretty much the only solid clues are the dates and locations of the robberies, which anyone who reads newspapers could have gotten."

"I'll give it a shot," said Benmont. "So is this really the Dukes of Hazzard bank robbery investigation?"

"All over the news," said Quint. "The Crime Stoppers TIPS line is flooded with calls, but the police aren't hopeful."

"Why not?"

"There's no connection to *The Dukes of Hazzard*."

"Then why are they called that?"

"One of our previous studies showed that robbers have a thirty-two percent higher chance of being captured if they're given nicknames. And a secondary analysis found that *The Dukes* has a fifty-nine percent favorable rating among people who like to tell on others."

"Okay, I'll get on it immediately," said Benmont. "Just curious about one thing."

"Shoot."

Benmont gestured across the office floor. "Those kids are so much faster with computers. Why not give the urgent police cases to them?"

"Because they're locked into binary tech-thought," said Quint. "But you're old-school and go with creative hunches. You have a place to start?"

Benmont stood and pointed. "The coffee machine."

"I'll get out of your way . . ."

. . . Just after five P.M., Quint was grabbing his coat when someone appeared in his office doorway. "Oh, hi, I was just about to see how you were doing."

Benmont stepped forward and handed a sheet of paper to his boss.

Quint put on his glasses and stared down at the page. "What am I looking at?"

"The names of the bank robbers."

"Wait, what?— . . . So fast? . . . Are you sure?"

"Sure as I'm standing here. I also included their home addresses and where they work, if that helps."

Quint finally closed his open mouth. "Okay, let's both take seats and you explain this to me. Don't skip anything."

And Benmont laid out his step-by-step method.

"Fantastic job," said Quint. "Grab your jacket."

"I didn't bring one. Why?"

"We're delivering this in person." Quint slipped arms into his own coat. "It's about customer maintenance, and we need to set a new price point for their next job."

The pair arrived at the police department with their news, and the stunned reaction was about the same as Quint's had been. They immediately dispatched the SWAT teams and took down a trio of construction workers in Fort Pierce. Then they summoned Quint and Benmont into a meeting room.

Quint slapped his employee on the back. "Time to dazzle them."

Benmont stood sheepishly and cleared his throat. "I only had the dates and locations of the robberies. So I checked all the cell-phone numbers that had pinged off towers in a ten-mile radius of each bank branch, limiting it to a three-hour window before and after the robberies."

"But that must have generated millions of calls," said a lieutenant.

"It did," said Benmont. "I simply mashed the lists together—"

Quint jumped in. "Of course, using our latest proprietary technology. Sorry for interrupting. Go ahead, Benmont."

". . . And the millions of phone numbers became just three. Your bad guys."

A captain removed his hat. "How is that possible?"

"Think about it," said Benmont. "Who is going to be in extremely specific parts of Jacksonville, Orlando and Boynton Beach at equally specific times on August third, ninth and twenty-first?"

Police brass glanced at each other around the table. "But I thought collecting this kind of data was illegal," said the lieutenant. "There's been a lot about it in the news."

"Compiling lists of what numbers they *called* would be illegal," said Benmont. "We weren't asking that. We just looked for what phones were turned on. The law hasn't caught up with that yet. It's all in the terms of agreement."

"And you got this information from where?"

"We have arrangements with most major cell carriers," said Benmont. "In exchange for lists to help them steal each other's customers."

"Doesn't that make them mad?"

"None of them can afford to be left out," said Benmont.

More glances around the table, followed by a round of nodding.

The chief stood. "We'll hold a press conference in the morning. Hope you don't mind if we take credit. It's in *our* terms of agreement."

"Just as long as you keep bringing us business." Quint got up from the table. "I'll be sending over our updated fee schedule, and the new contingency clause."

"Clause?"

"In addition to our regular payment, we get any rewards."

Chapter 3

SARASOTA

A Ford Falcon sped away from Pinecraft Park. Coleman looked out the back window. "The Amish aren't playing volleyball anymore, just watching our car."

"Watching in respect."

"I'm hungry."

"You're in luck." Serge hit his turn signal. "That's another cool thing about the Florida Amish. They've assimilated into our society, unlike AM radio listeners, and there's an unnatural concentration of fabulous country restaurants right around here like the Dutchman, Yoder's, the Amish Kitchen, not to mention Big Olaf's ice cream."

"Get me to the closest."

Moments later, the Falcon skidded into a parking lot, and the famished duo headed for the entrance. "It's not only the food," said Serge, "but these restaurants sell all their crafts as well, like candles and quilts. On the way out the door, instead of grabbing a toothpick, you can pick up a rocking chair."

"Why would you buy a rocking chair from a restaurant?"

"Not just any rocking chair." Serge opened the door and pointed at a piece of furniture. "An *Amish* rocking chair. That says state of the art. See? It's in high def."

"But isn't that because we're looking at it in person?"

"Exactly," said Serge. "I'm right again."

A waitress approached and smiled. "Two for dinner?"

"Unless the volleyball team followed us," said Serge. "By the way, pleasure to make your acquaintance. We're the weirdos."

"What?"

"I mean, not *the* Weirdos, you know, like a traveling circus troupe from Budapest that rides motorcycles upside down in round cages. The vernacular ones. We forge understanding." A big grin. "And we're absolutely starved after a day of building trust! To the butter churns!"

The woman grabbed a pair of menus. "Please follow me."

They sat in wooden slat chairs, by far the youngest customers in the entire restaurant. Coleman looked down. "What's barn-raising stew?"

"What an Amish neighborhood eats after everyone pitches in to help each other."

"Help each other? Who the hell does that?"

"I've just heard rumors." Serge flipped to the back page. "Let's cut to the chase. The homemade pies are what they're famous for."

The waitress arrived with glasses of water. "Need more time?"

"Did you hear that bell?" asked Serge. "Ding! Ding! Ding! That means it's pie time!" He handed his menu back. "I'll have your scrump-dilly-icious shoofly!"

"Me too," said Coleman.

She jotted on her pad. "Two slices of shoofly."

"No, the whole pie," said Serge.

She smiled. "Planning on taking the rest home for a late-night snack?"

"Nope," said Serge. "It's all for here."

She looked up from her pad. "If you don't mind me saying so, our pies are pretty big."

"That's what we hear!" Serge tucked a napkin into the collar of his tropical shirt and unfastened his belt buckle. "Bring it on! And two of your biggest spoons!"

Both Serge and Coleman were soon facedown over the table, scooping away.

"Know what the oldest retirement community in Florida is?" Serge asked with a mouthful. "Advent Christian Village, opened 1913, tucked in a bend of the Suwannee River near Live Oak. Totally immersed in nature instead of outlet malls." He pointed with the spoon. "Now that's vision!"

It wasn't long before Coleman tossed a napkin on his plate. "That's it, I'm about to pop. She wasn't kidding about the size of their pies."

"I knew it would be too big." Serge threw in his own napkin. "We'd never finish it on our own."

"Then why'd you order it?"

"To make friends. I've had the room under surveillance the whole time we were chowing down like wombats." Serge tilted his head. "See that booth in the corner?"

"The ones eating dumplings? They're like the oldest people in the whole place, and the others are freaking ancient to start with."

"That guy is wearing one of those military caps." Serge stood up from the table. "I love the old dudes in the military caps!"

"Why?"

"Another of Florida's natural treasures," said Serge. "We arguably have the highest concentration of war heroes retired down here with all these fantastic stories to tell. Except they're too humble to say anything, and you only know they're embedded among us when a TV station airs the latest in an unending series of stories about some stupid committee that makes one of them take down an American flag outside his house because it's too big."

"Where are you going?"

"They haven't ordered dessert yet." Serge carried the rest of their pie across the room and grinned. "Could you scoot over?"

"Uh, what—?" said the man in the cap. But Serge was already beginning to sit, and the man had to scoot by default.

Coleman arrived and Serge pointed. "There's room on that side with her."

"What—?" said the woman, hurriedly moving as Coleman began another inelegant plopping down.

"So! Military cap!" said Serge, stretching his neck around to see the front of the hat. "Wow! The marines, no less." He saluted. "Semper Fi!"

"Uh, do we know you?" asked the man. "Were you in the corps?"

"No and no," said Serge. "But I'm one of your biggest fans! Mind if I get out my tape recorder? It won't take up much room. I need to complete my oral history before you cats are all gone. I'm guessing by your age—what, Korea?"

"He never talks about it," said the woman across the table.

Serge swung the microphone. "And you are . . . ?"

"Mildred." A smile. "He never wants to brag. He only wears that hat so he can meet the other veterans in public, and even then they just say hi and don't talk about it. But he should be proud. He looked so handsome in his uniform. And they even gave him this nice star."

"Star?" asked Serge, checking the volume meter on his recorder.

"Yes, it's really pretty and silver."

Serge's head jerked up with sudden seriousness. "It's *silver*? . . . Wait, Korea? Where was he?"

"I don't know," said Mildred, looking at her plate. "I think it was like a canal or something."

"A reservoir?" asked Serge.

"That's it." She raised her face and nodded with another smile. "A reservoir."

Serge jumped to his feet and snatched the tape recorder off the table. "I'm very sorry for the intrusion . . . Come on, Coleman!"

"What's going on?"

"Just get up!" Serge looked down at his pie, then at Mildred. "That one's eaten out of. I'll send the waitress to take it away, and you order any one you want on me. I'm so sorry again. Enjoy your day." He grabbed Coleman by the arm.

"Ow, that hurts!"

They ended up back at their original table.

Coleman rubbed a red mark near his elbow. "What's gotten into you?"

Serge's hands covered his face. "There's something seriously wrong with me. I don't mean anything bad. I just get overexcited and spaz out. Too much enthusiasm is all. But I can't always be blustering around without consideration for who I'm imposing on."

"I still don't understand what's going on," said Coleman.

Serge stretched out a rigid arm. "Do you know who that is over there?"

"I don't think we got a first name."

"I'm talking about what he did."

An empty expression stared back.

"He was at the Chosin Reservoir," said Serge.

"What's that?" asked Coleman.

"Precisely." Serge swept an arm in the air. "Almost nobody remembers. We take everything for granted in our comfy cruise-control lives where the wrong wine with fish is a pants-shitting crisis. Totally oblivious to the sacrifices of people like him who self-lessly fought for the freedom of today's Americans to be childish."

"But I still don't know what the reservoir thing is."

"Snow, sub-freezing temperatures, brutal terrain when the Chinese came pouring down into the peninsula in late 1950. Thirty thousand of our troops completely encircled by a force that outnumbered them four to one with orders from Mao not to take prisoners. They were getting cut to pieces but never gave up, fighting seventeen straight days until they punched a hole in the enemy line and escaped. Some of the most brutal combat the world has ever seen." Serge shook his head. "Everybody deserved a Silver Star, but if that guy got one in the middle of that bloodiness . . . well, I've read some of the commendations. He must have done something ridiculously brave to save his brothers, like single-handedly capturing a machine-gun nest with only a pistol and a grenade, then using it to wipe out an entire enemy platoon . . ."

"Excuse me?"

Serge looked up with a start. "Mildred?"

She was holding the rest of his pie. "Mind if we join you?"

"Sure! Sure!" Serge jumped up and pulled out the other two chairs at the table. He noticed the old guy had a cane, one of those deluxe models with a small tripod of rubber feet at the bottom that you buy off late-night infomercials.

Serge returned to his seat more than a little surprised. "You really want to sit with us? After I bothered you?"

The sweetest smile. "It was no bother," said Mildred. "You were very nice and complimentary taking an interest in us. We're never been interviewed before."

"You should have reporters lined up around the block," said Serge.

"We like visiting with people. But we're some of the oldest out at the retirement park and have trouble getting around, and the others are busy with their activities. And we also love talking to younger people, but they have their lives, too. It can get a little lonely, you know."

"I'm not too busy," said Serge. "Actually, I am, but everything's on hold for heroes like you." He looked down at the table. "I said I'd buy a whole new pie."

"It's bad to waste," said Mildred. "Is it okay to share dessert together?"

"Are you kidding?" Serge turned around for the waitress, but she was already there with pleasantness.

"I see you've made some new friends to help finish that pie." She set down two more plates and utensils.

Serge held out a hand. "We were never formally introduced. I'm Serge and that's Coleman."

"Buster." The old man shook the hand. "Buster Hornsby. Eureka, Kansas."

"Well, Buster Hornsby of Eureka, Kansas," said Serge, "how did you end up in our fine state?"

"I read in the papers where Doolittle's Raiders sometimes held their annual reunions in Sarasota, and the pictures looked so nice. It always stuck with me."

"You're kidding! I went to the Doolittle reunions," said Serge. "Right on the bay front. If you were anywhere in Florida, how could you *not* go?"

"Dr. Doolittle?" asked Coleman. "The guy with the weird animals?"

"You'll have to excuse my friend." Serge wiped pie off Coleman's nose. "He has the historical memory of a tsetse fly."

"One of his animals had two heads, right?"

"Coleman, that's it!" said Serge. "We're watching *Thirty Seconds Over Tokyo* tonight."

"I loved that movie," said Buster.

"Me too," said Mildred. "They were so brave."

Coleman shoveled pie. "What's everyone talking about?"

"Just one of the most dangerous missions of World War Two," said Serge. "Barely four months after the sneak attack at Pearl Harbor, America was far from having her battle legs under her. That's when President Roosevelt decided the country needed a morale boost and ordered something beyond audacious."

"We would bomb Tokyo," said Buster. "It was an operation so preposterous that nobody ever saw it coming."

"That's right," said Serge. "It's hard to fathom today, but prior to the war, the U.S. military was ranked something like seventeenth in the world, behind Belgium. Japan had an iron hold on the Pacific, and we had nothing but an inferiority complex. So the president sent a tiny force across the ocean that slipped unnoticed through the Japanese fleets. On April 18, 1942, an enemy patrol boat spotted the aircraft carrier *Hornet,* still hundreds of miles too far from its target for the planes to take off and return safely. And you know what? The pilots took off anyway! Sixteen B-25s with only enough fuel to reach the target. It became a suicide mission!"

"They flew on and dropped their bombs," said Buster. "But as miracles happen, they'd picked up a tailwind, giving them just enough to overfly Japan and bail out in the ocean or the coast of mainland China."

Serge shook with goose bumps. "Did you know they secretly trained for that mission in Florida's panhandle at a base near Destin? . . . And decades later, it blew my mind that I got to see many of the survivors in the flesh in this city. The reunions are over now with the math of years. But there was a time not long ago when those gatherings just a couple of miles west of here were among the proudest moments in Sarasota's history."

"You sure know your stuff for such a young guy," said Buster.

"And you lived it!" said Serge. "I have the uncontrollable impulse to march around the restaurant singing the national anthem in your honor, but as you can see, I'm redirecting all my energy to sitting on my hands."

Mildred looked out the front window. "We need to make sure we don't miss our shuttle bus. It's getting close to leaving."

"Shuttle bus!" Serge's hands shot out from under his butt. "I won't hear of it! Any recipient of the Silver Star deserves a private driver! Your chariot awaits! Where do you live?"

"Boca Vista Lago Isle Shores, but we just call it Boca Shores."

"Coleman, let's give them a hand toward the door."

Minutes later, a 1970 Ford Falcon sped east toward the interstate.

Serge glanced up in the rearview at the backseat. "How are you two nutty kids doing back there?"

"Fine," said Mildred. "You really didn't have to do this. We always take the shuttle."

"Nonsense," said Serge. "Consider me your peace dividend."

Buster leaned forward and tapped Serge's shoulder. "What exactly is your friend doing?"

"Eating a pineapple."

"And setting fire to the top?" asked Mildred.

"New health craze. Eliminates free radicals."

In southern Sarasota County, Serge took one of the Venice exits and crossed over to the east side of the interstate. They approached the entrance of the Boca Shores retirement park with rows of coconut palms on each side and a small guard shack in the middle with a small TV and an Earl inside. Normally, Earl remained seated and waved people through without taking his eyes off the game shows. But none of the residents drove muscle cars. He stood and hiked his guard-uniform pants up to the stomach overlap.

"How can I help you fellas?"

"*. . . Wheel . . . of . . . Fortune! . . .*"

"You can't," said Serge. "I have everything under control."

"Is that a pineapple?"

"Yes, next question."

"Why is smoke coming out of it?"

"The Q-and-A portion of our program has just ended. Thank you for playing," said Serge. "Please raise that wooden arm blocking our way. We have precious cargo."

"*. . . I'd like to buy a vowel . . .*"

Buster leaned and waved out the window. "It's okay, Earl. They're giving us a ride."

"Oh, Mr. Hornsby. I didn't see you in there." He turned back toward his booth. "I'll open the gate."

"*. . . Is there an X in the puzzle? . . .*"

". . . Ooooooo, sorry . . ."

Straight ahead, a fountain weakly sprayed water into a square man-made lake. Boca *Shores*. Eight miles inland. A flock of bored swans listlessly circled the fountain. Serge's gaze turned toward the rows of aluminum trailers disguised as houses. "I already love this place!"

"They have a clubhouse and everything," said Mildred.

The wooden guard arm raised, and the Falcon drove through.

". . . Chico, your spin . . ."

Chapter 4

1957

Far down below, the planet Earth was big and blue and radiant with life. White, cottony wisps streaked all the way from California wine country to the Mexican Baja. The world continued to turn.

Up here, which would be 140 miles above sea level, the electromagnetic spectrum was doing all kinds of magical stuff. Some of it could be seen with the naked eye, which is why it was called "visible light." But the vast majority could only be detected through scientific instruments. X-rays, infrared, ultraviolet, radio waves.

They named this part of the upper atmosphere the ionosphere. That's because it had become mildly charged with radiation from the sun, which took eight minutes to get here. Among other things, the ionosphere does this: Some of the invisible radio waves coming up from Earth are bounced back down, where they skip back up, only to ricochet down again and so forth, covering great distances across the surface of the planet.

Slide back up the magnetic spectrum, and you returned to the visible world, where the distant view below toward Hawaii was turquoise and emerald. Clouds near Fiji began to swirl in the birth of a Pacific cyclone.

Suddenly, at close range, a shiny silver ball flew by at eighteen thousand miles an hour, perfectly round, three times the diameter of a basketball. It was beeping, like a softball used to play with the blind. The metallic orb, with four spider-like legs trailing behind it, continued zooming eastward across the sky for fifteen minutes until it sailed over a subtropical peninsula called Florida.

Straight down below, a thirty-two-year-old man named Theodore Pruitt had just finished cutting his lawn in West Palm Beach. It was a Saturday. Now it was time for iced lemonade in his den. The reward for perspiration. His right hand twisted a tuning dial on an elaborate radio. As he did, the radio waves outside hopping up and down off the ionosphere reached his shortwave set with what he usually listened to: official government broadcasts from Cairo, Buenos Aires, Prague, Bangkok. But this time he kept tuning past the medley of foreign languages until he reached the vicinity of twenty megahertz. His hand stopped as the radio picked up something new, and it wasn't an atmospheric skip. Today it was a direct downlink.

Beep, beep, beep, beep . . .

Sitting next to him in a child-size chair was a child, little five-year-old Teddy Pruitt. His father was from Hartford and worked for Pratt & Whitney, an aviation company with a giant new manufacturing plant in Florida on the edge of the Glades. There was growth ahead from government contracts in the postwar boom. Pruitt was a stand-up guy, always putting his wife and family first, his only vice an occasional Grabow pipe popular among the slide-rule types.

There were many awe-inspiring perks to being raised by an

engineer. Teddy sat next to his dad's knee, looking up with circular eyes needing approval.

Beep, beep, beep, beep . . .

"Hear that, son?"

The boy nodded with vigor, though not exactly sure why. It wasn't like those other things he heard from the radio. Strange tongues. Calm, screaming, monotone, but always an imagination-voyage to a faraway land. This time, just:

Beep, beep, beep, beep . . .

"What's that, Papa?"

"It's what they call *Sputnik*." He turned the volume up. "The Soviet Union launched it in October."

"Where is it?"

"Look up, son."

The child saw the ceiling.

"More than a hundred miles above us in outer space, circling the Earth every ninety minutes. Something new called a satellite. The Soviets put it on top of a big rocket."

Beep, beep, beep, beep . . .

"Do we have big rockets?"

"Yes," said the elder Theodore. "The Soviets beat us into space, but we're catching up. We're going to launch our own satellite in January called *Explorer*. It will try to detect radiation belts surrounding the Earth."

"Are the Soviets our friends?"

"Not anymore," his father said gently. "We used to be allies during World War Two, but then there were disagreements, and now we're in something called a Cold War."

"What's that?"

"Nobody's shooting right now, but we're not getting along," said his father. "You know those drills you do in school where you get under your desk for protection?"

The child eagerly nodded.

"That's in case the Soviets do something bad."

"Will I be okay?"

"As long as you stay under your desk, you'll be fine," his father lied.

"But what kind of weapons can reach my school?"

Beep, beep, beep, beep . . .

"They're known as nuclear weapons. The United States used to have the only ones, but some people called spies stole our secrets and gave them to the Soviets."

"Who were these people?"

"Other Americans."

"I don't understand," said the boy. "Why would Americans give our secrets away?"

"I don't understand, either, son. You have to love your country."

"I do."

The *beeps* faded from the radio.

His father smiled and reached under his desk for an unseen shopping bag. "I have a surprise." He handed it to Teddy, who pulled out a box with an illustration on the cover.

"Wow! A model rocket!"

"A new company called Estes is just starting, and I got an early sample. Their models really fly. A parachute pops out and everything."

"Can we build it?"

They got to work, cutting balsa wood, gluing cardboard tubes, taping strings to the plastic parachute. After letting it all dry a few hours, they went to a nearby high school football field.

The rocket was on the miniature pad that came with the kit. Theodore put his arm around his son's shoulders as they said the countdown together. "*. . . Three, two, one, blastoff!*"

The child pressed the control button, and the rocket whooshed skyward far higher than little Teddy had thought possible. He shielded his eyes and watched a tiny orange chute deploy at three hundred feet. Then the child took off running as the rocket safely drifted down and landed in the end zone.

That evening, little Teddy was in his bedroom, carefully inserting the folded parachute back into the rocket and refitting the nose cone. His father appeared in the doorway. "Son, do you want to *see Sputnik*?"

"Isn't it in outer space?"

"Yes," said his dad. "Except it's visible if you know when to look. It has to be just before sunrise or after sunset, when the sky is dark but the sun is still close enough over the horizon to reflect off the satellite."

"I want to see *Sputnik*!"

His father led Teddy back into the den. He tuned his shortwave to the same frequency as before. But there was no sound. "When we start hearing the beeps again, we go outside."

They waited quietly and stared at the equally quiet shortwave receiver set precisely at 20.0005 megahertz. Then:

Beep, beep, beep, beep . . .

They ran outside. His father pointed straight up. "There it is!"

"I see it! I see it!"

They watched together as the tiny dot of light streaked across the darkness at incredible velocity, and his father put his arm around the boy's shoulders again.

Little Teddy thought: *This is the best day of my whole life!*

THE PRESENT

A 1970 Ford Falcon pulled up to a green-and-white manufactured home near Sarasota. A row of azaleas ran along the front of the trailer, and another row of little white concrete domes ran along the edge of the grass at the street so people wouldn't drive on the lawn or else. An American flag on a stick hung from a brass bracket by the front door.

Serge looked up at a shiny steel tube rising high from the middle of the yard. "What's with the big flagpole?"

"Used to have a big flag," said Buster. "Now I have to settle for—...that one on the stick."

Serge stepped back. "What in heaven's name happened?"

"Young guy from the park office came around. Told me the flag violated some kind of governing rules that I don't remember signing. 'Out of proportion with the visual aesthetic,' or so he said. I had to take it down unless I wanted to pay fines each day."

"Motherfu—" Serge quickly covered his mouth. "Uh, not good."

"He had a point in a way," said Buster. "If my flag flew, they would have to let others fly any crazy flag: Red China, Russia, swastikas, Kentucky Fried Chicken. I finally agreed, partly because he had worn me down, and I had to get to the doctor for my leg thing."

"I wouldn't have been nearly as calm," said Serge.

"Neither was Mildred," said Buster. "After the doctor took a look at my veins, she was right on the phone to the TV stations. One of them sent out a truck with a big dish on top, and I was interviewed by a woman who looked like a swimsuit model."

"She was that attractive?"

"She was wearing a swimsuit," said Buster.

"Of course," said Serge. "The networks go belly-up anytime a condo committee or homeowners association tells a veteran to take down the Stars and Stripes because it's an eyesore. They probably have miles of stock video they can just splice in."

"They did," said Buster. "They aired their interview of me, but added footage of a different guy's house and another flag. That was three months ago."

"So how is the flagpole still up?"

"Some lawyer from the American Civil Liberties Union saw the story on TV and said he'd represent me for free. He filed for an injunction to keep the flag up under my freedom of expression, and filed another injunction to take it down for infringing on the park's right *not* to express. The judge convinced the ACLU to strike a compromise with itself to remove the flag but leave the pole."

Serge shook his head vigorously to clear his mental Etch A Sketch. "I know some other lawyers—"

"Life's too short." Buster flicked his wrist. "I still got my stick flag."

"Would you like to come inside?" asked Mildred. "I have coffee and Little Debbies."

"Come inside?" Serge took another step back. "Your cathedral of semi-wind-resistant construction? Say no more! . . . Coleman! We're golden! . . . I was trying to work up my best pickup line to view the inside of an actual senior-citizen terrarium, but she beat me to it!"

Mildred led the way, followed by Buster, limping with the aid of his tactical cane tested by the special forces.

The layout of all the trailers in the park seemed quite unorthodox and perplexing at first, then brilliant in its retirement function. The front *door* of each trailer was a sliding glass door. And in front of it was a screened-in porch that faced the street, just like all the old front porches up north, where people sat outside on balmy evenings and waved to their neighbors prior to the onset of the suburbs and pricks. But because it was Florida, these porches needed screens to keep out bugs, and metal roofs to keep out sun. So, if you arrived at one of the trailers from the street, you walked up the driveway, climbed two steps to a screen door, then another few steps past all-weather furniture to a glass door before entering the forgotten world of wall-to-wall carpeting.

Serge walked into an aroma-funk of baked apples and ointments. "Whoa!" He spun slowly in place, appraising a trailer that appeared to have been decorated by the Consumer Channel. "You've beaten back the concept of minimalism with a tree trunk!"

There were knickknacks and figurines and crystal crap, several ottomans, a chandelier that was out of scale for the space, a dusty set of encyclopedias, and an embroidered pillow that said WHO FARTED? Inside a glass bell jar was a clock with all the moving parts visible, powered by a ring of three shiny balls that spun one way and back the other. A row of matching flowerpots in descending order of size sat on a mantel below a painting of dogs playing poker.

Rrrrrring . . .

"I'll get it," said Mildred. She picked up a cordless phone from a base featuring a bronze eagle coming in for the kill. "Hello? . . . I'm sorry, we're having company right now . . ."

Coleman tripped over a knee-high ceramic frog. "Where am I supposed to walk?"

"This way," said Mildred, navigating a winding path to an embroidered sofa covered in plastic. "I'll get the Little Debbies. Are red velvet cakes okay?"

Ding-dong! . . .

"I'll get it." Mildred answered the door. "I'm sorry, we're having company right now."

Buster eased himself down into a large padded chair and grabbed its remote control that made him recline. Serge took a seat on the plastic-covered couch and stared at a marble coffee table supporting stacks of magazines representing fifteen successful magazine salesmen.

"So, Buster," said Serge. "How did you end up in Korea?"

"Enlisted." He finished adjusting his chair until his pale legs were out perfectly straight in his favorite position. He placed the chair's remote control with all the other remotes, stored in a special fabric organizer that hung from the armrest. He stared at a TV set showing bundled-up people straining to walk in a snowstorm. "Enlisting is what you were supposed to do back then. Most of my family was military. So was most of the neighborhood."

Serge pointed at the television. "What are you watching?"

"What's the point of retiring to Florida if you don't follow the weather back home?" Buster reached in the armrest organizer for a portable phone and dialed. "Roland, it's me, Buster. How's the shoveling coming?" He hung up and giggled.

Mildred emerged from the kitchen with a wicker tray of dessert cakes that she set on the magazines. She clasped her hands. "Would anyone like some coffee?"

"Uh-oh," said Coleman.

"Ooo! Ooo!" Serge waved a hand.

"Coming right up."

Rrrrrring . . .

"Don't answer it," said Buster.

"What if it's the children?" asked Mildred.

"It's not."

She pressed a button on the phone. "Hello? . . . No, we're having company right now . . ."

"Buster," said Serge. "If you don't mind me asking, how old are you?"

"Ninety-four. Mildred's two years younger."

A lace doily, saucer and cup were placed on a 1996 *Reader's Digest*. "I forgot to ask what you like in it."

"Black's fine," said Serge. "Sometimes ice cubes so I can chug."

"I'll get them."

"No, sit down and take a load off. It's cool enough."

Ding-dong . . .

"Is that the door again?" asked Mildred.

"Don't answer it," said Buster.

"The children."

"They're in Kansas."

She opened it. ". . . We're having company . . ."

"Buster," said Serge, quickly slurping his china cup, "who the hell are all these people?"

"Solicitors."

"Does this happen often?"

"All hours of the day."

"I'll bet you're on some kind of list."

"Gee, you think?" Buster pointed at a ring of spinning gold balls. "This room used to be pretty empty until we bought that stupid clock. Then all hell broke loose. I'm happy to sit in peace and quiet, but Mildred gets lonely and likes to talk to people on the phone. And at the door. Whenever an eight hundred number comes on TV, I have to change the channel or I'll be up to my nipples in nonstick skillets."

Serge glanced toward the kitchen. "Can I get more coffee?"

"Knock yourself out."

Serge was back in a flash with a fresh cup. "Hope you don't mind that I chugged an extra one while I was in there to save time . . . So where were we?"

Ding-dong . . .

Mildred was in the bedroom getting something. Serge jumped up. "Allow me."

He answered the door. A man in a tie held a briefcase of color swatches. He grinned and started opening his mouth.

Serge raised the front of his tropical shirt to reveal the butt of the pistol tucked in his waistband. "Go ahead, say a word! Say one fucking word!"

The man's mouth closed and his eyes opened wide.

"Good," said Serge. "And in case you're thinking of coming back . . ." He kicked him in the nuts. "Now, if you don't mind, we're having company."

The door slammed.

Buster had been watching the exchange in a gilded mirror on the wall. He started giggling.

Chapter 5

SARASOTA

Mildred Hornsby returned from the rear of the trailer with a leather-bound volume under her arm. "What so funny?"

"Just sharing a joke," said Buster.

She looked out the sliding glass door as a salesman limped away in a serious rush.

Serge was examining a frame on the wall displaying a Christmas card with a mechanical autograph from the second President Bush.

"We gave to his campaign," said Mildred. "And he was nice enough to send us that. He really signed it."

"Yes, he did."

She sat down on the couch and patted the spot next to her. "Have a seat." She opened the volume in her lap. "This is the family album."

"Family album!" said Serge. "Those are the two most terrifying words in the English language! Friends and relatives violently up-chuck, scrambling for escape routes . . . Whenever there's an emergency, forget yelling 'Fire!' If you really want to clear the building in a hurry: 'Here's the family album.' . . . But not me! I love photos of tots in high chairs covered with milk and Cap'n Crunch. Or the big family outing at the beach when everyone thinks they look like the Kennedys. And don't forget the school plays where you had to dress like butterflies or Pilgrims . . . Let's take a look, shall we? . . ."

An hour went by. Phones and doorbells went unanswered.

"Here's the letter he got from the marines with his Star," said Mildred.

"I guessed it," said Serge. "Machine-gun nest."

"And then on the next page . . ."

"No, no, no, I'm not finished with this one yet," said Serge. "Is there a magnifying glass anywhere in this place? You're supposed to have one."

Another hour . . .

Buster's and Coleman's heads rested back over the tops of their respective chairs, snoring. Mildred yawned. "Well, I'll just be putting the family album away."

"No, no, no, I want to start again at the beginning!" said Serge.

"But I need my afternoon nap."

Serge flipped back to the front of the book and bent over with a magnifying glass. "You go rest. I'm in command of the bridge . . ."

Near dusk, there was a contagion of stretching as people in the trailer slowly awoke.

Buster's eyelids fluttered open, and he found Serge's giant right eyeball staring back at him through a magnifying glass a few inches away.

"Ahhhhhhh!" The old man jerked alive in his chair. "What are you doing? How long have you been there?"

"Waiting for you to wake up. Half hour." Serge dropped back

down on the sofa. "The curiosity has been killing me! I didn't notice it before because of all the other junk piled everywhere, but what is that big metal thing with the air vents at the end of the couch? Everything else in here is decorative, and that's so industrial."

"It's the ionizer."

"What's it for?" asked Serge.

"Supposed to keep us from getting sick," said Buster.

"I don't mean to bring you down or anything, but I've seen home ionizers before. Sleek little models. That baby's meant for a small warehouse."

Buster shrugged. "The salesman said we needed it."

Serge pointed toward a humming sound from another direction. "What's that thing?"

"Air purifier," replied Buster. "To keep us from getting sick. Different diseases."

"What diseases?"

"Swans." Buster glanced out the front of the trailer at the lake. "The salesman had a brochure with pictures. The swans poop, and the droppings dry out and become airborne as little particles that come in the house and get you if you don't watch out."

"Did this salesman happen to sell you anything else?"

Buster worked a remote control to get his recliner to un-recline, then grabbed his cane. "Come with me."

They ambled down a short hall. The master bedroom was on the right. Buster opened the door on the left. They were hit with a chorus of sound that seemed quiet and loud at the same time: various soothing hums that combined harmonically in such high proportion to create a low-frequency, bone-tingling drone.

Serge was boggled by a sight that looked like the HVAC center in the basement of a major downtown hotel. Two crammed rows of more metal encasements with ventilation slits.

"You can't even walk around in there," shouted Serge.

"We don't use that bedroom anyway," shouted Buster.

"What *are* all these things?"

Buster pointed with the rubber tips of his walking aid. "That's the humidifier . . ."

"Humidifier?" said Serge. "It's Florida. The whole state's one giant free humidifier!"

"They said we needed it." The cane swung. "And that's the other humidifier."

"Two?"

"They said one wasn't enough."

"Jesus!" said Serge. "They're even bigger than the ionizer. Each of those suckers could handle an office building in Albuquerque."

"And this next row are the dehumidifiers."

"Dehumidifiers?" said Serge. "Is this some kind of Steven Wright joke?"

"We told them we were getting sweaty," said Buster. "Now we don't sweat."

"I'll bet not."

Mildred joined them in the doorway. "Isn't all that stuff great?"

"What's the thing installed in the back wall?"

"The master zone air-conditioning control unit," said Mildred. "Running zones one, two and three."

"But you already have central air," said Serge.

"They said it would save money."

"Even the Pentagon doesn't spend like this." Serge grabbed his stomach. "Did they sell you anything else?"

"Just the security system."

"Okay, security." Serge nodded. "At least something practical. Always good to have that."

Mildred nodded in return. "Also controls the smoke detectors and monitors for carbon monoxide, carbon dioxide, carbon trioxide . . ." She opened a closet and pointed at a flat screen. "Plus all the surveillance cameras are displayed on the same screen. I don't know how they do it."

"*Sixteen* cameras?" Serge began to shake. "I've witnessed all manner of predation before, but this is beyond the pale."

"Your face is all red," said Buster.

"Maybe you need to sit down," said Mildred.

They returned to the living room.

"Do I have this straight?" said Serge. "The same salesman sold you all this stuff?"

"Actually, there were two," said Mildred. "The first was such a nice young man that I ordered a small ionizer. And the next day an even nicer older gentleman showed up. By old, I mean older than the kid, about forty. And he said my ionizer was too small, but I could trade up for a discount since it was barely used. And then he got out his brochures for the humidifiers—"

"May I jump in?" asked Serge. "I can tell you how this works. They hire these young kids and pay them next to nothing to go out cold-calling. It's a low-percentage game, and it takes a lot of knuckles on doors to get a sale. But once they find a customer, the percentage rises appreciably. They give the kid a commission and yank him off the case. Then they send in the seasoned con men known as closers. They have absolutely no soul. They will sell and sell and sell until you either lose your house or call the cops."

"Oh my," said Mildred. "Is that what happened?"

"Hate to be the one to break the news."

"But he seemed like he really cared."

"That's the worst part," said Serge. "Call me old-school, but back in the day, we left the most vulnerable alone, and we respected our elders. That is, if I ever did anything requiring such choices, which I didn't. But this new breed lives by no code and goes straight for the weakest victims first."

"I told you," said Buster, staring at a snowbank on TV.

"But one thing I don't understand," said Serge. "You guys live in a gated community with a guard booth. And yet your doorbell's been ringing all day. I thought the guard would stop salesmen."

Mildred looked down in thought. "I was wondering about

that phone call. Earl said a man was at his booth claiming he had an appointment with me, except I didn't recall scheduling anything. But who knows with my memory? I would feel guilty if I inconvenienced him."

"And that's exactly what he was counting on," said Serge. "That you would have values. That you would care about *him*. It's their version of trying to get buzzed into an apartment building when you don't know anyone and just start hitting intercom buttons. And then they're inside the guarded retirement community, free to cold-call up and down the street."

"I had heard some people were like that," said Mildred. "But you could spot them because they looked like criminals."

"The new ones don't." Serge placed a reassuring hand on her shoulder. "But all is about to change for the better. Do you think you could find the receipts so I can tabulate how much you've spent on everything?"

"I can probably do that."

"Good," said Serge. "And one more item. Would you happen to have his business card?"

TAMPA

Benmont Pinch placed a sausage-and-cheese croissant on a napkin and turned on his computer for the day. He liked to arrive at Life-Armor early, before the others, to enjoy simple morning routines while it was still quiet. He blew on the top of a steaming cup from Dunkin' Donuts and checked his e-mail.

There it was, right at the top. An overnight message with an attachment from the police department. His newest crime-fighting assignment.

The previous afternoon, Benmont and his boss had met again at police headquarters. A string of unsolved home invasions. This time there wasn't a single flimsy file but box after box of evidence.

Quint slapped Benmont on the back. "Dazzle 'em, sport!"

Benmont took the cover off each carton in turn and fished through the sealed clear bags. Everyone leaned forward, expecting a dramatic Sherlock Holmes moment.

"Sorry," said Benmont. "I don't do forensics."

Shoulders sagged around the table.

"But let me see those lists of stolen items again."

Someone handed them over, and Benmont laid the pages side by side across the table. An index finger ran down each column. "I'm assuming you have all the pawnshops on alert for the most valuable possessions."

A lieutenant nodded.

Benmont tapped a spot in the middle of the last list. Then went backward, comparing and tapping similar spots in the others. He held up a page. "This item here. It's just a category. I need a detailed list from each crime scene."

"But that stuff's virtually worthless," said a sergeant.

The lieutenant held up a hand for silence. "Get it for him." The meeting dispersed . . .

. . . And now Benmont sat at his desk the next morning, sipping coffee as he pressed a button to open an e-mail attachment with extensive inventory.

"Now this is more like it." He grabbed a legal pad and began jotting. He called up websites. He grabbed the phone . . .

. . . Near the end of the day, Benmont approached the open doorway of his boss's office. There were family photos on the desk, next to a nameplate that said QUINT POWERS. On the wall behind him hung a framed novelty photo with a doctored scoreboard that said Quint had just hit a home run at Wrigley Field.

Quint was nearing his fiftieth birthday but still had broad shoulders from yard chores and lifting stuff. He used to work at a tax preparation franchise in a strip mall until QuickBooks came along. Now he was here.

Knock, knock, knock . . .

Quint looked up from his computer. "Benmont! Come in, come in!" He removed bifocals. "Have a seat."

A page was passed across the desk. The bifocals went back on. "What's this name?"

"The head of the home invasion ring." Benmont settled into a chair. "I also compiled a list of most likely associates from his metadata."

"I'm speechless again. How?"

"My gut. At most of the break-ins, a bunch of DVDs were stolen. But that's all it said in the police files: 'various DVDs.' That's why I asked for a complete list of titles."

"Movie titles cracked the case?"

"I called one of our clients, the people at Blue Box . . ."

"You mean those vending machines that now rent movies after Netflix turned all the brick-and-mortar video stores into nail salons?"

"Exactly. I plotted the robbery sites, pinpointing the geographic center, which I figured was their comfort zone. Then I located all the vending machines within a three-mile radius and requested a list of particular titles rented less than a week after each invasion."

"Why?"

Benmont shrugged. "People like to watch sequels."

"Sequels?"

Benmont spread a map across Quint's desk. "Two days after the first robbery, the next installment of the *Fast and Furious* franchise was rented here, then the next home was hit and the follow-up *Die Hard* was rented from the same machine, then the second *Hangover* and so on. Of course, dozens of people rented those movies, but when you narrow it by robbery dates and overlay the lists, only one credit card pops up. I checked, and the cardholder is a woman with a clean history, but her husband was just released last year from Raiford for B-and-E."

"Amazing." The boss picked up the phone. "Lieutenant, this is Quint at Life-Armor. Prepare to be pleased. You got a pen? . . ."

The conversion ended and Quint hung up. He put his hands behind his head and leaned way back in his leather chair. "Benmont, you have a big raise coming."

"Thanks."

"I thought you'd be happier," said Quint. "What's that look on your face?"

"Nothing." Benmont wiggled in the chair. "Just been thinking. You know how sometimes you get a vague feeling that something's out of place, but you don't know what? And then you can't get it out of your head, and it keeps nagging. Know what I mean?"

"Not really. Continue."

"It was an assignment I had last month. Another request for cyber-gibberish. One of those nebulous data crunches where you have no idea what the client is looking for, but who cares as long as they pay on time."

"Sounds like most of our clients," said Quint.

"This was about Social Security numbers," said Benmont. "We told them that legally we could only provide the last four digits, and they said that was fine. Just give them a list in numerical order. Doesn't that seem odd to you? Who has use for only the last four numbers?"

"Like you said, they pay on time." Quint sat forward. "And this is what's bothering you?"

"That's just the front end," said Benmont. "I performed the rest of their data collection, collated the other requested fields for names and birthdays, and e-mailed the finished project to you. I didn't give it another thought until Monday, when I suddenly woke up in the middle of the night and wondered: 'What the hell?' . . . I figured I must be imagining things, but I checked my files here the next morning and there it was."

"What?"

"Anomalies."

"Still nothing's registering on my end," said the boss. "Specifics?"

"Coincidences will always occur with this much information, but there's randomness and then there's *randomness*." Benmont reached into the briefcase by his feet. "I made printouts and circled each instance."

They stopped talking as a young man with heavy piercings and a ponytail came bobbing into the office to whatever sounds were in his headphones. He set a file on the desk without speaking and bobbed his way out.

Quint craned his neck to watch him leave, then turned to Benmont. "What do you think of the kids?"

"Their style choices throw off our generation, but after you get to know them, they're really quite nice. More so than we were at that age."

"What do you really think?"

"I feel threatened."

"Me too," said Quint. "They grew up with all this technology and know it inside out. The important thing is we can't let on . . . Where were we?"

"These printouts."

"Let me see that." The boss flipped pages. "Okay, it looks a little weird. You've got a few statistical clumps that may or may not be random. What's it supposed to mean?"

"That's the point. Who knows? I just have this vibe," said Benmont. "Dealing with all that raw data can get a little dry. Other than the police stuff, I rarely find anything interesting."

The boss held up the printouts. "And now it takes very little to amuse you?"

Benmont shrugged again. "I like puzzles. That's why the Social Security numbers caught my eye. You know how the government randomizes them?"

"Yes, I know they do."

"I mean, do you know *how*?"

"No."

"The first three digits are assigned to states, and the next two are group codes. To mix things up for security reasons, the groups go zero to ten by odd numbers, then eleven to ninety-nine even, then zero to ten even, then on up odd—"

"Stop. My head's starting to hurt," said Quint. "Someone got paid to think of that?"

"It's actually pretty clever," said Benmont. "Keeps the crooks guessing, and that's how fake numbers are spotted. All states have a bunch of unused groups scattered throughout the spread, so you can't just bet on low digits. Match the middle two digits to an empty state code group, and you got your bad guy."

"Now *I'm* getting bored."

"Maybe this will grab your attention. One of the client's requests is pretty suspicious. They wanted me to filter all adjoining Social Security entries with the same birthday."

Quint thought hard a moment, then a sudden look of understanding. "Why didn't you say that in the first place? And I'm surprised *you* didn't figure it out yourself. It's simply an ingenious way to create a large database of twins. They would have the same birthdays and consecutive Social Security numbers. Perfect for assembling some medical study, nature versus nurture, or a double-blind test on research drugs for a genetic disease . . . Well then, that's it. Mystery solved. There's nothing suspicious here at all."

"No, you're not following me," said Benmont. "They weren't asking me to filter and save the names. They wanted me to filter and delete. That just leaves non-twins."

"But that makes no sense." Quint looked back down at the data. "Why would anyone want such a list. Even odder, why would non-twins appear to *be* twins?" He reclined in his chair. "This is a new one on me."

"That's what I've been saying all this time." Benmont passed another piece of paper across the desk.

Quint sat back up. "What's this?"

"My theory. I also e-mailed you a copy."

"I thought you said you didn't know what was going on."

"I don't. That's why it's just a theory," said Benmont. "I realize it's pretty wild, so I wanted to warm you up first with all the background information."

Quint read down the page. "You're right. This is a pretty crazy theory. I think you've been watching too many action movies."

"It just hit me when I was driving to work. There's probably nothing to it, but I thought you might find it interesting."

"You do understand that if this is true, a lot of people are in serious danger, not to mention our company's legal exposure. But like you said, probably nothing." Quint set the page down. "Okay, I'll play with this. Now it's bugging me, too. I have an old friend at the Social Security Administration who might be able to help."

"So you'll send him my theory?"

"Not remotely," said Quint. "Your theory goes through our legal department. And don't give this to anyone else unless I say so. I'm just going to send my government friend your initial work product and see what he makes of it independently."

Another headphoned kid bopped in to drop off a file, then departed.

"Wine corks?" asked Quint.

"They seem happy," said Benmont. "I think *we're* the problem."

"Don't let them know."

Chapter 6

SARASOTA

Early mornings in the retirement park were almost religious. Especially just before sunrise. Still cool out, quiet enough to hear distant seagulls. The fountain hadn't been turned on yet, and the man-made lake remained still enough to see the occasional ripple from a turtle. A lone heron hunted insects in the reeds. A three-wheel bike circled the water with a poodle in the front basket. The cyclist waved at an oncoming pair of women power-walking in size-six sneakers. Fresh newspapers sat in plastic bags on dew-covered St. Augustine lawns. But most important: the beginning of a whole new day. Possibilities. The poodle's name was Banjo.

A sliding glass door opened onto a screened-in front porch facing the lake. Buster and Mildred Hornsby never missed a sunrise, never disappointed. Buster came out with his cane and Mildred in her slippers, carrying a tray of English muffins and orange juice. They sat in a pair of patio chairs with plastic straps. The chairs were the kind that mildly swung forward and back. They watched the swans in the lake, waiting for the fountain.

"Those sure were a couple of nice visitors we had yesterday," said Mildred, pushing the floor with her slippers to make the chair swing. "We don't get many—I mean, that aren't selling something."

"Serge was a good Joe," said Buster. "A mite rambunctious, but all in all."

"I hope we get to see them again."

"He promised we would."

"I wish I could have said good-bye. When did they leave?"

"I don't know." Buster swayed. "I fell asleep."

A peek of light to the east.

"Here comes the sun," said Mildred.

They stopped to appreciate the first warm, orange rays spreading out across the park. They hit the tops of the coconut palms first, and worked down to the sea grapes and birds of paradise.

The light glinted off the polished metal shaft of Buster's flagpole. He glanced up for the first time that morning. "Mildred, look."

"Someone raised a new flag," said his wife.

"It's bigger than my old one."

They stared as an immense rendition of the Stars and Stripes flapped gloriously in the onshore breeze.

"But why is it upside down?" asked Mildred.

Some people who don't know the protocol of displaying the flag might have considered it disrespectful. But those who revered it like Buster knew the real meaning.

He stood with his hands on his hips and gazed skyward. "It's a distress signal."

A man in a dress shirt and tie pulled into the parking lot of a sketchy motel in a long line of sketchiness on the Tamiami Trail. This particular length of road had officially been designated by the state as a scenic highway, and the scenery was undercover female police officers strutting the sidewalks in hot pants and arresting johns. Rigid rule of thumb in north Sarasota: If a hooker isn't meth-head ugly, she's a cop.

It was unusual to see a white-collar executive driving one of those large contractor vans, but there were always exceptions. The man behind the wheel was forty-four years old with a forty-five-dollar haircut. A laminated badge clipped to his pocket. CARL. The badge had a photo. The photo was meant to put senior citizens at ease about not being robbed and raped like all the talk.

Carl stopped the van in a small dust devil of blowing trash near the end of the motel. He checked the address on his clipboard and looked up at the room. "This can't be right."

The salesman had thought it was too good to be true at the time. Since when did customers cold-call *him*? And now it appeared his initial impression was correct. It was all a mistake. He threw the van in reverse.

Suddenly the door of the room opened, and someone in a tropical shirt enthusiastically windmilled his arm for the driver to come on in.

Carl glanced around. "I've already written off this sale, so what's to lose?" He got out, crunching broken glass under his oxfords, and approached the man in the doorway. Another look at his clipboard. "Are you Hank McKenna?"

"Nope; Serge." He extended a hand. "Nice to meet."

"Sorry, I've *definitely* got the wrong address." He turned to leave.

"No, you're at the best place of all," said Serge. "Let me guess. You got my brand-new X5000 Quantum Humidifier in the back of your van! Can't wait to check that baby out! So let's just roll that beauty right in here and rock my world!"

The man turned back around. A pause of confusion. "But you're not Hank McKenna, and . . . you're in a motel room. I thought this was getting delivered to a retirement park."

"It is," said Serge. "Hank's my grandfather and he told me you visited and left this." Serge flashed Carl's own business card at him, and returned it to his pocket.

Hmm, thought Carl. *That* is *my card, so this is starting to look legit after all.* "Then why not meet at his trailer?"

"It's a surprise. I'm planning to have it waiting in his driveway when he steps outside on his birthday. With a giant ribbon and bow on it, like on those new cars that people get as presents. But where do you even start looking for gift wrap that freaking size? Any help in this area would be most appreciated." Serge walked around to the back of the van and began hopping in excitement. "You want to sell this thing or not? There are plenty of other salesmen knocking on doors. It's like a goddamn conga line whenever I visit dear old Granddad."

"No," said Carl. "I've got your unit. I'll just follow you over to your grandfather's."

"Negative." Serge pointed at the open doorway. "It's not his birthday yet. In the motel room."

"But—"

"I'll provide final transport myself. You just point me toward the giant ribbon-and-bow store."

"I don't think it will fit through the door."

"Already measured from the specs in the brochure you gave Grandpa. Inches to spare on each side." Serge whistled. "You always drag your heels like this on a sure sale? Maybe you need to go back to salesman school. Always be closing, man! Even if you have to ram that cocksucker through the door! So let's put some elbow grease into this endeavor, shall we?"

Greed overcame Carl's skepticism as he opened the back of the van. The humidifier slid out on a rolling steel grate that became an electric lift lowering it to the ground. The unit had wheels, and they easily navigated the handicap ramp.

Serge flipped the beds upright against the walls, making room for the X5000 Quantum that now stood shimmering in the middle of the room. Coleman squinted at it and yawned.

"There she is," said Carl. "Just like you ordered. So I guess it's that time when we get out the checkbook."

Serge slowly closed and locked the motel room door behind him. "Yes, it is that time." He formed a toothy smile.

"Uh, okay," said Carl. "Where's your checkbook? That'll be sixty-eight hundred. I threw in delivery for free. And I'm sorry, but I'll need to see a driver's license."

"Oh no, no, no," said Serge. "Not my checkbook. *Your* checkbook."

"What are you talking about?"

"Buster and Mildred Hornsby, Boca Shores." Serge pulled out a spreadsheet. "According to my calculations, you've taken them for a whopping total of twenty-seven thousand." He handed Carl a pen. "You can make that check out to 'Cash.'"

"What the hell is going on here?"

"Customer service, and you're looking at the serviceman," said Serge. "That couple is very old and you took advantage of them. They neither want nor need what you sold them, so I'm asking for a good-faith refund. Believe me, this is as polite as it gets."

"I get it now. A do-gooder." Carl shoved Serge in the chest, knocking him against the wall and a dusty painting. "Well, fuck you and fuck the fucking Hornsbys! I work hard for a living. I was totally ethical! So what if they're old? They didn't save up all that money not knowing how to make decisions for themselves! And now it's mine!"

"How did you end up like this?" Serge calmly rehung the painting of ducks trying to take off from a pond. "Did your mother spit in your food? You saw that Marine Corps hat on Buster, and it didn't slow you down even a second?" He held out his hand. "I'm still waiting. Refund please."

This time Carl socked Serge in the jaw, dropping him to the floor. He reached down and grabbed a handful of Serge's shirt, jerking him up. Then he got nose to nose. "And you're paying for that stupid humidifier behind me! Nobody wastes Carl Effluent's time!"

Serge pulled the pistol from his waistband and stuck it in the salesman's gut. "Ding! Ding! Ding! That signals the end of our politeness round! . . ."

. . . Carl found himself hog-tied on top of the X5000 Quantum humidifier.

"On second thought, forget the check. I like the idea of hard cash much better," said Serge. "My tax position."

"But I don't have that much money in my account!" said Carl.

Serge slapped him with the back of his hand. "Wrong answer." Another wicked slap returned the other way. "What about your retirement account? I like the irony of that." The barrel of a gun pressed between Carl's eyes. "Do you have a retirement account? I'll know if you're lying."

"Yes." Carl began sobbing. "But there's a penalty for early withdrawal."

"And right now there's an even bigger penalty for late withdrawal."

"Okay, okay, yes, I have enough in my account."

"That's much better." Serge pulled out a pocketknife and sliced the ropes. "We're taking a little pleasure drive. And don't think I won't shoot you because we'll be in a bank full of people. I'm crazy! Ask anyone. Ask Coleman."

Coleman chugged from a bottle of Jack and nodded. "He's batshit."

Fifteen minutes later, Carl's legs barely functioned as he stiffly entered the bank. Serge whispered over his shoulder: "Remember what I told you to say. And remember I've got this gun on you, so no funny stuff! Especially not this!" He danced a wacky jig in a circle around Carl, before returning to his original position and poking the pistol in his back again. "I'm loony tunes."

Carl sheepishly stared down at the counter as he handed the teller his request.

"Sir, you do realize there's a steep penalty for early with-drawal . . ." She stopped to look closer. "Are you okay?"

"Medical emergency in the family," said Carl. "No other way we could get the money."

"But you're sweating like I've never seen."

Serge peeked over Carl's shoulder at the woman. "He sells humidifiers."

"Please, could you just hurry," said Carl.

"A life depends on it," said Serge.

"All right," the teller said warily. "How would you like that? Certified check?"

He shook his head. "Cash. Hundreds."

"Sir, are you sure everything's okay?"

A gun poked.

Carl slapped a palm on the counter. "Dammit! Can't you tell when someone's having a bad day?"

"Well! There's no need to be like that," huffed the teller, turning to get a money bag.

Chapter 7

BALTIMORE, MARYLAND

Leafless trees and brown grass surrounded a sprawling government office building at 6401 Security Boulevard. It was chillier than normal, and people became subconsciously irritable about not bringing the right coats from home.

The dormant landscaping could not be seen from a certain windowless office where a man named Symanski pressed a button on his computer that pulled up an e-mail.

"Shit."

He stared at a message from an old friend in Florida. One of those friends who continued to send Christmas cards every year, even though he hadn't sent one for the last five. Awkward.

But this was the kind of e-mail that required a response. He couldn't just ditch it.

He ditched it.

After lunch, the bureaucrat had second thoughts and called the e-mail back up. "What am I looking at?" Twins and non-twins and the last four digits. Made no sense.

To cover his butt, he took it to the division chief.

"What am I looking at?" asked his boss.

"I don't know," said Symanski. "Just got an e-mail from an old friend at one of those identity-protection companies. He doesn't understand it either and just passed it along out of due diligence. Probably nothing. But given all the recent memos about hacking . . . I mean, nobody's tried anything serious with our agency yet, but if it isn't a coincidence that these Social Security numbers look screwy—"

The supervisor held up a hand. "Say no more. I'll take care of this personally. Nice work, Symanski."

"Thank you, sir."

Symanski left, and the supervisor ditched it.

SARASOTA

Serge and company arrived back in their dicey motel room with a bona fide sack of cash.

"Carl, have a seat. On top of the humidifier will do." Serge pawed through the canvas bag of stiff U.S. currency and zipped it closed. "You did great!"

"S-s-s-so you're going to let me go now?"

"You must be thinking of the politeness round." He tossed the bag in the corner. Then bashed Carl on the side of the head with a pistol butt. His inert body rolled unceremoniously onto the floor. "Coleman, come over here and give me a hand."

"I'm busy."

"Dammit! Take off your beer vest. I can't do this alone."

"*Alllllll* right." Coleman mustered the resolve to rise from the floor. "What am I supposed to do?"

"Grab that side. We need to roll this thing into the bathroom."

Coleman grunted. "It's heavy."

"It has wheels."

The wheels squeaked as the industrial-gray box began the journey.

"It's a straight shot through the door, but a bit tight, so just watch your fingers."

"Ow! Shit!" Coleman hopped around, flapping his left hand.

Serge sighed and finished the job on his own. "Okay, next item . . ."

. . . Carl Effluent felt his cheek being lightly tapped with the barrel of a gun. He found himself tied to a straight-backed motel chair with duct tape across his mouth. A thousand points of light dotted the ceiling from one of those new educational projectors that make constellations.

"You're awake," said Serge. "That's great because it's fun time! Up there is Sagittarius, and down here is to-go food from Waffle House. I absolutely love Waffle House!"

Coleman nodded. "I like menus where you can just point at pictures."

Serge lowered the beds that he'd tipped up against the walls to make room for the humidifier. "I also made a run to Home Depot, but more on that later." He held something under Carl's nose. "Up for a waffle? No? Suit yourself."

"It's good," said Coleman, wiping syrup-hands on his shirt. A beer can popped.

Serge sat on the corner of the bed. "Ready to have fun? I sure am! You know what I just realized? I love the *word* 'waffle'! Say it three times and you can't be in a bad mood. It's just not possible. Try it!"

The duct tape was ripped off a mouth. "Waffle?"

"You have to say it three times."

"Waffle, waffle, waffle?"

Serge giggled and replaced the tape. "For some reason that just tickles me. You know what else is fun? Fun *facts*! And I've got a doozy for you! It's not exactly on point, but life doesn't stay on point, either, so why should we? You simply go out for a waffle one morning and end up in a motel room with a hostage and a humidifier. Ain't existence weird like that? Ready for your fun fact of the day? In Florida, Waffle Houses have a strategic role far more important than breakfast. When a hurricane bears down on our state, the Federal Emergency Management Agency employs a variety of traditional meteorological metrics, but they've also developed something called the Waffle House Index . . ."

Serge got up and emptied bags from Home Depot. Two large plastic pails, a half-dozen jugs and a windup timer.

" . . . A man named W. Craig Fugate came up with the index because, while weather data measures a storm's strength in the air, FEMA didn't have a real-time gauge on the ground of disruption to infrastructure. Fugate studied the problem and decided one of the most accurate measurements would be Waffle House status. Why? The Waffle House people are maniacs! They're absolutely obsessed with staying open no matter what, so they've developed cutting-edge disaster preparedness. To cope with supply lines being interrupted and power going out, many locations have installed generators and employ an emergency limited menu of non-perishables. I swear this is all completely true . . ."

Serge uncapped the jugs and began pouring the thick, gooey contents into the pails. "During major storms, FEMA estab-lishes direct lines to Waffle House headquarters to update their color-coded index. Green: restaurants open, all systems go! Yellow: limited crisis menu. Red: the unthinkable, closure. It all reached a pinnacle during Hurricane Matthew on October 16, 2016, when the index went solid crimson from Fort Pierce all the way to Titusville, and FEMA swung into action. So Waffle Houses are secretly a network of land-based weather buoys dis-guised as restaurants, you know what I mean?"

Serge went over to the bathroom sink, pouring water in the

pails and stirring with a stick. Then he sealed them in plastic wrap. He returned and plugged a portable DVD player into the motel's TV set.

"The main event!" Serge sat on the bed next to Carl and rocked with anticipation. "If this doesn't get your heart pumping, you're already dead. Sorry, bad choice of phrase. We're going to watch *Thirty Seconds Over Tokyo* with Spencer Tracy, depicting the daring bombing mission of Doolittle's Raiders! . . ." He turned on the movie and fast-forwarded. "For my money, the best scene is when the planes fly in for training at Eglin Air Force Base up in our panhandle. Can you dig it? How many people actually know that the famous mission was launched from my home state? . . . Look! Look! They're using actual black-and-white aerial footage of the military complex near Destin as they come in for a landing! And here's my favorite quote from the whole movie when one of the crew looks out the window."

"*. . . Florida, palm trees, alligators, bathing beauties! . . .*"

Serge checked his watch. "Thirty seconds. Show's over." The TV went black.

Carl struggled and whined.

"Right," said Serge. "Curiosity. Comes up a lot in my work. You want to know what's going to happen to you?"

He ripped the duct tape off Carl's mouth. A brief scream.

"Quiet," said Serge. "I carry an astonishing amount of tape."

"Don't kill me! Please, I'm begging!"

"Kill you?" said Serge. "Don't be ridiculous. You might kill yourself, but I just teach school . . . Coleman, assistance."

"Twice in one day?"

"Consider yourself an overachiever."

The pair began dragging Carl's chair backward toward the bathroom. The screaming started again, and the duct tape went back on.

Coleman stood in the doorway. "Where are we going to put him? There's no room anymore with that big thing in here."

"Help me get him on top of the humidifier . . ."

In minutes, Carl was lashed with braided ropes, naked, spread-eagled on his back across the cold metal.

"What's the plan this time?" asked Coleman.

"Wait here." Serge disappeared and quickly returned with the plastic buckets. He twisted open a cap on the machine and began pouring.

"But I thought these things just used water," said Coleman.

"They also allow you to add pleasantly scented aroma additives so your house smells like a pine forest or a chick's apartment. I've whipped up my own custom additive, but I had to seriously dilute it or the humidifier would gunk up."

"Hey, I remember that smell," said Coleman. "I was in kindergarten."

"Me too," said Serge, topping off the unit's internal tank. "Nostalgia always makes your job go faster."

Then Serge went to work with a screwdriver on the bathroom's light switch plate. He pulled the unit out of the wall and disconnected one of the wires. Then he grabbed his last purchase and wrapped wires around a pair of screws, introducing them into the light switch's circuit.

"What's that?" asked Coleman.

"One of those timers people use on lights to save electricity." Serge pointed at the ceiling. "In this case, the timer also controls the bathroom's ventilation fan."

"The light and the fan are still going."

"Because the timer's not on." Serge cranked the spring-loaded mechanical dial, and the light went out. "Six hours ought to do it."

"Six hours for what?"

"That big honkin' humidifier will make the air too moist—and that dude too sweaty. My science project requires that the room be vented once the machine's reservoir is empty." He pressed the power button, and the large device hummed to life with a salesman on top. "Which brings us to the bonus round!"

Serge and Coleman stepped just outside the bathroom, inter-locked arms and square-danced. Singing a duet:

"... *Ohhhhh!*... *The bonus round, the bonus round!*..."

"... *What the hell's up with the bonus round?*..."

"... *It's one last chance for this piece of snot*..."

"... *I'll bet he's thinking,* Thanks a lot!..."

"... *Got himself in a serious Serge spot*..."

"... *That big machine's getting red-hot*..."

"... *How much time has he got?*..."

"... *What else rhymes? Polyglot!*..."

"... *Will he make it? Will he not?*..."

"... *Is his life fucking shot?*..."

"... *Not*... *quite*... *yet*..."

"... *Why?*..."

"... *Ohhhhhhhh!*... *The bonus round, the bonus round!*..."

Carl screamed under the duct tape at the clearly insane antics of his captors.

Serge came back in and idly tapped his fingers on the sales-man's forehead. "This is a first! The bonus round has actually al-ready been decided. The results just haven't been tabulated. Here's the deal: We had an argument earlier, only a little dustup where crazy things were said in the heat of the moment that we'd all like to take back. I'll be the first to admit I was a tad harsh on you, hurling accusations when I don't know the first technical thing about humidifiers except they're totally stupid in Florida. And by stupid, I mean special, so don't get me wrong again. Still, I have a hunch you oversold the Hornsbys on the size of the unit. On the other hand, you claimed you were totally ethical. So if you didn't exploit them on the unit's capacity, my experiment won't work, and you'll just be clammy until they find you. If the unit's too big, however, yikes!... But why go there until it's time? You're a sales-man: Be Mr. Positive!"

Serge sprinted out of the bathroom and dug through his duffel bag, removing several small figures.

Coleman ambled over. "Whatcha going to do with those?"

"Observe." Serge ran back in the bathroom, pulled out the humidifier's reservoir, and dumped the figures inside.

"Jesus!" said Coleman. "Those are some of your favorite souvenirs!"

"My whole collection," said Serge. "But I'm an artist, and I'm taking one for the team. I'll order more on eBay."

They left the bathroom and closed the door. Serge used an entire roll of duct tape to create an airtight seal all the way around the frame.

Coleman cracked a Schlitz. "I can still hear him trying to yell, even with the tape."

"Must be afraid of the dark." Serge zipped up a duffel bag. "Let's rock."

Chapter 8

1970

Theodore Pruitt Jr. sat in his bedroom surrounded by shelves of impressive model rockets. On his desk was an assortment of the latest shortwave radio equipment. He slowly turned a dial and picked up Jakarta...

Everything had changed for Ted. It happened back in 1959. For the rest of his life, Ted Pruitt Jr. would never forget the day he found his mother sitting alone on the edge of her bed crying.

Teddy walked over. "What's the matter, Mom?"

She just clutched him as tight as she could and cried even harder.

His father was gone. She would later explain something went wrong with his blood. Try as they might, nothing would ever be the same.

Years passed quickly as Ted worked his way up through grade

school and then senior high. He was a slight youth, and he was picked on, not overly so, just the usual of what was going around back then. His mother always worried about him, as mothers do. Ted never showed the loss of his father, but it was there. Others his age were into sports and cars and music, and most parents had no idea where they were spending their Saturday nights. Ted spent a lot of time by himself in his room, working on that growing collection of rockets that filled all four walls. His favorites were working replicas of the Mercury and Gemini and Apollo programs. Then there were the elongated desks with three short-wave receivers, tape recorders, a small library of global listening guides, and wires everywhere, some going out the window to a special antenna now rising from the roof. He was compensating. He wanted to be his dad.

Could have been worse, his mom thought. She had barely made it through 1968, when parents' fears spiked. Martin Luther King Jr. and Bobby Kennedy had been shot. Protests in the streets, rebellious music, marijuana and LSD everywhere. Glenda Pruitt was almost relieved that her son was nerding his way through the times. But there was one thing it couldn't shelter him from.

Vietnam.

By 1970, Ted was nearing graduation, about to turn eighteen, and Glenda had nervously monitored the previous draft lottery. Birthdays picked at random, ranked 1 to 366. From what the other parents were saying, it wasn't good. The war was growing and they were taking practically everyone, deep into the lottery. As a single working mom, she didn't have money for college and a deferment. Unless his birthday drew an extremely high lottery number this year, she had already decided to drive him to Canada. She hadn't told her son yet because they both knew that her late husband wouldn't approve. He'd often spoken of duty to country.

Ted continued to fly his rockets and tune his radios. One of his passions was writing letters to foreign shortwave stations that broadcast for English-language audiences. Then Ted would turn on his tape recorder at the appointed time and hope his correspondence would be read on the air. It was something the hobbyists did. And it was a lot of disappointment. A lot. Some of his unsuccessful tapes had been recorded over twenty times. But then he finally got a letter read in Madrid, and another in West Berlin.

A month later, Ted raced into the kitchen yelling so loud that his mother almost had a heart attack.

"Don't scare me like that!"

"Mom! You've got to listen to this! It's great!" He set his recorder on the table and pressed the play button.

A thick accent rose from a tin speaker. *". . . This is Radio Moscow, and today we have a letter from Ted Pruitt, a high school student in West Palm Beach, Florida, United States. Ted asks, 'If in the Soviet Union all citizens are supposed to be equal, then why is there so little personal freedom?' Ted, if you're listening, it is a very good question. The reality is that you've only heard your own government's side of the story. Look at the violence in your own streets, government police attacking young people who are only expressing their rightful outrage against an unjust war. If you ever had the chance to visit and know us, you would have a much different opinion. We are a peaceful, freedom-loving people. Thank you very much for writing, Ted . . . And now a letter from Scotland . . ."*

Ted pressed the stop button and looked up with excitement. "What do you think?"

"Uh, that's very impressive," said Glenda. "But you do realize it's propaganda."

"I know, I know!" said Ted. "But isn't it cool they read my letter?"

"Yes, son, it is very cool."

He snatched the tape recorder and ran back to his room to write more letters . . .

. . . The next afternoon, a knock at the door.

Glenda answered. She immediately thought the person had

the wrong address. Standing on her front porch was a college-aged man in torn jeans, sandals and a tie-dyed T-shirt. In other words, a hippie. He had one of those big white man's Afros. And a guitar.

"May I help you?" asked Glenda.

"Yes." The man tilted his head to see past her into the house, which Glenda didn't really care for. "Does Ted Pruitt live here?"

"I'm sorry, but he passed away years ago."

"No, I mean the high school student."

Glenda stopped and looked him over again. "You're here to see my *son*?"

"Yes, is he in?"

From behind: "Who is it, Mom?"

"Nobody." She turned back to face the stranger at the door. "Exactly what do you want with him?"

"I'm a big shortwave enthusiast! And, well, not too many other people are," said the young man. "I heard Ted's letter read yesterday on Radio Moscow, and I thought, 'That is so cool! They've never read any of my letters.' Can I talk to him?"

Ted came up behind his mom. "Who is it?"

"Ted Pruitt?" asked the young man at the door. "I'm Tofer Baez. I love shortwave radio, and I heard Moscow read your letter. That is incredible! Do you think we could talk shop? Trade tips on equipment and stations?"

"Heck yeah! I don't know anyone at school who's into short-wave."

"Me neither," said Tofer.

"Mom, what are you doing? Let him in."

Before Glenda even realized it, she was stepping aside.

"Do you play the guitar?" asked Tofer.

"No."

"I can show you some easy chords," said Tofer. "I know the Beatles and Stones and Jefferson Airplane."

"That's groovy."

"Let's go to your room."

Glenda warily watched them trot down the hall, and Tofer glanced back just before closing the door.

She stood with folded arms. "I don't like that guy."

Two hours later they came out, and Tofer waved bye before driving away in a VW microbus.

"Son, can you come in the kitchen a second and have a seat?"

"Sure." Ted sat down. "What is it?"

"What were you doing all that time in your room with the door closed?"

"Nothing. Just talking shortwave and playing the guitar." He smiled. "I know three songs now."

"Something's not right about him," said Glenda.

"Mom! He's the coolest guy I know, even cooler than the coolest guys in high school who won't even talk to me. And he goes to college."

"You *don't* know him. He's a stranger," said his mom. "And since when does a college guy take such an interest in a high school student he's never met? I think he's trying to sell you drugs. That's how they get you hooked."

"Mom! Tofer doesn't do drugs. He said he's high on life."

"That's even weirder. I don't like him."

But Glenda, nonetheless, allowed Tofer into their home the next day, and the next. And even reluctantly let Ted go when Tofer invited him to his apartment. *If I pull back too hard with his new friend, he'll totally rebel.*

After hours of worry, she'd regretted her decision and sprang out of her chair that night when she heard the VW microbus dropping Ted off.

She met him at the door. "Let me see your eyes."

"Mom, I'm not doing drugs! You don't even know what you're looking for."

"What did you do all evening?"

"Talked about the war and politics and listened to Buffalo

Springfield. Can I go now?" He went into his bedroom and closed the door.

Glenda pondered. He did seem okay. And now she was less sure than ever what to do about the Tofer situation.

THE PRESENT

A few minutes after noon, a white sedan cruised north on the Tamiami Trail past Jungle Gardens, where parrots were roller-skating. The driver finished a pastrami sandwich and wadded up the paper. The vehicle approached a run-down motel where there was usually plenty of parking space. But not today. Police cars, Crown Vics with blackwall tires, a crime scene van and another truck from the Medical Examiner's Office.

The detective parked and dabbed mustard off his mouth with a napkin. He headed toward an open motel room door where evidence techs streamed out with sealed evidence bags. Inside, the activity seemed to be tilted toward the back of the room.

"I'm Detective Gannon. What have we got here?"

Space was at a premium in the bathroom, and the medical examiner had to stand on the toilet, leaning over the victim with a penlight. "Another weird one. But judging from the duct tape on his mouth, and how he's tied to the top of this humidifier, I'm ruling out natural causes."

"A humidifier?" said Gannon. "In Florida?"

An evidence tech stuck his head in the doorway. "Some asshole sold my parents one." The head disappeared.

"Why does he look that way?" asked the detective.

The examiner pointed at the humidifier's removable reservoir bin, sitting in the bathtub. "Still need to run chemical analysis on the residue, but—"

"Wait," said Gannon. "The condition he's in. It reminds me of something . . ." He stared at the floor a moment before snapping his fingers and looking up. "I got it. Those Mold-A-Rama machines at tourist attractions when I was a kid."

The evidence tech's head was back in the doorway. "Mold-A-Rama? I loved those! You'd insert a quarter and look through a glass dome as two halves of the mold came together hydraulically and made a plastic souvenir."

A forensic photographer peeked around the corner. "Are you talking about Mold-A-Rama? I still have a plastic mermaid from Weeki Wachee."

"And I have an albino alligator," said the tech.

"Ahem," said the examiner. "We have a body here. A little respect?"

"Excuse me," said Gannon. "You mentioned a chemical analysis?"

The examiner used gloved hands to twist the victim's head. Everyone winced at the crackling sound. "You weren't far off with Mold-A-Rama. There's a connection. Most of what was in that reservoir bin was probably Elmer's Glue, from those gigantic jugs at hardware stores. Too thick in its regular state out of the bottle and would gum up the machine. But it's water-soluble, so if you dilute it to the consistency of skim milk, the humidifier will evaporate it. Obviously, it voids the warranty and isn't recommended long term. But if it's a one-off homicide, then you're good to go."

Gannon inspected the rewired light switch. "What's this about?"

"The killer knew his stuff," said the examiner. "The humidifier would make the bathroom too moist to achieve his goals, so he wired in that automatic timer. Once the humidifier was empty, the timer turned on the ceiling ventilation fan to dry out the room so the vaporized glue could congeal and harden. Every surface in this room has a coating."

"Cause of death?"

"Need to get him on the table for that, but I'd bet either cutaneous suffocation from his pores being sealed, or generic asphyxiation from it clogging up his nose and sinus cavity. Either way, he was a victim of extreme rage."

"You mentioned some connection to Mold-A-Rama?" asked the detective.

"Take a closer look at the bottom of that bin in the bathtub."

Gannon got on his knees. "Looks like the top parts of an alligator, dolphin, mermaid . . ." He looked up. "What the hell?"

"They didn't melt completely." More crackling noise as the examiner pried a shoulder blade from the top of the machine. "The effect of those figures was more symbolic than anything, though they did add a little sheen across the skin to create the Mold-A-Rama appearance."

Gannon ran a hand through his hair as he considered the milky-white-encased victim. "I don't even know where to start. What kind of suspect am I looking for here?"

"One with a very interesting childhood," said the examiner. "He turned this guy into the state's largest roadside souvenir."

Chapter 9

Serge lowered his binoculars.

Coleman lowered his joint. "Why are we sitting here?"

"Another nature watch." Serge snapped photos. "For reasons unknown, this is where ancient genetic instincts cause them to gather each day just a few minutes from now."

"But it's a restaurant," said Coleman.

"God works in mysterious ways." Serge reached in a paper sack and pulled out a piece of fruit.

"I didn't know you liked to eat bananas."

"I'm not eating it." Serge held it in front of his face and stroked the yellow skin. "I'm having a religious experience. All life is connected, and I just heard last night on TV that humans possess half the DNA of a banana, so I'm checking it out to see if I can pick up a family vibe."

"But religious?" asked Coleman.

"Therein lies the rub," said Serge. "Some people think you can only have a religious experience if you're ordering others to stop whatever they're doing that's making them happy. On the other hand, you have the atheists. I've been to a lot of book and cultural festivals, and there always seems to be a booth for an atheists' association. That's the dumbest shit in the world. If you really don't believe in something, fine, then just move along. I don't believe in unicorns, but you don't see me sending out fucking anti-unicorn newsletters."

Coleman stared at Serge holding the yellow fruit. "Feeling anything yet?"

"Yeah, stupid." He peeled it and took a bite. "Makes me want to rent a booth."

"My stomach has those hungry noises again."

"We need to be going inside anyway." Serge opened the car door.

The pair entered the restaurant, and a cheerful waiter approached. "Table for two?"

"Yes, we're here for the early-bird special," said Serge.

The waiter checked his watch. "You're a little early."

"Isn't that the whole point?"

The waiter smiled. "By the time your food arrives, I'm sure you can get the discount."

"Beer," said Coleman.

Serge elbowed him. "We're not even at the table yet."

The waiter seated them and handed menus. "I'll get that beer."

Coleman looked around. "We're the only people in the entire dining room."

"I need to document the full arc of the migration."

The waiter returned, and Serge ordered a Cuban sandwich, and Coleman was told they didn't have buffalo wings or nachos.

"Then a beer."

"I just set one down for you," said the waiter.

"It'll be gone by the time you get back," said Coleman.

"Bank on it," said Serge.

They were left alone again.

Not for long. It took all of ten minutes, like a slow-motion stampede into a Who concert, until every table in the room was full.

"What just happened?" asked Coleman.

Serge looked out the front window. "Shuttle buses."

Coleman quickly pounded his second beer and ordered a third.

"Can you please stop the Belushi show this one time?" snapped Serge. He jerked a thumb sideways. "These are proper people. They know not of your ways."

"Maybe they do."

"What are you talking about?" Serge turned as a platoon of waiters began pouring into the dining room with teetering trays of drinks.

"Look at all those cocktails," said Coleman. "And a bunch are martinis. That's like solid alcohol."

"At four in the afternoon, no less," said Serge. "And I thought they took naps because they were old . . . Plus a whole bunch of them are getting multiple drinks at once."

Coleman pointed at a chalkboard near the entrance. "'Two-for-one special.' I dig the early-bird thing."

Soon the room was full of laughter and dropped utensils. Meals served and consumed. Serge glanced toward the back corner. "There's a rare couple not drinking. They should be lucid enough for my oral history." He started to stand and sat back down. "Okay, relax and get a grip and don't be off-putting like last time, because that's wrong. A calm and normal first impression. Their nerves can't take much at this stage. The key is to undersell."

They walked over to the corner booth. "I'm Serge! This is Coleman! We're taking retirement big! I have a white belt!" Serge began jumping in place. "Did you hear the latest on bananas? Isn't that insane? I also heard that our best telescopes are still picking up background radiation noise from the Big Bang, because it's so far away. They also said if you're watching TV with a snowy picture, one percent of what you're looking at is the Big Bang. Isn't that a trip? Last night at the motel, Coleman came out of the bathroom and saw me staring at static and asked what I was watching, and I said, 'Everything!'"

Coleman nodded. "He's really smart."

"Dammit!" Serge lowered his eyes and kicked the carpet with the toe of his sneaker. "I'm still doing it. Please erase that first impression." He turned and walked away five paces, then came back demurely, shuffling his feet with chin tucked to his chest, speaking in a low monotone. "I'm Serge. This is Coleman. I seek your wisdom in an underselling manner . . ." He looked up with a wince. "That comes off weird, too, doesn't it? . . . Sorry, but those are your only two choices right now. Can we join you to break bread?"

Despite another gone-astray introduction, Serge was surprised once again to find a couple that was happy to have conversation company. They scooted over to make room in the booth, and the man shook Serge's hand. "I'm Ethan and this is Sarah, the Gotliebs."

"Well, the Gotliebs, where do you hail from?"

"All over," said Ethan.

"We're military," said Sarah.

"Met when I was stationed at Maxwell Air Force Base in the fifties."

"Maxwell?" said Serge. "That's Montgomery. It would have put you in the middle of the bus boycott."

"It did," said Sarah. "What exciting times those were."

"Hold on!" Serge pulled out a pocket recorder. "If you don't mind . . ." He pressed a button. "Go!"

"After Rosa Parks refused to move to the back of the bus, the boycott began, and sympathetic people with automobiles carpooled the bus riders who needed to get to work. A lot of people don't remember the stuff about the taxis."

"Never heard of the taxis," said Serge. "And I've read all about this."

"When the city saw all these car pools, they tried to put a stop to it by passing racist laws declaring them taxis, which had to be a certain color, and follow this regulation and that, until it pretty much ruled out everyone giving rides to the boycotters," said Sarah. "Police pulling vehicles over, making people get out and walk or face arrest. So a bunch of us wives at the base banded together and decided to step in and give them rides. Now the city was dealing with the U.S. military, and they were unofficially advised through back channels not to mess with us, and we got the people to work. Looking back, it was a little more dangerous than we realized."

"Wow, you were there fighting the good fight from the beginning! You're my heroes!" said Serge. "What made you decide to retire in Florida?"

"Fell in love with the place during my next assignment down here," said Ethan.

Serge pushed his voice recorder closer to Mr. Gotlieb. "What assignment was that?"

"I flew a U-2."

"Wait," said Serge. "Not during 1962?"

"How'd you guess?"

"Lord above!" said Serge. "You flew reconnaissance during the Cuban missile crisis?"

"It wasn't called that then," said Ethan. "We were just doing our jobs."

"Coleman, this is what I'm talking about!" said Serge. "All these great Americans living among us that never get any recognition other than incontinence jokes . . . Oops!" He covered his mouth and turned back to the couple. "Sorry, my bad. You didn't need to hear that they make fun of you behind your back." He pounded a fist on the table. "Pay them no mind!"

"Uh, the shuttle bus looks like it's ready to leave," said Sarah.

"Forget the bus," said Serge. "Today, you're riding in style."

"I think we'll be fine with the shuttle," said Ethan.

"Nonsense," said Serge. "Where do you live?"

"Boca Shores."

"What a coincidence! I love that place! Do you know the Hornsbys?"

"Buster and Mildred?" said Sarah. "Sure."

Serge placed a hand over his heart. "Dear personal friends of mine. Buster served at the Chosin Reservoir."

Ethan gave his wife a glance that said, *These are pretty odd characters, but if they know Buster and Mildred . . .*

And so another retired couple hitched a ride back to a trailer park in a Ford Falcon. Serge cranked up Ray Charles on the radio.

" . . . O beautiful for spacious skies . . ."

Serge twisted all the way around to face his passengers. "How's it going back there?"

"Could you watch the road, please?"

"I'm right on it." Serge gripped the wheel and leaned with focus. "You're worth the extra effort. Did I mention you're my heroes?"

"It's come up a few times."

They pulled into the entrance of the trailer park and stopped at the guard shack.

" . . . Let's play Jeopardy! . . ."

Earl hitched his pants and stepped out. "Oh, you guys again."

" . . . I'll take palindromes for two hundred, Alex . . ."

Earl checked the backseat. "Hi, Mr. and Mrs. Gotlieb. I'll let you in."

He went back in his booth and raised the gate arm.

" . . . What is 'A man, a plan, a canal, Panama'? . . ."

The Falcon circled the artificial lake and pulled up to another manufactured house with bamboo wind chimes and a Gaelic yard gnome. A little-used Buick sat in the carport. A piece of string ran down from the carport's ceiling to a tennis ball that touched the Buick's windshield. It told the Gotliebs when to stop.

"Would you like to come in?" asked Sarah. "I can get you something to drink."

"Yes!" said Coleman.

"She doesn't mean it that way," said Serge. "But yes, we would love to come in."

The couple led their guests up to the screened-in front porch. Ethan began sliding the glass door. "I'll have to warn you it's a bit snug inside."

"We've been to the Hornsbys'," said Serge.

They entered.

"Whoa!"

"He warned you," said Sarah.

"Are you opening a restaurant or something?" asked Serge.

"Looks that way, doesn't it?" said Ethan. "This salesman pitched us on a new kitchen, and we figured we'd treat ourselves."

"You do realize that the oven and all these other appliances are commercial grade for restaurants and not designed for residential use."

"We do now," said Sarah. "It didn't look like this in the brochures. By the time we realized what was happening, we were just dealing with the installers, and the salesman wouldn't return our calls."

"Don't forget the hidden charges," said Ethan. "It was like buying tires, more than twice the original price, and it was all tucked into a contract that we couldn't get out of."

"Most of this over here used to be the living room," said Sarah. "But what are you going to do?"

Serge grinned. "You can start by giving me the salesman's business card."

TAMPA

A frozen personal pizza from a vending machine rotated in the lunchroom's microwave. Body-pierced people at the health-food kiosk ordered sesame-turkey wraps. Benmont Pinch removed the top slice of bread from a sandwich and nudged a wayward pickle slice back in line with the herd.

Sonic sat down across from him with a tray of vegan. "How's it going?"

"Can I ask you a question?"

"Fire."

"What do you think of us older people at the company?"

"You guys are radically cool."

"Seriously?"

Sonic nodded with emphasis. "You've got life all figured out, and you're happy in your own skin." He took a sip of soy milk. "No tats or piercings, and you wear your pants strange, regardless of what they say. You're like a rebel."

Benmont inflated slightly with pride. "People did used to say I reminded them of James Dean."

"Who?"

Benmont was good at changing subjects. "Did your nickname always used to be Sonic?"

"No, it used to be some variation of Ass-Hat until I took control."

"So how's your day?"

"Got off the phone with some guy in Fort Myers whose credit card just filled ten tanks of petrol in France—" He suddenly pointed up at one of the flat screens. "They're playing it again."

Benmont turned around. "Playing what?"

A Naples news station was broadcasting live from a middle-class stucco house with dozens of onlookers and crime tape.

"Double homicide, another retired couple," said Sonic. "Nasty stuff. They've been playing it all day. Can't believe you haven't heard."

"Staring at my computer all morning."

"I can show you how to get streaming video up in the corner of your screen."

"That's against the rules," said Benmont.

"Everyone does it and all the bosses know," said Sonic. "They never mention it."

"Because you work fast."

The youth looked back up at the flat screen. "Wait a minute. This isn't the double murder I was talking about. That was a condo…" He paused to read the details. "*Another* double murder?"

"It's a violent state."

Network cameras filmed FBI agents arriving at the residence. Flashing red and blue lights filled the screen as the names of the latest victims scrolled across the bottom.

Benmont squinted at the TV. "Why do those names seem familiar?"

"What is it?" asked Sonic.

"Do you have something to write with?"

Chapter 10

SARASOTA

A Crown Vic with blackwalls sped north on the Tamiami Trail. It passed the Bahi Hut Lounge and pulled into another unusually crowded parking lot of a decrepit motel. It wasn't hard identifying the room. The windows were blown out, and glass scattered all the way to the sidewalk. A good-looking hooker had been first on the scene and called in the explosion over her police radio.

This time the usual forensic vehicles were accompanied by the bomb squad. Detective Gannon went inside.

He stopped and stood in awe at the thoroughness of the obliteration. The bomb people were going over the room with special instruments and swabs.

"Gannon!" said a friendly bomb guy named Barrot. "Haven't seen you since that guy blew up his garage by putting gasoline in his washing machine to get motor oil out of his jeans."

"As I remember, the garage door was like a crumpled piece of foil."

"This one here's a first on me," said Barrot, appraising the charred walls and carpet. "An explosion without a bomb."

"What about a gas leak?" asked Gannon.

Barrot shook his head. "Nothing that flammable." He watched as one of his team swabbed the windowsill and stuck the cloth into an elegantly calibrated machine. "No traces of nitrates or anything remotely similar in chemical composition to known explosives. No accelerants, no fuel, nothing. Yet there was clearly a devastating blast, not to mention the shock wave that set off car alarms for blocks. It's like the room spontaneously blew apart all on its own."

"The victim?" asked Gannon.

"You're looking at him."

"Where?"

"That wall."

They both turned toward a victim-shaped charcoal stain.

"Ewwww!"

"See the shredded rope and pieces of chair embedded in the plaster? Looks like he was tied up at the time."

"I still can't believe we don't have a single clue to the blast," said Gannon.

"We did find one thing, which has me even more baffled." Barrot looked down at a tabletop that was missing its legs. "Detected a small spot in the middle that tested positive for pyrotechnic flash powder."

"Then there you go," said Gannon. "You've got your answer. Why were you making this out like some big mystery?"

"No, you're not getting my meaning," said Barrot. "When I said small, I'm talking tiny, no more than three grams of a potassium compound."

"In English?"

"A firecracker," said Barrot. "Maybe a ladyfinger or blackcat—at most a cherry bomb or M-80, but still just a firecracker." A hand swept across the destruction. "It doesn't make sense."

"That's it?"

"Have to wait on all the final tests," said Barrot. "For now, we're totally stumped. The killer must be some kind of scientific genius or a homicidal David Copperfield."

Gannon swiveled around to assess the destruction again. "How on earth could someone blow up an entire motel room with just a firecracker? . . ."

TWELVE HOURS EARLIER

"How on earth can you blow up an entire motel room with just a firecracker?" asked Coleman.

"Easier than you'd think," said Serge, setting the ignition source on the counter next to a bag from a grocery store. "You just need a basic grasp of physics and an impish sense of humor. I got the firecracker idea by thinking about atomic bombs."

"They seem different," said Coleman.

"A lot of people don't realize that A-bombs are actually two explosions." Serge reached into the grocery bag and began setting candles around the room. "The nuclear part of the detonation is the second. The first is a conventional blast that implodes the radioactive material in on itself, triggering the chain reaction that leads to a mushroom cloud and generations of frogs with two heads."

"Cool," said Coleman. "You've got some radioactive shit?"

"No, I've got this." Serge reached again into his supermarket bag and removed a pair of ten-pound sacks, setting them on the dresser.

Coleman scratched his head. "You're going to bake a cake?"

"Shhhhh!" Serge ran to the door and checked the peephole. "He's here."

Another salesman thought he had the wrong address. The van was about to pull out when Serge threw the room's door open. "Come in! Come in!" An arm waved enthusiastically. "We're suckers for flashy brochures!"

"But I'm supposed to meet someone about a kitchen remodeling job." He looked left and right. "This is a motel."

"You're on the ball! It's for my grandparents!" said Serge. "Can't have you showing up at their trailer and ruining my surprise! I saw the fantastic work you did at Boca Shores for the Gotliebs, and they gave you a glowing recommendation! As in atomic!"

"Oh, I understand now." The salesman shook Serge's hand. "The name's Art. Art Crumb. You do realize that if we decide to go forward, I'll need a down payment today."

"Naturally," said Serge. "Let's get to it! There's nothing to fear!"

Art entered the room and Serge locked the door behind him.

"Why are you peeking out the window like that?" asked Art.

Serge turned and smiled. "Witnesses . . ."

Thus began an increasingly familiar routine: a polite but persistent request for a refund. Serge getting socked in the mouth. A salesman marched at gunpoint into a bank to empty his retirement account. Swinging by Boca Shores with a hostage in the trunk to deliver the refund. Then back to the motel, the duct tape, another motel chair and science projects to follow.

Serge held one end of a rope and pulled a cow-hitch knot tight behind Art Crumb's back. "As you've probably deduced by now, this isn't my first rodeo."

Next: redecorating. Serge pushed the beds aside and slid the hostage against the far wall near where the headboards had been. Then he grabbed a square table and pulled it to the middle of the room. "Coleman, I need those bags. Coleman? *Coleman!*"

"I'm resting."

"Where the hell are you?"

"Right here."

"Keep talking. I'll follow your voice."

"What do I say?"

"The alphabet and counting might be outside your reach at this point." Serge searched the room with his eyes. "How about drug slang?"

"You got it . . . Grass, reefer, blunt, boo-ya, cheeba, colitas, endo, indica, mota, shake, hippie lettuce, fatty boom blatty, acid, blotter, windowpane, microdot, Owsley, electric Kool-Aid, Lucy in the Sky with Diamonds, coke, bump, yale, eight ball, gutter glitter, booger sugar, meth, crank, ice, crystal, chalk, Scooby Snax, smack, skag, scat, white pony, white lady, white death, Big-H, GHB, Special-K, X, Molly, Sally D . . ."

Serge slowly walked toward the back of the room as the voice grew louder. He slipped his hands down between a wall and a mattress, sliding one of the beds out, revealing Coleman lying on the floor and sipping a Heineken out the side of his mouth.

"Coleman, why did you just lie there while I was pushing a bed over you?"

"I didn't feel like moving."

"You idiot! I need your help."

Coleman struggled to his feet, and Serge pushed the bed back. "Now get those two grocery sacks and meet me at the table."

Serge grabbed another chair and sat with a roll of tape, an M-80 firecracker and a lighter.

Coleman joined him and placed the bags on the table. "I still don't understand what you're going to do with regular grocery-store flour."

Serge flicked open a pocketknife and carefully cut a circle in the side of one ten-pound bag. He laid the M-80 in the middle of the hole. Then he cut an identical circle in the other bag, and sandwiched the pair together over the firecracker. He peeled the edge of the roll of tape and wrapped the entire package together. Finally, he wiggled his fingers to create a small opening between the bags and jammed in a wad of toilet paper to leave the M-80's fuse exposed.

He pulled out a pack of cigarettes.

"But you don't smoke," said Coleman.

"I know I don't, but a cigarette is the perfect fuse extender when you need a running start." He tore off the filter and fitted the end over the tip of the regular fuse. "And there you have it!"

"Have what?"

"It's all about dust," said Serge. "That's why it's such a mystery to the general public. In the early industrial age there were countless dramatic explosions that initially baffled investigators because there was no explosive material to be found."

The hostage continued a shrill whine. He glanced around at all the Catholic saint votive candles with tall, frosted glass to prevent wind from blowing out the flames that the souls in purgatory were counting on.

Serge walked over and bashed the side of the salesman's head with a phone book. "Pipe down and pay attention! This concerns you . . . And now you made me lose my train of thought." Another bash with the phone book.

"Dust," said Coleman.

"Right!" Serge smiled and loped back to the table. "We're not talking about regular dust, where a shaft of sunlight comes through a window and all these particles are dancing in the air. If you can make out the particles, they're too big. We're talking microns, where the dust is so fine that all the naked human eye can detect is a foggy haze, like in a third-world factory where the workers have to wear surgical masks."

Coleman grabbed the lighter off the table and blazed a doobie. "I still don't understand how flour can be an explosive."

"Say I'm holding a piece of paper in one hand, and a stick of dynamite in the other."

"I'm holding a piece of paper in one—"

"Shut up." Serge raised one hand, then the other. "The paper will burn, but the dynamite explodes. So how do you get the paper to detonate like the dynamite?"

"Wrap it around dynamite?"

"Physics, I tell you!" Serge lowered his hands. "There's all kinds of everyday stuff that people would normally consider so non-explosive that they'd be shocked to witness it level a building. But if you know what you're doing, you can even make powdered milk explode. Heck, barely a decade ago, a sugar explosion in Georgia killed fourteen."

Coleman had his trademark glazed look.

"Picture a burning log." Serge pushed the cigarette farther onto the fuse. "You wouldn't consider a log to be explosive because it's not. It's just combustible, and it actually takes a lot of work to get one going in a fireplace. And after it's ignited, it just burns along the top with a gradual release of heated carbon dioxide . . . But imagine if you could make the entire log burn all at once in a tiny fraction of a second. The gas expansion would reach such ferocity that it would blow the house apart, just like a bomb."

"But, Serge! How is that possible?"

"The tipping point."

"What's that?"

"All physics has a tipping point, and in this case it's four hundred microns," said Serge.

"What's a micron?"

"Only the dead know," said Serge. "When something non-explosive burns, it's along the surface. The greater the surface area, the faster the burn rate, and scientists have done the math. If you can grind an entire log down to microns, you've increased the surface area many thousands of times until the burn velocity is up there with traditional explosives."

"Far out." Coleman exhaled a giant hit and nodded. "You mentioned something about an atomic bomb?"

"After grinding up a log—or flour in a flour mill—it's still safe. It's just a pile of dust. The key is to get it suspended in the air, so that each particle is floating separately. Then just add flame. As one speck burns, the next dozen particles are so close that the fire jumps to them, then those in turn each ignite dozens more and so on until you've got an uncontrollable chain reaction. More importantly, it all takes place in a tiny sliver of time . . . So, like an atomic bomb, you need a primary explosion—in this case the M-80—which will effectively disperse a white cloud into the room until it reaches the ignition source." He pointed at the candles placed along the windowsill and dresser. "If you notice, the tall religious holders will prevent the small, initial blast from blowing them out."

"I don't doubt you," said Coleman. "It's just that I'm, uh, I'm . . . what's the word?"

"Stoned?"

"That's it."

There was a little loose flour on the table from where the bags had been cut open. Serge scooped it into his right hand. "Follow me. And grab that mason jar you were drinking Seven and Seven out of."

They walked over to the dresser. "Now wipe the inside of that jar until it's bone dry and give it to me."

Coleman did. Serge took the jar and dumped in the flour. Then he covered the top and shook it like the devil. He set it on the dresser, with a milky cloud inside and wisps of white haze wafting out the top. "Stand back."

Serge pulled out a book of matches, struck one and tossed it in the jar.

"Whoa!" said Coleman.

"Mmmmmmmm!" said the hostage.

Coleman cautiously stepped forward. "That was some flame!"

"And that was just a jar," said Serge. "Imagine a whole room."

"But why did you pick flour?"

"Irony again. This salesman went big with the whole kitchen concept for the Gotliebs, so I'm going bigger. He's baked goods."

"Mmmmmmmmm!"

"Will you shut the fuck up?" More negative reinforcement with the phone book. "You're pissing in my irony punch bowl."

Serge opened his book of matches and struck another one. He held it to the end of the cigarette until he was sure it was going.

"Mmmmmmmmm!..."

"And that about wraps it up here," said Serge. "Let's rock!"

"Aren't you forgetting something?" asked Coleman. He whispered in his ear.

"Glad you reminded me! The bonus round!" He threw up his arms. "Almost forgot with all his whimpering nonsense."

"Mmmmmmmmm!"

"Pipe down! This is important!" Serge leaned toward the victim's face as the Marlboro continued to smolder. "Here's your bonus round: Come up with your own. I'm tired of doing all the work for your people . . . Just kidding. That would be mean. This bonus round is a physical challenge like those reality shows where people run goofy obstacle courses over water and take hilarious spills into the lake of shame. But more is at stake here than social embarrassment. See that cigarette? If you can shimmy your chair over to the table and figure out how to knock it free before it burns down and ignites the M-80 fuse, you're our grand-prize winner! But the M-80 fuse burns like a Fourth-of-July sparkler, and once you see that, start shimmying the other way in a hurry. Of course, it will be slow going in either direction because I went a little overboard with all the rope, and you now look like some damsel in a silent movie. Give me your honest opinion: Should I see someone about OCD?"

"Mmmmmmmmm!"

"That's what I thought. False alarm."

The pair left and the door closed.

"Mmmmmmmmm!"

The legs of the chair began tapping across the wooden floor a fraction of an inch at a time, even though the captive's thrashing couldn't have been more desperate. But after a couple of minutes he'd gotten the chair turned around and was now heading backward. He watched over his shoulder as the fingers of the hands tied behind him wiggled toward the cigarette ... Closer ... *Closerrrrrr* ...

Chapter 11

1970

Acoustic twangs came from the other side of a closed bedroom door.

The Byrds, Dylan, Joni Mitchell.

Theodore Pruitt Jr. was getting almost decent on the guitar,
thanks to Tofer's mentorship. The pair were laughing as they
came out of the room and down the hall. They turned the corner
and froze.

Glenda Pruitt sat crying into her hands at the kitchen table,
just like that day in 1959 when her son found her on the edge of
the bed.

Tofer came over and placed a hand on her shoulder.
"Mrs. Pruitt, what's the matter?"

She just cried louder. Sitting in front of her was a folded newspaper with a number circled.

"Mom, what is it?" asked Ted. "What's wrong?"

Tofer nudged his new friend. "I know what's up." He pointed at the paper. "Your birthday drew number thirty-seven in this year's lottery."

"What's that mean?"

"You're going to Vietnam."

"I am?"

Tofer sat next to Glenda and held one of her hands. "Mrs. Pruitt, it's not that bad. I have an idea so he won't have to go."

She shook her head. "We can't afford college."

"Not that," said Tofer. "And he won't have to flee to Canada and remain in exile until who knows when."

She looked up and wiped tears. "What is it?"

"He joins the navy."

"The navy?"

Tofer nodded. "They stay on ships and don't go into combat. Except I have an uncle who's a chief petty officer on the aircraft carrier *Enterprise* off the coast of Nha Trang, and they just had a big explosion. Planes are always crash-landing, and artillery batteries on destroyers blow up. There's a bigger risk on surface ships right now. But my uncle says very few people request submarines, which means they almost automatically get in." Tofer nodded again. "Ted should request submarines."

Glenda sniffled and blew her nose in a tissue. She never would have thought of the navy. For the first time, she was beginning to turn around on the Tofer thing. He was saving her son.

So down to the enlistment office they went the next morning. And out came future Seaman Third Class Theodore Pruitt, the newest recruit of the United States Navy.

Then, in quick succession, high school graduation, boot camp and a brief furlough home in West Palm before his first deployment.

Tofer and Ted hugged in the living room. The hippie rubbed Ted's practically shaven skull. "That haircut is a trip."

"I'm going to miss you," said Ted.

"Me too." Tofer held up his acoustic guitar. "One last jam session?"

"Let's go."

This time Glenda didn't give it another thought as they rushed down the hall and closed the bedroom door.

Tofer sat on the bed and strummed "Summertime Blues." "You got submarines just like I said! What ship are you on?"

"The USS——."

"Holy smokes," said Tofer. "That's the real deal. You're on one of the boomers."

"What's that?"

"The subs with the nuclear missiles." Tofer whistled. "Hope you're not claustrophobic."

"Why?"

"Missile subs are different from the others. They stay submerged for almost three months without surfacing, mainly under the Arctic Circle, because that's the shortest ballistic path to the Soviet Union."

"How do you know all this?"

"My uncle, the petty officer." Tofer glanced at the ceiling. "Man, Armageddon at your fingertips. That some heavy shit to lay on your karma."

"I think I'm just supposed to be a cook."

"I know, I know." This time he strummed something by Cream. "This Cold War is a mind-bender. I'm not worried about the standoff with all guns pointed at each other. I'm worried about either side gaining an advantage . . ." Then singing: *"In the white room . . ."*

"Why?"

"The Dogs of War!" said Tofer. "The political leaders don't worry me as much because they're somewhat rational actors, but if the generals get any temptation from an edge of superiority, they just can't resist the itch to go."

"Now *you're* worrying *me,*" said Ted.

"Oh, dude, sorry to freak you out. And just before you're about to deploy." New chords on the guitar from Simon & Garfunkel to tranquilize the mood. "Where you sailing out of? King's Bay?"

"Where's that?" asked Ted.

"Just north of Jacksonville in Georgia."

"Then King's Bay," said Ted.

"Hey, I have an idea." Tofer put down the guitar. "I know this professor at college, and he knows these other teachers in Europe and Asia, on both sides of the Iron Curtain. They're on like this global peace-initiative committee, you know, to keep dialogue open among level heads. Sort of the opposite of the Dogs of War. Anyway, they said today's biggest threats on the doomsday clock are missile submarines. They're an all-or-nothing game of cat and mouse with the whole planet's chips on the table."

Ted always respected Tofer's take on the worldview. "How so?"

"There are two kinds of submarines in the U.S. and Soviet fleets: boomers and fast-attacks. Boomers you already know about, lurking around below the Arctic at a few knots trying to be as quiet as possible. The fast-attacks aren't really attack submarines as the name might suggest. They're essentially surveillance subs, trying to find the enemy's boomers and hanging by their sides. If—and only if—the sonar equipment on the attack subs detects missile doors opening, then they fire their torpedoes before the atomic bombs are launched. Otherwise, they're just babysitting the missile subs."

"This seems very dangerous for the world," said a shaken Ted. "Very dangerous for the existence of the whole human race."

"It is," said Tofer. "But there's hope. While our professors and diplomats are trying to settle things down, the safest thing is for both sides to know where all the other's subs are. The best deterrent to preemptively launching nukes is knowing that you'll be stopped before you can even fire them."

"Then I guess I just have to hope our attack subs can track their missile guys."

"Me too," said Tofer. "The problem is that our equipment is more advanced and our guys do their jobs too well. It's ramping up the temptation for our generals and admirals."

"I hope they work it out," said Ted.

"You can't always bet on hope, but there's something you can do in the meantime," said Tofer, unfolding a plastic chart with a ruffling sound. "You're going up to the Arctic Circle, right? I brought along a shortwave radio map of the area you'll probably be traveling through."

"That doesn't look like any shortwave map I've ever seen."

"Because it's the latest, covering areas over oceans, ice caps and scientific outposts," said Tofer, smoothing out the noisy wrinkles. "These are the most likely routes you'll be traveling, up between Greenland and Iceland and onward to points north."

"I was going to ask how you know, but—"

"My uncle."

"Of course."

"Here are your quadrants." Tofer drew on the chart with a grease pen. "Erase all this when you're done."

"What exactly are you asking me to do?"

"Since you won't be surfacing and there's no way for anyone to communicate with the outside, it's pretty much an open boat." Tofer drew a black line past a frozen coast. "That means you'll be around material that's classified beyond your security grade. And since space is at a premium, the navigation team plots their charts out in the open where a lot of other stuff is going on. People are always walking by on their way to different parts of the ship. It's a third forward on the second deck. So you walk by."

"And do what?"

"Glance at the charts," said Tofer. "And seek out the navigators in the galley during chow time. Make friends. Give it a good few weeks, only seeing them at meals. Then after that, it won't seem unusual if you stop to chat while walking by and take longer looks at the navigation charts. You keep a diary, innocent stuff, but work out a personal code—maybe the first letter of each sentence—to embed stuff that will help you remember what you saw on those charts when you get back. And also get the depths and speed—those should be clearly visible on the control panels in the con where everyone also walks through."

"Hold it right there," said Ted. "You want me to spy on my own country?"

"Oh no, no, no, no!" said Tofer. "It's for these professors. They explained it all to me. The more they understand how close we are to the brink, the better they can try and work things out by bringing up your information at their symposiums. It's totally innocent."

"But why do professors need navigation information?"

"Like I mentioned, the safest world is when both sides know where all the subs are," said Tofer. "But right now America has pulled ahead in stealth technology to make our subs run quieter and less detectable."

"If it's not spying, then what's with all the cloak-and-dagger?"

"This sort of thing would definitely be frowned upon, but it's really no big deal," said Tofer. "You and I have talked a lot about politics and how insane the world has become with greedy corporations. Even a conservative like President Eisenhower warned of the military-industrial complex. We agreed on this, right?"

"Yeah, sure."

"It's your chance to make a difference." Tofer picked up the guitar again. "The bottom line is you'll be helping America. It's actually patriotic."

THE PRESENT

A Ford Falcon sped south on the Tamiami Trail. Serge drained an extra-large cup of 7-Eleven coffee.

Coleman glanced over—"Here we go again"—emptying his own mini Jack Daniel's with a tincture of hash oil.

Serge crumpled the cup and emitted a satisfied *ahhhhh*. "You know what I just remembered I dig from childhood? Old cartoons where the Florida Keys are actually piano keys. And that game Operation we played as kids. 'Remove wrenched ankle.' And Rock'em Sock'em Robots."

Boom!

Coleman turned around. "What was that?"

"The shock wave from the motel," said Serge. "Next question."

"Why do you like old people so much?"

"There's all the wisdom that I've mentioned," said Serge. "Second, *we're* old, too."

"We're not that old," said Coleman, exhaling a hit.

"That isn't what I mean." Serge pointed ahead out the windshield. "See that building? We perceive it like the rest of the world, in three dimensions, height, width, depth. There's also a fourth dimension, time, but humans are limited to perceiving this dimension one point *at a time*."

Coleman held his thumb and index finger a half inch apart in front of his right eye and squeezed them together. "I'm crushing that building."

"Try to stay with me," said Serge. "Some scientists theorize that all of time has already happened, and the dimension is completely laid out like the others, but it's just the constraints of our particular universe that create the illusion we're flowing through it."

"Makes sense to me," said Coleman, tapping an ash out the window.

"And thank God it's set up that way!" said Serge. "Can you imagine if we could see all of time at once, but lose one of the other dimensions? And then we're a bunch of flat people who can't move, like refrigerator magnets stuck to an infinitely large metal astro-plane stretching across the cosmos."

"I hate it when that happens."

"Scientists also subscribe to the notion that there are many other parallel universes operating right now under completely different rules of macro physics and quantum mechanics," said Serge. "The next one over from us might be the giant refrigerator door with all the flat guys who can see their whole lives in a single mural but can't scratch their noses."

"Those poor people," said Coleman.

"I should probably send some money or something," said Serge. "Anyway, that's why when I get up each morning, I close my eyes, straining real hard to break the shackles of my earthly construct and see time for what it really is. And it works! Suddenly I'm at the end of my life, living in a strange future land where there's no need for shoes because everyone hovers everywhere whether they want to or not, and food tastes a million times better, which is odd because it's all made from seaweed that has been harvested by the sirloin steak and ice cream ministries. Tell me if I'm babbling."

"You're good."

"So there I am lying in bed at sunrise with my eyes shut, contentedly reflecting on a life well lived. With one reservation. If I could have a single wish, I'd like to be younger. Then I open my eyes, and I've gotten my wish!" Serge nodded to himself as he raced through a yellow light. "When you begin each day like that, how can you not want to skip down the street?"

"Where are we going?"

"What time is it?"

"Almost four."

The Falcon skidded into a parking lot. Serge and Coleman sat alone in a dining room. A shuttle bus arrived and suddenly they were hardly alone. Trays of martinis rushed in.

"Coleman . . ." Serge tilted his head at another couple in another corner booth. He stood up and grabbed his coffee.

The pair arrived at the booth, and Serge bounded on the balls of his feet. He opened his mouth, but before he could say anything . . .

"You must be Serge," said the man.

"And you're probably Coleman," said the woman.

Serge went flat-footed. "How'd you know?"

The smiling couple scooted over to make room. "There's been a lot of talk about you guys," said the husband.

"You're getting quite the reputation at Boca Shores," said the wife.

"Uh, what are they saying?" asked Serge.

"That you got a bunch of money back for some of the residents who were swindled," said the man.

"Nobody's been able to do that before," said the woman. "And you're very polite and respectful."

"A little energetic, but appreciative and interested in our lives," said the man, offering a hand to shake. "I'm Lawrence, and that's Nancy. The Shepards from Springfield. Missouri, not Illinois."

"It's an honor." Serge slid into the booth. "Did you read about those teenagers in Fort Lauderdale who threw the sixty-eight-year-old woman in the swimming pool because she asked them to turn down their music?"

"Sadly. Sometimes I don't recognize my own country anymore," said Lawrence. "If anyone ever did that to Nancy . . ."

"You'd be in line behind me." Serge set his recorder on the table. "So what's your fantastic story? How'd you two lovebirds meet?"

"In the Peace Corps."

Serge nudged Coleman. "We're off to the races . . ." He grinned at the couple. "What did you do in the Peace Corps?"

"We were doctors," said Nancy. "Epidemiologists. In Africa."

"Holy shit!" Serge covered his mouth. "I mean wow. You could have made a lot of money with that specialty."

"People were suffering needlessly," said Lawrence. "But we missed the States and later opened a practice in Appalachia, because they didn't have enough physicians."

"Then we joined a free clinic in Oakland," said Nancy.

"Damn," said Serge. "You had me at Peace Corps . . . Coleman, meet our newest heroes!"

"Hooray."

"You could be living in a mansion," said Serge. "Instead you're stuck in a trailer. Okay, that came out wrong. A manufactured home, and a nice one at that."

"No, you're right. It's a trailer," said Nancy. "And we couldn't be happier."

Lawrence nodded. "What good is money if you know you could have helped others but didn't? Few realize the infant mortality rates we've seen."

Serge's mouth was hanging open in disbelief when a passing waiter noticed his empty cup.

"More coffee?"

"What? Yes! By all means!"

Nancy cut a piece of meat loaf. "So what do *you* do?"

"I didn't do anything!" Serge said defensively. "I mean it's a discreet business. I do favors for people. Social odd jobs. You could say I fill a vacuum."

Coleman sucked a martini olive and nodded. "People always wonder how he makes his money, where he gets his cool cars and a bunch of cash to travel all the time."

"That's right," said Serge. "Say you start a business and take on a legitimate partner, but then that partner goes seriously in debt—medical bills, gambling, who knows—and gets a black-market loan, and now you've suddenly got a new silent partner you didn't bargain for. I had a totally innocent accountant friend who was doing very well before this shady character from Hialeah put the arm on him. Turns out the shady character was working for an even scarier boss in Miami. Threats were made. My friend was out of his league, weeping on the phone. That's where I came in." He held an empty cup out in the aisle and a waiter refilled it. "I went to the guy's house in Hialeah. I think he was sleeping when I knocked, just because it was after midnight. Anyway, he asks what the hell I wanted, and I said to dissolve the partnership and never contact my friend again. So he reaches behind the door and becomes puzzled. I say, are you looking for your baseball bat? It's duct-taped to the ceiling fan. He looks up and is shocked to see it there. I also tell him his golf shoes are on top of the mantel. He says I'm a dead man, and gets out his phone to call his boss in Miami, and I say, 'While you're on the line, tell him his goldfish bowl is on top of the refrigerator.' Of course next to the fish bowl was a personal note that whoever put the bowl there could get back inside the house at will, especially when he's sleeping. And by the time the guy got off the phone with his boss, I had vanished. I remember him creeping around his yard in his pajamas looking for me, gripping that baseball bat like Pete Rose. Hoo-wee, what a hilarious image! Bottom line, they received the message loud and clear and decided the matter was more trouble than it was worth. My friend had no more problems, and I got a cool Ford Falcon!"

The Shepards' smiles had transformed into frightful stares.

"Uh, that's the exact reaction I was looking for," said Serge. "It's a screenplay I'm working on, but it'll probably end up a TV pilot. What do you think?"

"*Ohhhhhh . . .*" Nancy exhaled with relief. "You're a writer. You really had me going with that story!"

"Thank you for being a wonderful focus group," said Serge.

They enjoyed their meal and small talk—"Your thoughts on the Big Picture. Refrigerator door or what? . . ."—Serge manically shook an empty cup at the waiter again, who poured a third refill.

"Thanks!" Serge began vibrating as he sipped. "That and a dime will get you a cup of coffee, the sixty-four-dollar question, if I had a nickel for every time, a penny saved is a penny earned, penny wise and pound foolish, selling like hot cakes, since sliced bread, a New York minute, a country mile, the whole nine yards, ten ways to Sunday, everyone and his uncle, you and the horse you rode in on, all that and a bag of chips, don't count your chickens, don't burn your bridges, don't eat the yellow snow . . ."

"You're babbling," said Coleman.

"Sorry," said Serge. "Talking a blue streak, talking till blue in the face, talking through one's hat, talking a mile a minute, talking in circles, talk is cheap, money talks, like talking to a brick wall, talk the talk and walk the walk, running off at the mouth, diarrhea of the mouth, speak no evil, speak softly but carry a big stick, spill the beans, a picture is worth a thousand words, from your lips to God's ear, silence is golden . . ."

Coleman finished another oversize martini and fell out of the booth.

Lawrence and Nancy glanced at each other.

"So what do you say?" asked Serge. "Can we give you a lift back to the park?"

Chapter 12

BOCA SHORES

The Falcon slowed as it approached the guard booth, but Earl recognized the car by now. The gate arm was already raised, and Earl waved them through.

The car circled the man-made lake and parked. Serge pointed at a sign on the screen-porch door.

No Solicitors.

"I know," said Lawrence. "You wouldn't think we'd need a sign like that in a place like this, but we do. And it doesn't work."

They entered through the sliding glass door. "Look at all this space!" said Serge. "You've managed to stay off the list."

"I'm still amazed at the sheer volume of scam artists who prey on seniors today," said Lawrence. "It's become so bad that Mrs. Olsteen on the next street was burying her husband when some guy came up in the cemetery and claimed Mr. Olsteen had an outstanding debt, and she needed to write him a check immediately or lose her trailer. She's old, grieving, confused . . ."

"And she wrote the check," said Serge.

"It's a different world," said Lawrence.

Rrrrring! . . . Rrrrring! . . . Rrrrring! . . . Rrrrring! . . .

Serge glanced at the wall phone. "Aren't you going to answer that?"

"Why?" Lawrence went in the kitchen for a glass of water. "Nine out of ten times it's someone trying to scare us into coughing up information to get into our bank accounts. Fake tax collectors, fake lottery, fake medical billing."

"And the tenth time?" asked Serge.

"Someone who says, 'Hey, Grandpa, guess who this is?' That one's particularly devious. A lot of us are dying to get a call like that, and just as many are hard of hearing. So the person who picked up the phone guesses the grandchild whose voice sounds the closest. The person on the other end says 'Right,' and then the games begin. The Klostermans are out five grand to 'Jimmy.'"

"How come you don't get taken?" asked Serge. "How do you know all this?"

"I've seen more of the world in my life, and it's set the bar for depravity pretty low," said Lawrence. "I arranged for the state attorney to come here and give a seminar in the park's clubhouse on scams against the elderly, and without exception, someone inevitably raised their hand and said they'd been a victim of each scheme described."

Ding-dong . . . Ding-dong . . .

Serge jumped and looked toward the front of the house. "Who's that?"

Lawrence sighed. "The sign on the door still isn't working."

"I've got this one." Serge went out onto the screened-in porch and opened the door. "May I help you?"

"Yes, is Mr. or Mrs. Shepard in?" A young man in a thin tie smiled and cradled a folder of shiny brochures.

"I've been expecting you!" said Serge. "They can't wait to be swindled. Please, come right in!"

The man's smile dissolved into a quizzical look. *Wait, this is the guy the others warned me about.*

He ran off, leaving a trail of pamphlets.

Serge returned to the living room. "What got into him?"

Lawrence chuckled. "It's not just the residents who are talking about you. You're a hot topic with all the salesmen, too. Hornsby said you kicked that one guy in the balls pretty hard."

"You know about that?"

"Everyone does," said Lawrence. "It was the high point of the month around here. You're bigger than bingo."

Nancy came out of the bedroom in a one-piece bathing suit and rubber swim cap with plastic daisies. "Lawrence, did you forget?"

"What time is it? Crap!" He turned to Serge. "I hate to be a rude host, but we have our aqua-aerobics class."

"Aqua aerobics!" said Serge. "I'm all about aqua *and* aerobics! Can I join you?"

"You don't have a swimsuit."

"Always carry one in the car for the possibilities."

"What about him?" asked Lawrence.

Serge looked behind the sofa, where Coleman was spread out on the carpet in another signature chalk-outline pose. "I also carry smelling salts."

Minutes later, a group of seniors slowly descended the concrete stairs into the pool. The instructor came over with a clipboard.

"These are our guests," said Lawrence.

"That's wonderful," said a fit middle-aged woman named Heather. "Always happy to have a couple more."

"Wouldn't miss it!" said Serge, fitting a borrowed swim cap onto his head.

Heather stared up at the plastic daisies but maintained her smile. Then she turned and called out across the water: "Let's begin . . ."

Coleman nudged his buddy. "What do we do?"

"Just follow their lead."

The residents spread out across the pool in precisely spaced rows.

"Remember to warm up," said Heather.

The class grabbed their elbows and twisted side to side, then alternated raising their knees.

"Why aren't we warming up?" asked Coleman.

"I'm constantly in a state of overly warmed up, and you just did your stretching on the carpet."

"Let's begin," said Heather. "Kick! One, two, three . . . Kick! One, two, three . . . The other way. Kick! One, two, three . . ."

"This is harder than I thought," said Coleman, surrounded by bubbles.

"Did you just fart?"

"More to come," said Coleman.

Bubbles and giggles.

"Jesus!" Serge slid away in the water with a look of contempt. "You need medical attention. The kind where you're in a giant operating room at a teaching hospital with a glassed-in spectator section above so other physicians from around the world can observe."

A voice from across the pool. "Is everything okay?" asked Heather.

"You can smell it all the way over there?" said Serge. "Don't worry. The offshore breeze is dispersing it out to sea. Please proceed . . ."

The residents were soon all grabbing the edge of the pool and kicking lightly. Coleman clung motionless to the wall while Serge kicked the water into a roiling froth.

Heather smiled patiently. "And now our water ballet . . ."

"Water ballet!" Serge told Coleman. "This is my favorite!"

"This is stupid."

"That's because you're not used to seeing people with heads-on-straight priorities." Serge swept an arm toward the rest of the class. "Exercise, fresh air and friendship. These motherfuckers have their shit wired solid." He looked up. "What? . . . No, I didn't realize I was talking that loud . . ."

Heather turned on a boom box at the side of the pool. A recording from the metropolitan ballet. Everyone began twirling gracefully in the water.

Serge made his arms into a circle over his head like a ballerina. He twirled in synchronization with the others. Coleman twirled the other way.

The music picked up rhythm, and so did Serge. His spinning rate increased, slightly at first, then faster and faster, until he was at top speed, a splashing blur in the water.

Serge became seriously dizzy and stopped spinning, staggering side to side in the pool with his arms out for balance. He regained his bearings and looked up again.

The rest of the pool was silent and still. Everyone was staring at him.

"What?"

There was a barely audible *bloop* in the back of the pack. Nobody saw it because they were all still looking at their visitors.

But Serge did. He violently dove down in the water, paddling furiously until he reached the drain. Then he bent his legs and pushed off from the bottom. He broke the surface with a lithe woman over his shoulder and rolled her onto the cement along the edge of the pool.

People screamed. Heather came running.

"It's Rose!"

"What happened?"

Before the instructor could arrive on the far side of the pool, Serge had already vaulted from the water, expertly performing chest compressions and mouth-to-mouth.

"Dear God!"

"Call an ambulance!"

Serge made a final two-handed thrust, and Rose spit up water and coughed.

The paramedics arrived. Silent drama as they checked her out. The whole exercise class pregnant with worry.

An EMT stowed a stethoscope. "Probably just a fainting spell, but we're going to take her to the hospital for overnight observation just to be on the safe side."

The audience remained silent as the back door slammed shut behind the stretcher, and the ambulance drove away. Then they all turned and stared at Serge.

"What?"

THE NEXT DAY

A Nissan Versa sat at a red light in heavy morning traffic. The driver had changed his routine, listening to a new radio station in order to relate to his younger coworkers.

"... *Don't believe me, just watch!* ..."

Benmont Pinch bobbed his head and tapped fingers on the steering wheel. "This new music these kids listen to isn't that bad."

"... *Don't believe me, just watch!* ..."

The tapping continued as the light turned green, and the Nissan started through the intersection. "I wonder who this is?"

"... *You've just been listening to a commercial-free set from Beyoncé, Lady Gaga and Bruno Mars* ..."

"Who?"

A hand reached for the radio tuner. "Let me see what other young stuff I can find ..."

"... *Home, home, where I've wanted to go* ..."

The Versa pulled into the employee parking lot.

"... *This is WPPT-FM, the Party Parrot, and you've just been listening to 'Clocks' by Coldplay.*"

Benmont again was one of the first to arrive at the offices of Life-Armor. He went in the lunchroom to reheat a breakfast biscuit. The flat-screen TVs were on.

"... *Police are at the scene this hour of another double homicide*..."

Benmont froze to watch. Then he scrambled for a pen and paper, and let the cheese burn on his biscuit.

... A half hour later, Quint Powers and his expensive briefcase entered the building and strolled toward his office. He hesitated a step as he saw Benmont Pinch sitting in a chair outside his door. And not the usual chipper Benmont.

Quint got out his keys to open the office. "You look like something's on your mind."

"We need to talk," said Benmont. "And we need to close the door."

Anyone outside watching the silent exchange through the window would have thought someone's dog had died.

"I didn't expect this when I got here today," said Quint. "Can you back it up?"

Benmont reached into a folder. "I did an Internet search of news articles. Some are unsolved, others have been closed as murder-suicides, but all occurred after I turned in that Social Security project." He passed two pages across the desk. "I compiled the victims' names."

Quint held the pages side by side, looking at one then the other. "You gave me a duplicate copy. They're identical."

Benmont shook his head. "The one in your left hand is a list of victims from the news reports. The other is names I compiled for our client."

Quint practically choked. "You've double-checked this?"

"Over and over," said Benmont. "What do you think of my theory now?"

Quint solemnly set the two pages down on his desk blotter. "We're in new territory. Before, when the theory seemed far-fetched, I didn't want to pass it along because of legal issues. But knowing what we do now, it's an even bigger problem if we don't act."

"What are you going to do?" asked Benmont. "Call the lawyers back?"

"That's my *second* call. Because they won't want me to make the first," said Quint. "Do you mind if I take credit for this?"

"What?"

"I'm not trying to be a jerk," said Quint. "But this is too important, and your theory will still sound absurd at first impression. It will be far more credible to my contact in the government if it comes from me. I swear, after the dust settles, I'll sing your praises from on high."

"I trust you."

"Give me the room."

Benmont respectfully left and closed the door.

His boss picked up the phone and dialed a number with a Baltimore area code. "Jerry, it's me, Quint . . . Yes, the kids are doing great . . . No, don't worry about the Christmas cards. Listen, remember that last e-mail I sent you? There's been a development . . ." He pressed a button on his computer. "I just sent you another e-mail, but I wanted you on the phone when you opened it because it's going to seem like the craziest theory. Hear me out . . ."

The line was quiet as a person in a government building in Maryland read down his screen. "You're on the level?"

"Couldn't be more serious."

"Then as of now, this is all officially classified," said Jerry. "Who else has the list?"

"One of my analysts, the client and the lawyers."

"Secure them all. I'll get back to you." *Click.*

Quint held the disconnected phone in front of his face. "That was abrupt."

. . . A man named Jerry Symanski ran through a building in Baltimore and into another office. His division chief.

"You're all out of breath."

"Sir, remember the e-mail I sent you from Florida last week?"

The chief thought, *You mean the one I ditched?* "Yes, I recall it."

"It seemed innocent, but now we've got a big problem. We need to fold the FBI in."

"Slow down," said the chief. "You're skipping steps."

"Check your inbox."

The chief did. He read to the end of the e-mail. "Don't tell me you've turned into a conspiracy nut."

"A friend of mine in Tampa came up with that theory," said Symanski. "I checked it out on the Internet. All those people are really dead."

"Stop talking," said the chief. "Not another word to anyone, not even me. Go back to work and forget this conversation. Someone will come around this afternoon for a routine virus inspection of your computer. They may have to switch out your hard drive."

Symanski understood. Firewalling. He'd never see those e-mails again. "Yes, sir."

The door closed.

The chief: "Dammit! Why did I ditch that first e-mail? How do I fix this?" He picked up his phone. "Get me a secure line to the FBI..."

Two separate e-mails began zipping through the nation's most secure servers, up the food chain. Benmont's original work product from the previous month, and his current theory. They moved faster than normal through the bureaucracy because the whole mess had a giant, unspoken headline on it: THIS COULD END CAREERS.

The e-mails hit the computer screen of one particular FBI agent, who finished reading them and turned off his computer. He grabbed a heavy coat off a hook and decided to take a chilly lunchtime stroll through a public park.

He took a seat on a bench. Someone else sat down. They didn't talk.

The agent placed a newspaper on the bench and left.

The other man picked up the paper and walked away in the opposite direction.

Chapter 13

SARASOTA

The Shepards from Springfield, Missouri, sat in their screened-in porch enjoying their evening tea. They had company.

Lawrence set a cup in a saucer. "That was some fast reacting at the pool yesterday."

"It's the only way I know how to react," said Serge, pinkie extended from his teacup.

"If the park wasn't talking all about you before..." said Nancy.

"It's about to get dark." Lawrence tapped his wristwatch. "Scott."

"That's right, Scott," said Nancy, getting up to make preparations.

"Who's Scott?" asked Serge.

"Why don't we walk and talk?" said Lawrence.

The pair strolled along the edge of a peacefully empty street as the air cooled, and the Florida sky shared its burnished beauty. Three-wheel bikes and exercise walkers greeted them. The fountain in the lake gurgled to a stop, and a turtle crawled onto it.

Serge pointed at the water. "You have swans. Did you know that they're some of the most violent and aggressive birds on earth? It's true! People universally accept them as elegantly beautiful creatures, but that's our downfall. You don't even have to go near them; they're out looking for shit. You think you've got a comfortable life, just walking around wondering if you still have that pecan log back at the house, and then you're chased by swans. Deal me out of that program."

"Serge, forget the swans," said Lawrence. "This is important. I need to tell you about Scott, one of the greatest kids you could ever meet."

"Right, Scott. You mentioned he's the grandson of the Packers?"

"Buford and Wilma." Lawrence waved at a passing cyclist. "He lost his parents early, and they raised him from age two until he left for college. Now it's a decade later, and he's back staying with them for caregiving."

"That *is* a great kid," said Serge. "So young, yet sacrificing his social life to be a caregiver."

"No, the other way around." Lawrence shook his head. "Worst luck in the world. Big handsome kid, brilliant computer technician, until he was hit by a drunk driver. Bad insurance coverage, lost his job, car, girlfriend, emptied his bank account, everything. Had nowhere to live, so he's back with his grandparents. Doctors say he should recover almost ninety percent, but it did a real number on his back and will take at least twelve months, maybe eighteen."

"That's such a shame," said Serge.

"Nancy and I always have the best time when he comes over."

"Well, if you're having him and his grandparents for dinner, Coleman and I should probably be going," said Serge. "Tight fit."

"No, only him," said Lawrence. "And not just for dinner. He's spending the night."

Serge slowed a step. "Now I'm confused. If he's living with his grandparents, then why is he crashing at your pad just a few doors down?"

"Park rules," said Lawrence. "Nobody had heard about this one regulation because it's buried way down in the fine print of our contracts. Scott had been staying with them a few months when somehow the park management got wind. Not that anyone was trying to conceal it. Anyway, one of the managers came around and informed the Packers that one of the park's rules is that residents can only have visitors under fifty-five years of age for a maximum of thirty days in any calendar year. They said Scott would have to leave immediately, and they didn't mean the next morning. So his grandparents registered him and his wheelchair at a local motel that night."

"Don't they have a heart?" asked Serge.

"Apparently not," said Lawrence. "A bunch of us went to the management office the next day and asked for a hardship exemption, but they wouldn't budge. Can you believe that? Scott is like everyone's adopted grandson around here. So we had a meeting among the residents and decided to rotate him trailer to trailer each month to get around the rule. This is our month."

"You seniors never cease to amaze me," said Serge.

"Here we are," said Lawrence, turning up a walkway toward a screened-in porch where a radiant face was already poking out the door.

"Hi, Mr. Shepard."

"How many times have I told you to call me Lawrence?"

"Sorry, Mr. Shepard."

The grandfather already had the wheelchair open at the bottom of the steps. Scott slowly worked his way down to it with a cane, but his cheer never faltered. They helped him into the chair, and the young man placed his walking stick across his lap.

The grandfather furtively motioned toward Lawrence that he wanted to step aside for a private word.

"What is it?"

"Not sure, but it doesn't look good," said Mr. Packer. He pulled a letter from his pocket. "Just got this in the mail today. You said you know some lawyers. Could you look at it for me?"

"No problem."

Scott tried to see back over his shoulder. "What are you guys talking about?"

"Nothing," said Lawrence, tucking the envelope away. He walked up behind the chair and grabbed the handles. "Ready for a ride?"

Serge touched Lawrence's arm. "Please allow me. It's important."

"Who's that?" Scott called behind him.

"Serge, your newest best friend. And your chauffeur for to-night." He pushed the chair back down the driveway to the street. "And I know all about you nutty kids, so don't even ask me to do a wheelie. Okay, but just one . . . *Weeeeeee!*"

"Serge! Jesus!" yelled Lawrence. "He's in physical rehab! Can you please push him normal?"

"Just trying to find the edge of the performance envelope on this wheelchair," said Serge. "But you're right. It's probably safer to test it on Coleman first."

He resumed pushing at a slow rate with all wheels on the runway. "I've heard so much about you."

"You have?" said Scott.

"Got a girlfriend, right?"

"Well, used to."

"Damn," said Serge, stomping a foot on the pavement. "I've done it again. Wandered like an unattended toddler into insensitivity traffic."

"No," said Scott. "It's fine. Actually, it's great!"

"That's an interesting attitude." Serge pushed on in the growing darkness. "How so?"

"My grandparents raised me, and what a fantastic child-hood!" said Scott. "Ever since I can remember as a little guy, my grandpa was never too busy to play baseball with me or go fishing or help me build a fort in the backyard. And Grandma played Legos with me and Tinker Toys, and let me lick peanut butter off the spoon. The whole time encouraging me, always saying I was destined for great things."

"They sound wonderful," said Serge.

"They are," said Scott. "Bought me a computer when I was young, and I got really good at it. Beyond what I ever would have imagined. Guess I just had a knack, but my grandparents said they always knew. Then I got a job. I was rising up fast, even receiving offers from other companies for more money. One of them hired me to be the head of IT for the entire firm, the youngest ever, with a ridiculous salary and a company car. The weekend before I was supposed to start, bam, that guy hit me. Was in a coma three days. Fast-forward: I went to court and the guy seemed genuinely sorry, so I asked the judge to show leniency if he would agree to go with me to local high schools and talk to the kids about what had happened, because something good can come out of everything."

Serge glanced at Lawrence, who returned a look: *What did I tell you about this kid?*

"But here's the best part!" said the handicapped youth. "I get to live with my grandparents again! Most people grow up and leave home and try to stay in touch the best they can, but life is just life, and new responsibilities gradually drift you away until you're spending practically no time at all. But in my case, after missing them for ten years, we all get to live under the same roof again! I know I'll eventually recover from my injuries, so in the meantime I'm going to savor every moment with them. Most people never get a chance like this. I guess I'm just really lucky."

Now Serge gave Lawrence a look: *This kid is unbelievable.*

"My grandparents sleep in separate rooms, because he snores," said Scott. "Grandpa has an extra bed in his room, and he went to the lumberyard and had them cut a thick piece of plywood to fit between the box spring and mattress to support my back, and after we go to bed at night and turn off the lights, we just talk and talk about sports and memories like a couple of little brothers bunking together. Then he bought two flashlights and some walkie-talkies for us to goof around with in bed like we really were little brothers, laughing and cutting up until my grandmother has to come in the room and ask us to keep it down. But she asks nice . . . Anyway, now that I have to sleep at the other trailers, I miss those late-night talks with Grandpa. That's my only regret . . . Oh, sorry, Mr. Shepard . . ."

"It's Lawrence."

"I didn't mean to sound ungrateful."

"Believe me, you're not even in the ballpark."

They wheeled him up to the screened porch, and Serge ran on ahead inside while Lawrence helped Scott with his cane.

Serge waved at Nancy sitting on the couch, then called out: "Coleman! You have to meet this kid! . . . *Coleman?*"

"Here."

Serge looked behind the sofa, where Coleman was lying on the carpet again with his limbs defying anatomy. "What the hell are you doing down there?"

"Just what you told me to," said Coleman. "Visiting with her."

"Coleman, I believe in the rest of the English-speaking world, that means something different."

Nancy suddenly popped up with excitement. "Scott! Come in!" A huge hug.

The evening wore on, and the living room filled with Scott's contagious optimism. Nancy served pastries. They watched the late news.

Outside: *"Lean into it! Lean into it!"*

"I'm trying! Slow down!"

Crash.

"Ahhhhh!"

The Shepards ran out onto their porch in alarm.

Serge righted a wheelchair in the street and smiled. "Nothing broken. But I've established some important data on the envelope."

Coleman sat up on the tar and rubbed his knees.

"He's bleeding," said Nancy.

"Just a little road rash," said Serge. "Most of the time he doesn't even feel it."

"I'll get some Band-Aids."

They returned to the house, and chitchat resumed. "Then my granddad took me to like a million spring training games back before the mini-stadiums when they still played at the historic old fields and the players were up close: Al Lopez in Tampa, Al Lang in Saint Pete, Payne Park here in Sarasota. And all the baseball junk food I could eat! . . ."

Lawrence pointed out the sliding glass doors. "Show's about to start."

"What show?" asked Serge.

"Oh, you'll love this," said Scott.

They all went out on the porch and took viewing seats as fat raindrops began to plop in the lake.

"I still don't know what I'm looking for," said Serge.

"You know how Tampa Bay is accurately named the lightning capital of the world?"

"Intimately," said Serge.

"Well, weather doesn't obey county lines, and down south here in Sarasota, we still get more than our share," said Lawrence.

"At first, when we moved in, it was a source of concern," said Nancy. "'What's up with all this lightning?' Transformers blew and lights went out, and there were sirens. But the lights were always quickly back on, because the power company had beefed-up, round-the-clock emergency crews on standby."

Lawrence chuckled. "Workers in thick, blowing raincoats always out in cherry pickers in the middle of monsoons to get our favorite TV shows back on. Corporations aren't known for that level of service, but local politicians don't like receiving lots of calls about extended outages, especially from us seniors, who vote like maniacs."

The group noticed other residents emerging onto their own porches with drinks and snacks to take in the free fireworks show. It wasn't as odd as it sounds. Contrary to popular impression, much of the lightning here wasn't the classic scary bolts with crashing thunder. It tended to be heat lightning and distant air-to-air strikes that made the clouds glow in a dancing chain of flashes that was actually an enjoyable display of nature's beauty. And the thunder was more of a gentle, rolling rumble. Given the area's bounty of almost perpetually sunny days, it became welcome variety.

The palms started to rustle and rain began to pour. "Here we go," said Lawrence.

The flashes began, and horizontal streaks laced the sky. It seemed like it would continue forever.

"Only one thing missing . . ." said Lawrence.

"What's that?" asked Serge.

Bang.

A transformer blew, knocking out power in the neighboring, rival retirement park. An enthusiastic cheer went up from all the other trailer porches.

Then a Florida thing. Just as quickly as the storm had swept in, it was gone.

Lawrence got up. "Show's over."

They all went inside, and soon the yawns started as people prepared for bed. Lawrence stood in the kitchen. "Serge, could you come here a minute?"

"What is it?"

"Just when I thought the bar of human callousness couldn't get any lower." Lawrence was holding a piece of paper and almost shaking. "The Packers got this today via certified mail. Buford gave it to me before we wheeled Scott over."

"Let me see that."

Lawrence handed it over. "Letter from the park's attorney. They're reinterpreting the policy in the terms of agreement. Now they're saying that the thirty-day limit in any year applies to the entire park. They're classifying Scott as the Packers' visitor, regardless of which trailer he stays in. They want him gone again."

Serge read the correspondence and gave it back. "What's wrong with these people?"

"I don't know, but I'm calling an attorney first thing in the morning."

"Does Scott know?"

"Not yet."

"Then don't call an attorney," said Serge. "If I've figured Scott out, he'll feel terrible about the cost and strain of a legal fight."

"We can't just allow them to throw him out on the street."

"Trust me, that's not going to happen," said Serge. "Give me twenty-four hours."

"What are you planning?"

"It's better you don't know in case you're called to testify."

"I didn't hear that."

"Who owns the park, anyway?"

"Big local development company with lots of political clout," said Lawrence. "The owner has a giant beach house out on Siesta Key."

THREE A.M.

German binoculars focused on a full moon that had faded from bright white to a daffodil yellow as it prepared to set over the shimmering Gulf of Mexico.

"Just listen to that ocean. There's nothing more peaceful than waves quietly rolling ashore at night." The binoculars swept across the water to a post-modern beach mansion with lots of glass blocks and brushed-metal balcony railings.

Coleman was in the passenger seat, playing with a lock pick set. "Ow, I stuck myself."

"Give me that!" Serge snatched the kit and returned it to his pocket.

Coleman uncapped a flask. "That was a pretty cool pet store we went to. They had all kinds of strange creatures I never knew people wanted. What do you even say to a newt?"

The binoculars returned to the second floor of the residence, where all the lights were out. Serge pressed buttons on a cell phone. Understandably, it rang and rang. Until finally, a groggy voice: "Uh, hullo . . ."

Serge could hear the person on the other end fumbling with a bedside alarm clock that crashed to the floor. "Is this Mr. Dryden?"

"Who the hell are you? Do you know what time it is?"

"Listen carefully," said Serge, "because you won't get a second chance. Whatever you do, don't throw your legs over the side of the bed and put on your slippers."

"What is this bullshit?"

"Turn on the lamp instead."

Serge saw an upstairs light come on in his binoculars.

The scream was so loud he heard it in stereo: through the phone, and outside, echoing off the balcony.

Mr. Dryden clutched the side of the bed and stared down. A thread was tied to his left slipper. The other end acted as a kind of tiny leash, around a pissed-off scorpion.

"Hello? Hello?" said Serge. "Are you still there?"

"I'll kill you! I'll call the police!"

"Doubtful." Serge's binoculars watched an upstairs silhouette going through dresser drawers. "In case you're looking for your gun, it's in the refrigerator on top of the eggs. And it's time to throw out that milk."

The silhouette stopped. "What's going on? What do you want?"

"That's better," said Serge. "You own Boca Shores, right? There's a retired couple living there, and their grandson is going through a difficult period. You're going to let him stay at the park as long as he wants."

"Are you fucking joking? *That's* what this is about?" yelled Mr. Dryden. "They signed the terms of agreement, and that kid is taking advantage of me! You've threatened the wrong person, asshole. I have private investigators and I'll track you down. But first—just because of you—I'm kicking that kid *and* his grandparents out of my park!"

"You might want to check your jewelry box," said Serge. "You never know when someone could develop a case of sticky fingers."

"Son of a bitch! If you touched a single one of my Rolexes! . . ."

The binoculars watched the silhouette change course. Then another chilling scream in stereo.

"That would be a tarantula," said Serge. "I can do this all day long. All *year* long, because the weather's incredible down here. So many interesting insects and reptiles. In the future you won't be getting a courtesy call."

"I'll—! I'll—! . . ."

"Why don't you calm down and take deep breaths?" said Serge. Silence on the other end.

"That's much better," said Serge. "And for the record, the Packers don't know anything about this, and I don't know them. I just heard on the grapevine what was going on with this poor kid, and I thought, 'There's got to be some kind of mistake. The owner definitely must not realize this is going on,' so I'm doing you the favor of filling you in."

More silence.

"You've got it pretty cushy out here on Crescent Beach," said Serge. "So ask yourself this question: Is hassling that young man and his grandparents really worth inviting me into your life?"

"You're a madman!"

"That should make your decision a no-brainer."

A long pause. "If I let him stay, is that the end of this?"

"You have my word." Serge slapped himself on the forehead. "Almost forgot about the rattlesnake in the humidor for your Montecristos."

"Okay, okay, just leave me alone!"

"Oh, and a couple last conditions . . ." Serge told him what they were. "It's non-negotiable under *my* terms of agreement."

"You've got to be shitting me!"

"I wouldn't shit you. You're my favorite turd." Serge laughed maniacally. "I never get tired of that old joke. Have to admit, you opened yourself up for that one!" More unbalanced laughter.

"Fine! Anything! Just don't hurt me!"

And Serge hung up.

Chapter 14

Bright and early.
  Knock-knock-knock...
"Who can that be?" asked Wilma Packer.
"Even the salesmen don't knock this early," said her husband.
Knock-knock-knock...
"Hold your horses! I'm coming!"
Bam-bam-bam...
Buford opened the sliding glass door. "I said I was coming! What's the emergency?"
There was a golf cart in the driveway and a man in an Italian suit at the screen door. "Are you Buford Packer?"
"Yeah, who are you?"
"Trent Dryden, owner of the park."

"That's why you're banging on our door?" said Buford. "Because our grandson hasn't left fast enough for you? Have you no shame? . . . Well, don't you worry. His suitcases are in the car and he's ready to go. We don't know where, but he'll be out of your soulless life!" He began turning around to go inside.

Dryden's hands shot out. "No! No! No! Don't let him go! Please, make him stay! I'm begging you!"

"What?" Buford looked back. "I thought you wanted him out of here?"

"That's the last thing I want!" Dryden exclaimed. "There's been a horrible misunderstanding. I had no idea what my staff was doing, and as soon as I found out, I said, 'What kind of sick people are you? We're a family-friendly park, and you're treating this fine young man like this?' Then I fired them. Sam can stay as long as he likes."

"It's Scott," said the young man, joining Buford on the porch.

"Scott! Yes! I've heard so much about you! You can stay! You *must* stay!" He pointed at the Buick in the driveway. "I'll get your suitcases!"

Grandson and granddad looked at each other, puzzled. Dryden ran back to the porch steps and set down the luggage. "Anything else? Good. Great! Tell all your friends and any other interested parties that we're cool. Okay! . . . Almost forgot!" He reached out to Scott. "Here, this is for you. For all your inconvenience. Forget about the wheelchair."

"What are these keys for?"

Dryden pointed at the driveway. "Your new golf cart. Just tell your friends!" He ran away.

Buford shrugged. "Live long enough and you'll see everything." They went inside.

Scott's grandmother met them at the glass doors. "What are the suitcases doing there? What's that in the driveway?"

"You're not going to believe this . . ."

A Nissan Versa sat on the shoulder of the road as the morning rush hour blew by.

Benmont pumped the handle of a tire jack, lowering the back of his car after putting on the spare. "Darn, now I'm going to be late."

The office of Life-Armor was unusually quiet as Benmont arrived. Actually, it was almost empty.

He slowed his steps and apprehensively neared his desk. His eyes darted around as he set down a lunchbox. "Where is everyone?"

Answer: In the lunchroom, and there wasn't a breakfast special.

Benmont approached the crowd from behind. "What's everyone watching?"

A collective "Shhhhhh!" Then they all faced back up at the flat screens.

"*. . . The three double homicides in the last forty-eight hours still appear to be unrelated, as the victims had no connection to one another and were spread across three cities and different economic levels. However, murder-suicide hasn't been ruled out as all the cases took place at retirement communities . . .*"

Benmont saw a familiar head in the front of the audience. He wormed his way through the pack and lowered his voice to a whisper. "Sonic, what's going on?"

Sonic turned and startled. "Benmont! Jesus, come here!" He pulled his colleague out of the crowd. "Nobody knew where you were . . ."

"Had a flat tire on the way in."

"I need to give you a heads-up," said his friend, quickly looking around again. "The lawyers are looking for you."

"Lawyers? . . ." Benmont thought to himself: *It can only get*

Sonic in trouble if he finds out. For his sake, I need to play dumb. "I don't understand. What for?"

"The last two victims lived only ten blocks from here." Sonic took shallow breaths. "More alarmingly, they were on our frequent flyer list."

"What's that?" asked Benmont.

"You wouldn't know because you're not in the privacy division, but our type of business naturally attracts a lot of paranoid types who call every other day. Very high maintenance, and we put them on a black list and dump them with a brief, prepared script whenever they call. This particular couple, the Treadstones, swore that enemies were trying to track them down and kill them. So we told them that they weren't paying us good money for nothing. They had the very best identity protection available and would be alerted within seconds of the tiniest problem."

"Right," said Benmont. "Our company is the best."

"When we saw the news this morning with their names as victims, we got curious and did a system-wide search. Sure enough, their personal information had been compromised."

"How so?"

"We sold it."

"We?"

"Actually, you."

"I didn't sell anything!" said Benmont.

"Yes, you did."

"What!"

"A marketing list you compiled last month."

"But how is that possible?" said Benmont. "I just assumed that the names of anyone paying our company for privacy protection would be shared with us so that we would make sure not to include them in any of the data we sold."

Sonic shook his head. "Sharing their information with your division would be considered a privacy breach. We have to maintain integrity."

"That's insane," said Benmont.

"That's pretty much what our lawyers told us," said Sonic. "The entire company is circling the wagons for the lawsuits." He nodded toward the crowd watching the flat screen. "Starling knew the victims personally, the only one with the patience to take their freaked-out calls. She's devastated."

"Who's Starling?"

Sonic pointed. "Purple hair, crying inconsolably and blowing her nose into a planet-friendly Jamaican handkerchief."

Benmont didn't recognize the dizziness at first. Then he had to deal with it. "I need to get back to my desk . . ."

It was an arduous trek back across the building's second story. He entered the open office floor and saw his own little cubicle in the distance. His steps faltered as his legs malfunctioned, and he had to sit down to take a break at someone else's desk. He summoned resolve and struggled the rest of the way. He hit a power switch, and his computer came to life. With a blank screen. "What the hell?"

Benmont stood up and checked the back of the computer, where panels were missing and loose wires sticking out. He lost his balance and fell back into his chair.

From a nearby desk: *"Benmont? Are you okay?"*

"I have to see Quint." He tried to stand and fell back down again in his chair. Then another attempt with even worse results. But the chair had wheels, so Benmont shuffled his feet, propelling it backward up the aisle. Heads poked out the sides of cubicles as his chair squeaked by. The back of the chair crashed into the door of his supervisor's office. Benmont spun it around and knocked. No answer. He scooted over to the window and peeked inside. Nobody home. He called out: "Has anyone seen Quint?"

"He's not in yet," said a disembodied voice rising from a cubicle.

So Benmont just sat and conducted an emotional breakdown in a loud kind of way, and his colleagues rushed to his aid. A glass of water, a wet cloth for his forehead, an offer to call an ambulance that was turned down.

"Does he have a history of mental problems?"

"Don't think so."

"I need to talk to Quint!"

"He keeps saying that."

"Benmont, why do you need to talk to Quint?"

"The news on TV!"

"Wow, those murders must have really gotten to him."

"And we thought Starling was taking it hard."

The company had three huge office buildings that were linked by covered walkways in what they liked to call a campus. It was large enough to justify an on-site nurse, who currently raced down the walkway from Building Two on a Segway. Under certain circumstances she was allowed to administer a single tablet of Valium, and when she saw Benmont, there was no question. He was now flopping on the floor—"I have to see Quint!"—with others sitting on his arms and legs until she could get there. She crammed the pill between his pursed lips and propped up his head to insert a water tube from a sports bottle.

"Has anyone called an ambulance?" asked the nurse.

"He said he didn't want one."

"And you listened to him?" She pulled out her cell phone.

But by the time the paramedics arrived, the tranquilizer had dialed Benmont down a bit. The EMTs said it appeared to be a simple panic attack, and gave him an oxygen mask for a few minutes so they could say they did something in case it came up later.

Benmont's coworkers were finally able to get him back up in his chair. Word spread and others came to check on his welfare.

"Everything's going to be okay, buddy . . ."

Four serious men in dark suits arrived. "Which one's Benmont?"

"Who are you?"

"The lawyers."

Everyone stepped back and pointed accusingly toward the chair.

"The rest of you, scram!" said the lead attorney.

They scattered. One of the other lawyers unlocked Quint's office, and they wheeled Benmont inside and closed the door. Disaster control filled the air.

"My name's Ramsey," said the tallest. "I'm your lawyer, so anything you say has attorney-client privilege. Do you understand?"

Benmont nodded.

"Have you talked to anyone?" asked Ramsey.

"About what?" said Benmont.

"That theory your boss sent us."

Benmont began shaking again. "That's why you're here?"

"Not the theory itself," said Ramsey. "But your boss made the stupid move of sending it to a friend of his in the government. I really wish he'd talked to us first . . . Think hard: Have you mentioned your theory to anyone else?"

"Oh my God!" Benmont covered his face with his hands. "So it's true! The lists that I compiled for our client! Those poor people! What have I done?"

"Stop right there," said Ramsey. "Don't say another word and just listen. Your lists had absolutely nothing to do with this, so you can't be blurting out stuff when you aren't thinking straight. Not even to us, because then we're ethically bound not to tell you to lie on the witness stand or else it's suborning perjury."

Increased shaking. "You mean testify?"

"It won't come to that." Ramsey grabbed Benmont by the shoulders. "So lose that idea right now! We just have to get out ahead of this thing because heartless jerks are always looking to cash in on tragedies. Some asshole's bound to sue."

"How do you know?"

"Because we do it all the time," said Ramsey. "We're very good."

"But why are you sure that my lists are unrelated to that stuff on TV?" asked Benmont.

"Our forensic experts gave us an initial assessment. Do you know how many people were in your report?"

"Not exactly."

"Five-point-six-two million," said Ramsey. "Exactly."

Benmont whistled. "That many?"

"More than half the population in your geographical sample area," said the attorney. "Which means it would be stranger if some of these crime victims *didn't* appear on your list. Does that make you feel better?"

"A little," said Benmont. "But you're making me kind of nervous with all your seriousness."

Ramsey extended a used-car-salesman arm all the way around Benmont's shoulders. "It's like this: The whole identity fraud and protection field is still new. We're not worried in the least about your list causing these unfortunate incidents. What does get a little sticky is that a couple of the victims paid your company to guard their privacy, and then you went and sold it. You can see how some unscrupulous people might spin that the wrong way."

Benmont sighed and nodded. "Okay, I'm good. I'm feeling better."

"Then back to square one: Who have you told about your theory?"

"Just my boss."

"Keep it that way," said Ramsey. "Not even your most trusted friends or relatives. And this part is most important of all: Since your boss sent your report to the feds, they may be in contact. More like they definitely will."

"Jesus, what do I say?"

"Nothing. You're lawyered up." Ramsey handed him a business card. "You give them our number and tell them you're represented. After you say those magic words, they're not allowed to even *ask* any more questions or we'll rip them to shreds. You've got a whole team of junkyard dogs guarding your back."

"Thank you, I guess," said Benmont. "Now what?"

"Here's the plan. You take a much-deserved vacation." Ramsey removed a bulging money clip from his pocket and peeled off several thousand. "That's cab fare. Call us if you need more."

"Thanks." Benmont stood. "I just have to tie up some loose ends at my desk . . . I've actually been thinking about Aruba for a while."

"That's more like it." A hard slap on Benmont's back that jolted him.

The data analyst stood up to leave the office. He noticed something. "Hey, the back of Quint's computer has been ripped open. What's going on?"

"Oh, that," said Ramsey. "We sent an advance team before dawn to sanitize the scene."

"Wait," said Benmont, turning and pointing out the window toward his cubicle. "Are you the ones who took my hard drive, too?"

"No need to thank us."

"But why did you steal all my data?"

"To protect your privacy."

Chapter 15

BOCA SHORES

*L*et's play . . . The Price Is Right! . . ."
    Earl looked up from his small black-and-white TV as a contractor's van with a salesman at the wheel turned in the entrance of the retirement park. The guard stepped outside the booth and stuck his thumbs inside the hips of his pants, ready to serve and protect.

The van stopped short of the gate and pulled over to the curb. The driver noticed a new sign attached to the front window of the booth. He got out his phone.

The voice on the other end of the cell was so loud that Earl could hear it from the driver's open window: "*. . . Get out! Now! . . .*"

The van made a screeching three-point turn in the driveway and took off.

Earl chuckled to himself and went back in the booth.

He wasn't inside long.

A Ford Falcon rolled up and the driver hung out the window. "Hey, Earl, how's the sign working?"

"Like gangbusters. Salesmen have practically dropped off to nothing."

"That's great to hear."

The Falcon drove into the park, and Earl walked around to the front of the booth. He chuckled again at the hand-printed placard in the window:

Serge on Duty.

The Falcon pulled up in front of a white metal house with orange trim, careful not to run over the concrete domes guarding the edge of the lawn. Serge and Coleman bounded up the porch steps and were met by the owner before they could knock.

"You invited us to dinner?"

Lawrence Shepard had a slight smile as he shook his head at Serge. "I still don't know what to make of you."

Serge extended innocent arms. "What?"

"I'll play along," said Lawrence. "You don't know anything about what happened. That makes you the only person in the park."

"I still don't understand what you're talking about."

"Anything you say." Lawrence walked down the steps. "Follow me . . . Nancy, you coming?"

"Be right there . . ."

Serge looked back in the direction of the kitchen. "What about dinner?"

"It can wait," said Lawrence. "I want to show you something. It's a surprise."

"Come on, Coleman! It's a surprise!"

The foursome strolled down the quiet, darkening street. The fountain was still going in the lake, and a formation of pelicans glided low over the water. Unseen bullfrogs made their presence known in the reeds. The breeze carried a light taste of salt. A lizard ran across the road. A neighbor waved as he pedaled by on three wheels.

"I can see now why you like this place so much," said Serge.

"Our little piece of paradise," said Lawrence.

Another neighbor waved. This one was rocking in a patio chair on his screened porch. "Serge!"

"Mr. Hornsby!"

"Thanks so much."

"For what?"

"You know." Buster pointed upward. A new American flag—even larger than the first—flapped atop the pole. "The park's owner personally presented it to me for my service and even hoisted it himself. I don't know what you said to him."

"Me?"

Buster laughed. "He was real nervous the whole time and kept saying, 'Make sure you tell your friend!'"

Serge looked at the ground. "That's weird."

"It's sunset." Buster got out of his chair and opened the screen door. "Time to show proper respect. Flag protocol."

"Let me help you . . ."

Serge and Buster worked the ropes together, slowly lowering the Stars and Stripes. Serge reached for the lowest tip of fabric so it wouldn't touch the ground. Then the two grabbed the flag by each end and folded it toward each other until it was a small triangle.

Buster held it to his chest with one hand and shook Serge's hand with the other. "Thanks again."

"For what?"

"Right."

The quartet resumed walking. Serge did an impulsive cartwheel. "I'm dying to know what this surprise is."

"You're about to find out, because we're here." Lawrence stopped at the end of a driveway.

Serge looked at the trailer. "The Packers?"

"I know you're an unusual kind of person," said Lawrence.

"That's an understatement. And I know you're up to some stuff that's not exactly kosher and that I definitely don't want to know about. But deep down inside your heart . . . Well, anyway, I brought you here because you deserve to see how happy they are."

The group walked up the driveway past a new golf cart. Wilma was already at the screen door. "Come on in! The brisket is almost done."

"But—" Serge looked up the street toward the trailer they'd just left.

"I invited you to dinner," said Lawrence. "I didn't tell you where."

As they were about to enter through the sliding glass, Wilma spontaneously grabbed Serge for a tight, tearful hug. "You're a good person."

Grandfather and grandson were talking a mile a minute on the sofa. They saw Serge and lit up. Granddad shook Serge's hand so hard he thought his arm would fall off. Scott arrived belatedly with his cane and began misting up.

"Hey! Don't start!" said Serge. "I'm a sucker for tearjerker movies, so if you keep that up I'll begin bawling like a baby."

"Sorry." Scott dabbed his eyes. "Will you sit by me?"

"That would be an honor."

They all took seats around the dining table. It was time to say grace, which meant it was time for Coleman to reach for a biscuit. Serge slapped his wrist.

"Ow. Why'd you do that?"

Serge gestured at the others.

"Sorry." They bowed their heads.

Wilma led the prayer, and it took some time: a lengthy appreciation list of all the little things that most take for granted. ". . . Thank you for returning Scott to our home, and last but not least, thank you for bringing new friends into our lives. Amen."

Coleman looked around, then whispered, "Who's she talking about?"

"Us," said Serge, passing a serving bowl of salad.

"Wow," said Coleman. "Nobody's ever thanked God for us before."

"I told you these people were special."

"Don't be bashful," said Wilma. "Dig in."

Buford went to the refrigerator. "I didn't know if you guys drank, or what you liked, so I got beer and wine."

"Right here," said Coleman.

"Which?" said Buster.

"Yes."

Serge forked meat onto his plate. "Now serving chaos."

"Anyone want coffee?" asked Wilma. "I usually make it after, with the dessert."

"Oooo! Oooo!" said Serge.

"Coming right up . . ."

There was laughter and good times and second helpings. Serge got more coffee, and Coleman stuck himself with a fork. The conversation turned to current events.

Wilma took a sip of sweet tea. "Have you watched the news lately? It's gotten so depressing."

"You're not kidding!" said Serge. "I used to need more facts, but now everyone just makes up their own. You can accuse a politician of being a deep-sea squid with a giant eyeball under his shirt, and draw an overnight poll of at least twenty percent. And I hate to get religious, but now they want to teach creationism in schools as *alternate* science. Great! I'll be the first to give God credit for a job well done. But then I learned that they're saying the Earth is only five thousand years old. Seriously? Written history goes back that far, and yet not one mention of dinosaurs in the Dead Sea Scrolls. You'd think if the Earth were only that old, they'd be talking about nothing *but* dinosaurs: 'I was over at the Euphrates yesterday and another T. rex came out of nowhere and grabbed Billy, just his legs kicking out its mouth. This is no way to live.' More coffee, please?"

The plates were cleared, but nobody had to labor at the sink because of the industrial dishwasher the salesman had sold them. Wilma cut the key lime pie. "Let's all go in the living room."

"Let's watch the local news!" Serge ran over to the set. "It's a scream! Some bank robber used black electrical tape for a fake mustache, and another guy with a twelve-pack of beer put a propeller on a Weed Eater and sailed a little plastic tub out to sea until the coast guard told him to knock it off. And the family that was attacked by their own pit bull for trying to dress it in a Christmas sweater. You can't make this stuff up! Here's a photo on my smartphone of a hearse pulling a wood chipper. That's a red flag." Serge got up and reached behind the TV for the cable wire. "How about static? You don't know what you're missing. Everything!" Eyebrows pumped. "No? Okay, I guess it's *Dancing with the Stars,* an unforeseen consequence of the Big Bang."

"How about no TV?" said Lawrence.

An hour passed, and the living room chatter dribbled off. Arms stretched and mouths yawned. "I better be getting to bed," said Wilma. "Not as young as I used to be."

Buford patted his stomach and stood. "Me too."

"I'll get the walkie-talkies," said Scott.

Serge had gone uncharacteristically quiet, just staring at a point on the wall. The point was in the middle of a Norman Rockwell painting of a holiday feast. It was sinking in all at once. What a family. What great people the country still had. He wished it were his family.

"Then we'd better be leaving," said Lawrence.

"Yes," said Nancy. "Thanks for the dinner. It was wonderful."

"Serge, you coming?" said Lawrence. "Serge?"

"Huh, what?" He looked up from the trance.

"We're leaving."

"Do you think it would be possible for me to just sit here a little longer?"

Buford headed for the bedroom. "You can stay as long as you like. Just lock up on the way out."

Serge went back to staring and worked on keeping a lip from trembling.

Lawrence watched him a moment and smiled sentimentally. He took his wife's hand. In a low voice: "Let's go."

The living room became quiet. Coleman sat next to Serge, zonked, with his head far back over the top of the sofa in a way that his neck would remind him of in the morning.

A world of thought swirled inside Serge's head. He heard a distant, strange noise. He got up. It was coming from down the short hallway. He removed his shoes and crept across the carpet. The bedroom on the left was Wilma's, and the door was closed. Buford had the one on the right, and liked the door ajar to let the air circulate. The odd sound became distinct as Serge approached. The squawking of walkie-talkies.

Serge knew it wasn't appropriate, but he couldn't help himself. He flattened against a wall and slid the final few feet until he could eavesdrop.

Tshhhht! "Grandpa, remember when you took me to that spring training game in Saint Pete when I was six?"

Tshhhht! "I remember you got sick on hot dogs and peanuts."

Tshhhht! "It was the best day ever! Remember when you took me to get catfish at that tiny restaurant on the bay that's no longer there?"

Tshhhht! "Remember those great deep-fried hush puppies?"

Tshhhht! "I really love you, Grandpa."

Tshhhht! "I love you, too, Scott . . ."

Serge slunk back into the living room and took a seat again and stared.

Coleman came out of his self-induced coma like he was in post-op. "Serge, you're zoning. What's up?"

Staring continued.

"Is that a tear?"

Serge wiped it.

"What's the matter?" asked Coleman. "Why are you sad?"

"I'm not."

"Then what's going on?"

Serge looked toward the hall. "Life is good."

Chapter 16

1970

Palm Beach International Airport.

Starting in the late 1960s, airline flights from Florida were being hijacked to Cuba so regularly that it was considered more of an inconvenience than anything else, and passengers practically baked the potential delays into their travel schedule. It was the era before you had to walk through metal detectors, and families and friends were allowed to go all the way to the gate to greet loved ones.

Glenda Pruitt and Tofer Baez stood with homemade signs, watching eagerly as arriving passengers entered the terminal from a square tunnel. The two had become unlikely friends ever since Tofer had gotten Glenda's son out of Vietnam.

She pointed. "There he is!"

They both yelled and waved their signs.

Welcome Home!

Ted began running when he saw his mom, and they shared a tearful hug. Then she held him out by the arms. "Look at you, my big navy hero!"

Tofer and Ted grasped each other's hands in a freak-power handshake, and Tofer playfully elbowed him. "Better than combat, eh?"

It was a big celebratory dinner of Ted's favorites: Salisbury steak and tater tots with lots of A.1. sauce. Glenda allowed herself a rare glass of wine, then a second. She got emotional. "I'm so glad you're home!"

"Mom, take it easy. Everything's okay."

"I can't." Dabbing her eyes. "I'm so happy."

Soon everyone was stuffed.

While Ted was at sea Tofer had turned into Eddie Haskell.

"That was a fabulous dinner, Mrs. Pruitt!" Tofer stood. "Let me clear the table for you."

Glenda started to stand. "Let me help."

"I've got this," said Tofer, grabbing her plate. "You need to catch up with your son."

Once the kitchen was tidied: "Ted, let's go to your room . . ."

Tofer strummed his guitar. "How was the cruise?"

"It was great!" said Ted. "So exciting I don't know where to begin! We did evasive maneuvers, and blew the ballast tanks, and conducted torpedo hot-run drills, and security exercises where a small-arms team ran through the sub with pistols, and the guys in sonar let me put on headphones and listen to whales, and I got a blue-nose initiation when we crossed the Arctic Circle and crawled through all this slop in my underwear and had a raw egg cracked in my ass . . ."

"Ted . . ."

"And we conducted a mock missile launch while listening to Jimi Hendrix, and I got to sneak a look out the periscope when it was slow one night, and my bunk was right outside one of the missile tubes, and we played poker and watched movies and shared girlie mags and I learned karate and—"

"Ted, slow down . . ."

"No, wait, wait. I haven't gotten to the most excellent thing," said Ted. "You know how they get rid of your crap on subs? They have these huge sewage tanks that they pressurize with air, and then they open a valve and blow it out into the ocean. But since you're so far down with all that sea pressure, the air in those tanks has to be super compressed, and since the tanks are attached to the toilets where they get the crap in the first place, they have to be special toilets. They only pressurize the tanks a short time each day when you can't use the bathrooms, and the rest of the time you go through this funky procedure to use the toilet: Instead of regular flushing, they have these heavy-duty ball valves at the bottom. Now imagine the biggest cast-iron monkey wrench you've ever seen and triple it. That's your flush lever that rises straight up from the side of the toilet. When you're done, you simply pull the lever forward, which opens the ball valve, and you turn a knob that runs the rinse water, and finally you push the lever back upright again to close the valve—"

"This is all very interesting, but—"

"Hold on! I had to explain all that for the best part!" said Ted. "The ball valves have to be extra strong so they can withstand the super-pressurized air when it's time to blow the sewage tanks under the sea. But even then, if you look in one of the toilets during the pressurization, you'll see all these little fizzing bubbles around the ball valve. An ensign told me that if I ever see bubbles in a toilet, do not under any circumstances pull that big flush lever. Everyone knows this, and it's become the least likely mistake anyone will ever make on the sub."

"That's fascinating, but—"

"I'm not done! So one day, in the middle of pressurizing the sanitation tanks, they ran a drill called angles-and-dangles, where they run the ship through steep climbs and dives and everyone must secure their stations so pots and pans and stuff don't fly all over the place. And during one of the severe climbs, all of those extra-heavy cast-iron flush levers fell forward, spraying shit everywhere! Isn't that great?"

"I'm sure it was fun for all," said Tofer. "Do you have your diary?"

"Right here." Ted dug through his military-issue duffel bag for a small olive-green notebook. "I did just what you said, except I had problems with an alphabet code, so I drew a bunch of pictures of model rockets and shortwave equipment. And I hid little lines and circles in the drawings to help me remember."

Tofer flipped through the pages. "Good idea. Rockets and shortwave are your hobbies, so it would appear normal if anyone checked." Tofer reached into his own hippie backpack and unfolded a map on the desk. It was a different kind of map, highly detailed and scientific, with topography of the ocean floor.

"That map looks familiar," said Ted. "No, it looks exactly like . . . the navigation chart on the sub. Where'd you get it?"

"The professors." Tofer then opened a leather case with precision drafting instruments. "Now go through your diary and help me plot your course . . ."

. . . Thus was the beginning of a rigid routine that proceeded steadily for the next two years, until 1972.

"I don't want to be in the navy anymore," said Ted. "My draft requirement is over, and I'm not going to re-enlist."

"Good for you," said Tofer. "Vietnam's winding down, so what's the point of still being part of the war machine?"

"But I thought you'd be disappointed. You won't get your charts anymore."

"They've had their usefulness. It's time to move on." Tofer now had an electric guitar. He strummed it unplugged. "Hey, you know what you should do? Join the FBI."

"The FBI?" Ted recoiled. "That's about the last thing I thought you'd suggest."

"And normally you'd be right." Chords from "Harvest" by Neil Young. "That damn J. Edgar Hoover! He's turning our country into a police state! Keeping files on all my friends in the anti-war movement, as well as the civil rights movement, the women's movement, the farmworkers' movement. It's un-American! One of my professor friends was even threatened with violations of the Espionage Act, which by extension means you and me as well."

"What!" Ted jumped up. "You said we weren't doing anything wrong!"

"We weren't," said Tofer. "We're innocent, but that doesn't mean we don't have to worry."

"What does that have to do with the FBI?"

"You'd be in a position to hear stuff, and you could tell me, and I could warn our friends."

"Okay, now this definitely sounds like spying," said Ted.

"What the FBI is doing *is* spying! On its own citizens!" said Tofer. "If they're trampling the Constitution, then whatever we do in opposition is defending it."

"That makes sense," said Ted. "But you have to have a college degree for the FBI."

"Only to become an agent," said Tofer. "You can do filing or work in the mail room, and as soon as you can, put in for a transfer to counter-intelligence."

"But why would they hire me?"

"Why wouldn't they?" said Tofer. "Spotless military record, honorable discharge. And you enlisted when others your age were trying to avoid the draft. You're exactly what they're looking for."

A week later, Ted knocked on Tofer's door. "Guess what? They hired me!"

"Didn't I tell you?"

"And I'm on the clerical staff in counter-intelligence."

"What? You mean like immediately?" Tofer blinked hard. "*That* I wasn't expecting . . ."

. . . So started another era of Ted feeding Tofer a steady stream of information nuggets from the office. At first it was anything he might overhear concerning protests and radicals. Then Tofer abruptly requested something different: anything personal on the counter-intelligence agents themselves. Home life, vices, affairs. Five years passed, then ten. The eighties became the nineties. The Berlin Wall fell, and the Soviet Union became Russia.

The pair met for drinks in a balcony bar on Clematis Avenue.

"What do you mean you don't need any more information?" said Ted.

"This hippie's gotten old," said Tofer. "Protest is a young man's game."

They promised to keep in touch.

They lost touch.

Chapter 17

SARASOTA

The Ford Falcon sat on the grassy shoulder of a quiet county road.

Coleman picked at specks of dried salsa on his shirt. "What are you doing?"

Serge maintained attention with the binoculars. "Another stakeout."

"For what?"

"That." He pointed up the street.

A windowless white van with no markings entered the Boca Shores retirement park. Serge started up his car and followed.

The van stopped at a trailer, and the driver went inside with a small white box. The Falcon parked discreetly four doors down.

"Another scam artist?" asked Coleman.

Serge jotted notes on his clipboard. "Not this time."

The driver returned to the van, drove up ten more homes, and got out with another box. Serge clicked his pen again, recording the time and address. The process continued until the truck had stopped at a dozen more mobile homes and left the park.

"Who was that guy?"

"Meals on Wheels," said Serge. "I drove by their headquarters yesterday to see what kind of vehicle to expect."

"But why would you stake out Meals on Wheels?"

"So tomorrow we can beat him to the punch and deliver our own cuisine."

"You don't mean . . . ?"

"That's right," said Serge. "Xtreme Meals on Wheels!"

"You're taking retirement big."

"I've been meeting lots of wonderful people for my oral history, but only in restaurants. I'm not getting an accurate statistical sampling of those who can't get out much, and who would most appreciate our offbeat menu." Serge turned out of the park and headed for the grocery store. "Plus I didn't realize how slow the restaurant process would be for my project. Meals on Wheels is like senior-citizen speed dating."

They parked in the shopping center.

"Can I pick out some of the stuff?" asked Coleman.

"Absolutely . . ."

. . . The next day, the Ford Falcon pulled up to the first address on Serge's clipboard. He pressed a button next to the screen door.

Ding-dong.

Serge tapped an impatient foot. After a couple minutes, a voice inside: "I'm coming!" Then a few more minutes, and a woman in a nightgown stuck her head out the sliding glass door. "Who is it?"

"Mrs. Blutarski? It's Meals on Wheels. May I call you Olga?"

"You're early."

"I'm in a perpetual state of being early," said Serge. "All time has already occurred."

The woman stretched her neck toward the street. "Where's your van?"

"Traded it for a muscle car because we're now Xtreme Meals on Wheels." Serge held up an extra-large box of temptation and winked. "Have a surprise for you today."

"Okay, come on in." Olga left the glass door open and shuffled slippers across the living room. She sat down on a sofa covered in a quilt depicting the national park system. "The rack of trays is against the wall."

"I can never get enough of those old TV-dinner trays!" Serge snapped one open and set it over her knees. Then he opened his box on the lacquered surface. "I know you usually have to settle for whatever they bring, but today we have a selection. "Chili dogs, tacos, egg rolls, pulled pork with red-hot Hog's Breath sauce."

Coleman opened the cooler he was carrying. "Sparkling water, beer, hard lemonade, wine coolers."

Olga looked up at them like there had to be a catch. "You mean I can pick anything I want?"

"The world is your oyster." Serge laid out a paper plate. "And we have oysters in the car."

"You're my new favorite people!" She began snatching items out of the box, then pointed at what she wanted from the cooler. "I used to love applesauce and mashed potatoes, but now that goddamn stuff is coming out my ears."

Serge turned on his pocket recorder. "Mind if I ask you a few questions while you eat? For the official archives, of course."

She chased a big bite of chili dog with Coors. "Knock yourself out."

"Tell me about yourself. What did you do? What makes you happy?"

Now Olga was two-fisting, an egg roll and a chili dog. "My favorite was working for the USO during Vietnam. All those nice young boys drafted, and coming home in a daze. People don't remember now, but there were no parades, and some were even spit on, if you can believe it."

"Unfortunately, yes," said Serge.

"The war wasn't their fault, and most were the poor kids who couldn't go to college," said Olga. "I decided I needed to do something. I don't know how much comfort it was, but I couldn't just stand by."

"I'm sure it was a great comfort," said Serge. "But I know what the sixties were like. Not many young girls would have thought of doing what you did."

She noshed away. "Came from a military family. My father was a tail gunner of a B-17 Liberator and he taught me duty and honor. His name was Wojciech, first generation from the old country, so he still spoke Polish. He enlisted right after Pearl Harbor because he said that was the price of freedom. They were on a bombing run and got shot down outside Warsaw. He bailed out but was captured. The Germans marched all the prisoners in a line through the city, carrying their parachutes in balls in front of them. All the townspeople were watching, and some woman on a balcony said in Polish that the silk in those parachutes would make nice dresses, and my father looked up and said in the same language, 'Yes, they would make very nice dresses.' The women were shocked with embarrassment and ran inside. Then the Nazis tortured my father. Some of the Allied planes that used to be painted green were now just a shiny bare-metal silver color, and they wanted to know why. So they beat my father and pulled out some of his fingernails, but he never talked."

Serge winced and shook with the willies. "Jesus! . . . But it's obvious why they were silver. Paint adds weight, so it saved on fuel and gave the planes a longer range. They did the same thing with the space shuttle's external fuel tank."

"The Nazis didn't know that."

"And your father gave up fingernails instead of telling them such a small thing?"

"He was my dad," said Olga. "Next to that, me joining the USO was nothing."

"No, it was something all right. You're a true hero." Serge checked his watch. "But we have a lot more meals to deliver."

"Speed dating," said Coleman.

"Could I have another dog and beer before you go?"

"All yours . . ."

. . . A few houses down at the next address.

Ding-dong.

"You're early."

The pair began serving another housebound resident.

"You really have oysters?"

"On the half shell. Cocktail sauce and crackers, too."

"And cocktails," said Coleman.

The tape recorder was turned on, and Nikos Pinopolis slurped off a shell.

". . . I was a policeman in Louisville. Just like my father and grandfather. It's how we chose to serve."

"That's so admirable," said Serge.

"Why? We're all supposed to serve in some way," said Nikos. "Doesn't everybody know that?"

"Not today," said Serge. "Please continue."

"Anyway, I won a lot of medals in the annual marksmanship competitions. It was a really great police force, got along with the whole community. Then one day I'm walking my beat, chatting at the crosswalk with the little kids getting off the school bus. Suddenly these four armed guys come running out of the Farmers Bank. So I cut across the street, got down on one knee, and aimed my revolver. 'Freeze! Police!'"

"Four armed robbers?" said Serge. "Why didn't you call for backup first?"

"You're not familiar with police procedure, are you?"

"Familiar enough."

"Whenever you see a threat like that, you immediately oppose them regardless of odds." Nikos spread horseradish on a saltine. "You put yourself between them and the citizens because the community is depending on you. It's called the Thin Blue Line. So a gun battle starts..."

"I still can't believe you took on all four."

"Not as bad as it sounds," Nikos said with offhand humility. "See, the thing about bad guys is they can't shoot for shit. Give them rifles and it might be a problem, but short-barrel handguns aren't very accurate at any distance. You have to know what you're doing. The thing is to stay calm and not to hurry your shots."

"Sounds difficult when four guys are shooting back."

"Training," said Nikos. "Today's officers have Glocks and other automatics with much larger capacities. But back then, with a revolver, I had to make every bullet count. My first four shots all hit their marks, one for each robber. Two were killed, another went to the ground, but the last was only hit in the shoulder and still standing. And firing. So I dropped him with two more shots."

"That's amazing you were able to stay composed. What courage."

"Hemingway basically said courage is the ability to suspend the imagination. It was a busy afternoon downtown, and I was focused on all the civilians, especially the children... And you'd think I would have noticed it, but my adrenaline was pumping too hard. After everything settled, I had this tremendous pain. I looked down, and son of a bitch! That last guy had gotten off a lucky shot, a ricochet off the sidewalk no less. Right in the knee. Couldn't he have hit me anywhere else in the leg? But no, skipped off the pavement into the cap. No bouncing back from that to active duty, so it was a one-way ticket to a desk job my last seven years." He pointed in the corner. "I've got my new titanium cane now, but that old wooden one standing there is what I used on the force. I'm not usually sentimental."

"How can we ever repay you?" asked Serge.

"Leave the tacos."

"You got it."

Serge went back out to the car and opened the driver's door. "We need to speed this up."

"Why?" asked Coleman.

"The white van back there." He climbed in and started the ignition. "He's catching up."

The Falcon drove on. Down the clipboard list.

"I was a schoolteacher, thirty years." She pulled the pulled pork. "The school district in Mississippi didn't have enough supplies for all the kids, so I bought stuff out of my own paycheck. We all did back then . . ."

Next address: "Missionary in Africa. Spent most of our time just getting potable drinking water to the villages . . ."

Ding-dong.

". . . I volunteered at a retirement home. Ain't that ironic? . . ."

Ding-dong.

". . . The fire department was my family . . ."

Ding-dong.

". . . A janitor. I know what people think, but it was satisfying. Even met the president. I worked at NASA in one of the hangars, and Kennedy came around one day while I was sweeping the floor and asked how I was doing, and I said, 'Great. I'm helping put a man on the moon.' . . ."

T he Ford Falcon was on its way to the last address on the Xtreme Meals on Wheels clipboard. Dusk arrived. Three-wheel bikes, power walkers and pelicans.

Serge spotted a friend heading up a driveway. With a grave expression.

He jumped out of the car. "Lawrence, where are you going?"

"To check on Mrs. Butterfield."

"Good God! Is something the matter?"

"No, it's a regular check, but it's getting sad," said Lawrence, making purposeful strides. "I'm close to the family, and they asked me to look in each day. She's getting right up there against that dreaded nursing-home decision they'll have to make. They feel guilty."

"I'm sure it's a tough time all around," said Serge. "I'll eventually have to make that call on Coleman, probably sooner than later."

"Candace is a piece of work, independent and funny as hell, but she's in early dementia and has a year, tops, left at the park here," said Lawrence. "But I'm happy to make the checks because they cheer her up and give her someone to talk to before she goes to bed."

"Forgive me for saying, but you're walking faster than usual," said Serge. "Something *is* wrong."

"I can't put my finger on it," said Lawrence. "She just seems different. There's a little jumpiness, and a bit more forgetfulness. I asked her about it, but the dementia is getting in the way. It's early stages and doesn't seem to hamper her otherwise, except it always seems to get worse when I ask what's changed."

"When did this start?"

"When she got a new caregiver a month ago," said Lawrence. "She needs help with some of the small things during the day, and there was a nice older woman named Beatrix. Now a young guy named Gil. I've met him. He seems okay, and I'm sure he's doing a good job. I think it's just that Candace related better to a woman and someone closer to her age."

"I'm sure that's it," said Serge. "But what about the service company that sent him?"

"Impeccable reputation," said Lawrence. "I called to ask about the new guy, and they said they thoroughly vetted him. Excellent record. If anything is going on, it's something else."

They arrived at the trailer, and Lawrence led Serge onto the screened porch and through the sliding glass doors.

"Candace . . ."

"Oh, hi, Lawrence. Great to see you again." She was sitting

back in a recliner wearing socks with kittens on them. Then she saw Serge and startled. A quick, nervous snip: "Who's that?"

"Just a friend, Candace." Lawrence knelt next to her chair. "Are you sure you're okay?"

"Couldn't be better." She turned on the TV with a remote. "My family told you to ask, didn't they? I don't know why they keep talking about a nursing home. I'm fit as a fiddle."

"They just care."

"Care, schmare. This is my home."

"How are things with your new caregiver, Gil?"

"What? Why?" She jumped again. "He's fine."

Lawrence glanced at Serge. An old black-and-white episode of *I Love Lucy* came on.

"What do you talk about with him?" asked Lawrence.

"Him? Who?"

"Gil?"

"What about Gil?"

"What do you talk about with him?"

"Not much. He's too young." Candace pointed with a knitting needle. "This is one of my favorite episodes."

Lucy and Ethel threw cream pies at each other.

"You would tell me if anything's wrong?"

"Of course," said Candace.

"Do you need anything?"

"I need you to tell my so-called loved ones to forget about the nursing home." She turned up the volume on the set as Ricky arrived and took a pie in the face. "Everyone thinks I can't take care of myself."

"Okay, then. We'll be going."

"I'm sorry if I was being short," said Candace. "You're a good friend. You understand. I just want to live in my home."

"I do understand . . . Come on, Serge."

They left the trailer, and Lawrence stared back at the porch and sighed. "What do you think?"

"Perfectly normal reaction," said Serge. "Her self-respect and independence are threatened."

"I guess so," said Lawrence. "I just hope I'm still that feisty when I reach her age."

"You'll outlive us all," said Serge. "Listen, I just remembered I have to be somewhere with Coleman."

"Sure."

"You still look worried. Don't."

Lawrence headed one direction toward his trailer, and Serge drove off in the other.

The Falcon pulled into a nearby shopping center.

"Serge, what are we doing at the Baby Emporium?"

"Life comes full circle." They went inside and paced the aisles.

"A sippy cup," said Coleman, pointing at stains on his shirt. "I've been needing one of those."

Three more aisles, and Serge found what he needed. "Coleman, let's go. *Coleman?* . . . Damn!"

Serge retraced his steps and found his pal with his mouth hanging open, staring up at a spinning mobile with flying elephants.

"Coleman."

"Whoa! This thing's a stone trip."

"Coleman!"

"Yeah?" He turned. "What are you doing with a teddy bear?"

"It's not just a teddy bear." Serge turned it around and opened a small control panel. "It's a nanny cam."

"What's that?"

Serge marched toward a cash register. "You stick it on a shelf, and it records secret digital video to see if the babysitter is stealing silverware or having sex with her boyfriend while the unsupervised baby begins that long-distance crawl toward the highway."

They headed back to the park. Coleman puffed a joint and spun an elephant mobile stuck to the ceiling of the Falcon. Candace's trailer came into view.

"The lights are out. I think she's asleep." Serge turned. "Stay here. I can't have you crashing around and waking her up. She's jittery enough as it is."

Coleman filled the sippy cup from a flask.

Serge crept toward the trailer. The screen door was unlocked but no such luck with the sliding glass. He deftly popped it out of its track and slipped inside the dark living room.

Serge let his eyes adjust while searching for the perfect spot. Over the TV, a shelf with family photos and Beanie Babies. He checked the batteries in the teddy bear, turned it on and gently set it in place.

From down the hall, *"Is someone there?"*

"Shit." Serge ran out the glass door, snapped it back in the slot and took off.

Chapter 18

THE NEXT MORNING

The Savoy Arms was a beachfront landmark, built in 1926 with all the fanfare of Mediterranean Classic design. Stately to this day. Mornings featured mimosas and Bloody Marys on the wrap-around veranda under the wooden paddle fans. The idle rich browsed the shops filled with Swiss watches and yachting clothes.

But not this morning. The uniformed staff stood in a serious line along the front of the mahogany concierge desk. Whispers. On one of the upper floors, detectives came and went through the door of room 614. The bodies were still in the bed, and their clothes still on the floor.

The woman was known to police and hotel staff as a high-end escort, and the man had just been identified by the wallet in his pants. The pistol rested in his lifeless hand.

Murder-suicide was the initial finding.

A detective named Cheadle leaned over the bodies. "This isn't right."

"What's not right?" asked his partner, Sussman.

"There's no logic here."

"That's why they call it a senseless crime," said the partner.

"You know how you just get the sensation that a scene has been staged?" said Cheadle. "I'll bet my paycheck that there's no gunshot residue on the hand holding the weapon."

An evidence tech approached. "Preliminary test is positive for gunshot residue."

"That shoots your theory to shit," said Sussman.

"It just means the real killer placed the gun in his hand post-mortem and fired," said Cheadle. "Which means there's a third bullet."

"Except there's not," said Sussman. "Only one bullet in each of the victims. And the guests in the other rooms were all quite certain they only heard two shots about five seconds apart."

"Check the gun."

Sussman slipped on a glove. He removed cold fingers from the pistol and examined the chamber and magazine. "Only two bullets missing."

"Then whoever did this used a second gun."

"But what about what the witnesses heard? Two shots."

"Must have been a silencer," said Cheadle.

"Now you're deep-sea fishing."

"Am I?" The detective picked up a square foil pouch from the nightstand.

"Torn-open condom wrapper?" asked Sussman.

"With the condom still in it. He was ready for another round. Why shoot?"

"Who knows?"

Cheadle turned to everyone else in the room. "Check for a third bullet hole."

It was daytime, but they still used bright flashlights to make it easier.

An hour later: "Anything?"

All heads shook.

F or once, the alarm clock was off. The baby-blue digits said it was a lazy 8:48 A.M.

Benmont threw off the covers and stretched with a yawn. Then he remembered and smiled.

Aruba.

The law firm of Ramsey, Walcott & Kerfuffle had e-mailed the tickets overnight, along with photos of his cabana on stilts in the banana trees. Everything had been packed in his car the night before. For some reason he thought he'd need his old tennis racket. He felt nervous about carrying the four grand in cash from Ramsey's money clip.

He showered, dressed and got in his car. The radio came on a station for the It Generation.

"*... This is going to be the best day of my life...*"

"Wait, I actually know this one," Benmont said to himself. "It's from an ad for a motel chain."

He backed out of his driveway and checked his watch. Still four hours till his flight. The car idled, hanging halfway out in the suburban street. There was an itch in his brain he couldn't scratch. He really wanted to talk to Quint before he left. He dialed his boss's cell phone. It rang and rang. He hung up and sat in thought. Then: What the hell? He cut the steering wheel the other way...

Twenty minutes later, he stepped into the office of Life-Armor and glanced around the empty floor plan. "What *now*?" He looked toward Quint's office. Still dark with the door closed.

He left the empty cubicle matrix for the lunchroom. A crowd was staring up again at a flat screen. Most of them sobbing.

Benmont tapped someone's shoulder in the back of the group. "What's everyone so upset about?"

A discreet whisper. "Quint is dead."

"What!"

The young man pointed up at the screen. "Police found two bodies in a room at the Savoy. TV hasn't mentioned the names yet, but word got back to us." He lowered his voice again. "They're thinking murder-suicide."

"Quint?" said Benmont. "That's not possible!"

"I'm just telling you what I heard."

Benmont and the others gradually began drifting back to their cubicles. When they arrived, a police team was already there, gathered outside the door of Quint's office, just like the similar team currently going through Quint's house on the other side of town.

Benmont quickly marched down the aisle. "What are you doing?"

"Please stand back," said a detective.

"You're looking for a suicide note, aren't you?"

"This is just routine."

A maintenance man unlocked the office, and the police streamed in.

Benmont called through the open door: "You're not going to find any note!"

Detective Cheadle stood with hands on hips in the middle of room 614 of the Savoy Arms. The bodies were zipped up and wheeled out of the room on gurneys. The search had been called off for the magic third bullet. The police presence was now down to a pair of evidence techs dusting for a few final prints. And the two detectives.

"How could I have been so wrong about this?" Cheadle asked himself.

"It was a good theory," said his partner. "You were being thorough."

A knock came from behind them on the open door of the hotel room.

They turned around to find a new arrival.

"Reinforcements?" asked Cheadle.

"No, we just got another call," said the sergeant at the door.

"What kind of call?"

"Another guest didn't check out on time and wasn't answering his phone. You might want to see this."

Cheadle and Sussman glanced at each other, then followed the sergeant out of room 614, and just as quickly into room 615. They stopped silently in the doorway.

Lying peacefully on his back in bed, still wearing pajamas, was a paint salesman from Knoxville. On the left side of his head, the sheets soaked deep red.

Cheadle approached the victim and crouched next to the bed, examining the gunshot wound. His eyes followed an imaginary line of trajectory as he turned around and faced the wall. "Damn."

"What do you think?" asked Sussman. "Robbery? Revenge?"

"No, just one unlucky bastard." Cheadle got up and stuck the tip of his pinkie in a small hole in the plaster. Then he practically ran over everybody on his way back to the first room.

Sussman brought up the rear. "What's going on?"

"There it is," said Cheadle, this time probing with a pen from his jacket. "They missed it because it was right at the edge of the dresser."

"Well, I'll be," said his partner. "A bullet hole. So there were three shots after all."

Two more suits arrived in the room. The first displayed a badge. "Agent Baxter."

"FBI?" said Cheadle. "What are you doing here?"

"We went to his house first and found your uniformed officers already there, and they told us about this room."

"But why is the FBI interested in a local murder?" asked Cheadle.

"We didn't even know he was dead," said Baxter. "We just wanted to talk to him."

"So he was into something?" asked Sussman. "Drugs? Insider trading?"

"Not exactly." Baxter bent down and looked at a hole in the wall with a pen sticking out of it. "What have you got so far?"

"Staged murder-suicide with a prostitute."

Baxter glanced at his colleague. "That would fit."

"Excuse me," said Cheadle. "But could you please tell me what's going on?"

"No."

Chapter 19

SARASOTA

Residents from Boca Shores were out on their evening strolls when a Ford Falcon pulled alongside one of them.

Serge hung out the window. "Lawrence, checking on Candace?"

"How'd you guess?"

"Because you're at her driveway. Mind if we join you?"

Lawrence led the way again. "Candace, you remember Serge from yesterday?"

"Of course, I'm not senile, you know . . . *Ahhh!* Who's that?"

A wave. "I'm Coleman."

Crash.

"He knocked over my rack of TV-dinner trays."

"Sorry, I've got it." Coleman tried rehanging the trays, but ended up with everything on top of him instead.

"Dang it." Serge shot a grin toward Candace as he propped trays back against the wall. "I'm *his* caregiver."

"What's his problem?"

Hushed tones: "Put the sippy cup away and wait outside!"

"I always have to wait outside. There are bugs."

"Get going!"

"I like it in here. Lucy's on TV."

Serge threw another grin Candace's way. "Excuse us just a minute."

He grabbed Coleman's ear. *"Ow! Ow! Ow! Let go!"*

"Onto the lawn with you!"

Candace strained to see the commotion. "Are your friends all right?"

"They're fine," said Lawrence. "But how are you doing?"

"Same as every time you ask." A TV tray fell and she jumped.

Lawrence stood up and promised to report back to her family that all was good on the home front.

Serge came back inside. "Sorry about that. Where were we?"

"Leaving," said Lawrence.

Serge pointed down the hall. "What was that sound?"

"Where?" asked Candace, looking over her shoulder.

Serge snatched the teddy bear off the shelf. "My ears are playing tricks again. I need them checked."

"But you're so young."

Lawrence waved. "Good night, Candace."

They collected Coleman from the yard and got him into the Falcon. Lawrence glanced at the teddy bear under Serge's arm. "Do I even want to know?"

"Not really."

They departed again in opposite directions.

Back in his Tamiami Trail motel, Serge pulled the memory stick from the back of the teddy bear. He plugged it into his laptop and started the video.

Everything was fine for the first half hour, except Gil had

taken away the remote control for his own TV-viewing pleasure. That's when Candace said she was thirsty.

Gil got up from the couch. Serge inched toward the laptop's screen. He suddenly winced and turned away. He covered his face with a hand and turned back toward the computer, peeking between his fingers. Another wince. "I can't watch any more."

Coleman came over. "Why is she crying? . . . Jesus! He just slapped her for no reason!"

Serge ran into the bathroom, and Coleman followed. "Are you throwing up?"

"Just a little." Serge wiped his mouth.

"Man, I mean I throw up like ringing a bell," said Coleman. "But you never, ever do."

Serge rinsed with a handful of water from the sink. "This is a different ball game."

They returned to the laptop. Serge tried to be swift, but couldn't get the memory stick out before a final slap.

"What's the matter with that guy?" asked Coleman.

"Some people are just wired wrong," said Serge. "It makes no sense to the rest of us, but these bad units have a syndrome. They otherwise appear and behave totally normal. Then, in private, they abuse small children, really old people, animals. They seek out the most vulnerable, those without much of a voice." He grabbed his keys.

"Where are we going?"

"To the Party Store!"

T he next morning, Serge bounded up the steps of a screened-in porch and went inside. He knocked on the glass.

Candace slid the door open a crack. "Who are you?"

"Serge. I visited the last couple days with Lawrence."

"Your voice sounds the same, but you look different. You look so *old*. You have a big gray mustache."

"I'm in disguise. The Party Store has everything!" He held out a bouquet of freshly picked marigolds. "These are for you."

"They're beautiful!" She opened the door the rest of the way. "We better get those in some water."

"I'll handle it." He found a vase in a cabinet and soon the flowers brought cheer from the top of the TV.

"That was so thoughtful of you," said Candace.

"There's no good way to say this, so I'll just say it." Serge pulled a chair over and held her right hand. "I know what's been going on. I know about Gil."

"What are you talking about?"

"I left a surveillance camera in here. We watched everything." She covered her face. "I'm so embarrassed. So ashamed."

"That's what he's counting on," said Serge. "It's a common reaction to the loss of control, not to mention fear of the future."

"They'll put me in a nursing home!"

"Nobody's putting you anywhere while I'm around. You're a proud woman, and nobody can take that from you."

Sniffles. "Thank you. You understand."

"Yes, I do. But I'm going to need your help."

"How?"

"I called your caregiving service and said you had some appointment for the first couple hours, but your brother was visiting and would need assistance in the meantime. They're sending Gil over on the same schedule . . . All I need you to do is go in your bedroom with Coleman, lock the door and not make a sound."

"That's all?"

"Most important," said Serge. "Keep that door closed. Whatever you do, don't look."

They heard a car pull up out front. "That's him now," said Serge. "Get going."

The odd pair hurried down the hall and locked the door.

A knock at the sliding glass.

"It's open!"

Gil walked in. "Christ, you look even older than your sister."

An ancient accent: "I'm just a frail, helpless old man."

Gil went into the kitchen. Rummaging sounds. "What's good in the fridge? Nothing, as usual." He grabbed some chips from the pantry and returned. "Give me that remote control!" He plopped down on the couch for another rerun of *Baywatch*. "And don't talk to me!"

A crackly voice. "But I'm thirsty."

"What did I just tell you?" Gil hopped to his feet. "Now you're going to get it!" He rolled up a magazine and swatted Serge back and forth across his face—one blow for each word: "Shut . . . up! . . . Shut . . . up! . . . Shut . . . up! . . ."

"Why are you doing this to me?" asked Serge. "Why are you being so mean?"

"You don't listen for shit, do you?" *Smack, smack, smack . . .*

The last blow from the magazine pulled the costume glue loose, and a bushy mustache went flying.

Gil was about to strike again when he stopped in confusion, staring at a clump of gray hair on the floor. "What the hell?"

Serge smiled. "The Party Store has everything!"

"Who *are* you?"

"Not an old man. At least not as old as you like them."

Before Gil knew it, Serge had twisted his right arm behind his back, and he was pinned to the floor.

"How does it feel, asshole?" Serge pressed the face deep into the carpet pile. He reached in a pocket for a plastic zip-tie wrist restraint like police use at riots. Then he jerked Gil to his feet and pushed him toward the side door.

Just then, another door opened at the end of the hall. Serge looked up like he was caught in headlights, standing there seizing a handcuffed Gil by the back of his collar. Candace covered her mouth—"Oh my"—and slammed the door.

"Shit. Just have to deal with that publicity problem later." He reached the back door and peeked outside. No witnesses. Candace didn't own a car, which had allowed Serge to back his Falcon into her carport. He put his mouth right to Gil's ear. "Make one sound and I swear to God I'll break your skull!"

Gil stumbled and wept as Serge rushed him down the steps to the back bumper. He popped the trunk. "In you go!" *Thud.* "And I don't trust you about the quiet thing." A strip of duct tape was ripped from a roll and pulled tight across Gil's mouth. The trunk slammed shut.

Serge turned to face the back door and took a deep breath. "Now for damage control . . ."

He trotted back inside and knocked on the bedroom door at the end of the dark hallway. Then he took a few steps back so as not to startle Candace. "Everything's super! You can come out now!"

The door opened a half inch, just enough to reveal an eyeball.

"Really, it's okay," Serge said in a chipper tone. "There's nothing to be afraid of."

"Are you sure?" asked Coleman.

"You idiot! I thought you were Candace. Get out here!"

The two emerged from the bedroom and joined Serge at the kitchen table. "Candace, I'm very sorry you had to witness that. It wasn't my intention."

"Witness what?"

"When you opened the door and saw me and Gil."

"I never opened the door."

"Yes, you did."

"I don't know what you're talking about. I didn't see anything." She got up and went to the fridge. "Would you like some juice?"

Coleman leaned and whispered: "Man, her mind really is slipping."

"Just the opposite." Serge sat back and chuckled. "She's still sharp as a tack."

Chapter 20

On the campus of Life-Armor, police were back for a second day. Now that suicide had officially been ruled out, the office of Quint Powers needed a more thorough combing. All the desk drawers were open.

"Anything yet?" asked a lieutenant.

"Just that the hard drive and all physical files are missing."

"The attorneys have those," said the lieutenant. "They called and gave us a heads-up, but wouldn't say what was going on."

A woman with thin gloves looked up from one of the drawers and shook her head.

"So we've got nothing? . . ."

The employees were standing back at a safe distance, watching the police and starting rumors. They'd all been summoned by the company for police interviews, including Benmont. *Es-*

pecially Benmont. Besides Quint, he was the only person whose hard drive had been recently and unceremoniously ripped from his computer. He had to postpone that flight to Aruba.

"When are the lawyers going to get here?" asked the lieutenant. "We're in the dark on these hard drives."

The lawyers arrived.

They walked down the main aisle three abreast in a brisk manner announcing that the take-no-shit people had arrived.

"Listen up, everyone! Nobody says a word to the police without us present." Then to the lieutenant: "We'll be sitting in on all interrogations."

"They're not interrogations, just interviews," said the lieutenant. "Now, where are the hard drives?"

"Ramsey's bringing them," said an attorney.

"Who's Ramsey?"

"One of the partners."

"Where is he?"

"On his way."

They held the employees in a kind of standby area, and the police commandeered the executives' glass offices for questioning. They began leading the workers in one by one.

A cell rang. Then another. Finally, a whole chorus of electronic chirping from pockets. All the lawyers and all the cops simultaneously pulled out their phones and answered.

"When did this happen?" "Are you sure?" "The news people already have it?"

Another official person arrived at the proceedings. Black suit and thin black tie. A badge flashed. "FBI. Is there a Benmont Pinch here?"

The employees in the holding area stepped aside and pointed at the meek analyst, now standing alone in the middle of a dark-blue carpet with random paisley patterns to conceal dirt and coffee stains.

"Please come with me," said the suit.

"What for?"

"I'll tell you when we get there. But right now time is sensitive."

The agent led him into the lunchroom.

"Why are we going this way?"

"The back exit is best."

Benmont began shaking again. "You're scaring me."

"Nothing to worry about," said the agent. "It's standard procedure."

They passed one of the flat-screen TVs with local news.

"... *Well-known local attorney Thomas Ramsey was found dead this morning in his Bayshore mansion, an apparent suicide ...*"

"Ramsey's dead?" said Benmont.

"Hurry!" said the agent, pushing open an exit door.

Back outside the office of Quint Powers, the rumor mill was running on nuclear power.

Another suit arrived with another badge. "FBI. Is there a Benmont Pinch here?"

Empty stares.

"What's the matter?" asked the agent. "Is he here or not?"

"He just left with another FBI agent."

"What other FBI agent?" asked the suit.

Shrugs.

"Which way did they go?"

A dozen arms pointed toward the lunchroom, and the agent took off ...

... Just outside the back exit, Benmont stood in a rare moment of defiance next to the passenger door of a Crown Vic waiting at the curb. "I demand to know what's going on right now!"

"Once you're safe," said the agent.

"I'm in danger?"

"I'll explain later." The black suit put on dark sunglasses and glanced around. "Right now you'll just have to trust me. We have to get you out of here as fast as possible."

"I don't feel so good." Benmont grabbed the edge of the roof and began sagging.

"Shit, another limp one." The agent ran around the car and indelicately loaded Benmont inside like old luggage. He raced back to the driver's side and jumped behind the wheel.

Blackwall tires screeched as the sedan took off for the exit.

Suddenly someone on foot appeared before them, standing in the middle of the pavement. In a shooting stance.

Bang.

"Ahhh!" The windshield cracked, and the driver took the slug in the shoulder. He lost control of the Crown Vic and crashed into the rear of a parked Jeep Cherokee.

Benmont coughed in a white chemical haze as he pushed away the deployed airbag. His passenger door quickly opened as he looked up in surprise.

Someone seized his arm. "Hurry!"

"Who are you?"

"FBI."

"You shot one of your own agents?"

"No, he was an imposter." A firmer tug on the arm. "Come with me if you want to live!"

They sprinted over to another Crown Vic in the back of the lot and jumped in. Rubber spun again as they took off for the exit.

"Wait a second," said Benmont. "How do I know you're not the imposter, and the other guy was the real agent?"

"You'll just have to trust me."

"That's what the first guy said."

They raced past the scene where the other Crown Vic had crashed into the Jeep.

Bang.

"Ahhh!" The bullet came through the side window and struck

the driver in the arm. His sedan spun sideways into a parked Chevy Cruze.

Benmont pushed away another deflating airbag. "Fuck this!" He opened the passenger door and spilled onto the pavement, scampering away on hands and knees between rows of other parked cars with company stickers on the windshields.

Just when Benmont thought he might actually crawl to safe harbor, it started again.

Bang, bang, bang...

He flattened himself on the ground and peered under the parked employee fleet. Three rows over and twenty yards apart, two pairs of black dress shoes frantically shuffled behind the bumpers of crashed cars.

Bang, bang, bang...

The local police who had been inside rifling through Quint's office were drawn out to the parking lot by all the gunfire. They aimed their weapons at the two combatants, who were shielding themselves behind Ford products.

"Drop your weapons!" shouted a lieutenant.

They didn't. Just continued their firefight. But they didn't turn their guns on the police, either.

"I'm FBI!" called out the first agent, squeezing off a shot over the hood. "Shoot him!"

"He's an imposter! I'm the real agent!" *Bang, bang, bang.* "Shoot *him*!"

Confusion in the ranks.

The uniformed officers on the building's steps swung their pistols one way and the other, like they were following a tennis match.

"What do we do?" asked a corporal. "They both look like feds."

"But one's clearly not," said a sergeant.

"Then who do we shoot?"

"We'll just have to let this play out a little more."

The opponents changed out their guns' magazines and fired

some more, essentially killing a pair of cars. Then the second agent decided to take a gamble. A big one. It had to be timed just right.

He kicked his gun out and raised hands in the air, still crouched behind the bumper. "I give up." He began standing, and just as he was exposed, he immediately ducked back down a split second before his nemesis fired off a shot.

The police had their imposter.

Their first bullet winged him in the elbow, and he spun toward the cops to fire. Bad move.

It was all over in a very noisy ten seconds. The officers ran out into the parking lot and kicked the pistol away from the imposter's hand.

And while all the nonsense was going on, Benmont Pinch had crawled to his Nissan Versa in the parking lot's last row, slowly driving it out the side exit and toward the interstate.

Chapter 21

THAT NIGHT

St. Petersburg lies on a peninsula forming the western edge of Tampa Bay. On the other side of the city is the Gulf of Mexico. Running along the coast are a string of quaint barrier-island towns. Belleair Beach, Indian Rocks Beach, Redington Beach, Madeira Beach.

Gulf Boulevard connects them all in a lazy, winding drive past the souvenir shacks and swimsuit boutiques until it reaches Treasure Island.

The town has been lovingly passed over by time, leaving a nostalgic row of mom-and-pop motels with old Florida architecture and 1950s neon. The Arvilla, the Algiers, the Bilmar, the Ebb Tide, the Tahitian, the Thunderbird, the Trail's End.

The landmark Buccaneer Motel had been demolished in 2011 for condos, but the pirate on its roof that greeted visitors for decades was salvaged and adopted as the city's mascot. He now stands in a public park on his peg leg. His other foot, in a big black boot, rests atop a treasure chest. He's swinging a cutlass.

Headlights came on as light traffic trickled down the boulevard, and beach strollers took photos as the sun sank into empty water. A few claimed they had just seen the elusive flash of green. Back along the street, those trademark retro signs came on in succession.

The Sands, the Surf, the Satellite, the Sea Jay.

The evening wore on past midnight, and the sleepy coastal strip went to sleep.

The moon tracked down low over the Gulf as clocks in the motels reached three A.M. Any insomniacs up at that hour couldn't have missed a different complexion to the beach. A blinding bright circle of light flooded the edge of the waves, as if a UFO were about to land.

The light was supplied by several high-intensity, battery-powered lamps atop industrial-grade tripods arranged around the perimeter of the crime scene. Police also had erected a temporary plastic curtain, because the body was still on-site.

A sweaty man in a white dress shirt trudged across the sand. His jacket was back in the car. He stepped behind the curtain and bent down next to the medical examiner. "I'm Detective Parsnip. Caught this case in the middle of REM sleep. What have we got here?"

"Crafty fellow with anger issues." A gloved hand held up a small, charred metal rectangle.

"What's that?" asked Parsnip.

"Your murder weapon."

"A nine-volt battery?" said the detective. "You mean it was part of a detonation timer?"

The examiner shook his head.

"A remote-control triggering device? The power source of a small drone?"

"Nope, just a regular nine-volt." The examiner stood and dropped the battery into an evidence bag. "This was definitely your murder weapon."

The detective studied the ghastly discovery. "What's that all over his body?"

"A common grocery-store item that you probably have in your house right now and wouldn't think twice about." The examiner told him what it was.

The detective's head pulled back. "But that can't harm anybody."

The examiner held up the evidence bag again. "Not without this."

"But how can you murder someone with a single nine-volt battery? . . ."

SEVERAL HOURS EARLIER

In room 5 of a quaint mom-and-pop motel facing the beach, a caregiver sat tied and gagged in another unforgiving wooden chair.

"Gil?" said Serge. "May I call you Gil? I hate to be presumptuous. But I have great news! This is your lucky day! You're going to get the easiest bonus round I've ever concocted. Don't you feel swell?"

The captive thrashed and shook the chair, trying to wiggle the duct tape off his mouth as captives are known to do.

"What? Not totally swell?" said Serge. He stared off in thought, then raised a finger in revelation. "Of course! I completely skipped ahead in the conversation again! The bonus round doesn't make sense unless you know you're in a contest. And, oh, are you in a contest! I'm always jumping ahead, like when out of the blue, I just suddenly start yapping about the Spanish-American War— like now—leaving out the beginning when Teddy Roosevelt and his Rough Riders sailed from the port of Tampa, and his troops are now immortalized by Rough Rider condoms. If you don't believe me, look it up on the Internet. Some people question the taste of that product, but I'm a firm believer that anytime you can get in a history lesson just before boinking, it's A-OK!" Serge tore open a foil condom pouch. "The imprint on the memory is stronger during periods when you're paying attention, and I'm taking a wild stab that sex and being a hostage are near the top of that list." He reached in the little pouch and removed a Rough Rider. "Here, hold this . . ." He stuck the condom on Gil's nose. "I'll bet you're imprinting like a bastard right now, and you'll ace that next exam on San Juan Hill. No need to thank me. It's just how I roll."

Serge grabbed grocery bags off the dresser and dumped the contents on a musty bedspread with a pattern of vintage biplanes.

Gil looked down in confusion. All the products from the bags had the same box with the same design. A burst of red and orange and yellow around a single word:

Brillo.

"You're wondering about the scouring pads," said Serge. "Intellectual curiosity is one of my favorite traits. I just love to keep a clean crib, and steel wool is the bomb! Those boxes contain the extra-fine grade, which is best for our contest today."

Serge sat next to Gil with a fresh roll of tape. "As you can plainly see, I fitted you with a reflective-yellow caution vest before strapping you down because safety is number one! You've heard of the Michelin Tire Man? You're going to become the first Brillo Man!" He stopped and scratched his neck. "Although if this works the way I think, don't be expecting any TV endorsements. Advertising is a treacherous business!"

Brillo pads were taped down one side of Gil's chest, then up the other. Serge leaned him forward and affixed more to his back. Then a second layer and a third. Next, the pants, and even more pads stuffed into his pockets until he was a bulging mound of steel wool.

"Coleman, what do you think?"

Coleman popped a Pabst. "Brillo Man. Wooo."

Serge grinned big at Gil and slapped his back. "Hey, bud! Don't look so gloomy! You might need that look later." He rubbed his palms. "I'll bet you're itching to find out what your contest is! The key awaits in my final shopping bag!"

He snatched it from the dresser and dumped it on the other bed.

Coleman stumbled over. "Look at all those freakin' batteries."

"I'll admit I always go a little overboard when buying batteries, because you know that insane facial expression everyone gets when you're at home and need just one battery, and then you check the battery drawer and discover all these different sizes except the one you're looking for: 'Motherfucker!'" Serge sorted through the various types on the mattress. "People worry about the government, but it's the battery people who have us by the throat, always making us get out of our pajamas and drive to the store for some D-cells. And you're staring at the rack, thinking, 'I'll bet I'm also out of triple-As,' because when do you ever buy *that* size? Then you come home and open the drawer again: 'Goddammit! I always buy triple-As because I think I'm out, and now I've got an insane surplus of these little metal turds!'"

Coleman drained the Pabst. "Fuck triple-A."

"That's the spirit." Serge ripped open a pack. "But the small rectangular nine-volts are a whole different story. Smoke detectors, radios, alarm-clock backup power: nine-volts are the humbly dependable workhorse of the battery world. No guile or secret agendas." He nodded. "You always know where you stand with nine-volts."

Coleman sat on the corner of the mattress and cracked another cold one. "So you need all these dozens of batteries of every shape for your science contest?"

"That's the most fascinating part of the contest." Serge violently flung a pack of triple-As that burst against a wall. "I actually only need a single battery." He held a nine-volt in front of his eyes. "And it just happens to be my favorite battery friend."

"But, Serge! How can one battery make a difference in today's world?"

"Glad you asked." Serge headed for the bathroom. "Follow me. And while you're at it, bring one of those leftover Brillo pads on the bed."

Coleman joined him at the sink. "Here you go."

"Okay, notice how I stuffed Gil's pockets to the breaking point with scouring pads?"

"Definitely!"

Serge held a paper cup to his friend's face. "Pretend this is Gil's pocket."

"I'm pretending."

"You don't have to close your eyes."

"Sorry."

"Now, to increase the wow factor . . ." Serge turned on the faucet, thoroughly soaking the Brillo pad. Then he picked up a portable kitchen fire extinguisher that he'd brought into the room for the occasion. He stuffed the steel wool into the paper cup.

Coleman pointed. "Gil's pocket?"

Serge held the nine-volt battery to Coleman's face. "Observe and learn."

He tossed it into the paper cup.

Coleman jumped back. "Holy crap! It's all, like, on fire! Shooting up with smoke!"

Serge blasted it with the extinguisher.

Cole crumpled a beer can. "But how'd you ever think of this crap?"

"Three places." Serge sat down on the closed toilet lid, crossed a leg, and uncapped a bottle of spring water. "First, I learned about Brillo pads as a kid on the Fourth of July. If you were poor and couldn't afford sparklers, you'd straighten out a wire coat hanger. Then you'd make a loop on one end for your finger, and a hook on the other end for a scouring pad. You'd set the pad on fire, and spin it with your finger, shooting sparks off in a wild circle. Then it turned out that scouring pads cost more than sparklers, and everyone got spankings."

"What about the battery?" asked Coleman.

"Two sources of knowledge there. A Brillo pad and battery are a little-known survival trick to start a fire in an emergency," said Serge. "You're out camping, watching some birds, and then you're inside an avalanche. The matches are obviously soaked, but you have a scouring pad to clean your mess kit, and a nine-volt battery for your weather radio. So you have fire and live."

"You mentioned two sources," said Coleman.

"I knew this arson investigator. He told me they often got cases that looked suspicious because there was no readily apparent source of the fire, plus an unlikely spot of origin, a small drawer. Investigators began comparing cases nationwide, and they found that most of those drawers were *junk* drawers."

"I love junk drawers!" said Coleman.

"Me too!" said Serge. "They have no rules or social norms where the self-righteous can boss you around."

"I saw this other dude's junk drawer once," said Coleman. "It was fucked up!"

"That's the only governing principle of junk drawers," said Serge. "Everyone else's is fucked up, whereas yours are always quite reasonable. 'Hey, I have this extra cap for a pen, but I can't bring myself to throw it away because as soon as I do, I'll find its capless mate: Into the junk drawer!' . . . 'Hey, there's a molly bolt lying on the kitchen floor that fell off of something but I have no idea what. So just in case the door falls off the dishwasher . . .'"

"Into the junk drawer!" said Coleman.

"And for the record, I just like saying 'molly bolt,'" said Serge. "But the coolest aspect of junk drawers is their evolutionary development in humans. Everyone simultaneously came up with the idea on their own. There was no corporate Big Junk Drawer with slick TV ads of supermodels storing pipe cleaners. So there had to be a tiny amino acid marker in our ancient DNA, lying dormant, waiting for the dawn of drawers and junk on the planet. Greek philosophers were debating an Epicurean conundrum, when: 'What's in this drawer?' 'I don't know. It fell off the Acropolis, but it might be important.' And the human race never looked back: glue sticks, poker chips, thumbtacks, rubber bands, paper clips, broken scissors, one-cent stamps, Las Vegas key fob, magnet calendar from 1996, plastic ruler advertising a fabric store, a Canadian quarter, a Chicklet, Wite-Out, dead cockroach."

"The junk drawer!" said Coleman.

They both stopped and looked at each other.

"Serge, what do junk drawers have to do with anything?"

"I don't know."

The two stared at the ceiling, then the floor, then their fingernails, the ceiling again . . .

"I've got it!" said Serge. "Starting a fire! So the arson investigators discovered the surprising rate at which people keep loose Brillo pads and nine-volt batteries in junk drawers, and after opening and closing the drawer long enough, stuff begins shifting around, different things touch, and the whole place burns down. Look it up."

"*Mmmmmmmmmmm!*" said Gil.

"Sorry, the Internet café is closed for you. Just take my word." Serge grabbed a knife and sliced the ropes binding Gil to the chair. "On your feet, slappy boy."

Gil stood up, festooned with scouring pads, hands still fastened behind his back.

Coleman giggled. "He looks funny."

"It's about to become a laugh jamboree." Serge peeked out the window into the darkness and saw nobody. He walked back to Gil. "Okay, here's the skinny. Our room here is on the back of the motel facing the beach, and it's empty at this hour. If you're familiar with the area, you know it's a pretty wide beach. There are a few clusters of palm trees behind the motel, and then about a hundred yards to the water. We're going outside now. Don't try to pull anything to attract attention or it's no bonus round for you!"

Serge seized Gil by the back of the neck. "Coleman, open the door and check outside again."

Coleman trotted to the edge of the sand. "It's still clear."

Serge rushed onto the beach with the captive and took cover in the nearest clump of palms. "It's reckoning time, so pay attention." *Slap!* "It could save your life. Which brings us to the bonus round. As I said, this one's a piece of cake, as long as you don't panic. Panic is bad in the bonus round. I'm going to let you go now." Serge poked a gun into his spine. "But you can't come back this way. You have to head out across the beach toward the Gulf." He reached a hand around Gil's neck to show him a nine-volt battery.

"Mmmmmmmmmmmmm!"

"I see you remember this baby from my little sermon back in the room. That's great! That's marvelous! Because this is also your parting gift." Serge glanced down at the wrist ties. "I see your hands are occupied at the moment. Where should I put this? I know! I'll stick it in your hip pocket. But before I do, remember about the panic. The burn rate on steel wool ranges wildly depending on conditions. All you have to do is put out the fire before it gets to be, well, why dwell before it's time? I notice that you're looking at the water. Excellent idea. You're a young chap, and if you were any good at track and field, it's not that far to the shore. Get the fire out in time and you're free to go. You have my word. There'll be a pretty bad burn on your hip area for a while, but I can't think of everything." Serge's head swiveled one last time and, literally, the coast was clear. "Ready to make your bid for freedom? . . . Gil, you have to nod or this won't work."

Gil whimpered and nodded frantically.

"Good." Serge stuck the battery in his pocket, then shoved him in the back. "And you're off!"

"Look at him go!" said Coleman.

Serge leaned against a palm tree with folded arms. "And look at his pocket."

"It already ignited. It's setting off the other pads on the bottom of his safety vest."

"I don't think I could have made the bonus round any simpler." Serge sighed. "And after all I said about not panicking."

Flames began working their way down Gil's legs and up to his armpits.

"He doesn't look like he's panicking," said Coleman. "See? He's keeping his head and running straight for the water."

"Exactly," said Serge. "All he has to do is drop and roll in the sand. I *told* him it was easy."

"Maybe if he had used sunscreen," said Coleman. "People are always telling you that down here."

"But nobody listens."

The flames began spreading, pad by pad, across his chest, but Gil wasn't slowing down. If anything, he was running faster.

"I don't know," said Coleman. "I think he might make it. He's more than halfway there, and most of the pads still aren't lit."

"That's the double whammy of panic," said Serge. "He's not rolling in the sand, *and* he's still running. Remember me telling you about twirling Brillo on the Fourth of July? The faster he sprints, the more air gets to the pads, and the fire accelerates until he's engulfed."

"He's almost to the water!" said Coleman. "Oooo, he's engulfed now. Engulfed isn't good."

The pair watched the human torch reach the wet sand at the edge of the waves. He dropped to his knees, then tipped over facedown and fell still. The waves continued rolling in, eventually putting out the fire with a series of sizzles, but it was all epilogue.

"That was cool!" said Coleman. "I mean, I guess I shouldn't be happy."

"Someone has to thin the herd, but why do they always leave it to me?"

"Because you're thoughtful?" asked Coleman.

Serge turned back to the motel room. "Show's over."

"Cancel sunscreen."

Chapter 22

SOMEWHERE ALONG THE GULF OF MEXICO

Water jets sprayed from the giant fountain in the middle of the man-made lake. It seemed to be the big selling point at every retirement park up and down the west coast of Florida. The setting sun created the illusion that the flying water droplets were ablaze like molten blobs of lava. Three-wheel bikes and members of the Silver Sneakers fitness club circled the pond. American flags flapped from sticks in doorside brackets.

Inside one of the trailers, a phone rang. A man in a recliner got up and reached for the cordless receiver.

"Hello?"

"Ted?"

"Yes?"

"Is this Ted Pruitt?"

"Who's calling?"

"Tofer Baez."

It was one of those stunned pauses that might have gone on forever.

"Hello? Hello? Are you still there?"

More silence. Then: "Tofer, is that really you?"

"Yes, we need to talk."

"That's what we're doing now," said Ted.

"No, not on the phone," said Tofer. "In person."

"Slow down, I'm getting dizzy," said Ted. "I haven't heard from you in—what, almost twenty-five years? . . ."

"More than that."

". . . And you call out of the blue, acting all mysterious?" said Ted.

"You'll understand when we meet."

"I need to sit down." Ted eased back into the chair and popped up the footrest. "We're not as young as we used to be. I just turned sixty-seven, so that makes you . . ."—silently counting on his fingers—". . . seventy-one?"

"By your area code, I'm guessing you're on the Gulf."

"You guessed right," said Ted. "Where are you? Still in West Palm?"

"No, I switched coasts years ago. Now I'm in Saint Petersburg."

"Then you're just up the road from me." Ted finally relaxed and smiled at the old friendship. "Where do you want to meet?"

"A bar. It needs to be an out-of-the-way place with lots of exits and clear sight lines."

"Jesus, with the mystery again!" said Ted. "I don't know any place like that."

"Then I do," said Tofer. "Got something to write with? . . ."

. . . Two hours later, a black Oldsmobile cruised south through downtown St. Petersburg on Ninth Street. Ted thought Tofer was being paranoid, but he promised to watch for surveillance as requested. He'd been checking all his mirrors since hitting the Skyway Bridge over the mouth of the bay. Still no signs of intrigue as he crossed the intersection with Twelfth Avenue North. Ted almost missed the tiny neighborhood saloon with a white picket fence holding up a banner that said FREE POOL WEDNESDAYS. A framed black-and-white photo of a handsome young man was bolted to the front of the building. Over the door:

FLAMINGO BAR.

Ted pulled around back to park, passing door after open door exposed to the night. Yep, plenty of exits. He entered one.

It was a Wednesday and the rear pool room was crowded, one of the few places left where you could smoke, hence all the open doors. A TV was on the pro bowling tour. Someone sank a cue ball and groaned. Ted rounded the last table, eyes sweeping the elongated bar in the middle of the lounge. From the edge of his vision, an arm waved. The bushy black hair was now a gray ponytail, but even after all these years, Tofer was unmistakable. He sat alone at a small table tucked between an antique barber's chair and an old stand-up ashtray. Above, shelves with an unnatural volume of books for a bar.

Ted waved back with a giant smile, and the pals had a huge, backslapping guy hug.

"Man, you sure did pick out a funky place," said Ted. "What a dive."

Tofer sat down at their secluded table. "It was Jack Kerouac's favorite bar at the end of his life, close to his final home in nearby Pinellas Park."

"I picked up on that from the book titles on the shelves, the big photo of him out front, and all the signs advertising 'Kerouac Special: Shot & Small Draft, $2.' . . . The ponytail looks good. What was too weird to discuss on the phone?"

Tofer leaned in and whispered. "Putin."

"Putin?"

"Shhhh! Lower your voice." Tofer's head yanked around. "I thought back in the nineties that all this Cold War shit was over."

"It is," said Ted.

Tofer shook his head. "Heating up again."

"What are you talking about?"

Tofer stomped a foot on the floor under their table. "Dammit! How could I have been so stupid? I was just a naive young guy trying to change the world. There were so many injustices in America back then—race relations, poverty, the war—and I bought into their propaganda. But the Russians were worse, much worse. I idealistically thought we were comrades in the struggle, but they were just using me, twisting harder and harder. I got more jittery over time and said I wanted out, but they wouldn't let me. Vague threats of blackmail. Then not so vague. They had tapes. Began talking about how many years you get in America for espionage."

"That's terrible," said Ted. "What happened?"

"Luck. The empire broke apart, and most of the KGB went home, at least those agents who handled us."

"What did you do?"

Tofer flinched as someone loudly racked balls on the pool table behind them. "Went into hiding. Kept a low profile and worked odd jobs. But every day waiting for that knock at the door from the FBI. Or worse. You can't live like that."

"But you're here and safe," said Ted. "It's been so many years I doubt they even care anymore."

Tofer scooted his chair around as close as possible to Ted. "In the last couple months, I've been contacted by some of my old friends from back in the day. Rumors are going around and they're worried. The Russians are reaching out to some of their old assets they left behind, mainly younger guys we recruited in the eighties. They're trying to put the networks back together."

"Have they reached out to you?"

"No, I'm too old." Tofer absentmindedly stroked the ponytail.

"Then what's the problem?"

"Don't you see? It puts the spotlight back on. Any files our government may have had on me were mothballed, but now they're getting dusted off. One of my friends in Orlando got a visit from the feds. They didn't have any hard evidence or he'd be in jail. But it was like they just *knew*. It was an intimidation visit, and it worked. He's really shaken, says he can never call me again for both our safety."

"I had no idea," said Ted.

"Gets worse," said Tofer. "This Putin character is a bad actor. I worked back under Brezhnev, the architect of détente, but Putin is former KGB, assassinating journalists and political opponents, and not too subtly. Gunning them down outside the Kremlin, poisoning them with exotic radioactive isotopes that only the military has. It's all deniable, and yet at the same time he wants people to know."

"I don't see how this affects you," said Ted.

"When I mentioned they're putting networks back together, they're also tying up some old loose ends, if you know what I mean," said Tofer. "Some of us defected to the United States, and others like me are just still alive. But the Russians aren't making the distinction: 'Hey, if Tofer's not in jail, maybe he cut a deal, or maybe he was never caught, but why take the chance?'"

"You seriously need a drink."

"There was some talk back when we were working. Nobody really believed it, though it was always there. One thing the Russians are good at is getting people out of the country, but they're not perfect. If one of their foreign assets becomes compromised, they're often smuggled to Cuba as a way point, or some other friendly place. But if they're too late for an extraction, and an asset knows enough to expose an operation, then it's a cold, quick decision. They just disappear. Happened a number of times in the seventies. We were always told they'd been spirited off to nice apartments in Moscow, but who knows? . . . I think I'm being followed."

"I think you're making yourself crazy," said Ted.

"Am I?" said Tofer. "Remember my friend in Orlando? He's missing now, along with his wife. One of my other friends drove by his house to check up on him, and the place was crawling with FBI. And there was a crime scene truck."

"But that could be anything," said Ted. "It's a dangerous state."

"Don't you see now? I personally can identify dozens of those younger agents from the late eighties that they've just reactivated. Anyone who knows anything is in play now. That means you, too."

"But I don't know those agents," said Ted.

"Doesn't matter. You know me. They like to be thorough."

"You're already worrying enough for both of us, so I'm not going to lose any sleep."

"Ted, we've been friends for a long time."

"Yes, we have."

"I'm not cut out for this stress." He placed his face in his hands. "In case anything happens to me, I want a clear conscience. I need to make a confession. I recruited you."

"I kind of figured that out later," said Ted. "We both liked shortwave and became friends. You were into this other stuff, but once you felt you could trust me . . ."

"It goes beyond that," said Tofer. "I *targeted* you."

"What? Targeted?"

"They first approached me at an anti-war rally, and it was an easy sell. I told them I was in."

"These were other Americans?"

Tofer shook his head. "That's the thing. They were Russian, yet their English was so perfect, even idiomatic. They knew all the music and fads and everything else about what the youth was into. It was amazing how easily they infiltrated the counterculture. Except their backgrounds could only withstand superficial scrutiny. So they said they needed my help to recruit Americans born and raised here. First we tried the flag burners, because they had already disowned their country, but they turned out just to be assholes. Then we looked at the Weather Underground types, real hard-core organizers, because we figured they're *organized*. But they had so much internal politics that they were fighting themselves even more than the government. Finally, we decided to forget all that and go younger. It would require much more time and patience, but we could mold them from an early age. High school students."

"Like me?"

"We developed a profile. Misfits."

"Gee, thanks."

"We were looking for bright kids, but loners. Our profile said the most vulnerable were from broken homes, single offspring without the support of siblings. Even better if they lost their dads at an early age. You came to us on a silver platter with your letter to Radio Moscow. We put you under surveillance for a couple weeks: You had little interaction with classmates, rarely leaving the house except to launch your model rockets. Just waiting to be befriended by a cool college guy with a guitar. That's when they sent me in. I'm sorry."

A long pause as they stared at each other.

Ted placed his palms flat on the table and leaned back. "That's a lot to take in."

"Life is a list of things you wish you could go back and change," said Tofer. "But there it is."

"Indeed," said Ted. "Now there's something that I need to tell you. It might come as a bit of a shock. Remember the first time we met back in 1970? . . ."

Chapter 23

SARASOTA

In northern states, they have hail damage. In Florida, they have different damage. An hour after dark, a palm tree dropped a coconut through the windshield of a Lincoln parked outside a trailer.

A Ford Falcon arrived at the entrance of Boca Shores.

"... *Let's play* The Hollywood Squares ..."

Earl came out of his booth in loose khakis and bright spirits. "Back again? You might as well move in."

Serge threw up his arms in mock frustration. "Another dinner invitation. What are you going to do?"

"You're the man of the hour," Earl said convivially. "Enjoy it while you can."

Serge waved. "Don't do anything I wouldn't."

"From what I hear, that's a short list."

The guard arm raised, and the Falcon sped through.

"... *Whoopi Goldberg to block*..."

Serge and Coleman bounded up a screened porch and were met at the door. "This really isn't necessary."

"What can I say?" said Lawrence. "You're in high demand."

Serge saw an unready kitchen and a dormant dining room. "What's going on?"

Nancy reached into the fridge for a covered casserole dish. "A surprise."

"Follow me," said Lawrence.

"Someone else's place again?"

"Not exactly."

Serge gave Coleman a clueless glance. "Mysteries abound in this place."

They walked across the lawn by the pool, and Scott silently vectored over the grass in his fancy new golf cart.

"Look at you and those wheels!" said Nancy. "The women will flock!"

"This is so much better than that wheelchair," said Scott. "It's changed my life!"

"Can I get a lift?" said Coleman. "My legs are doing that spaghetti thing again."

"Sure!" They took off.

Lawrence put a hand on Serge's shoulder.

"What?"

"Look ahead."

Lights blazed around the Boca Shores clubhouse. Flames from tiki torches licked into the night. After a brief hike across a manicured lawn, they met Scott and Coleman at the double doors and entered the main hall.

"*Surprise!*"

Serge and Coleman stopped in shock.

A hundred people cheered and clapped and blew noisemakers. They quickly surrounded the pair, patting their backs and showering compliments. On the front wall was the electronic bingo scoreboard, and above it, a large banner:

THANK YOU, SERGE AND COLEMAN!

The crowd dispersed with motivation, uncovering all the pot-luck dishes arranged on long tables around the edges of the hall. Others opened steam trays and grabbed paper plates. Big-band music filled the room from the PA system's ceiling speakers.

"Look at all that food!" Coleman took off. "Chicken wings!"

Serge slowly turned to Lawrence. "Did you have anything to do with this?"

"Actually, no. It was rather spontaneous."

Coleman came back with a plate of wings and a large, circular stain in the middle of his shirt that looked like he'd somehow fallen on top of an entire pizza, which would be accurate.

"I see you're wasting no time getting your Coleman on," said Serge.

Coleman nodded and ate with hearty imprecision like a bear cub in a Taco Bell dumpster. "This party rocks! There's only one thing missing, but I'm not complaining. They're old and have to be mellow."

A retired union rep named Dudley entered the hall on a motor-ized scooter. He was bald with a full gray mustache, bent over the handlebars in a tropical shirt that featured ukuleles and volcanoes. The scooter did a blistering three miles an hour until it arrived at the only empty table in the room, sitting under the bingo board.

Dudley dismounted, and friends helped him unload the bulky cardboard boxes from the scooter's oversize basket. The table soon held a row of those gigantic liquor bottles with the handles. Vodka, gin, scotch, tequila, bourbon. Tongs went in the ice bucket, and the plastic cups were stacked. Dudley turned to the crowd: "Soup's on!"

If the bingo hall had been a ship, it would have capsized.

Coleman gasped. "The missing stuff isn't missing anymore!" He took off.

Another resident, Coyote Jim, arrived, pulling an industrial dolly with square metal travel cases. He began setting up in the corner.

The prodigal Coleman returned again with a red plastic cup of Captain Morgan. A rubber band under his chin secured the conical party hat on his head. He blew the noisemaker in his mouth. It unfurled, then fell from his lips to the ground. "Serge, someone brought a whole bag of these little popper things, where you pull a string and it goes bang, and shoots out confetti!"

Bang.

Serge and Lawrence stood silent with facefuls of paper specks.

"Got to run!" Coleman took off again.

The big-band music from the ceiling speakers stopped. Much larger concert speakers began blaring in the corner with the pounding beats of DJ Coyote Jim.

"*. . . Life in the fast lane! . . .*"

Dozens began dancing.

"Are all your parties like this?" asked Serge.

"It's still early," said Lawrence.

"*. . . Everything, all the time . . .*"

Serge looked at another wall. "You've got a flat-screen TV in here."

"Yes, we do."

"But it's only showing static."

"In your honor."

Coleman glanced around suspiciously before slipping outside the hall to a darkened corner of the patio surrounding the swimming pool. He leaned against the railing overlooking the lake and fired up a fatty.

"Excuse me?"

Coleman jumped and spun, hiding the joint behind his back. "What!"

He hadn't noticed the two older women out getting fresh air on the other side of the pool. "Is that marijuana?"

"No, no, no!"

"Yes, it is. You're hiding it behind your back."

"No, I'm not!"

"Can we try some?"

"Sure." He passed it. "The most important thing is to hold in the toke as long as you can."

The first woman held her breath, then coughed and passed it to her friend. "Am I going to trip?"

"You never know."

They finished the doobie, thanked Coleman and ran back inside for the steam trays.

"... *Straight outta Compton!* ..."

The two women filled paper plates with popcorn shrimp. "This is the best music ever!"

"I know."

Coleman staggered to the front of the room, worked his way behind a long table, and deputized himself as the dancing bartender. The conical party hat was now over his left ear. The crowd roared as Coleman boogied and poured triple-strength drinks. Mixers spilled, and ice cubes bounced on the floor.

Fifteen minutes later—"Dudley, take over for me"—and Coleman snuck back out to the patio again. Two women followed, along with four of their friends. Coleman fired up again. "Here you go. Pass it around ..."

"... *Disco inferno!* ..."

The steam trays ran low, but the liquor was holding strong. Coleman hammered a rum and Coke, poured a refill for the road, and made another clandestine trip outside to the patio. He turned around. Thirty people were staring back.

"Okay, to make this work, we need to form a circle."

They did as instructed. Coleman drained his big red cup and lit two joints at once. He held them out, one in each hand. "Pass these both ways ..."

The joints burned down and Coleman had a chemical inspiration.

"What's Coleman doing?"

Splash.

"He jumped in the pool!"

"Everyone! In the pool!"

Splash, splash, splash, splash . . .

Fully clothed residents laughed and bobbed. A black sock floated to the surface. Some joined Coleman doing cannonballs.

Serge came outside. "Coleman! What do you think you're doing?"

"Oh, hey Serge! This party is off the hook!"

Suddenly high beams lit up the patio. A Mercedes parked and one of Boca Shores' managers got out. "What the hell is going on? Everyone out of the pool! Now!"

The laughter and splashing stopped. Some got paranoid and hid behind Coleman.

Serge sauntered over to the gate. "What seems to be the problem?"

"What's the problem? Just look!" The manager trembled with rage. "It's against the rules to be in the pool at this hour! And look at the mess with all the cups and paper plates."

"We have official permission," said Serge.

"From who?"

"The owner."

"No, you don't!"

Serge got out his wallet and retrieved a scrap of paper. "Here's his number. You might want to make a phone call before you're wondering how you ever ended up working in a food court. The code word is 'humidor.'"

The manager exhaled angrily out his nostrils. He reluctantly dialed his cell phone just in case. "Hello? Mr. Dryden? . . . Yes, I know what time it is, and I'm sorry to bother you at this hour, but the pool is full of residents who are trashing the place, and there's a guy here who claims you gave them permission. I know it sounds silly, but he mentioned something about a humidor . . . I see . . . I see . . . I understand . . ."

The manager stared at Serge a moment before sprinting back to his car and screeching off into the night.

From the pool: "Hooray!"

Chapter 24

MEANWHILE . . .

Pool balls clacked in a smoky bar in St. Petersburg. Two old friends sat across from each other.

"Of course I remember the day we met," said Tofer. "What are you trying to tell me?"

"There's something you don't know," said Ted. "It started right after you left my place . . ."

1970

. . . Ted watched the VW microbus drive out of sight. Then he ran back in the house: "Mom, can I borrow the car?"

"Where are you going?"

"To meet some friends," said Ted. "There's a game at the school."

"Keys are in the kitchen. Have fun!"

Twenty minutes later, Ted was feeding dimes into a parking meter in downtown West Palm Beach. He looked up at a stark concrete building and went inside.

Twenty minutes after that: A man in a black coat and tie knocked on an open office door.

Another man in a black tie looked up from a classified report. "Yes?"

"Sir, you might want to come see this."

"What is it?"

The pair entered a conference room full of other serious men. And a single, skinny kid slouched in a chair.

"Who's that?"

"A walk-in. Says a Soviet agent is trying to recruit him. We checked him out"—the man held up a driver's license—"Theodore Pruitt, goes to the local high school."

"Is he unstable or something?"

"Doesn't seem to be, except for his crazy story." The man turned toward the boy. "Ted, this is FBI bureau chief Brennan. Could you repeat what you just told us?"

And Ted did, from shortwave to guitar lessons. He unfolded a scrap of paper. ". . . Here's the plate number on his van . . ."

The rest of the agents sat quietly as Brennan stared down in thought. Then: "Son, could you wait outside . . . Jackson, get him a soda and keep him company."

They had the room to themselves.

"What do you think?" asked the agent who first knocked on Brennan's door.

"The only spies we have in Florida are Cuban," said the chief. "A few Soviets have come through briefly on specific details like the missile crisis, but nothing remotely resembling a permanent operation like this."

"What are we going to do about it?"

"It has to be the wild imagination of a strange kid," said Brennan. "On the other hand, I can't take the chance that I'm wrong . . . Call him back in."

The door opened, and Brennan stood and smiled warmly. He shook Ted's hand. "We really appreciate you coming to us with this. More importantly, your country appreciates it."

"Great," said Ted. "What do you want me to do?"

"You told us nobody knows you came here?"

Ted nodded.

"Let's keep it that way. Don't even tell your mother, because she'll worry. Okay?"

"I can do that."

"Wonderful. We'll be in touch."

"When?" asked Ted. "Where?"

"We'll find you . . . Jackson, could you show this young man out? The back way?"

The door closed again and Brennan faced the room. "Someone check out this license plate . . ."

T he next afternoon.

The last bell of the day rang, and the high school emptied as they all do, like a jailbreak.

A skinny student strolled down the sidewalk with a sack of books slung over his shoulder.

From behind: "Ted! Ted Pruitt? Is that you?"

Ted turned around to find a taller, more athletic boy in a varsity jacket. "Do I know you?"

"We went to grade school together." He put out his hand. "Mark Christianson. My family moved away to Texas, but now we're back. It's my first day." He looked around. "Man, has this town changed. Almost all the other kids must have gotten rezoned to the new high school. You're the only person I know."

"I don't know you," said Ted.

"We weren't close. So where are you going?"

"Home."

"Walking?"

"It's not far."

"Let me give you a ride. I just got a Corvette! My dad's an injury lawyer."

"A Corvette?"

"Come on!"

The pair ran around the corner to the student parking lot, and Ted stood mesmerized at the sight of the flaming-red Stingray convertible. "It's beautiful!"

"Hop in."

They began driving south as Ted tapped the books in his lap. "You know, I've been thinking about it, and I really don't remember you at all."

"It was third grade. Who does?" Mark cut the wheel with a skidding of tires as high school kids are required to do.

"This isn't the way to my house."

"I remembered I left something at home I need to get." Mark checked his rearview before another skidding turn. And another.

"Mark, you're driving in circles."

"I've been away so long, the streets are a little fuzzy." A last check in the rearview. "Here we are."

They parked behind a two-story stucco house with a separate outdoor staircase in back leading to the upper floor.

"Ted, why don't you come on in. I just got *The White Album*."

"My mom will be worried—"

But Mark was already out of the car, and Ted ran up the steps after him. They went inside, and once the door was closed . . .

"Hello, Ted."

He turned around. Four men appeared from a bedroom. Black coats and ties, the same ones from the conference room the day before.

"What's going on?" asked Ted.

"This is a safe house," said Agent Jackson. "Please have a seat."

Ted began shaking as he eased himself down.

"Relax, there's nothing to worry about," said the agent. "First we want to thank you for what you told us. Last night, your new pal Tofer met with a foreign agent we didn't know about. So you've already yielded results."

"Cool! So what's my next move?"

"You don't make any moves," said the agent. "If our hunch is correct, Tofer is going to start coming around to see you. A lot. Just play along and be a normal high school kid. Make him feel comfortable so he keeps doing whatever it is he's up to. And no more writing down license plates or anything else to arouse suspicion. We'll take it from here."

"When will I see you again?"

"You won't. And you can never come to our office again. That's why we met here. If Tofer reports to his superiors that you're a promising asset, the other side will have you under surveillance soon. That's why you'll only be talking to Mark from now on."

"Another kid at my high school?"

"I don't go to your high school," said Mark. "I'm twenty-three."

"So we weren't in third grade together?"

"Not really," said the varsity jacket. "If we ever need to get in touch with you, I'll be outside the school like today. And if you absolutely need to contact us, leave a football in your front yard."

"I don't have a football."

An agent tossed him one.

Ted rubbed the leather Spalding. "You guys think of everything."

"That about wraps it up," said Agent Jackson.

"Follow me," said Mark.

"Is your name Mark?"

"Not really. I can't drive you home for reasons that are now obvious, and you can't walk out the front, so I'll show you a way to cut between the yards and leave from the next street."

The following day, Tofer came over and Ted behaved surprisingly natural considering the quite unnatural hairpin turn in his life. They messed with the shortwave, Ted learned new songs on the guitar, and Glenda was in the kitchen having a cow over the whole thing. It fell into a routine. The cool hippie and the nerd hanging out two or three times a week. Their meetings began shifting more and more to Tofer's apartment. He started talking politics and giving Ted books to read. They went to an anti-war rally at a nearby college.

The high school student had never seen such anger and yelling and so many police in helmets.

"This is really exciting," said Ted. "What are those guys burning?"

"Their draft cards. You'll be getting one soon."

"I don't think I should burn it."

"We better get moving," said Tofer.

"Why?"

"Don't want to get hit by batons."

Weeks passed. Ted learned to play "Blowin' in the Wind." He attended a meeting to end injustice. He launched rockets.

A varsity jacket caught up with Ted on the sidewalk outside his school. "What's up?"

"Oh, it's you," said Ted. "He's giving me more stuff to read about communism and the heroes of the revolution in Cuba and South America."

"Grooming you," said Mark. "You still steady? This is a lot for a high school kid. Just give the word if it starts getting to be too much."

"Piece of cake," said Ted. "I really think I'm doing something that would make my father proud."

"Glad to hear it. Keep walking straight." And Mark turned alone into the parking lot.

More weeks passed. More guitar strumming and political rants.

Another school day ended, and a varsity jacket joined Ted on the sidewalk. "Just keep smiling and don't turn around. They've got a Camaro on you a block back."

"That seems excessive."

"They've decided you're a promising asset, so the vetting is about to get intense," said Mark. "That's why I can't meet you like this anymore."

"I don't understand."

"They just took our picture with a zoom lens. They're going to be taking photos of you and anyone you talk to for a while. See who shows up most frequently, who your closest friends are, and then check them out," said Mark. "This is the first day we've picked up a tail on you at school, so they'll only have the one picture of us together. You'll probably never see me again."

"But how will we get in touch?"

"You'll find out." Mark trotted away.

Another month went by. Someone out for a morning jog saw a football lying on a front lawn.

Ted was walking home with his books when he dropped into a convenience store for a Coke. An Impala drove by taking photos. Ted approached the soda case.

A girl with straight brown hair and bell-bottoms walked up next to him and grabbed a Dr Pepper. "Don't look at me. I'm your new contact. I'll distract the clerk, and you go out the back door. A car's waiting."

Ted stepped into the alley behind the store and was practically mugged. Agents threw him in the backseat of a sedan and pushed him to the floor. They went to the safe house.

Ted was sitting at a table upstairs when the girl in bell-bottoms walked in. "We saw your football."

"He wants me to join the navy."

"We were anticipating something like that. Another reason they targeted you: nearing draft age with no money for college. I'm guessing he wants you on a submarine."

"How'd you know?"

"They've been working on this for some time. Looking for homegrown American kids whose backgrounds would pass a security check," said the girl. "Navigational charts, right?"

"So what do I do?"

"Join the navy."

T wo days later, Ted went into the convenience store as instructed. And right out the back door again into the sedan.

They all sat around the table in the safe house. The bell-bottomed girl was named Fawn. "Here's the plan. Tomorrow you enlist down at the local office and request subs, and you'll get it. Do your patrol, do everything you're asked, just act like a regular sailor. But don't mention any of this to anyone. The right people will know, but you won't know who they are."

"What about the navigational charts?" asked Ted. "I'm supposed to keep a coded diary."

"Forget the charts and codes," said Fawn. "But do keep a diary. An honest one of boring stuff going through your head. Nothing about the sub. When the time comes, you'll hear from us."

So Ted joined the navy and went to boot camp, got all his hair cut off, and one autumn morning carried a duffel bag up a gangplank. He'd seen pictures of the missile subs, but in person it was a wonder of the world. They were loading torpedoes on the forward deck as he climbed aboard.

He did his three-month tour and came back into port with a bunch of new friends and great stories of pressurized toilets.

Sailors streamed off the sub onto the dock, looking forward

to seeing wives and kids. One of his new shipmate friends had a bounce in his step. "I've got a son I've never seen!"

"Congratulations."

"You want to meet him? He's with his mom where the families are waiting."

"Love to," said Ted.

The pal led him into a stern building on the submarine complex and down a hallway. Ted pointed back. "But the others are going that way."

"I know a shortcut." He opened a door.

Ted froze, and they pulled him into the room. Armed guards were posted outside.

"Have a seat," said a lieutenant commander in a snow-white officer's uniform. It seemed to be the dress code. White uniforms with gold shoulder stripes all around the table.

"I'm Commander Larson, and I've heard a lot about you. We're Naval Intelligence working with the FBI."

Ted didn't reply.

"Do you have your diary?"

Ted nodded and dug through his duffel bag. "Here it is."

Another officer unrolled a navigational chart on the table. Just like the one Ted had seen in the sub, except with different coordinates and lines already drawn on it. "We've decided to come at it from this angle. Memorize what you see here."

Another officer handed him some drawings.

Ted glanced over them and looked up. "Shortwave sets and model rockets?"

"Some of your interests. It will seem normal, doodling in your spare time," said Larson. "Tell your handler, Tofer, that you embedded some coded stuff into those pictures to help with your recall. We want you to copy these drawings in your own hand in the back of your diary . . ."

Ted returned home and did as he was told. Tofer was impressed, and his Soviet superiors even more so. After time ashore, Ted went back out on another patrol, and the process repeated.

In the last year of Ted's enlistment, he sat in the same room on the sub base, hunched over his newest diary and copying more drawings. "I hope this is doing some good."

"More than you realize," said Larson. "Thanks to your disinformation on our boomers' routes, we now know where their fast-attack subs will be waiting, which helps us track *them*. Plus we've started connecting the dots in Tofer's Florida network and uncovering agents we never would have found otherwise."

"I had no idea." Ted continued scribbling. "But what do the Russians want with Florida? I'd think Washington, D.C."

"Most people aren't aware of all the sensitive military installations the state has," said Larson. "Eglin, Boca Chica, Patrick Air Force Base near the Canaveral station, where we launch our defense satellites. And we run most of our kinetic operations from Central Command in south Tampa. You know what a honey trap is?"

"I've seen spy movies," said Ted.

"After your info began paying off, it led us to one of their agents from Belarus working in a convenience store just a few blocks up the road from the main gates of the Tampa base. A drop-dead sexy young woman. And the store was in the perfect location where a hundred guys from the base stop by every day for smokes or whatever. We stepped in before the bleeding began. From there, we checked every convenience store anywhere near a base, and you wouldn't imagine how many honey traps we picked up." Larson shook his head. "To think this all started when some young high school kid just walked in off the street at his local FBI office . . ."

Ted finished his enlistment, joined the clerical staff of that very FBI office, and started feeding Tofer fake information about the character flaws of the staff.

One agent was reported to enjoy a particular strip club, which led to an undercover stripper from Romania, who led them to another cell. Another agent was said to have a taste for the sauce, which led to more spies posing as barflies. At the local dog track, Russians consoled an agent who was cursing and tearing up losing tickets.

A large chart with photos and colored string remained permanently up in the "secure" room at the FBI office. It resembled a spiderweb depicting a significant Soviet network across the state. In the middle of the web, a single point: Tofer. He was like Patient Zero, the first infected person that started an epidemic.

On the outer edges of the chart were red circles around certain mug shots. From time to time, the Bureau approached their targets, trying to turn them. If it didn't work, arrest. Other times, if a target knew enough but wasn't suitable for double-agent work, they simply disappeared into protection programs after agreeing to blab.

The Russians didn't know what was happening. The missing agents had them jumpy, changing routines, making mistakes. They never realized that most of their Florida operation had been effectively neutralized. Thanks to a secret weapon called Ted.

After the Soviet Union broke apart, the FBI operation was indefinitely suspended. They gave Ted a medal in a secret ceremony.

"What are you going to do now?"

"I'm in Florida, so what else? Retire," said Ted. "I'm kidding. I'm still too young."

They shook hands and parted ways.

Chapter 25

ST. PETERSBURG

A cue ball clacked, and balls scattered across the pool table.

Ted finished his story, and Tofer stared silently at him in a corner of the Flamingo Bar.

"You were working for the Americans all along?" said Tofer. "You betrayed me?"

"You betrayed your country," said Ted. "I would say I'm sorry, but I'm not."

"I was so sure about you." Tofer bit his lip. "What did I miss?"

"You didn't do enough research," said Ted. "Yes, being without a dad made me more susceptible. But you also didn't *know* my dad. He loved this country. I did what he would've wanted me to."

Tofer's heart began pounding. "Then why was I never picked up?"

"It was considered," said Ted. "But I thought what was the

point since you'd been deactivated. I convinced our guys to leave you out in the field because who knew what the future might hold and what use you might be?"

"I can't believe you're telling me all this."

"What are you going to do, share it with the Russians? I'm sure they'd be overjoyed to learn the damage you did."

Tofer took a deep breath and settled down. "Believe it or not, you've actually made me feel better. I've been regretting my actions for decades. If I wrecked their operation, even unwittingly, then I couldn't be happier."

"Life is strange."

"I still need your help," said Tofer. "I need you to hide me."

"And I still think you're overreacting," said Ted, standing up from the table. "But why not? You can come live with me until your nerves settle down or we figure out if something really is going on."

BOCA SHORES

"Guys and gals!" Serge yelled into the swimming pool. "You need to settle down. Coleman isn't supposed to be a role model. He's a cautionary tale."

"Where *is* Coleman?" shouted a voice in the group.

"I thought he was with you," said Serge.

A voice from the black distance: "I'm out here!"

"Where?" yelled Serge. "Keep talking and I'll track your voice again."

"Okay . . . Beans, Dexies, Benny and the Jets, study buddies, rojo, Tussin, velvet, tweak, angel dust, wet, moon rocks, moon blast, black beauties, China white, brown sugar, mellow yellow, orange sunshine, blue cheer, red devil, shrooms, caps, hillbilly highway . . ."

An old woman dropped her cane and stepped up on the bottom rung of the railing. "I see him!"

All eyes turned in the direction she was pointing.

"He's in the lake!"

Serge covered his face. He painfully looked up at the splashing, waving figure out in the middle of the black water next to the turned-off fountain. "Will you get out of there?"

"But the water's great," said Coleman.

"But it's *fresh* water!" said Serge.

"So what? I'm having a blast!"

"Coleman's having a blast!" came a voice from the crowd.

"Into the lake with Coleman!" shouted another.

Whiskey in plastic cups sloshed, and a circle of seniors rapidly toked revived joints before joining the thundering herd down the shore.

"Stop!" yelled Serge. "You don't understand! Fresh water in Florida means alligators."

"But it's a man-made lake," yelled a former civil servant from Buffalo.

"Doesn't matter," said Serge. "It's their job to find fresh water in this state. Ask anyone who's ever tried to retrieve a golf ball."

They began diving in. *Splash, splash, splash.* Hooting and hollering. The joyous upheaval in the water drew a dark form down from one of the banks.

"This is the best party we've ever had!" yelled a woman behind the fountain.

"What's that?" said someone else still up on the pool deck.

"It's a gator! . . ."

"And it's heading for Coleman! . . ."

It was indeed. Coleman just continued whooping and waving up at the pool deck.

"Behind you!" yelled Serge.

"What?"

Two of the residents near Coleman spotted the reptile from the trademark eye bumps tracking through the water. They were among the more fit men in the park, thanks to a local spa. The gator wasn't *that* big, they thought, and they were fortified by Coleman's turbo-cocktails. They moved in for the capture.

Serge was already sprinting down the bank and dove in the water, swimming breakneck. He arrived simultaneously with the old men, who were drifting into serious misadventure. When Serge broke the surface of the water, he could see they were about to make the grave error of grabbing the gator by the tail, the worst place possible. But Serge knew his Florida biology. A gator's jaws have a massive biting force of more than two thousand pounds per square inch, but very weak muscles opening the mouth. That's how alligator wrestlers can amaze crowds by holding the animal's closed jaws tucked under their chins.

Just as the old men grabbed the tail, Serge's right arm got the gator in a headlock. It was only a four-footer, but still enough to inflict nastiness. The reptile thrashed.

"Everyone out of the lake!" yelled Serge, maintaining his grasp.

"Boooo!"

"I'm serious."

They just laughed and splashed him.

"There's some duct tape in the clubhouse," said one of the men at the tail. "We can seal its mouth."

"Good thinking," said Serge. "Then we'll release him on that far bank."

"No," said the old man. "I think we should keep him!"

Coleman turned around. "What are you doing there? What's with the gator?"

Serge rolled his eyes skyward in exasperation. He considered options of least resistance. Getting the raucous crowd out of the water was now a fool's errand.

"Okay, first things first," said Serge. "Let's carry him inside and find that tape."

They lugged the gator up through the reeds and across the patio into the clubhouse.

Back in the water: *"Ahhhhh! Ahhhh! Help me! Dear Jesus!"*

"Coleman's in trouble!" a woman yelled from the bank. "The swans have him!"

The residents began splashing and shouting at the birds, and someone else grabbed the swimming pool rescue stick, helping pull Coleman free from his feathered foes. He briefly staggered around the mucky bottom. Then, like a house cat sitting in the middle of an empty room, he got another non sequitur urge to be somewhere else. He climbed out of the lake and all the residents followed like ducklings, winding their way around the pool and returning to the hall.

"Coleman," said Serge. "Is that blood trickling down by your ear?"

"A large bird grabbed me by the top of my head. I hate that when I'm high."

Soon the party was back in overdrive. Music blared louder, and Coleman delivered an encore performance as the happy, dancing bartender. DJ Coyote Jim turned on his light show to Run-D.M.C. and Aerosmith . . .

A hundred yards away, Earl stepped out of his guard shack, removed his hat and scratched his head. He had regularly heard party noise from the clubhouse, but not like this. The growing volume of whatever was happening had piqued his curiosity and now got the better of him. It was against the rules, but he raised the gate arm and hung a BACK IN 10 MINUTES sign.

Earl entered the rear of the hall and approached tipped-over dining tables. Where did his eyes even begin? Soggy people jitterbugged under strobe lights. Chef's salad splattered the walls, a shirtless Coleman stretched out across the bar for body shots of Patrón. A circle of residents openly passed joints by the steam trays, and someone drove by in a mobility scooter, blowing a noise-maker at him. An alligator with its mouth taped shut scampered across the dance floor.

"What the hell?"

"*. . . Walk this way! . . .*"

"Hey, handsome." A relatively young widow handed Earl a drink of pineapple juice and Absolut.

"I'm on duty."

She took the guard hat off his head and put it on hers. "So am I..."

A half hour went by. Coleman was now out cold, but it didn't stop the body shots. Someone had tethered the alligator in a corner with a strong rope, untaped its mouth, and the residents took turns tossing him Swedish meatballs.

"I can't watch anymore," Serge told Lawrence. "They're old enough to make their own mistakes."

"Where are you going?"

"Out for air."

He walked up the street and cordially waved as he passed the guard booth. "Good night, Earl."

"Good night, Serge."

Earl resumed having sex in the shaking guard booth, and Serge left the park on foot for a night stroll.

The booth continued creaking in the darkness. Suddenly piercing headlights swung around the corner, catching Earl like a thief. He had wide, guilty eyes until he shielded them and recognized the Oldsmobile.

"Stay down," Earl told his partner. Then he raised the guard arm and stuck his head out the window. "Nice night."

"Are you okay?" asked the driver. "You're sweating like crazy."

"Just had to change someone's tire."

"Okay, take care."

The Oldsmobile drove around the lake and parked at a trailer.

"This is your retirement place?" asked the passenger.

"Home sweet home," said the driver.

And Ted and Tofer went inside.

Chapter 26

THE NEXT DAY

The conference room of the local FBI office was once again filled to capacity. And once again, everyone watched a video that they now knew by heart. The surveillance tape went frame by frame through the firefight in the parking lot of the Life-Armor corporation. Agents paid particular attention to the end of the video and an old brown Nissan nonchalantly driving off the top of the screen.

The TV went black, and the agent in charge faced the room.

"Well, that certainly was an entertaining little goat-fuck. Anyone care to share thoughts on how this could have happened? Agent Lang seems to be the only one who knew what he was doing."

"By the way, how is he?"

"Just a shoulder wound," said the bureau chief. "In the hospital, binge-watching TV and waiting for medals of valor."

There were personnel from every local field office and some top brass from D.C., plus the always nerve-racking unofficial observers from the CIA and Department of Justice.

"This is Tom Mansfield from Virginia," said the bureau chief. "The whole mess is starting to get a lot of moving parts in a hurry, so he's going to give the latest update. Tom?"

A veteran agent with full gray hair and an American flag lapel pin stood up. An indescribable aura of gravity that commanded respect. "As of zero-nine-hundred, we've shifted the focus of our task force to this man . . ."

An assistant held up a glossy eight-by-ten photo of someone who looked perpetually self-conscious.

"His name may or may not be Benmont Pinch. We're still checking his background, but as of now it appears so clean that it's suspicious. And this next part is especially unsettling, but the growing body of evidence can no longer be ignored. It appears we have a spy at one of the top echelons in Washington."

That set the room murmuring.

"Pipe down!" said the bureau chief.

A hand went up. "Is this Benmont the mole in the Bureau?"

"No," said Mansfield. "We believe he's the agent's outside contact. Here's the chronology of what we know so far: There were a number of homicides here in Florida that didn't initially get our attention until your Agent Lang in the hospital sent an inquiry memo to the main office. Turns out his hunch was right. All the victims' identities were contained in one of our most highly classified files. The only possible conclusion at the time was that the documents had been compromised by someone on the inside. We did a thorough housecleaning that came up empty . . . Then we caught a lucky break."

The assistant held up another glossy photo.

"This is a man named Quint Powers, who was found murdered with a prostitute in a local hotel. Clearly staged. Expert spycraft," said Mansfield. "Mr. Powers was a supervisor at the Life-Armor office where we had our little shootout. Apparently Mr. Powers stumbled upon something suspicious in one of his employees' computers . . . Now this next part is a little hazy, and we're still trying to put it all together, but separate e-mails began circulating through the Social Security Administration until we realized we had a mole."

Another hand. "What finally tipped us off?"

"The two Social Security bureaucrats who handled the e-mails are now dead," said Mansfield. "That's how we're certain there's a mole. Nobody else but someone in the company would have been able to see the internal routing of those e-mails . . . Use your imaginations. Probably passed along in a newspaper on a park bench."

More murmurs.

Mansfield reached for a carafe and poured a glass of ice water. "Which brings us back to the late Quint Powers. It appears he came up with a far-fetched theory that is now rapidly gaining credence at the highest levels. We initially thought the list of victims had been stolen from the Bureau, but it now appears that our spy in Washington knew enough about our intelligence procedure to direct the reconstruction of those lists by an outside contact. He needed a professional data analyst. Enter Benmont."

"But how was it possible to re-create such a list?"

"Quint Powers figured it out. His so-called crazy theory," said Mansfield. "Given the recent series of events, we reverse-engineered all the steps in Mr. Powers's hypothesis, and it completely checks out . . . For whatever reason, he discovered that Benmont Pinch had assembled a list that was prioritized by numerical ordering of the last four digits of Social Security numbers. We surmise this was what first attracted Quint's attention, because who would prioritize anything by just the last four digits? The second sequencing priority was alphabetizing and isolating all instances of juxtaposed names. Then, after deleting sets of twins by flagging identical birthdays, what do you have left? A list of people with the same last names—husbands, wives, children, aunts, uncles—

who weren't twins but somehow had sequential Social Security numbers. And who does the government issue such sequential numbers to? . . ."

The audience slowly began nodding.

"Exactly," said Mansfield. "Shocking as it may seem, a low-level data analyst, using the resources of a private company, was able to generate a massive list of Florida residents in government protection programs."

Abject alarm swept the room.

"If I may continue," said Mansfield. "In this case, none of the witnesses who testified against organized crime have been touched. The only victims are former Soviet defectors and double agents who worked for us. Given when the Cold War ended, most are now living in retirement communities."

Another question. "But I thought we stopped issuing sequential cards."

"We did," said Mansfield. "It became necessary when technology accelerated and identity theft started to get big. But nobody thought to go back and reissue the old ones, which we're doing right now like the Manhattan Project."

Mansfield stepped aside and allowed the bureau chief to take the floor again.

"I know there's a lot more questions out there, but the main item you need to be aware of is that we have agents fanning out across the state at this very moment to pull in everyone on the list who hasn't been hit yet. Second, everyone who has touched the e-mail and the attached report is dead: Quint, the lawyer, the two Social Security guys in Baltimore. This is as serious as it gets . . ."

An arm raised high at the back of the conference table. "But what about the fake FBI agent who Lang shot in the parking lot at Life-Armor? Isn't it possible that this Benmont character was just another innocent witness they wanted to eliminate, and that was why the fake FBI agent was sent in?"

"Now, *that's* a far-fetched theory," said Mansfield. "Benmont

Pinch may look unthreatening in that photo, but he is to be considered armed and extremely dangerous. He's already tried to kill one FBI agent."

A hand went up. "I thought Agent Lang was shot by the fake FBI agent."

"We believe that whoever the mole is in Washington saw the internal e-mails about Quint Powers's theory and realized we were about to uncover Mr. Pinch, so they sent an associate to pose as FBI and extract him," said the bureau chief. "Benmont's as guilty as his colleague who pulled the trigger. I hope I'm not speaking only for myself here, but they came after the Bureau this time, which means it's now personal."

The chief turned and wrote on a whiteboard:

TOP PRIORITY: FIND BENMONT PINCH!

SARASOTA

A Ford Falcon sat parked outside an Amish restaurant. Inside, two men occupied a rounded corner booth eating pie.

"I've been doing some thinking," said Serge, sipping coffee. "You know how I'm always talking about possibilities others miss?"

"All the time," said Coleman, spiking his orange juice with vodka.

"Like how you can get away with all kinds of stuff if you have a clipboard, or safety cones, or a windbreaker with letters on the back. Everyone just assumes you're authorized."

"Don't forget hard hats."

"Right, a hard hat is another magic wand. Wear a hard hat and people just melt and bend to your will. 'Clear the building! There's a gas leak!' Then everyone runs out into the parking lot and leaves you alone while you fill your pockets with candy."

"I still have Skittles left over from last time."

"But I've come up with a new one that I can't believe I never thought of before." Serge finished his coffee and signaled a waitress for a refill. "We've watched a lot of college sporting events on TV. Have you noticed the one person who can do anything they want, no matter how far against the grain of society?"

Coleman shook his head.

"The mascot!" Serge pounded the table with a fist. "Those costumes are an all-access pass to outside-the-lane behavior. Tigers, eagles, hornets, devils, bulldogs, cowboys, Spartans, gamecocks . . ."

Giggle. "You said 'cock.'"

". . . Wear any of those outfits, and you're free to run in crazy circles, twirl your arms, do push-ups, grab strangers for hugs, lead cheers in public against your rivals."

"I've seen what happens when you do that in street clothes," said Coleman. "We're usually asked to leave."

"More like *grabbed*," said Serge. "But mascots are applauded for the same antics. Is that fair? They can even beat up the other mascot if they want."

"That's hilarious," said Coleman. "I've seen them put on that act before."

"It's not always an act," said Serge. "Once a guy really hated the guts of this other mascot, and he was like, 'Just wait till we put our costumes on.' Then on the sidelines he beat the shit out of the guy. A felony assault is going down, but thousands of onlookers are laughing and taking pictures as a leprechaun stomps an owl half to death."

Coleman looked at the feathered costume head sitting on the end of the table. "Is that why you're dressed like a duck today?"

Serge stretched his wings. "I'm taking this baby for a spin."

"But don't you think it only works when you're at a sports event?" asked Coleman. "We've been getting a lot of strange looks since we came in here."

"That's just the culture of the people who run this restaurant.

When have you ever seen the Amish in freezing weather at a football game with bare chests painted in team colors?"

"You're really smart."

Serge grabbed his costume head and stood. "Let's roll . . ."

The Ford Falcon eased up to the guard booth at Boca Shores. Earl stepped out, rubbing his chin. "A duck today?"

"I'm authorized."

The gate arm raised. The Falcon cruised inside.

Serge slowed as he passed the parking lot in front of the clubhouse. A crowd milled aimlessly. "That's interesting." They circled the square lake and returned.

Residents checked their watches and monitored the entrance. A duck got out of a Falcon. "What's going on?"

A woman with binoculars and a straw sun hat pointed at an empty shuttle bus. "Our driver is late for our field trip."

"Field trip!" Serge flapped his wings. "I love field trips! Can I go? Please! We can sing songs and have snacks and touch stuff! Please, please, please!"

"I'm sure there's enough room."

"Great! Where are we going?"

"Myakka River State Park," said the woman, applying sunblock.

"Myakka! I've been there a million times! Even escaped once," said Serge. "There's the boardwalk, the canopy bridge, the dam, country store, log cabins! At thirty-seven thousand acres, it's one of the largest Florida parks, developed by the Civilian Conservation Corps and dedicated 1941. It thins the tourist crowd down to only the most worthy because the attraction is nothing but nature just rippin' out there! I'll get my camera! . . . Coleman! . . ."

Something had caught Coleman's attention, and he was drifting over toward a pair of retirees standing behind the bus.

"What's that bozo doing now to attract attention?" Serge waddled over in his duck suit.

Coleman slipped an old man a ten-dollar bill. "Thanks." A

blue pill was furtively exchanged in a handshake. He popped it in his mouth and started back toward the Falcon.

"What the hell are you doing?" asked Serge.

"Retirees rule!" Coleman pointed behind him as another old man joined the candid meeting behind the bus. "They're doing drug deals!"

"Coleman, you realize it's simply a black market in Viagra?" said Serge. "It's going on at almost every retirement community in the state."

"Viagra?"

"Another thing that burns my ass," said Serge. "Not the pills themselves, but the men in charge of the system; another shame to my gender!"

"How so?"

"A lot of insurance companies cover Viagra while at the same time excluding birth control, even though a pregnancy would cost them much more. Why would they do such a counter-intuitive thing, you ask?"

"I didn't understand all the words," said Coleman.

"Insurance executives correctly figure that if a woman is responsible enough to seek birth control, she'll buy it anyway. You'd think the same reasoning would apply to Viagra. But if Viagra increases the chance of pregnancy, who cares? They've already passed that cost along to the women."

"Dear God, how is that allowed to happen?" asked Coleman.

"It's the composition of the people making the decisions," said Serge. "Let me put it another way. Can you imagine an exclusively female boardroom: 'Yeah, denying birth control coverage is a shitty thing to do to our sisters, but we're running a business here after all. On the other hand, excluding Viagra? That's just crazy talk!'"

"Never thought of it that way," said Coleman.

"You took the pill, didn't you?"

"Sort of."

"Congratulations, you're sort of pregnant." Serge checked the memory on his digital camera. "Just keep your shirt untucked and don't bump into people."

One of the old guys from the bus ambled over. "Hey, Serge!" He glanced around suspiciously, then held out a prescription bottle. "Need anything? It's on me."

"I don't mean to brag," said Serge, "but that would be over-kill. It's why I can't read historic markers when there are children around."

"If you change your mind . . ."

Time went by. People began to sweat.

"That's it!" yelled Serge. "We're leaving on the field trip!"

"But our driver isn't here yet."

"Yes, he is," said Serge, climbing in behind the steering wheel.

"But you're not allowed to drive the shuttle bus."

Serge waved feathers. "I'm authorized."

Chapter 27

STATE ROAD 72

A shuttle bus sped east on a two-lane road through pasture-
land. Serge held the steering with one hand, and the other
waved a wing over his head like an orchestra conductor. The passengers swayed back and forth.

"...*The wheels on the bus go round and round... round and
round...*"

"Serge..."

"What, Coleman?"

"Uh, I've got a problem over here."

Serge turned. "That's disgusting." He placed the duck's head
on Coleman's lap.

Fifteen minutes later, a shuttle bus pulled up to the park rangers'
station.

"...*Ninety-nine bottles of beer on the wall...*"

Serge got out his wallet to pay the admission. "I'm authorized. Pay no attention to the duck head. Any questions?"

The shuttle bus drove along the southern lip of the lake and made its first stop at the bird-watchers' boardwalk. Serge charged down the wooden planks to the end and spun around. "I'm sure you're all new to this, so I'll just help you identify the wondrous assortment of species . . . Okay, that one over there is a little far away, but I think it's a heron—"

"Tricolored heron . . ."

"And there's a sandhill crane . . ."

"Black-necked stilt . . ."

Serge got out his camera. "Uh, very good . . ." He raised it toward an osprey.

All around him: *click, click, click, click, click . . .*

"Serge." Coleman walked up holding a duck head over his crotch. "They're taking more pictures than you do. And you take like a million."

"I know. I think I've found my people."

"A red-shouldered hawk . . ."

"Wood stork . . ."

"Limpkin . . ."

Click, click, click, click, click . . .

"Ibis . . ."

"Roseate spoonbill . . ."

They boarded the shuttle and took a tranquil, winding drive through a long tunnel of oaks draped with Spanish moss. Cameras out the window. *Click, click, click.*

"Stop the bus!"

Serge slammed the brakes and spun around. "What's the matter? Is everyone okay?"

"We're fine," said a woman up front, standing and adjusting her sun hat. Everyone else began standing as well, bunching toward the front of the shuttle. "Can you open the door?"

A curious Serge did as requested. "Bathroom break?"

"No, you almost missed the trail."

The bus emptied. "What's going on?" asked Coleman.

"I think they want to hike," said Serge. "Let's go."

The seniors had a good head start, and the pair trotted after them. Myakka boasts a wickedly healthy ecosystem with all manner of life fighting for elbow room. Serge and Coleman ran down a narrow, shaded path of dirt and leaves, snaking through a dense marsh with a vibrant green covering. Tree frogs, and insects dancing in the water, and oaks shrouded with ferns and moss. The two pals had almost caught up to the others in a stretch of scrub and hardwood hammock.

"Coleman, spiderweb."

"What? . . . *Ahhh!* Get it off me! Get it off me!"

"Home wrecker," said Serge. "Hold still."

"What is it?"

"You don't want to know." Serge watched the pointy yellow-and-black legs of an orb weaver creep onto Coleman's shoulder. He humanely brushed it off.

The seniors were still on the move, pulling granola bars and trail mix from fanny packs. *Click, click, click, click . . .*

"Now we have to catch up again."

They resumed trotting.

"How can old people hike like this?" said a panting Coleman. "I just threw up in my mouth."

"Maybe if you didn't have to hike with a duck head in front of you."

"I'm starting to get scared. The pill might not wear off."

The seniors had stopped at the foot of a wooden ladder and called behind them. "You coming?"

"Right there!" said Serge, muttering. "This stupid costume."

They were all one group again.

Coleman looked up. "Now we have to *climb?*"

"It's only twenty-five feet."

They reached a primitive wooden footbridge suspended by cables in the tree canopy.

Coleman seized the railing. "I think I'm still hungover."

"No, the bridge really is swaying. Check out our friends up ahead . . ."

Click, click, click, click, click . . .

"Pop ash . . ."

"Gold-foot ferns . . ."

"Shoelace ferns . . ."

"Butterfly orchids . . ."

"False pennyroyal . . ."

"Red blanket lichen . . ."

"What's this funky thing?" asked Coleman.

"Pineapple air plant," said a senior in a long-billed fishing hat. "They collect water in their bowls."

The retirees climbed another fifty feet up the observation tower for a panoramic view of the park's prairies and cypress domes.

"I'm staying down here," said Coleman, dropping the duck head and bending over to clutch his knees.

"Me too," said Serge. "I feel stupid around these people. They've forgotten more about nature than I'll ever know. On the other hand, I couldn't be happier. I knew seniors had the answers, but these people are amazing. How can I ever pay them back?" He snapped his fingers. "I know! I'll take them on a surprise second stop on this field trip! But first we'll have to go by the store . . . They're going to love this! . . ."

Two hours later, deeper into the state.

The giddy gang stood on the edge of an abandoned limestone quarry.

Serge demonstrated like a baseball coach. "You have to swing your arm like this. Let the momentum do the work."

A petite woman nodded. "I think I've got it."

"Then let her rip!"

A mild grunt as she threw.

Whoosh.

Quick steps backward. "My goodness!"

"Okay, I don't mean to be critical," said Serge. "But you need to heave it a little more downrange—"

"Dammit, Serge!" said Lawrence. "Don't you think this is a bit dangerous?"

Serge turned blankly. "What do you mean?"

"First flaming Brillo pads and all kinds of Roman candles, then giant slingshots made from inner tubes, and exploding bags of flour."

"I know! Ain't it great!"

"And now Molotov cocktails?"

"I specifically chose those little Coke bottles because I knew they couldn't throw that far."

"That last one almost went off at Gertrude's feet!"

"She didn't follow my instructions, but she'll get the hang of it." Serge turned and waved an arm toward the group. "Look, they're having the time of their lives! Not to mention learning important counter-insurgency skills."

"Give me the gasoline."

"Who's got the lighter?"

"All right. Here goes nothing!"

Grunt.

"Ooo, shit!"

"Just splash some water on it. My turn . . ."

"Serge!" said Lawrence.

"But I bought all these giant boxes of assorted fireworks that are the rage in Florida. See all the cool stuff through the cellophane display window? We've just gotten started."

Lawrence sighed. "Can you simply trust my judgment on this one and head back to the park?"

"Normally, I wouldn't do this," said Serge. "But because it's you, all right. I'll just hand out all these leftovers for the gang to use on their own time . . ."

E arl stepped out of the guard booth and waved at the passing shuttle bus full of foot-stomping residents.

"*. . . We will . . . we will . . . rock you! . . .*"

The residents debarked in the parking lot of the clubhouse, but they didn't disperse. It was the after-party. A trunk was popped and beer and wine handed out. Nothing remotely as wild as the other night. Just the park's regular sunset social after another fun-filled day on the planet. A few pointed skyward as a honking V formation of Canada geese flew overhead. All was good.

A lime-green MINI Cooper pulled into the parking lot, and the driver got out with a tray.

"Heather?" said Lawrence. "What are you doing here?"

"I baked cookies for your sunset gathering."

Coleman handed the duck head back to Serge. "I'm better now . . . Isn't that the swim girl?"

"Aqua-aerobics instructor, to be specific."

Coleman rubbed his stomach. "My body tells me it needs cookies . . ."

And so it went, friendship and laughs and a setting sun you couldn't pay for. As it went down, a few of the residents drifted toward the patio for a view out over the lake. They gathered along the railing.

It became still and quiet as the natural wonder of the glowing sky took hold. The least little sounds appreciated. A bullfrog, a cawing seagull, a plunk in the water from a turtle.

Then a new sound they hadn't heard before. Not very loud, just different. What was it? Where was it coming from? More residents meandered out onto the deck. The sound grew louder . . .

Ten minutes later, a wooden door opened. It was on the ply-wood shack that stored all the pool equipment.

Serge stepped out and hiked up his duck costume. He froze.

Staring back at him were two dozen completely silent residents of the park.

Serge spread wings. "What?" He headed back to his car.

The residents inched closer to see inside the dark shack.

Heather stumbled out with tousled hair, cleared her throat at the sight of the group, and walked away in the opposite direction. Two old guys in the back of the group slapped high fives.

The gathering continued a little longer and was about to break up.

Suddenly, back at the guard booth, Earl quickly raised the entrance gate.

An ambulance flew into the park.

The residents watched it race by the clubhouse. They'd seen it many times before, and they didn't speak. All eyes watched as the red-and-white vehicle rounded the lake and began slowing like a roulette wheel. Whose number was up this time?

Paramedics stopped in a driveway and ran inside.

"It's the Duncans," someone whispered.

"Ike and Judy?"

"They're so young."

And, as many times before, the onlookers had two silent questions: *Which one, and how bad?*

The second answer came first, when the coroner's wagon entered the park, followed by three police cars.

The group migrated to the near side of the clubhouse to continue their grave vigil on the pool deck. Two hours later, a stretcher came out, and the sheet was all the way up over whoever was underneath.

Residents said prayers inside their heads.

Then a second stretcher came out.

Two? This they had never seen before. The collective thought: *What's going on?*

More vehicles arrived. First, the unmarked cars with the detectives, then a van: CRIME SCENE INVESTIGATION.

Speculation took off like a grease fire. *"Murder-suicide? Nah, not the Duncans."* *"Robbery? Here? Are you kidding?"* *"Revenge? Who didn't like them?"*

And right when the intrigue seemed to have maxed out, a cobalt-blue Buick Regal pulled up to the guard booth.

"Earl, are you okay?" asked the driver. "You look like you've seen a ghost."

Earl opened his mouth, but nothing came out.

"What's going on. You're acting really strange."

Earl just raised the gate. The driver shrugged and drove into the park.

The crowd at the railing of the swim deck was still riveted on the trailer with all the emergency vehicles. Someone on the edge of the crowd nudged the person next to him, pointing at the Buick slowly rounding the man-made lake. Then that person nudged the next, until word swept down the entire railing in seconds.

The trailer was ignored, as all eyes now followed the blue car.

"Doesn't that belong to the Duncans?"

"But if they're alive in the car, then who . . . ?"

Chapter 28

BOCA SHORES

The residents solemnly watched the Buick approach the scene. A police officer stepped into the road and held out a hand for them to halt. He walked around to the driver's window and shook his head, pointing for them to go back. Then the driver showed his license, and the officer turned toward his colleagues with an urgent waving gesture.

Two detectives rushed over to the car. The couple was courteously escorted over to one of the unmarked Crown Vics and placed in the backseat. The detectives got in the front. The car sat.

Back behind the clubhouse: "What are they doing?"

"Looks like they're being questioned." A woman raised bird-watching binoculars. "One of the detectives is taking notes."

The residents at the patio railing began a fierce volleyball game of conjecture. *"Murder suspects? Nah, not the Duncans . . ."* Nobody was going anywhere. Not missing any of this.

A half hour later, the doors on the Crown Vic opened. Paramedics knelt down outside the car and gave the retired couple a quick checkup, considering the wholesale shock of all they had just been told. Stethoscopes listened, and blood-pressure bulbs pumped. The couple turned down the two Xanax tablets they were offered. The EMTs stood and gave them a clean bill.

The detectives were deferential again as they walked the couple back to their Buick. They were handed business cards and asked if they could avoid traveling out of town for the next few days.

Ike and Judy Duncan got back in the front seat. The car started, but didn't move for a few minutes.

One of the detectives walked back over. "Is everything okay?"

Ike slowly looked toward all the crime scene activity flowing in and out of his trailer. He turned back to the detective. "No."

"I understand," the detective said sympathetically. "It's still sinking in. Please call the number on my card if you need anything, day or night."

The Buick began moving and hit a peak five miles an hour as it passed the swimming pool, and everyone scrambled toward that side of the deck. The car eased over into the nearest parking space at the clubhouse and sat still again. Residents came pouring around the side of the building and surrounded it.

"Can everyone move back and give them some air," said Lawrence. "They've been through a lot."

The Duncans stepped out of the car. They were happy to be among all their friends. At a time like this, it's what they needed. And their friends needed answers. But they just didn't want to push. "Would you like us to get you anything? Water?"

A resident pointed with his cane. "What the hell is that?"

Fiercely bright spotlights came on along the road outside the park, the closest that Earl would allow the satellite trucks.

"The reporters are here," said Lawrence. "Let's get the Duncans in the clubhouse so they can relax."

They entered the hall, and the large-screen TV was on next to the bingo board. Local news.

"... *This is Veronica Dance reporting outside the sleepy retirement village of Boca Shores near Sarasota, where police have just discovered the bodies of two senior citizens who appear to be the victims of a grisly double homicide...*"

On-screen, a 1996 DeVille with grocery bags filling the backseat approached the park's entrance. One of the residents simply returning from an uneventful trip to the supermarket. The car slowed at the guard booth, and Veronica ran over with her microphone.

"*Excuse me, how do you feel about the murders in your quiet retirement park?*"

"Murders?"

"*Are you worried that the killers might strike again?*"

"Killers?"

A camera aimed into the backseat.

"*What's in the bags?*"

"Leave us alone!"

The car raced inside the park, and Earl came out to block the camera lens with his hands.

The news crew retreated back across the street without breaking narration. "*Often a pair of deaths in one of Florida's retirement communities turns out to be a mercy killing due to a long-suffering terminal disease, followed by the suicide of the surviving spouse. But a confidential police source is telling me that has been ruled out, as both victims sustained trauma—*"

Inside the clubhouse, Judy Duncan began sobbing inconsolably into her hands.

"Someone turn that goddamn TV off!"

"*... Who could be the next victim of these savage night stalkers? Sarasota, lock your doors!...*"

A plug was jerked from a wall socket, and the flat screen zapped to black.

Ike put an arm around his wife's shoulders as she raised her tearful face. "I can't believe this is happening."

As gently as Lawrence could: "Do you have a place to stay tonight?"

"No," said Judy.

"Then you're staying with us."

"We don't want to impose."

From the surrounding crowd: *"We're all your family." "We're here for you." "Do we need to run to the store for anything?"*

Ike shook his head.

A door opened and a bright spotlight filled the hall. *". . . Are you hunkering down in here in terror? . . ."*

Earl yanked the TV people back outside and slammed the door.

"I— . . . I— . . ." Judy covered her mouth.

"You don't have to talk if you don't want to," said Serge.

"No, I need to get it out." She placed trembling palms on a table. "We just flew back into Sarasota-Bradenton and picked up our car from long term. It was such a great time, a family wedding up in Braintree, Massachusetts, that we decided to stretch into a weeklong reunion. All the grandchildren were there. And now we come home to this. Oh my God! The poor Baldwins!"

"Who are the Baldwins?" asked someone on a mobility scooter.

"Please," said Lawrence. "Let her go at her own speed."

"That's okay," said Judy. "Anyway, we were talking with some old friends before the trip. We've known the Baldwins since when, Ike? . . ."

"Before I was in the army."

". . . We kept telling them how beautiful Florida is, and they should visit. But they said they couldn't afford it. I told them, nonsense, they could stay at our house for the week while we were up at the wedding. That we'd spend another week together when we got back. We were all looking forward to it, catching up on old times, the whole thing planned, shopping at Saint Armands Circle, visiting Mote Marine, the botanical gardens, a sunset cruise, and Mel always loved golf, but all the courses are frozen up there right now. I said everyone plays year-round down here, and that convinced him—" A hand went to her mouth again. "Dear Lord! If I hadn't mentioned the golf, they might still be . . . still be—"

More sobbing.

"You can't be doing this to yourself," said Lawrence. "There's nothing anyone could have foreseen or done."

"I realize," said Judy. "I'm just thinking of all the other times we spent together. You know how two couples have that chemistry? Now I'll never see them again." She turned her head toward a blank wall.

Lawrence stood and faced the rest of the group. "I think it would be best now if we got them over to my house so they can wind down from this."

Everyone nodded and stepped backward to loosen their human circle of stress.

They left the hall, and good old Earl was already waiting outside with a six-seater golf cart. They climbed in, and he pressed the pedal for silent electric power.

Ike looked back at his Buick. "What about our luggage? There's valuables."

"I'll grab it after I drop you off," said Earl. "You just take your mind off everything this evening."

They made their way inside the Shepards' trailer, tentatively, like walking on the moon.

"Just make yourself comfortable on the couch . . ." Nancy's voice trailed off as she entered the kitchen. "Can I get you anything?"

"I don't have an appetite," said Ike.

"Me neither," said Judy.

"When was the last time you ate?"

"Lunch," said Judy. "More like brunch."

"You have to eat something. I insist."

Nancy prevailed on the concept of soup. They sat around the kitchen table with steaming New England clam chowder. Large spoons clinked bowls, a clock ticked.

Ike and Judy exchanged a knowing look. *They guaranteed us that this could never happen. We can't tell anybody.*

Chapter 29

Trailer-park residents began filing into the clubhouse hall shortly after noon.

Folding chairs had already been arranged in a grid for their viewing pleasure, facing the large-screen TV on the front wall. Some residents brought cushions, others entire chairs, because the stiff plastic ones provided by the park weren't all that.

Serge entered the hall with his trademark zest for another day breathing on earth. "What's on the menu?"

"Our regular Wednesday matinee movie," said one of the regulars.

"Oooo! I love movies!" said Serge. "Which one is it? . . . No, let me guess. *The Graduate*? *Blue Velvet*? *Last Tango in Paris*? *Birth of a Nation*? *City of God*? *The Third Man*? *Fellini Satyricon*? Truffaut's *400 Blows*? Kurosawa's *Dreams*? *This Is Spinal Tap*? *E.T.*? Am I close?"

"We're watching *Cocoon*."

"*Cocoon*?"

"It's a coming-of-age film."

"I love *Cocoon*!" said Serge. "One of my all-time favorites! I need one of those pod things! . . . Coleman, we're watching *Cocoon*!"

A drone of happy conversation filled the seating area. Then the volume ramped down until there was silence. And it wasn't because the movie was about to start. Everyone was now staring at the side door, where Ike and Judy Duncan had just entered the room. They took seats on the end of a row and looked ahead. Then everyone else realized the silence was awkward and started talking again.

"I never expected to see them here," a neighbor whispered to Lawrence.

"There's no anticipating how each person will react to grief," he replied. "Some people need a distraction like this to occupy their minds or they'll dwell into a spiral. All things considered, they were in pretty healthy spirits this morning. I think this is a good thing."

A tap on Coleman's shoulder. "What?"

A whisper. "Got any more weed?"

"Yeah, sure."

"Great. We have a few minutes before the movie starts," said a resident with a walker. "I want to see this movie in a whole new light."

"This shit's so good, it'll be 3-D with Dolby surround sound," said Coleman. "Let's go out to the pool deck."

The pair left the hall, and ten other residents got up from their chairs and followed.

"What can possibly go wrong?" said Serge, watching them

leave as he took a seat next to Lawrence in the back row. He uncapped a travel mug of coffee.

Minutes later, the film began as Wilford Brimley arrived at a retirement community in a vintage Cadillac.

"I'm crazy about this movie!" said Serge. "It sets the record straight on Florida retirees! Did you know it was shot almost entirely on location in Tampa Bay back in 1985? And Brimley was actually only forty-nine at the time and had to dye his hair gray, so it's not much of a stretch that Coleman and I can jump into the good life. I'm just saying . . ."

The film progressed with a silently attentive audience in the darkness, especially those who'd come in from the pool deck.

"Do you see the nautical chart that Brian Dennehy is showing Steve Guttenberg to find the cocoons at the bottom of the bay?" asked Serge. "You can actually see where the chart says Panama City at the top, if you freeze the frame and get your face right up to the TV set. That's what I did. It jazzed my world . . ."

A few more scenes passed.

"That's the pool house, where the old guys swim with the cocoons for the first time and get stiffies and go home to their wives, and, well . . . It's really a love story," said Serge. "The pool house where they filmed it is located over on Boca Ciega Bay and was just a slapped-together Hollywood set, but the homeowners liked it so much they constructed a permanent one after the movie cats left town . . ."

Someone turned around. *"Shhhhhh!"*

"Do you always talk this much during movies?" asked Lawrence.

"Yes!"

"Can you stop?"

"I can try." Serge sat on his hands and pursed his lips. "How was that? The cast had their wrap party at the Dalí Museum . . ."

The movie proceeded toward its climax. Serge sat with his mouth open as the coast guard chased the retirees' boat through a tropical storm until it was beamed up into a spaceship. "Can you imagine working on the metro desk of a newspaper *that* night?..."

The credits rolled to thunderous applause.

Then a slow-motion stampede.

"Where's everyone going?" asked Serge.

"To the shuttle bus," said Lawrence.

"Another field trip?" Serge clapped like a grade schooler, then joined the exodus.

The official driver was waiting, and Serge handed him a C-note. "You're in retirement."

The bus filled and the door closed. Serge bounced in his seat behind the steering wheel. "Where to today?"

One of the passengers leaned forward and handed him a list.

"What this?"

"Local filming locations from *Cocoon*. That's why we watched it just before today's trip."

Another resident nodded. "So we could get all amped up before seeing the real places."

"Wait a second..." said a momentarily stunned Serge. "You mean you researched the movie to find these filming sites? You dig visiting authentic Florida spots where the state made iconic celluloid history?"

Another resident held up a camera. "And taking lots of pictures."

Serge clutched Coleman's shoulder, digging in fingernails.

"Ow," said his pal. "What's the matter? Are you okay?"

"These people are all my soul mates."

The vehicle started up and so did the singing.

"... *Don't stop ... thinking about tomorrow!* ..."

The latter-day Ken Kesey bus crested the 430-foot-high peak of the Sunshine Skyway Bridge over the mouth of Tampa Bay.

"... *If I had a hammer* ..."

Serge kept glancing in the rearview.

Coleman snuck a swig from a flask. "What are you looking at?"

"That Impala's been back there for a while."

"You think we're being followed?"

"I don't know," said Serge. "We may have a tail. Or it might be my habit of playing make-believe spy."

They reached the bottom of the bridge and took the exit for Fifth Avenue North. Serge checked the mirror. "The Impala went the other way. But it was fun while it lasted."

The bus slowed as it drove along the waterfront homes on Park Street. "Remember to show respect because this is a private residence," said Serge. "As much as I want to swim in that pool, we must defend the social code . . . Fire away!"

Serge slowed the bus to a crawl and lenses poked out the window.

Click, click, click, click, click . . .

"God, I love that sound," said Serge. "It sounds like . . ." He sniffed the air. "Victory."

From there it was a mad dash around the county.

"*. . . Go, Serge, go! . . .*"

The bus approached 125 Fifty-Sixth Avenue South.

"Coming up on your right is the Westminster Shores retirement community, which was named Sunny Acres in the movie, home base for the gang. Funky tidbit: The sign in the movie retained the actual address . . . You'll notice there's been major work and the resemblance is lost, but it's still a solid spiritual stop on our tour . . ."

Click, click, click, click, click . . .

Serge double-checked the mirror.

"What now?" asked Coleman.

"That Jeep's been back there awhile . . ."

They cruised down to 405 Central Avenue.

"And here's the Rutland Building, home of the old Snell Arcade from the post-coital shopping-spree scene . . . The Jeep is gone. You weren't supposed to hear that last part . . ."

Click, click, click, click, click . . .

The shuttle screeched around the corner. "Saint Petersburg holds the *Guinness* record for most consecutive days of sunshine at seven hundred and sixty-eight, hence its nickname, the 'Sunshine City.' To tout this tourism headline, the city's first newspaper, the *Evening Independent,* enacted its famous 'Sunshine Offer' in 1910 that gave away free papers on any day the sun didn't shine. From then until it folded in 1986, it only had to make good on the promotion less than three hundred times. I know that's a lot of math, so see me later if problems arise . . . Now we've picked up a Lexus . . ."

"How many cars are following us?" asked Coleman.

"Either three or zero depending on my mental state," said Serge.

"But they can't be following us," said Coleman. "You're only spotting them one at a time."

"That's how the best spies work. They switch out cars so you don't know you're being followed," said Serge. "Either these guys are really good or they're just guys."

The shuttle bus rounded the serene park at Mirror Lake in downtown St. Petersburg.

"*. . . Go, Serge, go! . . .*"

"Soon appearing on your left with its trademark green-and-white paint scheme is the home of another memorable *Cocoon* scene, the Saint Petersburg Shuffleboard Club, founded in 1924. The world's oldest and largest. If you don't believe me, when have you ever seen stadium seating *at a shuffleboard court? . . .*"

The bus stopped. *Click, click, click, click, click . . .*

"This cathedral to old Florida fell into nasty neglect as young people basically said fuck shuffleboard, but a heroic fund-raising effort in 2008 restored the ruins to its former glory. Please visit when in town to live the history. That last part was for our home audience . . . The Lexus is gone."

Click, click, click, click, click . . .

The shuttle pulled into a parking lot on Fifth Avenue.

"And last but not least, one final stop on the tour. Also constructed in 1924, the fabulous Coliseum, known far and wide and without exaggeration as the Finest Ballroom in the South." Serge stood to face his passengers. "And according to this list I was given, they're having an afternoon tea dance right now, complete with the big-band sounds you all know and love! Shall we? . . ."

Serge stood outside the door and extended an arm to assist exiting passengers. He noticed that more than a few had tiny coolers. "What are those for?"

A woman reached the pavement. "These tea dances are BYOB."

"Now they're my soul mates, too," said Coleman. "Serge, what's that look on your face?"

"There's an Impala again."

"Where?"

"Don't be conspicuous, but it's parked a block up the street on the other side," said Serge. "Except there's no possible way it can be the same one."

Coleman used his right hand as a sun visor over his eyes and craned his neck toward the road.

"Thanks, Captain Obvious. Let's go inside . . ."

The pair brought up the rear of the gang entering the majestic, cavernous space featuring curved wooden roof beams strung with cabaret-style lightbulbs. The dance floor looked identical to the one showcased by Don Ameche, Tyrone Power Jr., and Maureen Stapleton.

The music was already under way as the residents of Boca Shores began gracefully twirling their partners across the venerable wood.

Serge twirled Coleman.

"This feels weird."

"It's the Coliseum," said Serge. "We're required to dance."

Coleman looked up at the arched ceiling. "I have to admit this is a pretty cool place."

"That's what I'm talking about!" Serge spun Coleman again.

"First, the big shuffleboard complex we were just at, and now this grande dame ballroom, both almost a century old. There's fantastic history to be found all around us if you're just paying attention, but most people are looking at their phones."

"How did you first get so into old people anyway?"

"It was a specific, vivid moment in time." Serge dipped his partner. "About ten years ago I was strolling around Mirror Lake without a soul in sight."

"The one we passed by the shuffleboard place?"

"The water's surface remained perfectly still like glass, and I was in an odd state. I wouldn't say glum, more like pensive. And as I circled the shore, I heard faint music, like a radio station from the forties. I was drawn to the source, continuing my way around the lake. And next door was a retirement home. It was a balmy Sunday afternoon, and the doors and windows were propped open to let in the breeze. As I drew closer, I heard big-band music coming from one of the doors. I was still about twenty yards away, but I could see inside. A handful of couples were dancing, just like they are here, except on a much smaller floor. And I don't know why, but I locked on to this one couple. They were easily in their eighties, dancing slowly near the front of the room. The thing that caught me was their eyes. They were gazing into each other's like nothing else in the world mattered. And I tried to imagine everything contained in those gazes: two lifetimes of thousands of wonderful moments spent together that led to this one. Marriage is hard, believe me. But these two were now more in love than the day they first fell for each other. They didn't have much time left on this rocky planet, and it didn't matter. They'd gotten life all figured out, and nothing was as important as *right now*."

"Man, that's a fucked-up story," said Coleman.

"Because we don't have it figured out," said Serge. "I continued watching them dance in slow circles, still gazing with the hugest smiles. They were in a place of pure, distilled happiness. And as my eyes followed them across the dance floor, I suddenly realized that I had the biggest smile, too. I was drawing off them. Their happiness was filling my body."

"That's called a contact buzz," said Coleman.

"Okay, let's try not to ruin this with drugs," said Serge. "Anyway, I remember straining to capture that moment, which I stored in the happy box inside my heart. Ever since then, when mundane shit starts skewing my mood toward negativity, I'll open my box and take that memory out for a look, and all is right in life."

"I'm getting tired of dancing." Coleman pointed. "I want to drink with that couple. The little cooler on their table is *my* happy box."

"Go for it," said Serge. "I need to do something."

Coleman went his way, and Serge returned to the front of the Coliseum. He climbed a staircase to the balcony overlooking the dance floor. Then he grabbed a chair and sat by himself, watching the couples from Boca Shores sway and spin and gaze into each other's eyes.

A smile broadened across his face.

Serge was adding something to his happy box.

C oleman!"

"What?"

"Wheels up!" said Serge. "That means lift your head from the table."

Coleman's big melon rose from the wood. A mat of stray hair. "What's going on?"

Serge looked toward the front doors, where seniors were filing out of the ballroom. "We're leaving now. You're the sole deadweight."

"Okay, let me get it together . . ."

The rest were all in the shuttle bus when Serge guided Coleman up the steps.

A big cheer went up. *"He lives! . . ."*

Coleman looked confused at his buddy. "I don't remember anything. What happened in there?"

"You tried to break-dance like Don Ameche in *Cocoon*," said Serge.

"But I don't know how to break-dance."

"We're all now keenly aware of that," said Serge. "There was some table and chair damage that I had to cover."

The bus pulled out of the parking lot.

". . . Sweet Caroline! . . . Oh! . . . Oh! . . . Oh! . . ."

Serge drove east toward Tampa Bay, then up North Shore Drive. A heated movie discussion about *Cocoon* swept the bus.

"I would have gone on the spaceship."

"Not me."

"Are you kidding?"

"I don't need to live forever."

"I do!"

"And never see the grandchildren?"

"They don't write as it is."

"What if it's clammy and my sweats get worse?"

"We're clammy here."

"It could be a ruse, and they end up experimenting on your organs while you're awake. Who knows what kind of people these are?"

"It's worth a shot."

"Please direct your attention to that park on the right side of the street and the old men in the long white pants," said Serge. "That's Saint Pete's famous senior softball league, where you have to be at least seventy-five to join. Quite amazing to watch. There's only one major rule change: no sliding."

The shuttle bus headed south into downtown. "On our way home I'd like to sprinkle in some bitchin' history. And one cool thing about Saint Pete is they like to keep the past alive when naming stuff. Ready? Who's with me?"

". . . Go, Serge, go! . . ."

"This is First Avenue, and that brick building with the giant courtyard is Jannus Landing, home of outrageous open-air rock concerts. It was named after Tony Jannus, the aviator who started the nation's first scheduled airline flights from here to Tampa in 1914. And part of the venue is a joint called Club Detroit. Why is it called that, you ask? . . . Go ahead, ask."

"*. . . Why, Serge? . . .*"

"I'll tell you!" He made a right turn on Central Avenue. "Believe it or not, there was a fifty-fifty chance that this city would be called Detroit! Totally true! The co-founders flipped a coin for the naming rights. The winner, Peter Demens, picked the city in Russia where he'd spent some of his youth. The loser, John Williams, got to name the city's first building after his birthplace. Please look out your left windows at the illustrious Detroit Hotel, constructed in 1888, playground of such notables as Franklin Roosevelt, Will Rogers and Babe Ruth. Now it's gone condo with rumors of demolition. Let's pray . . ."

The shuttle headed back south toward the Sunshine Skyway Bridge. Serge's eyes were on the rearview.

"Are we being followed again?" asked Coleman.

"Yes."

Coleman turned around. "Which one?"

"All of them."

"But we're in traffic."

"That's right." Serge adjusted the mirror. "All traffic is following us. Just because they don't know they're following us doesn't mean they're not."

"And I thought weed made *me* paranoid."

"I think seeing that Impala got me rattled. I need to think of something mellow," said Serge. "Everyone, look out the right side at the bridge's railing, where you'll see a series of a half-dozen special phones. What are they? Suicide-prevention hotlines for people who've lost the last ribbon of hope and want to jump and splat themselves. Isn't that great? . . ."

The bus finally arrived back at Boca Shores, and Earl waved them through.

They all collected in the clubhouse parking lot, stretching and yawning.

"... *Time for a nap* ..."

"... *I need my medicine* ..."

"... *Check it out! They took down the crime scene tape at the Duncans'* ..."

Indeed, they had.

"Looks like you can sleep at home tonight," said Lawrence.

"I better check with the police first," said Ike, pulling out the detective's business card and dialing a cell phone. "Yes, this is Mr. Duncan from Boca Shores. You said I could call day or night ... Well, I noticed the tape is down at my house ... What? It's clear? We can go back in? ... You tried to tell me today? Six times? ..." He held out the phone and adjusted his reading glasses. "Oh, I have six missed calls. That must be you ... Okay, thanks." *Click.*

"Sounds like you're good to go," said Lawrence. "Think you're ready?"

"More than ready," said Ike. "Between the vacation and last night, I want nothing more than to sleep in my own bed."

The couple climbed into their Buick Regal.

Everyone else felt relief that the Duncans seemed to be bouncing back, but there was still the whiff of concern. They waved as the Buick left the lot, rounded the lake and pulled into their carport.

The sun began to set over the aluminum roofs as the rest of the residents dispersed back to their own trailers.

Hours later, a regular evening phenomenon that you could set your watch by: One by one, the mobile homes' lights went dark in a specific sequence according to respective circadian rhythms.

Finally, they were all out, except for the dim, bluish glow from an insomniac's TV showing a blizzard in Buffalo.

Lawrence sat up in bed. "Did you hear that?"

"What?" asked a groggy Nancy.

"I'm not sure," said her husband. "I think something woke me up."

Ding-dong...

Nancy grabbed the bedside alarm clock. "Who can it be at this hour?"

Lawrence swung pajama legs over the side of the bed. "I'll find out."

He padded his way through the trailer, switched on the porch light and peeked. Then he quickly opened up.

"Ike! Judy!" He urgently unlocked the screen door. "What on earth are you doing over here?"

Chapter 30

MIDNIGHT

J udy had to take a seat in one of the porch chairs. "It was just too soon."

"We thought we were ready," said Ike. "But we got in there and lay down with just our thoughts, and it was way too creepy."

"People were just killed in there," said Judy. "People we knew."

"As soon as we got in bed and turned off the lights, the whole room glowed with that stuff the police spray to look for blood," said Ike. "How can anyone go to sleep like that?"

"We're sorry to impose," said Judy.

"You know you're always welcome here." Lawrence stared out at the dark lake, where fat raindrops began to plunk. "And it looks like you made it just in time."

They all took seats on the porch to relax and take in the

weather show. The sky began to flash again. A few other still-awake residents emerged onto their porches.

"When we first moved in, this lightning stuff spooked me." Judy rocked in her swinging patio chair. "Now I look forward to it."

"Me too," said Ike. "Just as long as I have surge protectors on everything, it's relaxing."

A streak of light crackled sideways across the sky, then a second. Clouds glowed and pulsed on the horizon.

There was a faraway pop.

"Transformer." Ike nodded to himself. "I can always tell now."

Porch chairs continued rocking. Lawrence got up and grabbed the handle on the glass door. "Would you like something to drink?"

"I'm good," said Ike.

"Maybe a little orange juice?" asked Judy.

"You got it." Lawrence went inside and bent down in front of the refrigerator. "There you are . . ." He pulled out a carton and began pouring.

A louder pop, and lights in the trailer flickered.

"Transformer." Lawrence set the carton down. "That one was really close—"

Then:

Boom!

A glass of orange juice shattered on the floor. "Okay, that was no transformer."

He raced back to the porch. Everyone was on their feet. And not just his porch, but every single one in the park. Even those where the residents hadn't been sitting out to take in the storm.

The lake flickered bright orange from the reflection across the way. On the other side of the water at the Duncans' trailer, a blue Buick Regal lay in pieces. What hadn't been blown apart was now fully engulfed in flames, licking at the roof of the carport and beginning to set the mobile home on fire.

"What the hell?" said Lawrence.

"Maybe lightning hit the gas tank?" said his wife.

Lawrence turned to see an ashen, trembling couple. "Geez, are you okay?"

"Why don't we all go back inside?" said Nancy.

Soon sirens streamed into the park. The fire department quickly had the hoses going, and two brave souls with air tanks and flashlights ran into the smoke for the bedrooms. They quickly dashed back out and pulled off their masks.

"Well?" asked their chief.

They shook their heads.

"They're gone?" said the chief.

"Yes, literally. The house is empty."

The rest of the team quickly sprayed down the flames. Photo albums and other sentimentals might be salvaged, but otherwise a total loss.

Then more drama as the police arrived. There was excited pointing and other gestures between the officers and firefighters. Unmarked cars screeched up, and detectives joined the scrum. They got on the radio for reinforcements.

Minutes later, an official van pulled up to the house.

Lawrence rubbed his chin. "The bomb squad?"

Earl was out in the road, holding back the TV trucks. More flashing lights poured through the entrance. Someone in thick armor and what looked like a welding helmet approached the Buick's smoldering chassis. Phones were ringing around the park. Rumors.

"Ike," said Lawrence. "Can I have a word inside?"

"Uh, sure."

They went into the kitchen nook and lowered voices. "What's going on?"

"I don't know," said Ike.

"I've known you for a while, and all of this would have been incredible if I hadn't seen it for myself," said Lawrence. "First your houseguests and now this. It's too much of a coincidence.

Either you have some serious enemies, or this is a terrible case of mistaken identity, but either way we need to go over to the police right now."

"No!"

Lawrence looked down at his right arm, where Ike had seized him. "Tell me what you're not telling me."

"I can't right now."

"Are you and Judy in some kind of trouble?"

"Yes."

"That settles it," said Lawrence. "If you won't go the police, then I will."

"Please don't! It's much bigger trouble than that." Ike fell into a chair. "I'll tell you everything. I just have to collect myself first. It's a long story, so for right now, promise me you won't go to the police or tell anyone else we're here. For the moment we're safe. People think we died in the fire."

Lawrence pointed in the direction of the trailer. "The authorities already know you weren't home."

"But the people who did this don't. Not yet. And even when the authorities announce that nobody died, the culprits might think it's disinformation, a cover-up."

Lawrence dropped into his own chair. "This is way too much intrigue for me."

Red and blue lights filled the kitchen as a dozen more patrol cars rounded the lake and parked at various points. The first hours would be the most critical.

Lawrence went to the window. "Cops are starting to knock on doors."

"They're canvassing," said Ike. "Get Judy in here."

Lawrence slid the door open and calmly asked the two women to come inside. "Ike, Judy, go in the spare bedroom and close the door and don't come out till I say."

"What's going on?" asked Nancy.

Lawrence stared down the hall until he'd confirmed they were safely in place. He led his wife to the couch. "I don't know, but it's something serious. Ike's so scared he's afraid to go to the police."

"That's nonsense," said Nancy. "If it's something that bad, then they *have* to go to the police."

"You didn't see his face," said Lawrence. "Until he tells me the full story, I'm going to abide by his wishes. We can always approach the authorities later, but if he's right about whatever he's hiding, then that's a bell we won't be able to un-ring."

"I don't know—"

He grabbed her hands in both of his. "Will you trust me?"

"Okay, but I'm not a very good actor—"

Ding-dong...

Lawrence went out on the porch. "Yes, Officer?"

"Sorry to bother you at this late hour, but may I come in and ask you a few questions?" said a corporal.

"No problem at all. How can I help?"

They made use of the patio furniture.

"The other neighbors said you were close to the Duncans..."

"Yes, very close."

"When was the last time you saw them?"

"This afternoon on our field trip to Saint Petersburg. We said good-bye outside the bus at the clubhouse."

"Have you seen or heard anything from them since..." The corporal glanced across the lake.

"Wait. What?" said Lawrence. "They're still alive? I was just assuming the worst."

"Unfortunately, I can't say anything because it's early in the investigation," said the officer. "Is your wife up?"

"Who?"

"Your wife. Is she awake?"

"Um, uh, sure."

Lawrence stepped inside the glass door and didn't expect the corporal to follow, but there he was in the living room. "Honey, can you come here?"

"What is it?"

He quickly hugged her. "You're not going to believe this, but the Duncans are alive!"

"Really?"

"The officer can't say anything official . . . Isn't that right? . . ."

The corporal nodded.

". . . But I read between the lines. They weren't home."

Nancy gasped. "Oh my God." Then she glanced down the hall before crying into her hands. "They're alive! They're alive!"

Jesus, Lawrence thought. *That really* is *bad acting.* But the corporal seemed not to notice because of the uncomfortable nature of the moment.

"Ahem, I know this is difficult," said the cop. "But time is of the essence. Have your friends had any recent visitors? Someone new, not known to you?"

They shook their heads.

"Any changes in their behavior lately? Seemed jumpy or nervous?"

"You know," said Nancy, "they did appear worried yesterday."

Lawrence: *What are you doing? Just shake your head no again.*

"Worried?" asked the officer, flipping open a notepad.

"Yes, they wanted to cash in some CDs, but there was an issue about their taxes."

"That's it?"

She nodded.

The corporal closed his pad. "Here's my business card. Please call if you remember something, even if it seems insignificant. Sorry again for the intrusion. I'll let myself out."

"Anything to help the police," said Nancy.

The screen door closed and the officer moved on to the next trailer.

Nancy turned to her husband. "What's that look you're giving me?"

"What was that business about the CDs?"

"I didn't think he was buying it," said Nancy. "I wanted to make it believable."

"*Un*-believable," said Lawrence, heading down the hall and stopping outside a closed door. "The officer's gone. You can come out now."

A muffled voice from behind the locked door. "We don't want to."

Ding-dong . . .

"Stay put," said Lawrence, trotting away. "Who now?" He slipped back onto the porch. "Serge! Coleman! What are you guys doing here?"

Serge bounded up the steps. "We came as soon as we heard. Is everyone okay? What about Nancy?"

"We're fine," said Lawrence.

Serge looked across the lake. Halting words. "Your . . . friends . . . ?"

"They're fine. Come inside, quick." They gathered near the sofa. "God only knows why, but right now I feel you're the only person I can talk to."

Serge smiled and raised his eyebrows. "Because I've become a good, trusted friend?"

"Because you're shady."

"Okay, among your tribe I guess that's the same as a trusted friend. What's on your mind?"

"We've got a situation. Have a seat."

"Lawrence, don't make me play twenty questions."

"I think someone is trying to kill the Duncans."

"I *know* someone is trying to kill the Duncans."

Lawrence's head pulled back in puzzlement. "You do?"

Serge nodded severely. "Textbook car bomb like that?"

"But how do you know it wasn't a lightning strike on the gas tank?"

"Because that's improbably rare. It would have to be a direct hit," said Serge. "But if I was going to build a car bomb, and I'm not saying I would, but it would be wired to the ignition." He pointed toward the wall socket next to the TV. "You have a surge suppressor. Excellent. When lightning hits nearby, it fills the air with static, gets into the power lines and shit. It doesn't even have to hit very close to knock out your cable shows."

"I'm not seeing where this is going."

"We've had a ridiculous electrical storm tonight. Any transformers blow?"

"A couple, like usual."

"The closest?"

"On one of the poles next street over behind . . . the Duncans'."

"Their car was probably rigged to blow when they started it up tomorrow," said Serge. "An ignition bomb trigger runs on a tiny amount of electricity, but it doesn't have a surge suppressor. Lucky for them, the static in the air from that nearby strike tripped it early."

"How do you know all this?"

"An excellent childhood." Serge clapped his hands a single time. "Now, what's the situation you mentioned?"

"This way." They walked down the hall, and Lawrence knocked again. "You can come out."

"We don't want to."

"Let me take a wild stab." Serge looked up at ceiling tiles and tapped his chin. "The Duncans?"

"They're in serious trouble. The kind where they can't go to the police."

"What other kind is there?" Serge stepped up and knocked harder on the door. "Please come out."

"Lawrence, who the hell's there with you?"

"Candygram," said Serge. "Special delivery."

"Everything's okay," Lawrence said through the door. "It's someone you can trust, although it might not initially appear that way."

An extended pause. "We're not coming out."

Serge knocked again. "I'll huff and I'll puff—"

"Will you quit that?" said Lawrence.

"Just trying to add levity."

"Ike, listen . . ." Lawrence's mouth was almost against the wood. After several minutes, he was able to alleviate the tension and talk the Duncans in off the ledge.

The door cautiously opened.

The ensuing gathering around the kitchen table was more bizarre than the most dysfunctional holiday dinner. Coleman's head was already down, his right cheek taking on the pattern of a place mat. Serge squeezed stress balls advertising an oral surgery center that was liberal with the nitrous oxide.

"I'll be direct," said Serge. "I'm not with the police or anyone else. *I follow nobody.* And I've been in jams like yours more than you'll ever know, so lay it on me, bro!"

Ike exhaled a hard sigh and grabbed his wife's hand. "Where do we start? It was the sixties and the country was tearing itself apart. If you think things are divided today, you weren't there. Revolutionaries bombing government buildings, students shot at Kent State. So we joined the anti-war movement and that's when we did some things we regret and everything went crazy."

"I get it," said Serge. "You were a couple of those flower children who pulled something idealistically stupid and ended up fugitives. They're still finding people on the run who robbed a bank in Fresno in '68 to fund the cause."

"I wish it were that simple," said Ike. "Everyone knows J. Edgar Hoover hated the hippies as well as Martin Luther King Jr., and it was an open secret he was trying to infiltrate the movements. So *we* infiltrated."

"You were FBI agents?"

"It was so easy," said Judy. "We started out by simply marching and waving signs at the demonstrations, and just like that they invited us in. Everybody was smoking dope, and the organizational meetings were *dis*organized meetings, playing records, drinking wine, voting whether to throw red paint on an army recruitment office."

"I don't get it," said Serge. "Then what's the big secret? Why were you acting all suspicious just now?"

"What Hoover hated even more than hippies were communists," said Ike. "Most of the agents infiltrating the meetings were looking to get dirt on the leaders of the war protests. But Judy and I had a special assignment. We weren't the only ones undercover. The Soviets also used agents to get inside the counter-culture, to stir things up. They had just as easy a time infiltrating as we did, probably easier. Our job was to infiltrate the KGB."

"Hold on," said Serge. "I need a program to keep track of the players. So the FBI sent you into the anti-war movement to cozy up to the Soviets, who were also sent to infiltrate the movement? . . . I guess it makes sense on a certain level."

"Worked like a charm," said Judy. "Some young guys with beards befriended us at a coffeehouse after a march. They asked how we felt about Cuba and Che Guevara and Karl Marx. We must have given all the right answers because they took us out to another protest that night. And then came the hardest part. The test. They gave us a Zippo lighter and told us to burn the American flag. Isn't that the entire mixed-up sixties in a nutshell? We had to burn the flag to stand up for the flag? Anyway, after we did that, they were convinced and recruited us."

"But here's where it gets really complicated," said Ike. "You think your head hurt before?"

"I'm already at the Complicated Party," said Serge. "Hit me!"

"The Soviets thought we were doing such a great job that they called us in and offered us a plum assignment: counter-intelligence."

"What's that mean?" asked Serge.

"They knew that the FBI was also infiltrating the war movement, so they asked us if we could infiltrate them," said Judy. "We became *triple* agents."

"Is that even a thing?" asked Serge.

"That's the spy world for you. Nobody trusting each other until it gets so convoluted you spend half your energy chasing your own tail. It became so ridiculous that I swear I thought there were no protesters at the meetings at all, just FBI and KGB reading bad poetry."

"I don't see the problem," said Serge. "You performed a noble service for your government."

"The problem is, it's a world of secrecy and wholesale lack of trust," said Ike. "If the Bureau asks you to go undercover, you become the subject of routine security checks. The Soviets were even worse. If they think you're really loyal, they'll ask you to infiltrate. Then, because you're infiltrating, they flag you as a loyalty risk because you might turn sides."

"It all came to a head the day we were walking down Flagler Drive in Miami. Broad daylight," said Judy. "A van pulled up, and these guys in ski masks snatched us off the street and sped away."

"Holy shit!" said Coleman. "Did they kill you?"

"Will you shut up?" Serge turned back to the couple. "Sorry about that. What happened?"

"It was our guys," said Ike. "They'd just received an imminent threat warning that we might be marked for assassination."

"The Soviets?"

Ike nodded. "Either they thought we'd defected to the Bureau or, just as bad, that we were about to be arrested, which they couldn't allow because by then we knew too much about their operation over here."

"Jesus." Serge leaned back in his chair. "At first glance, nobody would ever guess you were capable of leading such a life. Didn't mean anything bad by that."

"No offense taken," said Judy. "That's when they set us up with new identities. Our real name is Mulroney. We worked in a hardware store in Topeka, fish packers in Big Sur, a syrup bottler in Burlington, and too many others to mention, until we dropped anchor here. Nobody realizes how many Americans have to be hidden within their own country because foreign bad guys don't stop at our borders."

Ike nodded. "Just look across the lake."

Chapter 31

THE NEXT MORNING

A Nissan Versa remained under the speed limit as it zigzagged west across Tampa. Eyes darting from mirror to mirror.

Panic time.

Benmont Pinch had spent the last week holed up in a sub-dive motel with dirty linens, eating delivery pizza and jumping at every sound. He felt the walls closing in. Time to eject and put some distance between himself and whatever was happening.

White fingers strangled the steering wheel, and all the mirrors were checked again.

"I'm not cut out for this," Benmont Pinch told himself.

Benmont didn't realize it, but he was uniquely *cut out*. His job had provided the skill set. Benmont disabled his phone's GPS locator, and made no calls that could ping off towers. He avoided toll roads and only paid with cash. He wore baseball caps pulled down low to thwart facial-recognition programs. He detoured through neighborhoods to avoid traffic cameras. Not the ones that catch people running red lights. The other ones, unobtrusive in white boxes, on tall poles sitting farther back from the traffic lights, which digitally recorded license plates, matching them to lists of stolen cars, fugitives, and anyone else the government felt like chatting with.

The big trick now was getting across Tampa Bay. The bridges were all watched, so he looped over the top by land, into the rural cow and horse pastures of central Pasco County, then back south into the beach communities along the Gulf of Mexico.

Another tense check of the mirrors. So far so good.

But what was going on? A murdered boss and lawyer, plus federal agents trying to both protect him and kill him. That last part meant if he trusted the wrong person, he could end up dead, so he didn't trust anyone. Why did he have to come up with that stupid theory? Even Benmont had thought it was half-baked at first. Not anymore. Benmont didn't have a plan, but he had a destination, which was plan enough for now.

First things first.

Benmont crossed over a strip of water and turned south onto Gulf Boulevard. He suddenly snapped his fingers. The Nissan pulled into an independent convenience store, parking around the side to shield his license plate from the surveillance cameras. He went inside and bought a disposable cell phone for fifty bucks. He dialed from his car.

"Sonic? It's me, Benmont."

"Benmont! You should see the chaos over here! Where are you?"

"I can't say on this line."

"The FBI has been asking all kinds of questions."

"I need you to trust me," said Benmont. "And you can't trust the FBI."

"What's going on?"

"I don't know, but I'm going to need your help soon. I have nobody else I feel safe talking to. And you can't tell anyone I've contacted you. I'll call again soon."

"Benmont—!"

Click.

The Nissan pulled up to a series of three mom-and-pop motels. The first two needed ID and a credit card to register, so he quickly left. This third happily took cash without questions. He backed into a parking space. Again, the license plate.

Benmont lay down on top of the bedspread and stared up at a ceiling that was textured in 1956. No sound except the rattling air conditioner. Okay, relaxing was not an option. He got up and parted the curtains, looking across the wide beach on Treasure Island. The sun still had an hour left. *Think, think!*

He decided to turn on the old tube TV.

Benmont jumped.

His face filled the local news. *"Authorities are still searching tonight for this man, believed to have passed along classified intelligence information to unknown foreign agents. A recent FBI shootout at his workplace left one dead, and he is to be considered armed and dangerous. Do not approach . . ."*

He quickly turned the TV off, taking fast breaths until he calmed. Then something else made Benmont jump again.

His disposable phone was ringing. Only one person knew the number. He checked the caller ID. Not Sonic. He didn't dare answer, or authorities could triangulate his location.

Benmont got back in his Nissan and drove. A few miles south, he found a much larger hotel with a spacious lobby below two hundred rooms. If they came looking, good luck here. He took a seat near the reception desk, pulled out his phone and stared at the last incoming number. A deep inhale. "Here goes nothing."

He dialed. But didn't speak.

"Hello? . . . Hello? . . . Is this Benmont? . . ."

Silence.

"Benmont, I know you're scared."

"Who's this?"

"Thank God you're safe! This is Agent Carlson with the FBI."

Benmont winced. "What do you want?"

"Right now I want you to remain calm and listen. You're in danger."

"I know that. Two of your agents tried to kill me."

"Only one, and he was an imposter."

"Is that supposed to make me feel better? And what was that nonsense on the news about me passing along classified information?"

"Assets we were supposed to be protecting have been eliminated. Careers are in jeopardy, and the wagons are circled. It was your computer project, so you're a convenient patsy."

"What are you saying? That I could go to prison?"

"Since you're a patsy, it's neater if you aren't apprehended alive. This thing is already gathering momentum."

"But I'm innocent."

"Doesn't matter. Who knows where you are?"

"Nobody."

"Stay put."

"I thought this was the part where you ask me to come in to your headquarters."

"No, whatever you do, don't do that," said Carlson. "It's not safe. The Bureau is currently searching for a mole who is supposedly your contact. I'm sorry to say this, but until they uncover him, you'll be on your own out there."

"This isn't keeping me calm," said Benmont.

"But I can help with that," said Carlson. "I'd like to meet in a remote location."

"That sounds like something an imposter would say to lure me to my death."

"An understandable conclusion," said Carlson. "But it's an unusual circumstance. I dug into the files, and your boss sent up a theory about a list of our protectees. I also read a bunch of his old e-mails about how you had a knack for thinking outside the box and solving crimes for the local police. Everyone thinks it was your boss's theory, but it was yours, wasn't it?"

"Keep talking."

"I need your cooperation, so I'll tell you what's going on. At least what I can on this line. Are you sitting?"

"I'm ready."

"We've identified the fake agent who was killed in the parking lot. Turns out to be former special forces, now civilian military. A cutout."

"What's that mean?"

"It means that he works for the highest bidder, and that's often one of our intelligence services. Or theirs. Greed knows no allegiance. Guys like him come in handy when things might go wrong . . . I can't say any more over the phone."

"Call back when you have more."

"Don't hang up!" said Carlson. "All I can say is that I'm the only person in the government right now who's absolutely sure you're innocent and knows the danger you're in. But until I can put more evidence together to convince others, I have to help you stay safe out in the field for now. We really need to meet."

"I still think this is a trick."

"How about if I bring someone along that you know and trust?"

"Who?"

"Where do you think I got this number? Sonic."

"Dammit!" said Benmont. "I told him not to."

"He's worried sick about you," said Carlson. "If I bring him, will you agree to meet with me?"

"Did you watch a spy movie or something?"

"Yes. Two hours enough time? You name the place," said Carlson. "Got somewhere in mind?"

"As a matter of fact I do. Don't bother to dress up."

Chapter 32

A Crown Vic with blackwall tires and law enforcement antennae cruised slowly along the Gulf of Mexico, down through Madeira Beach and Indian Shores. The driver checked addresses.

He reached the number in his notepad and pulled over. "You've got to be kidding me."

At 19201 Gulf Boulevard sat a small, low-roofed yellow-and-green building. Out front, an abandoned Cadillac with missing doors, painted red, purple, orange and lime. For some reason there was a stool next to the car, also in wild colors. Dirt, weeds, broken cinder blocks. A neon Heineken sign hung in the window, and another wooden one hung out front:

Mahuffer

(Wurst Place on the Beach!)

"Wow, he wasn't kidding," said Agent Carlson, leaning over

the steering wheel as he pulled around back to more visual confusion: striped multicolored crab-trap floats, channel-marker buoys, and a derelict boat splashed with paint like the car in front. Nautical ropes, stray dogs, surfboards. Inside, the clutter only cranked up, as if it were a reality show about hoarding intervention where they finally said, "Screw it. Just paint everything and get a liquor license."

Carlson led Sonic inside, past a pool table with its green felt covered in graffiti. Bras, panties, newspaper clippings, street signs, and drooping strands of Christmas lights in the near darkness. The agent digested it all and thought: *Benmont should be a spy. This is one of the hardest bars to maintain surveillance because of all the obstruction and noise. Or even* find *a target.* He continued winding through the Indiana Jones catacomb of dive-ness. Scribbled-on Naugahyde chairs, photo collages, hubcaps and a row of astrology drawings depicting positions from the *Kama Sutra* for each birth sign. Gemini was doggie style. A live dog lay beneath.

"Over here." A waving arm.

"There you are." Carlson looked over next to a warehouse exhaust fan. "I'll have to remember this place. For business."

"Hey, Sonic!" said Benmont, hugging his pal. "Sorry I got you into this. All good?"

"You didn't get me into nothin' I can't handle. We're always good."

Benmont turned to the agent. "What's the word?"

"The good news is I'm here meeting with you."

"That means there's bad news."

"It's the folly of group mentality. Once the train started down the tracks with the wrong idea about you, everyone got on board and it's only picking up steam," said Carlson. "Right now all we have is that the trail starts and ends with you compiling that list, so you're left holding the bag."

"But what about the company that hired us?" asked Benmont.

"Traced back to an abandoned private mailbox in Fort

Lauderdale at one of those parcel shipping offices," said Carlson. "Registered under a fictitious company name. Standard spycraft, which only turns up the heat on you even more. There's a nationwide alert that you're assumed to have a stockpile of weapons and possibly wearing a suicide vest."

"That puts me in sort of a pickle," said Benmont.

"You could say that."

"You said you wanted a pickle?" asked the bartender.

"Maybe later."

The bartender exited behind collections of pool cues and signed undergarments.

"So what do you think?" asked Carlson. "Do you trust me now that I brought Sonic?"

"*Más o menos.*"

"Fair enough," said Carlson. "Let me buy you a drink."

"I'm not in the mood."

"That's the point. You *need* a drink. You both do." Carlson turned. "Bartender, three shots of Jack. And Cokes on the side."

"You got it."

The bartender walked away, and Benmont's index finger idly made a circle in bar-top dust. "I'm not feeling so good."

"Hold that thought . . ."

The building itself might have been atrophied, but the drinks came lickety-split.

Carlson raised his shot glass. "On three! . . ." He wasn't an afternoon drinker, just going by the training manual.

A trio of glasses slammed back down on the maritime counter. A chorus: "*Ahhhhhh!*"

Then the esophagus burn, glassy expressions and a lunge for the Coke chasers.

"This is too much to take in," said Benmont. "I just had a farfetched hunch when I came up with that theory. So you're saying that it really was a list of people in the witness protection program?"

"Almost right," said the agent. "People watch TV and movies, and they mainly think of mob informants in our programs, but there are many others. For instance, we've got a lot of foreign nationals in South America working for the CIA. They occasionally get compromised and we have to get them out. For some reason they request Orlando. You wouldn't believe how many death squad informants from the Pinochet regime are now selling time-shares near Disney."

"That's what I uncovered?"

"Actually, your list dates back to the Cold War."

"Didn't that end decades ago?"

"Yes, but we've seen an unmistakable resurgence in espionage activity that coincides with Putin taking power. Back in the day, spies were living among us in numbers the public never suspected. We were able to turn more KGB agents than we anticipated. We thought it would require painstaking psychological ops or blackmail leverage, but some of them lived here a few months and simply dug it. Then there were the Americans that the Soviets approached, who in turn informed us and volunteered to play along."

Another round of shots arrived. Benmont and Sonic did theirs. Carlson pretended to, then furtively dumped it out under his stool.

"Once one of our agents' tenure got a little long in the tooth—Russian or American—the risks rose exponentially. It wasn't exactly Stockholm syndrome, but humans have a habit of establishing emotional bonds with those they deal with over periods of time, even hardened spies. The Soviets boiled this down to a science and were notorious for randomly reassessing agents at various milestones. Lie detectors, counter-surveillance. We started having to get people out in a hurry. Many of them ended up scattered all over this state, hunkered down in small towns, peeking out windows and driving home making four right turns in a row. Then the Soviet Union collapsed under the weight of failed ideas, and everyone relaxed. Most of those we protected have now reached an age where they're proud members of our retirement communities, living out in the open, carefree in their golden years."

"Not so carefree anymore?" asked Benmont.

Carlson's look became grim. "The Cold War's heating up again, and you tripped over something. Or rather you were assigned to. Computers have progressed faster than our imaginations, and nobody saw it coming."

"I certainly didn't," said Benmont.

"Someone out there was sharp." He whistled in grudging admiration. "In the old days, it was tiny cameras in cigarette packs, microfilm in pumpkins, and listening devices in cuckoo clocks. Today it's computers. And forget the government. It's corporate America with their marketing software who've amassed larger stockpiles of private data on our citizens than we ever dreamed possible."

"'Terms of agreement'?" said Benmont.

Carlson nodded. "Why hack into the federal system when our enemies can buy all they need from a company such as yours?"

"Lucky me it fell on my desk." Benmont's head drooped. "And I just handed it all over on a platter. In bulk."

"You didn't know," said the agent. "And you did us a favor in a way. New numbers are being issued all over the country as we speak."

"Please tell me you have a plan."

"Yes," said Carlson. "First we need to get you someplace safe, temporarily. Then I need to find a way to prove you were only an unwitting bystander."

"How are you going to do that?" asked Benmont.

"Unfortunately, your company's law firm grabbed the hard drives, and then they were stolen from the home of that murdered attorney, so all records of your project—and anything that could prove your innocence—are gone. The only thing you've got right now is my belief in you. Please tell me you still have a memory stick or something."

"Of course," said Benmont. "Who doesn't back up their work?"

"Where is it?"

"In my car up the street. I didn't want to park here."

"Excellent. I'll need it." Carlson pulled out what looked like a cell, but more elaborate.

"What the heck's that?"

"A secure satellite phone." The agent punched buttons. "I'm calling in a favor, the next part of my plan. Like I said, until we know who the mole is, I don't know who I can trust at the Bureau. With one exception. There was an instructor of mine at the academy in Quantico. He's risen fast through the ranks and is now essentially the assistant, assistant, assistant director. Name's McCreedy."

"Doesn't sound that high up."

"High enough to be above the fray and start an internal investigation that will clear you." Carlson listened to the phone ring. "I haven't told a soul about my findings with your list, because if the wrong person gets wind, I could be in as much danger as you— and more importantly, my efforts to exonerate you will be buried. Some gears will need to turn in the meantime, but as soon as my theory reaches McCreedy's ear, you're practically home free."

"Is he answering?"

The agent waved for him to be quiet.

"*. . . Wait for the tone . . .*" *Beep.*

"Hi, George. It's Nelson calling again. They've said you've been in meetings all day, but I have something top priority that I can't leave in your voice mail. Call me as soon as you can."

Click.

"McCreedy's a great guy," Carlson told Benmont. "He's actually coming down to Florida soon for a professional retreat in Sanibel, so hopefully if all this has blown over by then, you might get to meet him." The agent slid a matchbook across the bar.

"What's this?" asked Benmont.

"Your contact at the safe house. I'm taking you there personally, so that number is only a last resort in case we get separated for some reason, like taking evasive maneuvers to lose a tail." The agent threw cash on the bar. "Number's inside. It's written in reverse in case you're captured."

"Captured? You said I was almost home free."

"You are. Just standard procedure." Carlson stood up. "Let's get to your car and secure the files on that memory stick."

The Crown Vic drove slowly down Gulf Boulevard.

Benmont pointed behind a dry cleaners. "It's the Nissan."

Carlson pulled up, and everyone got out. "Where it is?"

"In the trunk." Benmont pulled out his keys and popped the lid. "There it is, next to the spare."

Carlson grabbed it and slammed the trunk lid when his satellite phone rang. "We're in luck. It's McCreedy. Here's the beginning of your freedom . . ." He raised the phone to his head. "Yes, sir, thank you for calling me back. You know that situation in Florida? I've caught a break. It's about that data analyst everyone's looking for . . . Believe it or not, he's right here with me. Sir, you need to know that—"

Pop.

Benmont and Sonic looked at each other, then down at the agent with the spreading red stain in the middle of his chest.

"Is he fooling around?" asked Sonic.

"I think he's dead," said Benmont.

Pop, pop, pop . . .

Pings and sparks off the back of the car. The windows didn't shatter because the rounds were too high velocity. Just a neat, horizontal row of holes surrounded by spiderweb cracks.

The pair hit the ground, slithering through hot gravel to the Nissan's doors.

Pop, pop, pop . . .

They crawled inside and kept their heads low as Benmont threw the car into gear and took off.

Sonic looked over the back of the seat out the cracked window. "I don't see anybody."

Benmont drove in a box of four consecutive right turns.

"What are you doing?" asked Sonic.

"I don't know, but it's something Carlson said, so I think it's good."

"Still nobody following," said a turned-around Sonic. "How on earth did we escape?"

"Don't jinx us." Another right turn. "Whoever ambushed us was probably set up for our meeting at the bar, and was waiting until we got to my car, but didn't know it was parked that far away. I know a little about high-powered sniper rifles. The first shot was chambered and steady, but then he had to bolt the rest in a hurry."

They sped across a drawbridge for the mainland.

"Still nobody back there." Sonic faced forward in his seat and covered his eyes. "What are we going to do now?"

Benmont pulled a matchbook from his pocket and opened the cover.

Chapter 33

BOCA SHORES

The carpeting was wall-to-wall and eggshell, two quilted chairs, a sofa, oversize cushions. In other words, just like every other trailer in the retirement park.

With one exception.

A houseguest slowly moved along one of the walls, examining showpieces lovingly displayed on custom glass shelving.

"I never asked," said Tofer. "Are you married?"

"Not anymore," said Ted. "And if *you* were ever married, you'd know a husband could never decorate the living room with model rockets."

"Man, it's like you kept them all," said Tofer, squinting up close to a Mercury capsule. "I remember a lot of these from your old bedroom but never realized all the detail you put into them . . . So I guess you gave up shortwave?"

"Follow me . . ." Ted led his old friend down the hall and opened the door to the spare bedroom.

"Holy smokes," said Tofer. "It's like the radio room of an early NASA tracking station in the South Pacific."

"Pretty much." Ted pointed up. "Used to have a big antenna that could pick up everything to Antarctica, but the management here made me take it down because it didn't conform to the park's aesthetics. I mean, it's a *trailer* park."

"There's a lot of that going around."

A phone rang somewhere in the mobile home.

Ted grabbed it off the kitchen wall. "Hello? . . . Who? . . . My name? Why don't you tell me who you are first? . . . I'm sorry but I don't know anybody by that name. You must have the wrong number . . ." He was about to hang up. ". . . Wait, what? Could you repeat that last part? . . . Okay, do you have something to write with? . . ." A few minutes passed. ". . . Right, see you then."

He hung up.

Tofer was staring. "That was a most mysterious call."

Ted opened the fridge. "You should have heard it from my end."

"Don't keep me in suspense," said Tofer.

"I'm starting to think you might not be as paranoid as I first thought." Ted bent down and reached for the top shelf.

"What are you doing?"

"Something a husband would never be allowed." He drank straight from a container of orange juice.

"Holy shit!" said Tofer.

"What are you, my wife now?"

"No!" He held up the morning's newspaper. Two mug shots on the front page, next to a larger photo of a crime scene.

"Oh, that," said Ted. "We saw a pretty interesting fireworks show the other night. The Duncans had a close one."

Tofer shook his head. "These aren't the Duncans. They're the Mulroneys."

"What are you talking about?"

"Some years have passed, but I'm sure. Ike has aged well." Tofer sped-read down the article. "I knew them from way back when."

Ted took another swig of OJ. "Who are the Mulroneys?"

"A couple of our assets who became double agents for the U.S.," said Tofer. "Or maybe they were working for the Americans all along. They did quite a bit of damage, exposed a lot of our Cuban counterparts in Miami. We eventually figured it out and they were marked to be 'disappeared.' All these years, that's what I thought had happened."

"Clearly our side was a step ahead and got them out," Ted said wistfully. "Well, I'll be. Living across from a couple of protected agents and never guessing in a million years."

Tofer shook the newspaper. "It mentions a car bomb."

Ted put the carton of juice away. "Hmm, your story, the Duncans, and now that phone call I just received." He slowly began to nod. "It looks like I might be coming out of retirement."

LATER THAT AFTERNOON

Earl didn't recognize the car as it approached the guard booth at Boca Shores. He stepped out and hitched his pants from second nature.

"How can I help you fellas?"

They gave their names.

Earl grabbed a clipboard from inside the booth and found a spot in the middle of the top page. "Yes, he's expecting you . . . Have a nice day."

The guard arm raised.

"*. . . Let's . . . make . . . a deal! . . .*"

The car circled the lake until it found the address and pulled up the drive. Nervous eyes glanced around before the passengers ran for the screen door.

Ted opened it and they rushed inside.

The two new guests were hyperventilating, standing on random spots on the carpet and looking around in a general state of bewilderment like they'd never seen furniture before.

"Why don't you have a seat on the couch?" said Ted. "Just take slow, deep breaths and calm down. You've been through a lot."

They did.

Ted went to the fridge again and brought them each a soda.

Shaking hands tried to pop the metal tabs.

"Let me give you a hand there," said Ted. *Pop, pop.* "Now then, which one of you is Benmont?"

A hand went up. "Here."

Ted turned the other way. "That would make you Sonic."

A head nodded and sipped a soft drink.

"I have a question," said Benmont. "Why did Carlson give us *your* phone number?"

"Long story short," said Ted, "he was a rookie agent when I was winding down my career. We hit it off like a son I never had, and stayed in touch all these years. Some of the field agents are instructed to make their own emergency arrangements that nobody else knows about in case an operation goes sideways and security is breached. So I agreed to fill the void. My phone number and trailer are his aces in the hole."

"But why you?"

"Because I'm retired, off the grid. Which makes my safe house even safer." Ted pulled up a chair and sat. "Now then, where's Carlson?"

Benmont set his can down on the coffee table. "Dead, I think."

"Dead!" Ted was back on his feet. "What do you mean, you think?"

"We didn't stick around," said Benmont. "Bullets were flying everywhere. Someone must have found out he was going to meet us."

"Why didn't you tell me this on the phone?" Ted demanded.

"We didn't want you calling anyone," said Benmont.

"That's exactly what I should have done." Ted reached for the wall phone. "That's what I'm going to do now."

"No! Stop!" said Benmont. "Carlson himself explained why *he* couldn't call anyone. He figured everything out, but didn't know who to trust. Someone killed him just for meeting us. Don't you see?"

Ted took his hand away from the phone and returned to his chair. "Okay, now you are going to tell me everything. From the beginning, and don't leave anything out. What the hell was this theory of yours?"

"It all started when I received this assignment as a data analyst, but something bothered me, so I wrote up a report . . ."

And for the next hour, Benmont laid it all out: dead boss, dead attorney, shootout in the company parking lot, all the way up to meeting Earl at the guard booth a few minutes earlier.

Ted sat in thought. "Now I understand why Carlson couldn't exactly just bring you in according to procedure. And he did give you my phone number after all, so that fits."

"There is one person you need to call," said Benmont.

"Who's that?"

"At the bar Carlson mentioned a guy named McCreedy."

"Who's that?" asked Ted.

"Someone who's supposed to be way up in the Bureau," said Benmont. "Carlson told me that McCreedy would trust his version of events, and he had enough power to launch an inquiry and straighten everything out. He mentioned that McCreedy is supposed to be coming to Florida soon for some kind of professional retreat."

"Then it's simple," said Ted. "We just have to keep you two hidden until we can reach this McCreedy character. Piece of cake."

"Really?" said Benmont.

"That was sarcasm."

Night fell and Ted Pruitt put on a light jacket. "You three stay here. Stay away from the windows and don't answer the door."

Benmont, Sonic and Tofer sat in a row on the couch with expressions that said they wouldn't have to be told twice.

Ted locked the screen door behind him. He strolled down a few homes and rang the doorbell on another screen door.

Lawrence Shepard came onto the porch. "Ted, what are you doing here?"

"You still hiding the Duncans?"

It was an open secret in the park. The Duncans didn't want to be found right now, and an exploding car was a good enough reason for everyone. The residents closed ranks, no matter how many cops came to their door: "Nope, don't have the slightest idea where they are." Instead of the blue wall of silence, it was the silver wall.

Ted entered the living room. "The Mulroneys, I presume?"

The couple was stunned. Lawrence spun around. "How'd you know?"

"I've got a situation, too," said Ted. "And I've just learned some things that shed light on your guests' predicament . . ."

The bathroom door opened, and two people came out.

"But, Serge, I can go by myself."

"I'm not about to leave you alone with the guest towels."

"But I just wanted to wash my head."

"Coleman, I think you're the only adult with cradle cap."

They entered the living room.

"Oh, hi, Ted," said Serge. "Haven't seen you since the big party at the clubhouse. Sorry about Coleman. We'll pay for the shirt."

Ted turned. "What are they doing here?"

"It's okay," said Lawrence. "He knows."

"Everyone in the park knows the Duncans are here."

"No," said Lawrence. "He *knows*. The Mulroneys."

"What?" said Ted. "Why did you tell him that?"

"I trust him," said Lawrence. "And I needed some advice. He can navigate worlds that I didn't even realize existed. So you said you had a situation, too?"

Ted stared at a grinning Serge for a moment. Well, if Serge knew about the Mulroneys, and the sky still hadn't fallen . . . "Okay, you'll all need to sit down for this . . ." And Ted got them up to speed on everything going on back at his own trailer, especially the Benmont List.

"Let me see if I have this straight," said Lawrence. "If this so-called theory is correct, then the Duncans—I mean Mulroneys—were on that Social Security number list, which would explain the car bomb, as well as their dead houseguests a few days earlier?"

"It also means they're still not safe," said Ted. "Much bigger problem than the cops."

"Now we *have* to go to the police," said Lawrence.

"No," said Ted. "This means we definitely can't come forward. At least not until I can work this out and reach someone high up in the Bureau. I've been given a name."

"I'm getting dizzy," said Nancy Shepard. "I can understand a couple of retired spies living under assumed names here. They have to be somewhere, so why not? But now you're telling me you're also a former agent running a safe house with three more people lying low? That's way too much of a coincidence for one retirement park."

"I'm just retired FBI," said Ted. "I never anticipated my trailer would ever actually be needed."

An eager hand thrust toward the ceiling. "Ooo! Ooo! Ooo! Pick me!"

Lawrence sighed. "What is it, Serge?"

"In Florida, it's *barely* a coincidence. Have you heard of the island of Sanibel near Fort Myers?"

"Sure," said Nancy. "We went shell collecting there."

"There are so many retired spies living there that if you threw a rock, it would ricochet off at least three spooks."

"What are you talking about?" asked Lawrence.

"In 1974, a man named Porter Goss led an effort to incorporate the island and became its first mayor. He later was an eight-term congressman before being named by George W. Bush as director of the CIA, where he had spent much of the sixties as a clandestine agent in Latin America . . . If you need any further understanding why Sanibel is such a popular locale for our agents to retire, just check this map." Serge thrust out his smartphone.

People leaned and squinted.

"What am I looking at?" asked Lawrence.

"The island of Useppa just off the coast of Sanibel," said Serge. "Used by the CIA to train Cubans for the Bay of Pigs. Guess the agents put out the word that it was a comfy climate."

"Excuse me?" said Ted. "We're in the middle of a problem here."

"Sorry," said Serge. "I just like to bring things back to reality."

Ted looked at Lawrence. "We need to get all these people out of here. The car bomb says they've already zeroed in on this place."

Serge pounded a fist into a palm. "And that's exactly what we want! They'll walk right into our trap!"

"Lawrence," said Ted, pointing back at Serge. "What exactly were the positives about this guy?"

"The Impala," said Serge.

Ted's head swung. "What?"

"The Impala," he repeated.

"What Impala?"

"The one that was following us the other day when we took our *Cocoon* movie field trip to Saint Petersburg," said Serge. "Actually, there were three cars that kept switching out, but I like to call the whole phenomenon 'Impala' to keep it digestible."

"Anything else?" Ted asked impatiently.

"Lots," said Serge. "The same Impala is now parked at the end of the street outside the entrance of this trailer park."

"It is?" said Lawrence. "Why?"

"That had me wondering, too," said Serge. "But I just now put it all together. They're keeping the park under surveillance. They don't know whether the Duncans are alive or not."

"Who are you talking about?"

"I'm guessing the people who ordered that Social Security list from Benmont," said Serge. "Like Ted just told us, they found the Duncans' address on it."

"But if that's so," said Nancy, "what are they waiting for? Why are they just sitting out there? It's not like they're afraid of being bold."

"The newspapers described the blast and quoted the cops as saying the Duncans were missing," said Serge. "It could mean they're really missing, or that the authorities weren't thorough looking for remains, or that the cops are outright lying as a ruse to lure the culprits back to the scene of the crime. Whatever the case, it gives me a huge advantage!"

"I'm afraid to ask." Ted rubbed the bridge of his nose. "Advantage for what?"

"My big spy plan!" Serge nodded and grinned.

"Okay, I've heard enough," said Ted. "What we need—"

"Wait," interrupted Lawrence. "Can we please just hear him out? I know he sounds unorthodox, but I've seen the results."

"I'll defer to your judgment," said Ted. "But only for the courtesy to listen."

"Thanks!" Serge hopped up and clapped his hands. "It'll be an espionage thriller of epic proportions! Double crosses, shady deals, code signals like bending down to tie my shoes. I'd like to call it *The Serge Sanction*. Let's get started!"

"Uh, where?" asked Ted.

"First I need to talk to this Benmont you've got stashed in your trailer." Serge began bouncing in place. "If what I think is happening, I'll need to know every last thing he does and get a look at what's on his backup data to set my plan in motion. You've already painted a vivid picture: They've started waxing people—his boss, the attorney—and stolen their hard drives. Plus a couple more bureaucrats in Washington who read the e-mails. The shootouts in Tampa and Treasure Island, the houseguests across the way, the car bomb. It's getting to be a regular bloodbath. This is going to be so much fun!"

"What's wrong with you?" asked Ted. "This isn't close to fun."

"It sure feels that way," said Serge. "Am I missing something?"

Chapter 34

Cigar smoke and cognac.

The seaside resort sat on the north end of the island of Sanibel, and loud singing came from the bar. It was somebody's alma mater, and it was off-key.

A row of men with arms around each other's shoulders swayed as they belted out the next verse. Some of their tuxedo shirts had port-wine stains. They couldn't remember any more lyrics, and the singing sputtered out. So it was back to war stories and glory days: secret societies in college, fraternities where they'd been recruited, then initiation ceremonies involving nudity, alcohol, and being blindfolded before reaching into a toilet to squish a banana.

It was an inter-agency retreat—CIA, FBI, NSA, and the rest of the alphabet soup. Yale and Princeton had the biggest annual alumni reunions. This was a smaller one from a Pac-10 school on the West Coast.

Someone crashed into the bar and waved an empty brandy snifter. "Another round on me!"

The bartender would have rolled his eyes, but the tips were fantastic.

A stool tipped over with a crash. "From the top!" And the mangled college song began again.

Mid-verse, someone stopped and pointed at the door. "Check it out!"

"That's hilarious!"

"The perfect end of the evening!"

The college mascot flapped its wings. *"Quack, quack!"*

Fond memories flooded back from the University of Oregon.

The gang staggered and gathered round the duck. *"Quack, quack!"*

One of the alums knocked on the feathered head. "Who's in there? Is that you, Harold?"

"Quack, quack!"

The duck stepped back and began dancing. The hokey pokey, the Harlem shake, the Electric Slide, Gangnam Style. The crowd hooted and hollered and clapped in rhythm.

The duck got tired and joined them at the bar to a round of appreciative slaps on his back feathers. He stuck a bottled water in his bill.

"Seriously, who's in there? Steve? Mort?"

"Quack, quack!"

"This asshole's going to make us guess." Laughter.

"Fair enough. He paid for the costume . . . Victor? Walt? . . ."

The evening wore on, and the celebrants in turn made repeated, stumbling trips to the kind of high-end men's room with wooden-slat stall doors and stacks of neatly folded washcloths at the sink instead of a paper towel dispenser.

More brandy, people slouching lower over the bar. One of the taller alums broke off from the group and stumbled down the marble hall. He entered the men's room. The duck caught the door before it could close, went inside and locked it.

The alum unzipped at a urinal, looked over at the noise behind him and chuckled. "I have no idea who you are."

"George McCreedy?"

"Yeah?"

The duck removed his head.

Then a much different tone. "Now I really have no idea who you are. When did you go to Oregon?"

"I didn't. I've come to give you a message."

It had just gotten weird in a hurry. A security breach. McCreedy tried to fight off his inebriation. "Are you with an agency?"

"Carlson was trying to reach you before he got shot."

McCreedy strained his memory. Yes, a few missed calls from Carlson while he was in meetings, then the bad news about the agent. "Are you the one who shot him?"

"No, he was trying to tell you the truth about the list that's getting people killed. And the mole. Everyone's got it all wrong about this Benmont fellow."

"How could you possibly know about that list?"

"The only credible answer is: How else would I know the name Carlson? And that you were his instructor at Quantico?"

McCreedy did the calculus in his head. "Okay, you just bought yourself another five minutes."

"You probably saw an e-mail about a theory . . ." Serge walked him through the rest.

When the story was over, McCreedy whistled. "That is one unbelievable story."

"And if it's true and you don't act on it," said Serge, "think of the possible damage."

Drunken knocking at the door. *"What's taking so long in there? Why is this locked?"*

Serge and McCreedy yelled in unison: "Not now!"

The pair stopped and stared at each other.

"All right," McCreedy finally said. "Bring this Benmont in and you have my word he'll be safe. I'll give this whole matter a fair hearing."

Serge shook his head. "Benmont stays with me. You straighten things out internally and find the mole."

"While you do what?"

"Deliver the entire secret operation behind all this. Just be ready."

McCreedy stared again. "Who *are* you?"

Serge spread his wings. "I'm the duck. I'm authorized."

"Okay, how will I get in touch with you?" asked McCreedy.

"You won't," said Serge. "Give me your cell phone."

"Do I have a choice?"

"Yes, but the other has a downside."

McCreedy handed it over, and Serge entered the number in his own disposable phone. Then he removed the battery from the agent's phone—"Sorry, even though you're pretty hammered, you might be able to call before my getaway." He handed back the cell.

"But I can just call from one of my friends' phones."

"That's why I'm also locking you in one of the stalls." He held out a metal door wedge. "When it's time, I'll phone with the location. I assume you'll know what to do."

"What's your plan?"

"Draw them out into the open like bait. You guys haven't exactly been tearing up the league."

"And I assume you'll be the bait?"

"Bait gets eaten," said Serge. "I'm more like a bug zapper."

"Now you're mixing metaphors."

"I'm impressed. Look at the grammar on your ass." He stuck the disposable phone somewhere inside the feathers. "Just get another battery and keep your cell on. My code name is Serge. It's also my real name, so it's easier for me to remember. Your code name will be Mr. Buttons."

"What kind of a code name is that?" asked McCreedy. "And why do I even need one if you'll be calling me and already know who I am?"

Serge swung feathers in the air. "Do you want to do this professionally or not?"

Chapter 35

BOCA SHORES

Another typical clandestine meeting in a retirement trailer park involving national security.

This time the whole gang was there: Ted and Tofer, Benmont and Sonic, the Duncans, and Lawrence and Nancy. Coleman was behind the couch.

A Ford Falcon pulled up the drive, and Serge came in wearing a duck costume. "Everything went like glass. All your troubles will soon be over."

"Where have you been?" asked Benmont.

"Meeting with McCreedy."

"But how?" asked Ted.

Serge removed the duck head. "I'm authorized."

"So McCreedy's people have picked up everyone who's a threat to us?" asked Benmont.

"Not *exactly*," said Serge. "I need to put my Master Plan in motion first." He pulled out some notes from beneath feathers. "Lawrence, you have the most important tasks. First thing tomorrow morning, quietly start evacuating the entire park. Pass the word around on the hush-hush. Say it's a field trip and order as many shuttle buses as you need. But have them leave at staggered intervals so it looks normal as opposed to a mass exodus."

"Why?" asked Lawrence.

"Because there's a Russian agent in an Impala watching the park from the end of the street. He's been out there two days pretending to look at road maps."

"What?" He jumped up. "Then why aren't we calling the police?"

Serge shook his head. "And pick him up for what? Being lost and looking for directions? Plus I need him there for my plan to work . . . So, Lawrence, I'm counting on you. Every last person has to be out of the park or they will be in grave danger. Coleman, too. Can you handle that?"

"Sure, but where do we go?"

"Anywhere," said Serge. "Check into a hotel on Lido Beach if you want. It's very relaxing this time of year."

"Where will you be?"

"Right here," said Serge. "That road past Earl's guard booth is the only entrance or exit to this place. I'll draw our adversaries inside, and then it's just a matter of me keeping them occupied until the good men and women of the FBI swoop in to save the day. I've got them on standby. Easy-peasy."

Everyone glanced at each other.

"Trust me," said Serge. "What can go wrong?"

THE NEXT AFTERNOON

Senior citizens whispered among themselves as they boarded a series of shuttles lined up behind the clubhouse.

The first bus pulled out on schedule. It passed unnoticed by an Impala parked on the shoulder of the road before heading into town. A half hour later, the next bus left, then the next.

Serge returned from where he'd just hidden the Ford Falcon in the back of the park. He stood beside the guard booth and waved as the final bus departed shortly before sunset. "Earl, it's time for you to go, too."

"But I was going to stay here with you and fight them off, shoulder to shoulder."

Serge shook his head. "Who knows if my plan will work? I can't have you on my conscience."

"But you told everyone it was foolproof..."

"That's what they needed to hear." Serge gave Earl a hug. "Please, for me."

Earl locked up the booth, got in his car and followed the last shuttle into the city.

The sun went down, and the fountain in the lake turned off. The park was quieter than it had ever been. And darker. Not a single light on in any of the trailers. Serge walked out to the entrance and the masonry wall with the park's name spelled out in granite. There was something rolled up under his arm. He unfurled a hand-painted banner and hung it over the sign. Then he went back inside and waited ...

An hour later, Serge left the Shepards' mobile home on foot and walked out of the park.

Now it was just bullfrogs and crickets.

Stars twinkled and palm fronds rustled.

Eventually a pair of Impala headlights quietly swung around the corner at the entrance, and the vehicle drove into the park. It passed the lake and pulled up the driveway to a trailer.

Serge walked around to the back of the Ford and popped the trunk. He aimed a gun down at the driver of the Impala, who shielded his face. "Don't shoot me."

"Then don't pull any shit. You're still of use." Serge motioned with the pistol. "Get out! . . . Now turn around and lean forward with your hands behind your back."

Serge handcuffed him and led the bewildered captive into the trailer.

"Have a seat. The couch will do." He shoved the man down. "Don't take it so hard. Even the best training couldn't have prepared you, because who would ever expect a duck to be armed?"

The hostage glanced around the trailer for clues but only saw knickknacks.

Serge kept the gun aimed as he pulled out his cell phone. "I want you to call your friends."

"What friends?"

Serge delivered a frightful pistol-whipping until blood spattered the cushions.

"As you can tell, there's not going to be any clever preliminary chitchat like in the movies." The pistol butt caught the man in the Adam's apple. "Give me the number."

The captured spy caught his breath and spit out the digits.

Serge punched them into the phone. "It's ringing." He put it to the man's head.

Watery eyes looked up at Serge. "What do you want me to say?"

"Tell them there's someone here who wants to talk to them."

"*Hello?*"

"Boris? It's Alexi . . ."

"*You know you're never supposed to call this line unless it's an emergency. And you're not even calling from a secure phone.*"

"There's someone here who wants to talk to you."

"*Who?*"

Serge pulled the phone back to his own ear. "Boris, my man! We need to have a sit-down."

"*Who is this?*"

"I work freelance. They know me as Serge the Duck. Not as threatening as Carlos the Jackal, but I'm building a rep. Listen, there's been a series of misunderstandings that I'm sure we can clear up with an intimate conversation."

"What are you talking about?"

"The list of defectors and double agents, all the murders across the state, except you missed the Duncans. *Twice.* Plus the data analyst who came up with the theory and has the only remaining original set of your files that can expose your network's operation. Minor stuff like that. What do you say?"

"Uh, sure we can meet. Absolutely. We've got this house—"

"Oh yeah, right, I don't think so," said Serge. "I know you still don't trust me, so I need to take precautions. Sorry, spy rules. There's a gas station nearby. When you get there, give me a call, and I'll give you directions the rest of the way. Got a pen? . . ."

The person on the other end of line finished jotting down the address. *"Seriously, I've never heard of the Duck. Who are you really with? The Americans? Israelis? Arabs?"*

"You can absolutely take this to the bank," said Serge. "I follow nobody."

Click.

MEANWHILE . . .

The new mall was winding down for the evening. Customers walked back to their cars carrying large shopping bags with logos for name-brand bullshit.

At the empty end of the parking lot sat a row of jazzed-up street racers with raised hoods. Young people drank beer, admiring custom-built engines and shock absorbers.

Next to them was a row of shuttle buses. Retired people milled about, discussing options.

"What's going to happen to Serge?"

"He can take care of himself."

"What if he can't?"

"He's risking himself to protect the whole park!"

"That's right. Look around at all of us that he's helped in the past weeks. The Hornsbys, the Gotliebs, Candace . . ."

"Not to mention me," said a young man named Scott Packer.

"After everything Serge has done for us, we're just going to drive to a hotel?"

"We can't leave him alone back there."

"It's not how we were raised."

"I want to go back."

"Me too."

"Let's put it to a vote," said Earl. "All in favor?"

A unanimous show of hands.

They piled back into the shuttle buses.

E arlier in the evening, Serge had broken into the main junction box at the clubhouse and killed all the streetlights around the lake.

The only remaining light in the entire trailer park came from the blue-white glow of a TV. Serge sat cross-legged with his face six inches from the screen, staring at static. Where he'd been for the last hour.

In practically a trance: "All the answers are so obvious. They're all questions. Why didn't I see it before?"

He looked over his shoulder at a gagged and hog-tied Russian agent. "You ought to try this. It puts the whole enchilada in perspective, like, we really don't know anything at all about everything. Up, down, good, evil, life, death, one *or* two fingers up the ass—"

Rrrrrrrrring.

"I'll get that." Serge snatched the cell phone off the coffee table. "What's up, dog? You just got to the gas station? Then you're about fifteen miles away. We're all at the Boca Shores retirement park . . . That's right, the place your buddy in the Impala was watching.

Threw you a curve ball with that one, didn't I? Because that's the last place anyone would think we'd still be after my phone call to you. But I'm just the kind of cat who zigs when others stop for selfies. See you in a few."

Click.

He dialed again.

"Mr. Buttons? It's Serge. We're on. It's going down at the Boca Shores retirement park. You know what 'it's going down' means, right? . . . Oh, of course, you've seen *Miami Vice*. . . . What address? Believe me, you won't miss it."

Click.

Serge got up and playfully kicked his hostage in the ribs, over and over, like he was performing some kind of soccer ball-handling drill. Playful only to Serge.

"*Oomph* . . ." The captive made the sound of air wheezing from an under-inflated balloon.

"Isn't this great? I'm going to meet all your chums! The laugh fests that are to come! . . ." Serge jumped up and touched the ceiling, then lay stomach down on the carpet next to his captive because that's really the only way you can talk to someone who's hog-tied. "When I mentioned earlier about no movie-style wry banter, see, I have these wild mood swings that range from positive to fantastically positive! Unfortunately, you caught me on a down-swing, so the broken nose is all on me. But if you're starting to feel sorry for yourself, think about having to explain a blood-spattered couch to a retired couple from Kansas. That last sentence has rarely, if ever, been uttered in human history. My mind is racing. Shit, shit, shit—" Suddenly something caught his eye. Gasp! "Coleman!"

"Whuut?"

A head of disheveled hair had just eerily risen into view like a fog-draped scene in *The Creature from Behind the Couch*.

"What are you doing here?" yelled Serge. "You were supposed to go with the others."

"I missed the buses, but luckily I had a chunk of hashish."

"You idiot! This is no time to fool around!" said Serge. "I understand this is going to be a difficult request, but for the duration can you remain inert?"

"What's that mean?"

"Stay down on the carpet and don't move until I get back."

"I'll try." Coleman reclined with a smile on the thick beige rug and closed his eyes.

Serge's knuckles rapped on the captive's skull. "Do your people have this kind of aggravation? Probably not, because you guys build up a tolerance in grade school from your vodka Popsicles." He pointed out the door. "Another ultra-positive mood swing has arrived, so it's out the door and off on the wings of hope . . ."

Serge grabbed a shopping bag and a black trench coat and dashed into the street: "We rock tonight!"

Then a series of piercing headlights lined up at the guard shack.

Serge froze. "Oh no!"

The first driver used a magnetic card to open the gate, and a procession of shuttle buses rolled slowly through the entrance. They stopped in the parking lot behind the clubhouse.

Serge took off at a sprint.

The residents were calmly climbing out of the vehicles when Serge arrived out of breath.

"What are all of you doing back here?" He pointed urgently at the road. "They're going to be arriving any second! You have to go!"

"Not a chance."

"We can't just abandon you in your time of need."

"It isn't how our parents raised us."

Serge whined and stomped his feet. "Why did I get mixed up with some of the last people in the country who have character?"

"After all you've done for us."

"We'll fight whoever it is together."

"No! No! No!" said Serge.

A few of the residents folded their arms resolutely.

"Our minds are made up."

"We're not leaving the park."

"Nobody pushes us around on our own turf!"

"Okay, okay," said Serge. "How about this? You all go hide in your homes, where you can monitor as the Master Plan unfolds. If I get in any trouble that I can't handle—which I won't—then you're free to come to the rescue. That way you'll be my backup, with clear consciences. Deal?"

Murmuring at first, but then heads began to nod.

"Great!" said Serge. "Now my plan is already in motion with lots of variables on a tight schedule, so you've got to get inside your trailers as fast as possible!"

As fast as possible was relative. Serge grimaced with impatience at the slow-motion deployment, repeatedly checking back at the park's entrance gate for any sign of headlights.

Minutes later, it was down to the last dozen residents inching up their driveways with walking aids and oxygen tanks.

Headlights appeared.

Serge clenched his fists as he watched the last, straggling seniors. "Come *onnnnnnn*! Get inside!"

Two BMWs stopped, and the occupants stared curiously at a hand-painted banner covering the entrance sign for Boca Shores. In large bloodred letters:

HELL.

The driver of the first car looked at his four tightly packed passengers. "I'm already tired of this guy. No fucking around. He stays alive only long enough to help us find the other targets."

The final residents stepped inside and closed their screen doors as the first BMW smashed through the gate arm, sending splinters across the windshield.

Serge jumped in a golf cart and quickly circled the far side of the lake in the darkness.

The BMWs slowly cruised the opposite shore, checking houses.

"What are we looking for?" asked a backseat passenger.

"Anything," said the driver. "He wouldn't give an exact address, so just keep your eyes peeled."

"It's not late enough for all the house lights to be off," said another. "It's like something's going on."

"Give the man a cigar," said the driver. "Now will everyone just shut up and watch? Is that too much to ask?"

The Beemers continued on, even more slowly now, with the windows down. Insects and distant thunder. Tires crushing little stones in the road.

Suddenly an arm from the backseat pointed dramatically out the windshield.

"Look!"

The lead sedan stopped in the street.

It was a moonless night, with no artificial illumination in the park. But then more thunder, growing closer, and the heat lightning started cooking.

Clouds flashed randomly over the eastern horizon.

With each brilliant flash, the BMWs' passengers strained harder to see. And what they saw made them not trust their eyes.

Ahead in the middle of the road—lit up in a sequence of background lightning—stood a black silhouette with a flat-brimmed cowboy hat. A long trench coat flowed in the wind.

"Un-fucking-believable," said the first driver, cocking his gun and opening his door. "I am so going to enjoy killing this guy!"

The sedans emptied into the street. There was a loud clatter as the rest of the guns were racked.

The silhouette remained like stone.

The others spread out evenly in a line from one side of the road to the other. Once the leader was satisfied, they began marching in deliberate, individual steps. Cautious glances to the sides in case it was a trap. Senses heightened. The only sounds left were the thunder and shoe soles menacingly grinding on pavement.

The silhouette still didn't move, feet straddling the road's center line.

"Is this guy insane? There are ten of us!"

"Just stay alert. We don't know what he's up to."

As they drew closer to the mysterious figure, they could make out the orange glow from a thin black cigar.

This time the lightning was bright and crashing. The trench coat inflated and flapped.

Ten sets of shoes took another step in unison.

Serge removed the cigar from his mouth and held it to a silver tip.

The tip began to sizzle, and Serge held the rest of the device at a forward angle.

The marching gang froze and looked at each other.

Then, suddenly, multicolored flaming balls came flying and whizzing through their ranks.

"He's got incendiary rounds!" "It's like flying napalm!" "Take cover!"

Half dashed toward the bushes in front of some trailers, and the others dove in the lake.

Their leader stood back in the street, staring down in disgust. "You idiots! It's just Roman candles!"

Serge ignited a sizzling pinwheel that zoomed and exploded over their heads.

They ducked back down. "Are you sure?"

"Dammit! Will you get back up here?" screamed the leader. "There's nothing to be afraid of. This guy's clearly a clown who has no idea what he's doing."

Heads poked up from behind bushes, and others grabbed reeds as they trudged out of the water and up the banks.

"Dmitri!"

"What?"

"Behind you! In the lake!"

He spun in alarm. Then relief. "You had me scared there for a second. It's just a few swans. They're really beautiful.

And look: They're coming right up to me . . . Well, hello there, swans— . . . *Ahhh! Ahhh! Fuck! Ahhh! Get them off me!*" Down in the water he went with a froth of violent splashing. His head broke the surface, and the end of his nose was bitten. *"Help! Help! They're killing me . . ."* Then back under again.

The other men threw rocks at the swans, which caused the birds to run up the bank and start chasing them in circles in the grass. *"It's nipping me!" "Me too!" "Ouch!" "Help!"*

The leader hung his head.

They finally dragged their injured colleague out of the water.

"Leave him!" The leader pointed up the street at a silhouette with a billowing black trench coat, slowly marching out of sight behind a row of trailers.

The gang took off running.

But Serge knew the park well by now: which backyards had fences, which ones you could scoot through, which golf cart paths were dead ends. It was like a giant corn maze of aluminum siding.

The pursuing gang quickly became disoriented.

"We can't get through here. There's a fence."

"Go this way."

"A rock wall."

"That way!"

Woof, woof.

"A Doberman!"

"Everyone, back to the street!"

They all ended up by the lake again, panting and keeping a lookout for swans.

"What's wrong with you guys?" said the leader. "Go get him!"

"It's scary around here."

The leader pointed again. "There he is!"

The shadowy figure in a trench coat darted across the road and disappeared behind the clubhouse. He checked his glow-in-the-dark watch. "Where the hell is the FBI?"

The gang took off across the lawn toward the building.

Scores of eyes watched from behind curtains in nearly every darkened trailer, as they had been doing since the beginning. The intruders running one way, then another, then behind the homes, the swans, everything. Dozens of phone calls began crisscrossing the park . . .

The intruders rounded the clubhouse and stopped in the parking lot with a clear view of all escape routes.

"Where did he go?"

"It's like he just disappeared."

A shrill whistle.

They spun around.

"Over here!" yelled Serge.

"How did he get behind us—"

They shielded their faces as another fusillade of fireworks streamed toward them. Bottle rockets screamed and exploded all around, enveloping the gang in a cloud of pungent smoke.

"After him!"

Serge took off again behind the trailers. The group split up to encircle him. Serge glanced over his shoulder as he hurdled a birdbath. He still had a decent lead. Then he looked forward again as the rest of the gang raced around the corner of an upcoming trailer. Serge hit the brakes. "Uh-oh." He vaulted a fence and sprinted down a cart path.

The others scrambled over the fence, less gracefully, and resumed pursuit.

"I didn't expect this many," said Serge. Another glance at his watch. "What's taking the FBI so long?"

Eyes behind curtains followed the chase. More and more phones rang all around the park.

The gang was quickly learning the back routes of the park, and Serge kept finding himself in more and more close calls, hopping fences and hedges, until he was finally flushed back into the open by the lake . . .

A wife pleaded with her husband. *"Don't go outside!"*

"To hell with it." The old man trudged across his front yard.

The leader noticed the second silhouette. Squatter and slower. "What on earth?"

The old man snapped two clips on a rope and began hoisting. All the other eyes in the park watched as a giant American flag rose to the top of the pole and flapped in the growing wind.

Screen doors began opening.

"Stay inside!"

"I can't just stand by."

Serge found himself alone again in the middle of the road. This time exposed without a plan.

The pursuers emerged from behind trailers and regrouped in the street.

"What are you waiting for?" yelled the leader. "There he is!"

The small herd stampeded.

"Shit." Serge shed his trench coat and dashed up the street, passing trailer after trailer.

The group was gaining.

Just then: "What was that?"

A screaming, fiery rocket zipped through their ranks before striking one in the shoulder and exploding.

"Where did that come from?"

"Between the trailers!"

They picked up their pace. More whizzing, crackling rockets streaked across their path as they passed each trailer. Other fireworks soared into the sky for colorful air detonations.

The gang was running at top speed now, not after Serge, but from the pyrotechnic assault.

Near the end of the road, one of the residents ignited a set of glued-together cardboard tubes designed to launch molten balls like a Gatling gun.

The group retreated back to their leader.

"What the hell do you think you're doing?"

"We're outnumbered."

"They're just old people with fireworks." The leader pulled a pistol on them. "Don't make me use this!"

One of them pointed straight up. *"Look!"*

Something with a flaming tail tumbled in flight as it arced through the night sky.

It exploded at their feet with a tiny pool of fire.

"They're throwing Molotov cocktails at us!"

"You idiots!" The leader stomped out the flames. "It's just one of those tiny Coke bottles. It's harmless. They can't hold enough gasoline to do any real damage."

Serge reappeared near the end of the road, jumping up and down. He cupped hands around his mouth. "Yoo-hoo!"

The leader gritted his teeth. "Get him! And no more screwing up! I swear to God I'll shoot the next one of you who retreats!"

They took off again.

Up the road, halfway between Serge and the gang, an old man stood at the edge of his lawn with a large pail and sloshed the contents into the street. Then he hurried back inside.

The intruders ran hell-bent. Another flame curved across the sky.

"Look!"

"It's just another little Coke bottle."

They kept running.

It shattered a few feet ahead of them, igniting the gasoline slick that had been splashed onto the pavement.

"Ahh!" "Ahh!" "Ahh!"

They hopped around, swatting flames from their clothes. Those who were more seriously on fire dove in the lake, where they sizzled and were attacked by swans.

The leader watched in the distance and smacked himself in the forehead. He fired a shot in the air for motivation.

The survivors took off running again.

More phones rang in trailers. A number of war vets opened glass display cases and removed keepsakes.

Bang, bang, bang.

"Who's shooting?"

"Sounds like all of them."

"Where did these old people get guns?"

"Our leader has a gun, too. Keep running!"

Bang, bang, bang.

Of course with age and diminished eyesight, the gunfire was well off target, but sufficiently distracting.

The pursuers accelerated again as they rounded the corner of the lake after Serge, like a track meet at a high school. Then all the fireworks let loose, crisscrossing the whole park, horizontally, vertically, loop-de-loops, rockets' red glare, bombs bursting in air, lighting up that glorious American flag.

Bang, bang, bang.

Two of the residents stood back between their trailers, where they had attached a giant inner-tube slingshot to a pair of coconut palms. They worked as a team to stretch the long rubber cord as far as possible. They loaded their ammo and waited.

Serge ran by the gap between the trailers.

"Now!"

The pursuing gang never looked up because the projectile was dark. It exploded in their midst. They stopped and were as puzzled as they were surprised.

Then another giant slingshot cut loose from between other trailers. And another, and another.

More dim, quiet explosions on the pavement.

The gang began coughing in a large white cloud, waving their hands to clear the air. They looked at the broken bags at their feet.

"Flour?"

"Flour?" said Serge, turning around to see what was happening. "God bless 'em. They used my idea but forgot the ignition source."

Just then, everyone heard a whizzing sound as a brilliant sparkler spun in a wide circle between two of the trailers. The person doing the spinning let go.

The gang watched upward in continuing confusion as a flaming Brillo pad fell down into the cloud.

Flash!

The ferocious fireball knocked half to the ground, and the rest ended up in the lake again.

The leader slapped his forehead.

Serge pumped a fist in the air. "They didn't forget the ignition source after all. They were taking it to the next level! I *love* these people!"

The residents began emerging from their trailers, slowly, an army of dark forms like a zombie movie. The ones with old military pistols and rifles led the way.

"Uh-oh." The leader slipped out of sight by the pool deck, and the residents converged on the lake. The injured were in no mood to resist.

"Don't shoot!"

"We're coming out!"

They struggled through the reeds up the banks from the water.

Ted Pruitt carried a vintage Colt .45 as he approached the west end of the lake to prevent any escape of the first swan-attack victim. He stretched out his shooting arm. "Hold it right there!"

Hands went up. *"I'm not resisting."*

The leader had his back against a palm tree, shrouded in darkness. Cursing under his breath. Heart beating faster, and face growing hotter in escalating fury at the fiasco that had unfolded. Until all control left town. He snapped and charged into the open, sprinting down from the pool deck toward the lake.

Ted was paying attention to his prisoner and never saw what was happening behind him. The leader closed the distance to ten yards and raised his weapon in full stride.

"Noooooooooo!"

Ted heard the shout and spun around, just in time to see Tofer Baez dive in front of him.

Bang.

Tofer took the bullet and crumpled. Just as fast, Ted got off three shots, all hitting the leader in a tight group in center mass. His running momentum took him tumbling down the bank of the lake, until he ended up floating facedown in the water.

"Tofer!"

Ted turned his old comrade over, a spreading red stain across his chest. He cradled Tofer in his arms. "What did you go and do that for?"

"He was going to kill you."

"Jesus!" Tears began to well. "Just hang in there. You're going to be okay."

"No, I'm not." Shallow breaths. "Please promise me one thing."

"You name it."

"Tell them I was a patriot."

"You're going to tell them yourself," said Ted. "And you'll have many more years to do it . . . Tofer? *Tofer?*"

Tofer's head slumped to the side.

Ted looked skyward. "Ahhhhhhh!"

Tofer blinked and opened his eyes. "What is it? You startled me."

"You're still here?" said Ted.

Eyes closed again. "I'm just feeling really tired."

Epilogue

BOCA SHORES

A procession of dark sedans and tactical trucks flew past the guard booth so fast you could hear intervals of wind. They made skidding turns and stopped behind the clubhouse.

The FBI agents had been preparing to launch a blitz attack. Instead they slowly got out of the vehicles and tried to comprehend something they'd never seen.

Across the parking lot were two neat rows of prisoners lying on their stomachs, fingers interlaced behind their heads. Standing over them were the residents of Boca Shores, holding rifles, golf clubs, canes and gardening rakes.

The top FBI official on the scene led the agents across the pavement. "What on earth do we have here?"

"McCreedy!"

The agent turned and squinted. "Serge?"

"I was dressed different."

"You locked me in a toilet," said McCreedy. "If I hadn't found the mole you mentioned, I'd be seriously pissed at you. Actually, I still am."

Serge glanced toward the prisoners. "What took you so long?"

"Big smashup on the interstate below Venice."

"That made it a lot more interesting than it had to be . . ."

An ambulance arrived, and they loaded Tofer.

"You're going to be fine," Ted told his pal just before they closed the back doors and sped off.

Then he joined the confab.

"You McCreedy?"

"Who are you?"

"Ted Pruitt, retired FBI, counter-intelligence." They shook hands. "Ever since Carlson got shot in Saint Pete, I've been sheltering his protectees . . . Now that it's all played out, I think I can draw you a map of this whole mess."

"I already have a pretty good idea," said McCreedy, turning toward the crowd. "Which one of you is Benmont?"

The analyst bashfully raised his hand.

"Good work with your theory," said McCreedy. "Once we found the traitor in the Bureau, everything else fell into place. Sorry you were a suspect . . ."

". . . And that I was shot at. A couple times."

"That too," said McCreedy. "You've performed a great service for your country. You'll be getting a civilian medal."

A prisoner started to get up, and a rake knocked him back down.

"Who *are* these people?" asked McCreedy.

"The best our country's got," said Ted.

Agents began handcuffing the foreign agents and loading them into vans.

"That just about does it," McCreedy told Ted. "Of course we

need to take you and Serge in for debriefing to make it official. And we'll need to do it now while your memories are fresh."

"Of course," said Ted. He turned to Serge. "Go back to my trailer and get that paperwork."

"What paperwork?"

Ted raised his eyebrows and mouthed the words *Get lost*.

"Oh, *that* paperwork," said Serge. "Be right back."

McCreedy watched him trot off toward the mobile home and chuckled. "A duck costume! ... What agency did you say he works for again? ..."

Serge ran into the trailer and raced behind the sofa, vigorously shaking a shoulder. "Coleman, wake up! We have to get out of here! It's that time again!"

"Another adventure?"

"Afraid so."

The two dark figures exited the rear of the trailer and took a golf cart path until they arrived at the location where Serge had hidden the Ford Falcon along the overgrown back edge of the park. He used bolt cutters to cut through an old wire pasture fence covered in vines.

Coleman got in, and Serge turned around for one last look back.

Pow, pow, pow, pow, pow ...

The fireworks had started up again, but this time in celebration. Roman candles and starbursts filled the sky, lighting up Mr. Hornsby's proudly waving American flag. Serge smiled as he put the image in his happy box, and he took off.

ABOUT THE AUTHOR

Tim Dorsey was a reporter and editor for the *Tampa Tribune* from 1987 to 1999, and is the author of twenty-one other novels: *Florida Roadkill, Hammerhead Ranch Motel, Orange Crush, Triggerfish Twist, The Stingray Shuffle, Cadillac Beach, Torpedo Juice, The Big Bamboo, Hurricane Punch, Atomic Lobster, Nuclear Jellyfish, Gator A-Go-Go, Electric Barracuda, When Elves Attack, Pineapple Grenade, The Riptide Ultra-Glide, Tiger Shrimp Tango, Shark Skin Suite, Coconut Cowboy, Clownfish Blues,* and *The Pope of Palm Beach.* He lives in Tampa, Florida.